"YOU ARE STUCK
WITH ME IN HERE, RED."

For a second, she couldn't move, couldn't think, couldn't breathe. But then she dropped her eyes to Adrian's finger, still hot on her lips. She reached up to wrap her hand around his, moving it from her mouth as she stepped in close enough to erase any daylight between them.

"Did you just *shush* me so you could say your piece?"

Adrian paused, his body going rigid against hers even though his gaze didn't waver. "I guess I did."

"Mmm." Teagan pressed up on her toes, relishing the taste of his shock as she brushed her mouth over his. "I'll let you slide exactly once, but if you make a habit of it, you *will* be sorry."

He drew back, but only enough to pin her with a wide-eyed stare. "You're going to let me help you?"

Something that had no name loosened in her chest, and she felt her body slowly unwind against the strength of his frame as she tucked herself into his left side. Suddenly, it didn't matter that the words bubbling up from inside her were ones that would normally scare her to death. Right now, for the first time since she'd walked into the Double Shot to find her father half passed out behind the bar, Teagan wasn't scared at all.

"Yeah, Superman," she said, wrapping her arms around the broad expanse of Adrian's shoulders and holding on tight. "I'm going to let you help me."

Fire Me Up

KIMBERLY KINCAID

ZEBRA BOOKS
KENSINGTON PUBLISHING CORP.
http://www.kensingtonbooks.com

ZEBRA BOOKS are published by

Kensington Publishing Corp.
119 West 40th Street
New York, NY 10018

All Kensington titles, imprints and distributed lines are available at special quantity discounts for bulk purchases for sales promotion, premiums, fund-raising, educational or institutional use.

Special book excerpts or customized printings can also be created to fit specific needs. For details, write or phone the office of the Kensington Special Sales Manager. Attn.: Special Sales Department. Kensington Publishing Corp., 119 West 40th Street, New York, NY 10018. Phone: 1-800-221-2647.

Zebra and the Z logo Reg. U.S. Pat. & TM Off.

First Printing: February 2015
ISBN-13: 978-1-4201-3655-5
ISBN-10: 1-4201-3655-0

First Electronic Edition: February 2015
eISBN-13: 978-1-4201-3656-2
eISBN-10: 1-4201-3656-9

10 9 8 7 6 5 4 3 2 1

Printed in the United States of America

To my father, Tony,
for making it all too
easy to write a heroine
who's a daddy's girl.
I love you.

Acknowledgments

From the minute sous-chef Adrian Holt hit the page in *Turn Up the Heat*, I always knew he had a story in him. But this book never would've left my head if not for the support of the following people: My spectacular agent-and-editor team of Maureen Walters and Alicia Condon, who have both loved this series from the beginning, I am so grateful for your nurturing. To the incredible team at Kensington (Vida Engstrand, Alex Nicolajsen, Michelle Forde, I am looking at all three of you!) who is always so excited to see the next Pine Mountain book and get the word out far and wide, I couldn't do it without you.

To my besties, Robin Covington and Avery Flynn, our daily texts, inside jokes, and Friday Man Wars make this the best job ever (it's research!). Alyssa Alexander and Tracy Brogan, having your eyes on this book in its various stages was invaluable. I owe you Bailey's in your coffee, times infinity. Also, huge thanks to Susan Donovan, Jill Shalvis, and Bella Andre, for supporting Pine Mountain "out loud" with their amazing cover quotes.

Retired firefighter Chris Kulak and paramedic Jeff Romeo were both utterly instrumental in sharing their knowledge of procedures and treatments given by first responders at accident scenes. This book simply wouldn't have happened without their generosity or their high threshold for my off-the-wall questions about motorcycle wrecks, IV painkillers, and rehab timetables for broken bones. You guys are the true heroes. All the knowledge is yours. All the liberties taken are solely mine (like the one

I took in borrowing your names for the firefighters in this book!).

A huge shout-out to my fantastically rabid street team, the Taste Testers. I love how impatient you all were for this book, but not as much as I love being able to give it to you now. Adrian is finally yours, ladies. You are the best cheerleaders I could ever hope to have.

Finally, to my daughters, who don't think it's at all weird when Mommy starts scrawling down plot devices and character arcs on the back of grocery store receipts, and to my unbelievably patient husband for taking bedtime duty (and playdate duty . . . and rainy Saturday duty . . . and takeout Chinese food duty . . .) as I wrote this book. My happily ever after is you.

Chapter One

Adrian Holt got three steps past the back door at La Dolce Vita before the dangerous combination of fear and anger cemented him to the kitchen tile. He fisted the keys to the building in his palm, hard enough to feel the metal bite into his calloused skin.

Someone was in the kitchen.

He was supposed to be the first one in and the last one out, just like he had been for the past twelve days while Carly was on her honeymoon. She'd made it clear, both as his boss and best friend, that the kitchen—*her* kitchen— was in his hands. The place should be a ghost town, especially at nine o'clock on a Friday morning.

Muffled noise sounded from down the hallway, filtering past the dishwashing station and the tidy, darkened office, sending his heartbeat into a staccato, adrenaline-soaked rhythm. The telltale *clink* of pots and pans grated on his ears from the center of the kitchen, and Adrian's muscles thrummed with instinct.

If some chucklehead from the resort was back here messing around, he was going to be seriously irate. Just because La Dolce Vita served as Pine Mountain Resort's only full-service restaurant and shared a wall with the main lodge, that didn't give anybody free rein to—

What was that smell?

Adrian followed his nose through the dishwashing station as quietly as he could, although admittedly, at six-foot-five, stealth had never been his strong suit. Damn it, he wasn't even in the position to get a parking ticket right now, much less jump in some wannabe chef's face for being here un-invited and unattended. But Carly had trusted him, and no way was he going to let some deviant creep his way into the place like he had a claim to the real estate. Dicey or not, Adrian owed it to Carly to at least keep the kitchen she'd worked her ass off for intact.

Actually, he owed her a hell of a lot more than that, but now wasn't the time to split hairs.

He rounded the corner by the pastry chef's prep space at the back of the kitchen, the keys put away but his fists still curled into place. The warm, mellow scent of caramelizing onions tempted his anger to slacken, but Adrian didn't bite. The intruder could be making European white truffles drowning in Cristal for all he cared. Whoever it was had picked the wrong fucking kitchen for playing house.

Adrian hit the back of the line with the edgy tension of twelve days' worth of double shifts in his stride and his pulse playing chicken with his blood pressure. The perpe-trator had his back turned and body crouched, head halfway into the lowboy for God-knows-what, but that didn't change Adrian's snap first, ask questions later mind-set.

"Hey!" He threaded his arms into a thick knot of black leather and menacing intentions over his chest. His voice matched his tension with every razor-sharp syllable as he planted his boots on the tile. "I don't know who you are, but you're about three seconds from getting tossed out of here on your ass, and I started counting two seconds ago."

A pair of slim shoulders hitched upward in surprise before the person unfolded to a slow stand, and recognition slammed into him, too late.

"All things considered, that might not be your wisest plan, Chef Holt."

The familiar timbre of Carly's voice scattered Adrian's edgy irritation like bread crumbs in a shallow bowl, although it left a trail of unease in its wake. Okay, so her braid had been slung over her shoulder where he couldn't see it, and yeah, he wasn't expecting her for another two days, but had he seriously been strung tight enough not to put two and two together?

"You're not supposed to be back at work until Monday," he accused, although the smile tugging at his lips canceled out the sting of the words.

"I missed you, too. Even if you did just technically threaten to throw me out of my own kitchen." Carly's eyes glinted, brown and knowing, as she met his gaze over the stockpot in front of her. She gave the fragrant contents one last stir before eyeballing them with a stern look, as if willing them to behave while she broke rank to place an affectionate kiss on each of his cheeks.

"Sorry." Adrian hid his sheepish expression over her shoulder as he returned her embrace, his heartbeat finally rediscovering neutral ground. "And you just spent twelve days in Italy on a honeymoon you postponed for three months due to your work schedule. Not to put too fine a point on it, but I hope you didn't miss me. In fact, I hope you didn't even *think* of me."

He might've been her sous-chef for five years, and friends with her for nearly as many before that, but airtime in Carly's love life had always been a polite but firm no-thank-you in Adrian's book. Despite the fact that most chefs had no trouble blurring the boundaries, as far as he was concerned, mixing work with pleasure had *bad things* scribbled all over it. Being Carly's sous-chef—and staying as busy as humanly possible in the kitchen—trumped all that personal stuff by leaps and bounds.

After all, his *nonna* had always said idle hands were the devil's workshop. And testing the theory wasn't on Adrian's agenda.

Been there, done that. Complete with the battle scars and rap sheet to prove it.

"Okay, okay." Carly laughed, yanking his attention back to the kitchen. Her knife skimmed over the tomato in front of her with an insistent *tat-tat-tat,* and damn, it was good to get back to business as usual. "But we flew back yesterday like we planned, and Jackson got called in on some work emergency. I figured it wouldn't hurt for me to come in a few days early to get back in the swing of things and work off the jet lag. I'm totally rusty."

"Please," Adrian cracked, easing into a grin. "You've got to stop moving to get rusty." Carly might not have thought about *him* while she was gone, but no way had she ditched thoughts of food. She'd once tried to chop a butternut squash with one hand while getting stitches in the other, for Chrissake.

Never one to pass up an opportunity for some good ribbing, Adrian continued. "I'm sure the chef at the villa where you stayed was just thrilled to share his space with you. How long did it take before you caved and had to cook something? A day? Two?"

But Carly just shook her head, wiping her hands on her low-slung apron before returning her attention to the stockpot. "Actually, I didn't cook at all."

"Uh-huh. And I'm Derek Jeter. Seriously, how many

recipes did you come up with while you were gone?" Fifty bucks said the number was well into the double digits, and Adrian's mouth watered at the thought.

"I'm dead serious, Ade. I ate a lot and jotted down some suggested wine pairings, but I didn't do any hands-on cooking the whole ten days Jackson and I were in Italy."

He opened his mouth to go for round two of giving her a hard time, but her serene, honest-to-God smile sent a pop to his gut like a back alley brawler.

She really hadn't given the kitchen—or anything in it— a second thought while she was gone.

"Oh." He shifted his weight, fingers suddenly itching for something to chop, stir, or whisk together. "Well, I didn't think you'd be back until Monday, so we prepped for specials through the weekend. I can get the pantry set for the produce delivery if you want to get reacclimated with the food."

Between managing the produce delivery that was due in about twenty minutes, whatever tweaks Carly wanted to put to things now that she was back, and the typical busy Friday dinner shift on tap for later, he'd be good and exhausted by the time today ticked into tomorrow.

Outstanding.

"Adrian." The single word slashed his movements to a halt, and she turned to fasten him with a no-nonsense stare. "Normally, you come in here smiling and humming old Sinatra tunes. Today you barged in like a one-man commando unit. Why don't you take the weekend off and relax?"

"Work relaxes me."

Her hand went to her hip like a harbinger of *not so fast*. "You've been here for the past twelve days with no sous-chef."

"I'm the sous-chef, *gnocchella*." Oh hell. Now Carly

had that look on her face, the one that reminded him of a pit bull, only more tenacious. "Seriously. We're booked solid this weekend. Plus, I'm fine."

She took a step away from the bubbling stockpot, as if she didn't want to contaminate the food with the sharpness of her frown. "I don't think so. There's more to life than just the kitchen, you know?"

Frustration curled in his chest like steam fingering out of a teapot, but he tamped it down. They'd gone through this Zenmaster, bigger-picture, this-is-your-life song and dance a couple of times now over the last few months, and his standard answer springboarded from his mouth.

"For you, that's true, and I'm glad. But I'm good with just the kitchen."

For a second, he was certain she'd plow forward with the next line in their now-scripted argument, to the point where he preloaded his next response about how he really *was* happy. He should've known she'd come back from her honeymoon all brimming with uncut bliss, and if anyone deserved it, Carly did.

But guys like him? Not going the hearts and flowers route in a million years. Plus two. Stuff like that only spelled trouble in the long run, and no way was he splitting his attention between the kitchen and . . . well, anything. He belonged here.

Period.

After a lingering glance, Carly simply nodded, and Adrian's breath eased out at the unexpected gimme.

"Okay, you win. But I've got the produce delivery. At least go home and get a little sleep before the dinner shift. I don't want to see you back here before two."

"Come on," he said, only halfway joking, but she shook her head with zero wiggle room.

"I'm saying this with love, *gnoccone,* but you look like

shit. Get some rest." Carly's sugar-sweet smile belied the seriousness of her words, but she didn't back down.

Ah, hell. The pit bull thing only got worse if he argued with her, and if Adrian stuck around—or worse, put up a fight—she might rethink letting go of the topic at hand. Probably better for him to take the hit for a couple hours now and come back for the dinner shift, when they'd have so many plates flying around, the topic would be forgotten. Until next time, anyway.

"You're the boss. I'll see you at two." He pulled his keys out of his pocket and forced a crooked smile as he made his way back out of the kitchen, his belly so full of unease, he'd swear he ate a bowl of it for breakfast.

Which was stupid, really. Carly was back, they had a full house on the books every night for the next month, and in a handful of hours, he was going to dive headfirst into a dinner service that would keep him too busy to breathe, let alone think.

Okay, maybe he *could* use a little shut-eye.

Adrian swung one leg into place over his Harley-Davidson Fatboy, finding familiar comfort on the bike as he skinned into his riding gloves and buckled his helmet with a snug pull. The bike rumbled to life with all the subtlety of a twenty-pound sledgehammer, and as he put it into gear and started to drive, the weariness of the last few weeks invaded him down to his marrow. He'd always thought sleep was pretty overrated—plenty of time for shit like rest when you were dead, and all—but yeah. He'd been cranked tight enough to not even recognize Carly in her own damn kitchen. Maybe he could stand to loosen his grip on his hours. Maybe Carly was right, and there was more to life than filling tickets and firing up the grill.

Or maybe he was just getting soft. After all, wasn't that

"something else" how he'd screwed up his life in the first place?

Adrian's knuckles hardened over the polished chrome handlebars as he downshifted to turn off of Rural Route Four. A flash of movement, time-warp fast, blurred in his rearview mirror, filling his mouth with the bitter taste of foreboding, black and awful like the scrapings from a forgotten skillet. Ominous recognition shot into place, bringing the rush of motion in a swift, too-close-to-avoid-contact push, and cold sweat slid its clammy fingers beneath his helmet.

He was going to die, right here on the asphalt, and his last earthly vision was that of a minivan.

Christ, that thought alone was enough to kill him.

The vehicle behind him clipped his Harley's back tire in a tight, forceful arc as it swerved away too late, the impact knocking his teeth together with an unrepentant *clack*. The force sent him toward the road's yellow center line at a sick angle, every one of his muscles in lockdown.

The gut-twisting screech of metal on pavement slammed into Adrian's ears like a violin concerto gone horribly wrong, but it only lasted a bare second before the ground rose up to meet him in a rush of asphalt and imminent danger. His well-worn survival instinct crashed together with undiluted adrenaline, making him jerk the handlebars hard to the left in a Hail Mary attempt to avoid getting pinned to the pavement—or worse yet, crushed outright.

In a stroke of blind luck, the torque was just enough to propel the bike out in front of Adrian instead of on top of him. He exhaled a heartbeat's worth of relief that his reflexes hadn't seized in fear.

That relief met a quick death, however, when the same sixth sense that kept him from becoming road pizza sent his left arm out to brace his unavoidable contact with Rural Route Four.

White lightning ricocheted from Adrian's leather-gloved hand all the way to the center of his chest, stealing his oxygen as his arm crumpled beneath him and he fell from the bike. Time hung in an eerie, slow-motion balance, delivering a slideshow of images that didn't seem to belong together. Shiny, sharp-edged bits of safety glass exploding from his rearview mirror, the lilt of his *nonna*'s voice as she hummed along with Sinatra on the radio, the velvety red of a perfect summer strawberry.

And here he'd thought the whole life-flashing-before-your-eyes thing was bullshit.

As quickly as it had slowed to allow him one last glimpse of his life, time yanked back and hit fast forward. Adrian made the rude, full-bodied acquaintance of the wet spring asphalt, turning everything to an indistinct blur but the ripping agony in his chest. Up became down and then up again, hitting his vision like a Tilt-a-Whirl with a busted kill switch. For just a heartbeat, Adrian was weightless, soaked in the sweet, preternatural darkness beckoning from the edges of his consciousness.

And then he sucked in an ear-popping breath, his lungs expanding as if they'd been taken by surprise, and he tumbled back into his body on the serrated edges of all the pain in the world.

Chapter Two

In the six years Teagan O'Malley had been a paramedic with Pine Mountain's Fire and Rescue Squad, she'd seen boatloads of terrifying things. None of them scared her quite so much, however, as the sight of her name posted next to the words *clean out the fridge* on the station's chore calendar. She battened down over the dread clenching her stomach like an industrial-grade vise and popped the thing open, taking a peek inside.

Takeout containers marked with cryptic scribbling and questionable food stains lay strewn about the dim interior, smelling about as appetizing as the Styrofoam they were made of. Two brown bags, both grease-tinged and labeled *Touch this and lose a limb!* sat stashed in the far corner, where they'd likely been for two weeks, easy. She didn't even want to ponder the possibilities for the leftovers-slash-science experiment jammed on the bottom shelf, affectionately known among her colleagues as Where Food Goes to Die.

There might be an upside to being a woman in a male-dominated profession, but living with heathens sure as hell wasn't it.

"Ugh." Teagan slammed the refrigerator shut with a

chorus of *oh hell no* jingling through her head. Getting out of this was going to cost her, but some prices were worth every red cent.

She kicked her legs into a purposely casual saunter across the station's common room, sliding her fingers into the pockets of her careworn navy blue uniform pants. Although the station manager scheduled ten people on any given shift, four of the firefighters were out clearing a small-time call with no injuries. The remaining four were napping away the still-early hours of the morning in the sleeping quarters down the hall, leaving Teagan to set her sights on the couch where her partner sat sprawled with the *Pine Mountain Gazette*.

"Hey, Evan. What do you say we swap chores this week? I totally don't mind taking the floors off your hands."

"Let me guess. You've got the fridge." Evan didn't even look up from the sports section, the pain in the ass. But that refrigerator was her own monogrammed version of hell on earth. No way was she giving in without hauling out every last thing in her arsenal of please, pretty-please, and do-this-or-I'll-spill-your-deep-dark-secrets-on-the-ten-o'clock-news.

"I'll do the floors and whatever you get next week, too. Consider it an act of camaraderie among paramedics." As a pair, she and Evan were half the certified paramedics on Pine Mountain Fire and Rescue's payroll, plus they were partners. There had to be honor in there somewhere.

Right?

"Camaraderie, my ass. That chill chest hasn't been properly cleaned out since Christmas. It's going to take more than next week's chores to move me, O'Malley."

Teagan dialed her pout up to ten and tried for some good old-fashioned sympathy as she upped the ante. "I'll buy you a drink at the Double Shot after shift."

"A pretty woman offering to ply me with liquor. Sweetie, I think you've made a bit of a tactical error." Evan buried his smile in the newsprint in front of him, but it held way more amusement than heat.

She returned the expression with genuine ease and deadpanned, "You're already busy tonight?"

"Uh, that, and I'm still as gay as I was when we met four years ago. You didn't seriously think that lower-lip thing was going to work on me, did you?"

So much for the pout being a universal ploy for sympathy. It had been worth a shot, anyway.

Teagan released her breath in slow increments, discouraged enough to give in, but too stubborn to actually follow through. "I don't suppose you'd just cut me a break? I get enough interaction with the fridge at my dad's bar."

God, was that the truth. Teagan's fingers did double duty as prunes at least four nights a week from all the cold bottles of beer she served up. It was enough to make even the toughest person want to run screaming from anything culinary, including the appliances. And lately, it had only gotten worse.

"You've been at the Double Shot a lot this month, huh?" Evan's sandy brows kicked up in question, prompting her to force a shrug. She was no rookie when it came to an honest day's work, but even she'd been running on fumes since their day cook ran off with their only good waitress and they had yet to replace either one.

But if Teagan had it rough spending a few extra shifts behind the bar, her father had it exponentially worse trying to keep the whole damned place afloat. A little sleep deprivation was the least she could do for the man who'd raised her all by himself.

"Yeah, we're a little short-staffed, that's all." She laughed, because it was either that or cry. "Know any gourmet chefs willing to work for peanuts in a small-town bar and grill?"

"Maybe you should bite the bullet and learn how to cook, T. Or does your fear of the refrigerator extend to the entire kitchen?" Evan lobbed a good-natured smirk over the edge of the paper as he folded it up.

Heat prickled at the back of her neck, but she swiped it away before he could catch the flush that surely went with it. In this profession, the only thing worse than fear was *showing* fear. And anyway, you didn't last more than a day at this job by getting all girly about a little ribbing.

Even ribbing about the stuff that hit home.

"Let's just say I'm all fridged out." Relieved to have a segue out of the conversation, Teagan went full circle. "Look, if you switch chores with me, I'll even take the next belligerent patient we get, no matter what the injury. Scout's honor." She held up one hand in a show of good faith, throwing on her very best doe-eyed look. "Please?"

Evan's laugh was as agreeable as his smirk, and Teagan heaved a silent sigh of relief through her too-tight smile as he caved. "Okay, okay. I'll take the fridge, but you can sell that innocent-girl routine somewhere else." He dropped his thick-soled boots from the futon to the floor, allowing himself a good stretch before heading over to the refrigerator.

"Thank you!" She paused, tacking on, "And ouch on the innocent-girl thing."

But Evan wasn't having it. "Teagan, please. You single-handedly broke up two bar fights last week alone. It's pretty clear you're not rocking a halo."

Eh. He had a point. "Okay. Maybe innocent isn't the best word for me," she said, crossing the dove-gray linoleum to rummage through the supply closet for a broom.

"Innocent is the *last* word for you." Evan's quip came

out more endearment than insult, and Teagan pointed the broom handle at her partner with a grin.

"Aw, stop. You'll make me blush."

He opened his mouth, presumably to launch an obnoxious comeback, but the piercing alarm signaling an incoming call from dispatch interrupted him. The broom was barely an afterthought as Teagan shoved it back toward the closet and yanked up the handset from the desk acting as command central between the kitchen and the common room.

"This is Pine Mountain Fire and Rescue. Go ahead, dispatch."

The radio hissed out a quick breath of static before carrying the reply, "Pine Mountain Fire and Rescue, this is dispatch. Requesting fire and EMS for a two-vehicle MVA on Rural Route Four, a mile north of Pine Mountain Resort. Police have been dispatched, over."

She shot Evan a look, but he was already moving with brisk steps toward the in-house intercom that would rouse the rest of their team from sleep.

Teagan cradled the handset against her palm, her thumb finding the smooth groove of the *reply* button with the same ease she used to draw in breath. "Received, dispatch. Engine Seven and Paramedic Two responding to Rural Route Four for an MVA, out."

Adrenaline raised Teagan's heart rate another level as she replaced the radio handset with methodical resolve, but she was far from holy-shit panic mode. Car crashes were pretty ordinary fare for a paramedic, and all things considered, a two-car bang-up was usually pretty tame since it was tough to go terribly fast on most of Pine Mountain's winding roads.

Still, she relayed the information to Evan and the rest of the responding team in clipped tones that meant business.

Taking care of whomever was on the receiving end of this accident might be her job, but she sure wasn't in it for the money or the glamour. Somebody needed help, plain and simple, and she had the knowledge and tools to take care of business.

Plus, if she wore herself out saving other people, maybe nobody would notice that she couldn't patch her own life together if someone spotted her a needle and thread.

Teagan squashed her thoughts like the contents of an overly full trash bin, yanking open the ambulance's passenger door with barely enough time to haul herself inside before Evan threw the thing into *drive*.

"Dispatch, this is Paramedic Two. We are en route to the scene. ETA eight minutes." Teagan caught Evan's look of approval out of the corner of her eye as she returned the radio in the rig to its perch.

"You know we're probably a good ten minutes from the resort, right?" Evan hitched the wheel to the left, steering the ungainly ambulance up Pine Mountain's main road with mind-boggling finesse.

"Mmm-hmm. I also know you could get us there in six if you push it." After all, not every MVA was a fender-bender. Even if the cops beat them to the scene and had it secured, someone's life could well be on the line.

That fact got hammered into place as soon as she caught a distant glimpse of the black and chrome Harley lying belly-up on Rural Route Four. Shit. *Shit*. This had *very bad things* written all over it. In block letters. With a Sharpie.

Teagan shouldered her first-in bag and jumped out of the rig, her boots barely making contact with the pavement before one of the cops securing the scene had fallen into step beside her. "Morning, Officer. What've we got?"

Although her eyes were locked in on the scene about thirty yards away—which was thankfully blocked from incoming traffic by a pair of police cruisers—Teagan's attention was just as sharply focused on the cop's response.

"Motorcycle versus minivan. Motorcycle driver is over there, single rider, wearing a helmet. Denies losing consciousness, no visible head injury, but he's combative and complaining of left arm pain. I've got an officer on him now, just to make sure he didn't fly before you got here. He's going to be a handful."

"Oh goodie. I eat those for breakfast," Teagan said, moving swiftly past the barricade. "How about vehicle two?"

The officer tipped his chin at a dark green Honda Odyssey sitting halfway on the shoulder of the road, hazard lights flashing in perfect orange rhythm. "Minivan driver has her two kids in the backseat, all parties belted in. Everyone appears stable with no visible injuries, no complaints of pain. Scene is secure. Just let us know what you need."

"Got it, thanks." She swung her gaze at Evan before letting it land on the Honda. "You want the minivan before the cops take her report? I'm grabbing Chris and Jeff from Seven to help nail down this single rider and make sure he's stable for transport."

Evan shook his head and shot her a wry grin. "I know you owe me, but I can take the cranky biker."

As if on cue, strains of a heated altercation filtered past the scene noise, pulling a sardonic laugh from Teagan's throat. "Call it even for the fridge. I've got this."

He turned with a shrug toward the nearby minivan. "You're a glutton for punishment, O'Malley."

Understatement of the frickin' year.

Teagan called for the two firefighters before turning her attention toward her patient, who stood arguing with one of Pine Mountain's finest in the middle of the road in spite of the fact that she was certain he'd seen better days.

Holy big-man-on-a-stick, this might be more than she'd bargained for.

Even though his back was half-turned and she was a good ten paces away, the guy was obviously huge, and from the sound of it, he was no stranger to being righteously pissed off. Still, the unmistakable edge of pain bled through his tone as clear as sunrise over Big Gap Lake, and the way he clutched his left arm at such an awkward angle against his body told her all she needed to know. Pissed off or not, she was getting her hands on him, pronto.

"Hey, Chris, run and grab the backboard from the rig and roll the cot over here, yeah? Jeff, you're with me for trauma assessment. I get the feeling it's going to be an adventure." She lasered her focus from her crew to the injured man without breaking stride or waiting for answers.

Time to get to work.

"Sorry to interrupt, gentlemen, but I heard this is where the party is." Without a second thought, Teagan slipped into the hairbreadth of space between the cop and her irritated patient, assessing the latter with a critical eye. Her subconscious gave a whisper of recognition as she looked at his rugged, stubbled face, but the tickle of familiarity took a backseat to the visual assessment she needed to do in order to gauge his injuries.

The guy had nearly a foot on her, which was pretty freaking impressive considering she measured in at five-foot-seven. The physique that went with his height left impressive in the dust, though, especially since his chest was as thick as a double-wide trailer and every ounce of it appeared to be muscle.

Make that leather-clad muscle, which had probably saved his ass, quite literally. As best she could tell, thanks to his now-banged-up jacket, the guy's road rash appeared shockingly minimal, although she'd have to get the garment off to be sure.

Too bad the rest of his injuries didn't match, namely that arm he was cradling like a helpless newborn. She didn't even want to get started on the laundry list of other injuries that could be lurking beneath the dirt-streaked denim and leather.

She passed the first-in bag to Jeff, who caught it without looking while the police officer stepped to the background to give them a wide berth.

"My name is Teagan O'Malley, and I'm a paramedic with Pine Mountain Fire and Rescue," she said, her hands a flurry of movement as she geared up to do a rapid trauma assessment. "Can you tell me your name?"

The guy lifted a pierced eyebrow toward his spiky platinum hairline and speared her with a stare caught somewhere between hazel and cold gray. God, how did she *know* him?

"I'm fine," he ground out, his voice pure gravel and aggravation. "Which I already told that fucking jarhead, but he wouldn't let me leave."

Yeah. It was going to take a little more than a bad attitude and some uncut testosterone to get her to back down. "That fucking jarhead, as you so eloquently put it, might've saved your life by keeping you here until you can be medically cleared. While I doubt there's a gift registry for that kind of thing, a simple thank you might be nice. Just to be on the safe side."

Her would-be patient took a step back, his stare going from cutting to calculating in the span of a breath. "I don't need to be medically cleared," he said, although it didn't escape her notice that he caught the cop's attention to toss him a tight nod.

Teagan bit back the temptation to point out that, from the looks of things, he was a walking, talking version of the game Operation with that arm bent up like it was. "Okay. Why don't you let me give you a quick once-over to be sure?"

"No." The word fell between them without subtlety, and she drew back with a frown. The tough guy routine was cute really, but nobody was indestructible.

"Look, I know this isn't fun, but it's necessary, so—"

"If you think I'm getting in that ambulance, then you don't know shit."

Jeff locked eyes on her in a nonverbal communication of *say the word,* but Teagan gave a quick shake of her head. She'd handled enough tough guys to fill a stadium, and this one was no different.

She craned her neck and stepped close enough to see the numerous abrasions peppered in with the guy's dark stubble, meeting his stare head-on even though it sent an involuntary shiver down the plumb line of her spine.

"Let me tell you what I *do* know." She dropped her voice to just a notch above a whisper and threw on a smile as thick and sweet as store-bought frosting. "I know your arm is broken, and I think you know it, too. I know you don't want me to look at it even though it hurts like a bitch. And I also know that's not an option, because it's possible that broken arm is the least of your worries. So here it is. You can either cooperate with me and we'll do this the easy way, or I can sedate you and work you over so thoroughly, I'll be on a first-name basis with every last part of you. Are we clear?"

A muscle tightened in the hard line of his jaw, drawing out the silence for a beat, then two before he turned toward her ever so slightly, as if waiting for her to get on with it.

Good enough, she thought as she lifted her hands to start checking him out.

But before Teagan could even start on his pulse, the guy's free hand had turned to form an ironclad circle around her wrist.

Chapter Three

Heat shot all the way up Teagan's arm and her heart whacked against her ribs like a hockey puck dropping at center ice . . . right up until she realized the guy had simply reached out to get her attention.

"Adrian." The word, little more than a harsh affirmation, pushed past his lips quietly, and it snapped her focus back into place.

"Excuse me?"

As fast as he'd touched her, he loosened his fingers, as if the movement of getting her attention in the first place had drained his strength to fumes. "My name is Adrian. And yeah. My arm hurts like hell."

And just like that, she was moving again, even though her skin still prickled with strange and residual warmth. "Can you rate the pain on a scale of one to ten, ten being the worst pain you've ever felt?"

Something Teagan couldn't get a gauge on flickered across his expression, darkening his eyes to a steely green gray, but he snuffed it out with an audible exhale. "If I don't move it, it's fine."

"And if you do?"

Adrian paused. "Six."

Damn. She'd hate to know what had given him his ten. "Okay, Adrian, here's what we're going to do. I'm going to have you sit on this cot." Teagan stopped to acknowledge Chris's impeccable timing as he rolled the thing over, and she reached for the trauma shears Jeff had wordlessly taken from the bag before she continued. "And I'm going to ask you a couple of questions while I check you out. You okay with that?"

He dropped his chin a fraction, and the wince it produced wasn't lost on her. "What're those for?" Adrian asked, gaze firm on the shears in her grip.

"I'm sorry, but in order to get a good look at you, that jacket's got to go."

The feral expression she'd just lulled off Adrian's face made a vengeful comeback. "You're not cutting my jacket."

Oh, come on. She was a paramedic, not a magician, and that arm probably resembled a jigsaw puzzle right out of the box. "You got any better ideas on how to get it off over a broken limb, Einstein?"

"As a matter of fact, I do."

In the time it took her to blink, he had the jacket halfway off his shoulders even though the move had to hurt like nothing else, and Teagan's gut gave an uncharacteristic yank.

"Wait—stop!"

But before her words could make it all the way out, the deed was done. "There . . . you go," Adrian grated, his face roughly the color of the sheet on the cot as he gripped the jacket in his free hand. "Problem solved."

"Are you out of your mind? I can't help you if you're only going to make things worse!" *Christ*. If there were broken ribs in that granite wall of a chest of his, he could've single-handedly punctured a lung with that little stunt.

His voice only held the slightest hitch as he fixed her

with a stoic glance. "You said you needed it off to get a good look, right? Now you're free and clear, Red."

Jeff reclaimed the trauma shears and put them in the bag with a sheepish grin. "Hate to admit it, O'Malley, but he's kind of right. What do you need first?"

Teagan sucked down a deep breath and shot Jeff the mother of all death glares. "I've got the RTA. You work on getting the stuff together to splint that arm." She turned her glare on Adrian as Jeff began to rummage for what he needed. "Park it," she said, jutting her chin at the cot.

Miraculously, he settled against the reclined back of the rolling bed and let her take his vitals without argument. The numbers were startlingly good for someone who'd just turned his motorcycle into spare parts in the middle of the road, but she'd seen vitals nosedive without warning too often for that to mean he was in the clear.

No better way to assess an injury than to let your fingers do the walking. Starting at the top of Adrian's platinum blond head, she skimmed her hands over him, missing nothing as she worked her way down the corded muscles in his neck and chest. The injury to his forearm indicated an obvious break, but since the skin was intact, she placed the limb carefully at his side to await a splint before sliding her hands to his abdomen.

"Careful. Any more personal and you're going to have to take me to dinner first."

The comment, and the hint of dark humor that came with it, caught Teagan totally off guard under the circumstances, and her fingers stuttered over the left side of his rib cage. She'd done thousands of assessments, and never once had they been anything other than a hundred percent perfunctory.

But right now, with her hands about an inch above the low-slung waistband of Adrian's jeans, her brain heaved forward into forbidden territory, and her girly parts were all too happy to shake off the dust and go along for the unexpected joyride.

Teagan cleared her throat. Twice. "I'm, ah, just making sure nothing else feels broken. Did you lose consciousness at any time? Any dizziness, nausea, trouble breathing? Anything like that?" She reset her hands and forced herself to concentrate as she moved them over the rest of his upper body.

Wow. He really was . . . wow.

And she really needed to knock it off.

"No, and no. Like I told the cops, I'm not an idiot. I don't ride without a helmet."

She worked her way down the lower half of his body, satisfied that everything was in working order before returning her attention to his face. "Good intentions aren't always enough to save people, you know."

His pupils looked round, reactive, and a lot less pissed than before, and his gravelly voice held a hint of amusement as he said, "Spare me the lecture, Red. I'm a big boy."

Teagan fought both the urge to agree with him and the burning desire to roll her eyes. "Gee, I've never heard that nickname for a redhead before." She sent her gaze up toward her strawberry-blond hairline before reaching out to help Jeff with the splint.

"It's not for your hair. *Ow!*"

Her pulse went double-time, eyes darting to where her hand rested with only bare pressure on Adrian's shoulder. "What?"

"Nothing." But the painful grimace pulling tight over Adrian's face said otherwise. Teagan wasn't anywhere near his forearm, and Jeff hadn't even touched him with the splint yet. The slight contact from her hands shouldn't have produced so strong a reaction.

Unless that broken arm had company.

"Let's get a better look at this shoulder, shall we?" With the gentlest motions she could call up, Teagan worked her hands over his collarbone, which was still as intact as the first time she'd checked it. Her brain spun with possibilities—what the hell could she have missed?—and then she slipped her fingers all the way around the back of his rotator cuff to find the gut-squeezing answer to her question.

"Can you rate the pain back here on a scale of one to ten?" Damn it, his shoulders were muscular enough that it was hard to tell if he'd partially dislocated the joint or simply sustained a nasty bruise. Her pulse hammered out an uncharacteristic lurch at the flinch her movements produced, even though she was barely making contact with his body.

"It's just a little sore. No big deal."

Rather than argue, Teagan surprised herself by softening her tone to match her ministrations. "Okay. Can you rate it for me like you did with your arm?"

His mouth turned into a hardened line. "Six."

Shit. She'd bet the shirt on her back it was dislocated. "Okay, Jeff, we're going to need to immobilize this arm. Chris, get a status on Evan. I want to be en route to Riverside in no more than five."

Adrian jerked forward, separating himself from the back of the cot to sit at rigid attention. "Hold on a second. I already told you, I'm not going to the hospital." Another jerk brought his arm tight against his body and his boots off the cot with a heavy, effort-laden grunt.

"Whoa!" Teagan splayed a hand across his chest, her fingers spreading over his faded T-shirt like a determined sunburst. "You agreed to get checked out, remember?"

"I agreed to let *you* check me out, which you did," he bit

out, pain clearly etched on his face. "And now I just want my arm fixed up so I can get out of here."

She opened her mouth to argue, to just let Jeff and Chris restrain him and be done with it. But then his calloused right hand covered the one she had pressed to his chest, gluing the words to the roof of her mouth.

"Please."

Adrian gave himself a mental beat-down for not balking harder when Carly had sent him home for a nap he didn't need. He should be deep in the belly of La Dolce Vita's kitchen, helping her experiment with specials and supervising that produce delivery. Nowhere on his agenda did it say to wrap his fingers around a feisty paramedic in a living embodiment of how pain could turn you into a total moron.

Fuck. The pain was killing him, too. But no way was he getting in that ambulance. If he did, it would only be a matter of time before his life became profoundly difficult.

After all, hell hath no fury like a crusty parole officer. The fact that Adrian hadn't done anything wrong wouldn't make a dent in Big Ed's reaction if he saw a police report with Adrian's name in the headline. The guy had been looking for a reason to drag Adrian back to Rikers ever since he'd left New York a little over a year ago. He was going to salivate over this like it was a steak dinner with all the fixings, twisting it up like a pretzel until somehow, the blame lay right in Adrian's lap.

He just had to go and get knocked off his block with forty-seven days left to go, didn't he?

Teagan turned her hand to squeeze his fingers, shocking him back to the here and now of Rural Route Four. "Adrian, listen to me. You need to be treated by a doctor at the hospital. I can't just splint you and let you walk. That's not how it works. There could be something wrong that I can't see. Something serious."

The murmur came out in quiet tones, and anyone taking in the rush of the accident scene—including the firefighters helping close by—would probably assume she was just doing her job. He was tempted to tell her he knew damn well his shoulder wasn't quite in its socket, and since the third time seemed to be the charm with this particular injury, he also knew damn well how to get it back where it belonged without wasting a trip to the hospital. But from the warm whiskey flash of Teagan's eyes, it was blindingly clear she would fight until she dropped to get him into that ambulance.

And if *that* crossed Big Ed's desk, Adrian was flat-out screwed.

"Okay, fine." As amusing as it would be to watch her give it her all, the pain in his arm was really starting to piss him off. Plus, dealing with a bunch of white coats was better than dealing with the cops, even if only by a hair. If they got out of here now, maybe he could avoid the latter. "Let's go before I change my mind."

"Really?" Teagan tucked her brow in tight, but started moving before he could answer, as if she was afraid he really would change his mind. "Okay. It might be a little uncomfortable getting you splinted, but the less your arm moves until the docs can take a look, the better." She scooped a hand under his mercilessly throbbing forearm, and even the featherlight touch felt amplified and covered in nails.

"I think you need to reevaluate your definition of un-comfortable," he hissed, bracing himself against the cot. Even the mundane movement of lifting his arm to put the splint underneath it sent tremors of borderline agony into his chest, and it flattened the breath right out of his lungs.

Damn it, he needed something to distract him from the pain, because right now it was enough to make him want to scream.

"I'm sorry. I'll try to be quick." Teagan leaned in close, and he latched onto the sight of her with all his waning might.

Her flame-colored hair was fastened into a no-nonsense ponytail at the back of her head, and it smelled fresh, yet not fragrant in a perfumy sense, kind of like rosemary right off the stem. Every time she shifted to adjust either her movements or her gaze, it swung against her lithe shoulders in a little arc, leaving the scent in its wake. Determination shaped her pretty features, bringing a serious bent to the high curve of her cheekbones and the soft dusting of freckles on the bridge of her nose. But her mouth was the crown jewel of her face, as red and ripe as a strawberry on the vine, and for a dark sliver of a second, Adrian wanted nothing more than an impulsive taste.

And then she tightened the splint into place over the train wreck of his arm, and he was right back at square one, wanting to scream.

"Hey, T." A guy with light brown hair and a uniform that matched Teagan's came up behind her, slinging his bag over one shoulder. "Minivan checks out fine, with the exception of being a little shaken up, so I gave the cops the okay to take her report and start to clear. What've you got?"

"Injury to the left forearm, left shoulder, no visible head or neck injury, no LOC." She rattled off a bunch of numbers and phrases that might as well have been ancient Sanskrit before turning to the firefighter guy who'd helped with his arm. "Jeff, tell the cops we're rolling out. Ev, we're stable for transport if you want to grab this thing."

Teagan swung the cot around into the other paramedic's

waiting hands, and Adrian snapped forward with sudden realization at the scene over her shoulder.

"My bike." Scraped up or not, no way was he leaving his Harley here unattended. "I've got to—"

"You've got to relax." Teagan's hand was right back in place over his solar plexus, and hell if it wasn't the only spot on his body that didn't hurt. "The cops will make sure your bike gets to the impound, where it'll be safe until you can send someone to get it. Now stop fighting and let me do my job, would you?"

She nodded to her partner without waiting for a reply, and the guy pulled the cot into motion. Adrian blinked hard against the sudden sensation. He opened his mouth to argue with her yet again, but the pain radiating from his shoulder to his fingertips dulled the edges of his periphery. It was fifty-fifty at best that his bike would start up right now, not to mention the shitastic odds that he could even get off this freaking cot to try. The impound wasn't ideal, but it also wasn't the middle of the road. As much as he hated it, the compromise would have to suffice until he could call Carly to help him out.

Yet another thing for the this-is-going-to-suck section of his to-do list. Carly was technically still on her honeymoon, for God's sake. She was going to lose her mind with worry over this. That was, if she didn't kill him first. Maybe if he pushed it, the docs at the hospital could get a cast on him before the dinner shift started.

The metallic *bang* of the ambulance doors halted the thoughts pinballing through his head, and he shifted awkwardly, trying to prioritize. The pain in his shoulder was going to settle in for an extended stay unless he got everything back where it belonged, and taking care of it before the pain took care of him was his top order of business.

Teagan's voice sounded behind him as she delivered a

status report to the hospital over the radio. Adrian reached up to unclip the safety harness over his chest, surreptitiously pressing his injured shoulder into the back of the cot to test how much pressure he could work up without noticeable movement.

Damn. Getting his shoulder to play nicely with the rest of his upper body was going to take a little more than a love tap. But it would skip a step at the hospital, and get him out of there faster, to boot.

And wasn't that just a win-win.

With one swift move, Adrian pitched forward to his feet and gave a sharp turn, slamming his shoulder with all his might into the vertical edge of metal cabinetry flanking the ambulance wall.

"Jesus, you've got some brass on you!" Teagan scrambled around from her seat by his head while he blinked back every star in the galaxy.

"Funny," he gasped, the blinding pain making his words looser than usual. "I was thinking . . . the same thing . . . about you earlier."

"You good back there, T?" came the voice of the other paramedic as he climbed behind the wheel, leaning into the narrow space that blocked off his seat from the rest of the ambulance.

"I'm fine." She hit Adrian with a high-level frown and molded her hands to his shoulder, forcing him back to the cot and strapping his seat belt tight. "And as long as Superman here doesn't try any more man-of-steel bullshit, I'll be stellar. We're good to roll out."

The guy pushed himself back through the space, the ambulance growling to life a second later.

Adrian gasped at another breath, but yeah, oxygen was still at a premium. He let go against the back of the cot with a wince. "Trust me. It wasn't . . . a picnic on my end, either."

"Well, you'd better hope you didn't just make matters worse. There's more to a shoulder reduction than just whacking it back into place like a Neanderthal."

He returned the favor of a frown. "I know exactly what I'm doing."

Teagan's eyes narrowed to pretty brown slits. "Oh, I'm sorry, I must have missed the MD after your name."

She ran her fingers over his upper body in swift but thorough gestures, and despite the jagged pain running the entire length of his left arm, he threw on a smile.

"It's back where it should be, isn't it?" he asked, more statement than question.

She paused. "I don't feel a dislocation, no. But that doesn't mean there isn't any damage to the tendons. It was a stupid move."

"And still not my worst by far." He let go against the thin padding of the cot, suddenly very aware of the soreness sinking into him like teeth.

"Yeah, well, it's definitely the last one you'll pull on my watch." She turned to pop the lock on the glass-walled cabinet behind her, sending that earthy rosemary scent his way as her hair snapped over her shoulder. "How much do you weigh?"

Okay, couldn't say he'd been expecting that question. "Two fifty. You want to know if I like moonlit strolls on the beach, too?"

Her scowl didn't even sway an inch. "You don't strike me as the type. Do you have any allergies to medication?" She pulled some paper-wrapped squares of gauze from another cabinet and laid them next to her before rummaging through a box on the shelf by her chair.

"No. Why?"

"Well, your tattoos are going to make this interesting, but if worse comes to worst, I can always tap the vein on the top of your hand."

"Tap the what?" he asked, realization trickling in like ice water.

Teagan lifted a brow and gifted him with an angelic smile that worked its way through his veins in about two seconds flat.

"Don't worry, Superman. It's only a prick. But then again, it looks like that's your specialty."

Chapter Four

The astringent bite of rubbing alcohol reached Teagan's nose as she tore into the packet in her hand, and she measured the intricate black tattoo on Adrian's right forearm with a casual glance. Placing a line was more about feel than anything else, but it didn't make this a cozy jaunt down Main Street, either. Still, procedure was procedure, and she wasn't about to tell the docs in the emergency department that she didn't start an IV en route when she knew damn well they were expecting her to do it. Explaining the shoulder thing was going to be bad enough.

Taking her eyes off a guy like Adrian in the first place had been the highest order of stupid. She wasn't screwing up his care again.

"So how come you're sticking me, exactly?"

His much-softened tone snagged her attention, and she adjusted hers to match. "Because you need painkillers on board before we get to Riverside. The doctors there are going to give you a pretty good workup. It's not going to be fun."

"I'm okay with the pain," he said, although the thin sheen of sweat on his brow coupled with his skin's growing pallor said otherwise.

Teagan shrugged. "You need the IV regardless. Might as well let the meds take the edge off." She sat on the bench seat at Adrian's side and flipped his right arm palm-side up, running her fingers down the corded length from elbow to wrist in search of a good spot.

"So what language is this, anyway?" she asked, folding his hand into a fist before tracing the thickly scrolled letters spanning his skin from wrist to elbow. Maybe if she distracted him, he'd let her do her job without complaint.

"Italian." He didn't elaborate, but he also didn't balk as she ripped open the IV kit she'd pulled from the med box.

"Oh. What does it mean?" Teagan tapped the pad of one gloved finger against the vein now standing in relief against his skin right above the words *vivere senza rimpianti*.

"You ask a lot of questions, don't you?"

The edgy little smile that had caught her so off guard in the middle of the road was back in full force, and it hadn't lost an ounce of steam in its absence.

Teagan's cheeks prickled with the unfamiliar sensation of a blush. "Sorry. Little pinch here. Ready?"

He nodded, keeping his smile locked in place. "Whenever you are, Red."

Right. Because that nickname hadn't haunted her enough in the third grade. "Just hold still."

She guided the IV into place with a few deft movements despite the fact her pulse had just taken on all the properties of a freight train. "I'm going to put some Fentanyl in here to ease some of your pain. It works pretty quickly, so you should be able to relax soon."

"Whatever will get this over with faster." Adrian looked away, the smile slipping from his face as he shifted his weight against the semi-reclined surface of the cot. It figured he'd go and get all agreeable when they were halfway to the hospital, but truly, Teagan knew better than to complain.

She drew two hundred micrograms of Fentanyl into a syringe and worked it into the IV, doing a visual sweep to make sure all systems were go. "I'm just going to recheck your vitals here and see if we can manage some focus assessment before those pain meds get in the way."

"Focus assessment sounds like something my high school guidance counselor tried once. Hate to break it to you, but it didn't work out so well then. Doubt you'll have much luck with it now."

Teagan's laugh popped out before she could swallow it, and she palmed the penlight from her bag. "Don't worry, it's not that tough. Look up for me."

Adrian fastened her with a dead-on stare, and whoa, there was a lot roiling around in those hazel eyes of his. No matter how big and bad, most car accident victims experienced some form of shock or another in the aftermath. Her social skills might not be impeccable—or hell, even good—but it was time to keep this guy as calm as possible.

"So, tell me," she said, slipping the pulse ox clip over his finger. "What do you do, Adrian?"

His forehead creased, making his surprise a dead giveaway. "I'm a chef."

Looked like surprise was catching. "And how long have you been a chef?"

"Since the day I was born."

The laughter pushing past her lips caught her off guard for the second time in as many minutes. "You've been busy, then. You must work at the place in the resort." That tiny tickle of recognition fanned over her again, but as soon as she flicked her attention toward it, it was gone, like smoke in a stiff breeze.

"What makes you say that?" He canted his head to the side, his shoulders seeming to loosen slightly.

Teagan noted his current vitals before continuing with

the exam. "Because unless you count the bakery on Main Street, there are only two other full-service places to eat in Pine Mountain, and there isn't a *chef* in either one."

The thought of Lou, the lanky guy who worked his magic at her father's bar and grill, working up a hoity-toity dish like on those reality shows was downright laughable. Not that Adrian really fit that mold either, but still. He'd been the one to use the c-word, not her.

As if he'd just climbed into her head for an easy look-see, Adrian teased, "Careful making assumptions over there. I ditched the tall white hat as soon as I graduated from culinary school."

She held up her hands, busted. "Okay. But for the most part, we townies tend to just sling hash and be done with it." Teagan examined him carefully, and this time the vague recognition darting around in her brain snagged and held. "The restaurant at the resort! You were there last year, when we responded to that call for the other chef. A woman."

The tumblers and gears of her memory locked into place over the image. They'd been first on scene, and Evan had gone to secure the patient—a nasty facial trauma, if she remembered right. Teagan had been too busy securing the rest of the scene, namely trying to peel Adrian off of Jackson Carter, a local guy she'd known since middle school.

The fight had been short-lived. And Adrian had been boiling-point furious.

"She's my boss," Adrian said, dispelling only a touch of the mystery running through her head. "You remember that?"

"Small town. And you have a memorable right hook."

His eyes flared, in way more panic than irritation. "It wasn't like that, exactly." A pause, and it looked like hers weren't the only gears sliding into place. "Wait, that was you who jumped in the middle of things."

Teagan nodded, sliding down the bench toward his feet and laying the flat of her hand against the bottom of one monstrous boot. "Securing the scene to administer care is part of the job. Press forward as far as you can."

He did, and when she prompted, he gave a quick repeat on the other side. "You could get hurt like that, being in the wrong place at the wrong time."

"Said the guy on the gurney," she said, unable to bite back a wry smile. "How's your arm feeling?" Now that she'd had more time for a more focused exam, it was clear the broken arm was likely the only injury he'd sustained, and even that looked pretty straightforward. Lucky bastard.

"Pretty good." He closed his eyes for a fraction too long to be a blink, and that, coupled with his answer, signaled the Fentanyl was starting to kick in nice and hard.

"Good. We should be at the hospital in another seven minutes, give or take. You can close your eyes if you want."

Another blink, this one shuttering his eyes just enough to be sexy as hell. "That might not . . . be the best idea."

Concern splashed through Teagan's chest, and she leaned forward from her perch on the bench seat at his side. "Are you sure you're feeling okay?"

"Relax." A lazy smile joined his bedroom eyes, sending an entirely *different* sensation through her chest. "I'm not going to code on you or anything. It's just, ah, easier to forget about the pain if I'm distracted, that's all."

Oh, buddy. If you only knew. "Okay, but consider yourself forewarned. I'm not sure I'm the best person for the job." Teagan bit her lip over a pause. "Polite conversation isn't exactly my forte."

"Polite conversation is for amateurs," he said. "Tell me something important."

A streak of shock popped through her veins. "You want me to tell you something personal?" That Fentanyl must be knocking him sideways if he thought she was going to spill her soul.

"Yeah," Adrian said on nothing more than a rumble. "Personal. What's your favorite ice-cream flavor?"

More laughter escaped in an unexpected burst, but at least it was a painless question. Poor guy probably *was* a little loopy from the meds. "Umm, wow. Coffee, I guess."

"I could see that." His voice was slow, and it dashed all the way down her spine, lingering only when it reached the lowest point between her hips. Desperate for something clinical to keep her busy, Teagan snatched a few packets of alcohol wipes. She tore one open and leaned in, dabbing methodically at a scrape above Adrian's eye.

"Ah." She shook her head, giving the cut a closer look. "You've got a pretty nasty lac here. It's small, but looks kind of deep. I hate to tell you, but you're probably going to have to lose this piercing to have it stitched up."

"Great," he said, although the sarcasm didn't quite stick. "You can go ahead and take it out, I guess."

Teagan made quick work of removing the stainless steel barbell, sliding it into a plastic bag before giving voice to the question in her head. "So how about you?"

"How about me what?" He angled the side of his face so it fit tight into the curve of her hand, and she scooped in a shallow breath at the increased contact.

"What's your favorite flavor of ice cream?" she murmured, surprised to find herself actually wanting to know.

His eyes went from warm hazel to smoky quartz in the time it took her to exhale, and he dipped his gaze to her mouth.

"Strawberry."

"And what's so great about strawberries?" Oh hell. Was that her voice, all breathy and ridiculous?

"They're perfect." He curled the fingers of his uninjured hand around hers, pulling her in and reducing the space between them to a mere sliver. With his stare resting right on her lips, he said, "And red."

Before the word even sank in, Adrian lifted his mouth to hers in a slow stroke. His lips were the exact opposite of the rest of him, soft and accommodating, and Teagan gasped against them. He tasted like cinnamon, spicy and dangerous, and he tightened beneath her like he had every intention of parting her mouth with his own and discovering all of her. Her brain screamed that she should pull back, give him what-for, do *something* other than just sit there and let him kiss her, but all her good intentions fell prey to one simple fact.

She didn't want him to stop.

But then, just as quickly as he'd closed the space between them, Adrian pulled away, and the resulting rush of cool air brought Teagan back to earth with a hasty snap.

"Sorry. I . . ." Adrian trailed off, eyes at half-mast. "I'm so tired."

"Close your eyes." Thank God she'd at least faked her way back to her normal speaking voice. The sound of it steadied her ever further. "We'll be at Riverside in a couple of minutes."

As if on cue, Evan leaned back and aimed his voice into the narrow pass-through, one eye still on the road as he hollered an ETA of ninety seconds. Teagan shucked her gloves and swept up the debris in the rig, double-checking Adrian's vitals even though her own probably looked like a skyline shot of Mount Everest. His eyes were closed, his chest rising and falling in smooth rhythm. She'd given him enough Fentanyl to knock out a basketball team, so it really wasn't a shock that he'd gotten a little goofy. He probably wouldn't even remember kissing her when his eyes opened up again.

The smartest thing she could do was forget it, too.

* * *

"Mr. Holt, my name is Dr. Russell. I'm one of the specialists down here in the emergency department." The guy crossed the curtained-off area to shake Adrian's good hand, but thankfully didn't dive into any more pleasantries. He'd been here for hours as it was, and he'd been itching to leave from the minute he'd been rolled through the door, half-cocked and thinking of summer fruit.

Holy shit, kissing Teagan had been stupid. And hot.

And stupid.

But the cadence of her laughter had been so oddly soothing, he'd been helpless to stop. The rich, velvety sound had covered him like warm honey on fresh-baked bread, sliding over his senses until he could taste it on his lips and under his tongue. Everything had disappeared save the push and pull of the moment, until her lush, red mouth was the only thing on the planet.

Definitely hot.

Dr. Russell cleared his throat and pulled out a stack of X-ray printouts, placing them on the rolling table next to Adrian's gurney. "Your workup shows you're clear of any head or neck injuries, and your chest and lungs look fine." He flipped through the paper copies, referencing the stark, grainy images as he went. "You're going to feel the bumps and bruises for the next few days, though. A discharge nurse will be in to talk to you about it before you're released."

Right, right. It was nothing a little time at work wouldn't fix. "What about this?" He nodded down at the splint on his arm, which was now throbbing to the beat of a marching band on game day.

"Ah, that. Well, the good news is that your shoulder

looks intact on the X-rays. No dislocation, although you've got a pretty nasty contusion. Mind if I take a closer look?"

"Help yourself." Adrian grunted as he leaned forward, and man, his body felt so much heavier than it had when he got out of bed this morning. Dr. Russell's hands moved over his shoulder with purpose, sending ripples of pain toward Adrian's sternum like shards of glass.

"I take it from the scar tissue you've sustained a dislocation in the past?"

"Twice." Three times if you counted today, which Adrian didn't.

Dr. Russell nodded. "So you know it can be sore for up to a few weeks."

Adrian dropped back into place on the gurney, and the limb in question squalled in protest. "You said that's the good news. What's the bad news?"

"You have a clean break of your radius, which is one of the bones in the forearm." The doctor flipped the printouts toward Adrian, pointing to the long bone on the thumb side of the X-ray. "It's pretty straightforward as far as breaks go, although that doesn't make it hurt less. It won't require surgery, but I'm not going to lie to you. You've got a pretty long road to recovery ahead. May I ask what you do for a living?"

Adrian's brow cranked in confusion. "I'm a chef."

"I see. And is this your dominant side?"

Dread leaked through his chest, knotting things up as it went. "No."

"Good." The doc readjusted the stethoscope hooked around his neck. "That should make things a little easier for you as you take time off to recover."

Oh hell no. "I don't need time off. My left hand is fine."

Dr. Russell pitched his voice to sympathy level, fixing Adrian with a patient look that told him nothing good would come from what the guy said. "Yes, but it's attached to your arm, which isn't fine. This break, in conjunction with the shoulder bruise, is going to have you in a sling for at least a week, and a cast that will include your thumb for six, maybe even eight. Your mobility will be seriously limited, and lifting anything, however light, is out of the question."

The dread in Adrian's chest morphed into panic. "Come on, Doc. People break bones all the time. Throw it in a cast and I'll be good to go. I don't need a sling." Sure, a cast might slow him down on the line a little bit, but he'd manage. He couldn't be idle.

He couldn't be out of the kitchen.

"I'm sorry, but with the damage you've sustained today on top of your past shoulder injury, it's really imperative to err on the side of caution if you want a full recovery."

"So what are you saying?" Adrian's throat threatened to close, but he forced the words out. "I can't cook at *all* if I want this to get better?"

Dr. Russell shook his head. "We can reevaluate the shoulder in a week to possibly eliminate the sling, and the cast will allow some functional use of your fingers, although your thumb will definitely have to be immobilized for the bone in your forearm to properly heal. But the best way to avoid significant repercussions from this injury is to rest the arm completely during that time."

The words hit Adrian like a delayed reaction, and he sank into the gurney as Dr. Russell finished.

"I'm afraid with the nature of your profession, six weeks would be the absolute minimum before you'll be back in the kitchen."

Chapter Five

Adrian leaned against the aging doorframe of his apartment, fumbling his keys twice before dropping them onto the threshold with a harsh metallic clatter.

"God damn it." He shifted his weight to bend down and go for a repeat performance with the finicky door, but Carly knelt down like nothing doing to scoop up the keys.

"I've got it." She maneuvered them into the lock with effortless finesse and a tiny smile. "Come on, let's get you situated. Your arm must hurt."

"It's fine." Sure. As long as *fine* was synonymous with *this sucks out loud,* Adrian was absolutely stellar.

"Mmm." Carly nudged her way into his apartment, eyeing the stark walls and lack of furniture. "You're supposed to take those pain meds with food. Why don't I throw something together and we'll talk?"

"I don't really need the medicine. Why don't we go back to the restaurant? You're cutting it close for dinner prep, and I'm sure I can . . . do something," he finished lamely. Christ, he should be up to his elbows in *mise en place* right now, giving their pastry chef, Bellamy, a hard time and barking orders at the line cooks. Had that really only been yesterday?

"Bellamy and Gavin have dinner prep under control for now. You and I need to talk."

Adrian nodded. As much as he wanted to avoid yapping about what was already done, they really did need to come up with a plan. Just because he wasn't cleared for the kitchen didn't mean he couldn't work.

He lowered himself onto the time-battered stool at the breakfast bar separating his tiny kitchen from the tiny rest of the place. "So I've been thinking. What if I help run payroll and kitchen inventory for the next couple of weeks?"

Carly's brows arced skyward. "With a broken arm?"

"I know it's not ideal, but at least it's something. And now that the garden is starting to bear more produce, I can oversee that, too."

The project had been Carly's brainchild last year, and a brilliant one at that. The resort's two-acre on-site garden had already reduced their costs and allowed produce to go from plot to plate in hours rather than days or weeks. He might not be able to do any of the manual labor, but they had a gardener and landscapers for that stuff anyway. Maybe they could use his help somewhere out there.

Carly leaned against the thin expanse of Formica counter space between them, putting on a wistful smile. "Are you going to accomplish all that with one hand tied behind your back?"

Adrian shrugged out of instinct, and his shoulder and arm ganged up on him in an epic game of *we hate you*. He sucked in a breath, but steadied his voice over the echoing pain. "I've done worse."

"I know, *gnoccone*. But we have a lot to consider. Things are different now."

"Different how?" It was just a broken arm, for Chrissake. Six weeks and he'd be good as new.

Carly paused, her voice going quiet and uncharacteristically soft. "For starters, I'm pregnant."

Adrian felt his jaw unhinge, and all the breath left his lungs on a hard *whoosh*. "You're . . . what?"

"I was going to tell you when you got back to the restaurant tonight. I'm due in October." Her hands went from the aging counter to the lower section of her chef's whites, right between the twin rows of buttons.

His gut gave a healthy combination of twist-and-yank. "Holy shit. Are you . . . are you okay? I mean, you're happy, right?" Damn, he was doing a spectacular job of botching this. They were supposed to be best friends! But the only stuff he knew about making babies was how *not* to. Since when had she wanted a kid?

But Carly simply laughed, waving off his verbal bumbling. "Yes, I'm happy."

"Wait a second." The math filtered past the shock and into his brain. "You're due in October? That's only six months from now. How long have you known about this?"

She dropped her gaze to her hands, but he'd be willing to bet it wasn't because they were suddenly interesting. "I wanted to wait until the second trimester to tell anybody, to be sure the baby was healthy."

"So nobody knows?"

"Almost nobody." Carly fiddled with a loose button on her chef's jacket, rolling it between her pinched fingers. "Obviously Jackson knows. And Bellamy guessed when I spent those couple of days throwing up last month."

Adrian froze to his seat, toeing the line between confused and frustrated. "I thought that was food poisoning." He'd even triple-checked all their food-handling procedures because of it to make sure no one else got sick.

"I didn't know what else to say, Ade, and I was scared. I swear to God, expectant mothers shouldn't be allowed on the Internet. The medical jargon alone is terrifying."

Her wide-eyed expression showed her words for the

truth, and it stemmed his frustration. "I'm sorry," he said. "I'm just surprised."

She'd never mentioned wanting a baby before, let alone trying to actively have one. While he wasn't exactly a talk-about-your-feelings-by-the-campfire kind of guy, they *were* still best friends. At the very least, something this major deserved a mention.

"I know, and my timing sucks." She gestured to his arm. "But this baby is going to mean big changes. For all of us."

Despite the smile blooming over Carly's face, her words peppered holes in Adrian's chest. "You need me in the kitchen now more than ever."

She shook her head and moved around the breakfast bar to look him right in the eye. "For now, I'm going to ask Bellamy to move back up to the line. She knows the menu from before she switched to pastry, and she's got great experience as a savory chef."

"Who's going to be your pastry chef?" Adrian asked, hating the sting in his tone. Was he really so easily replaced?

"I have to talk to management, but I think we can set up a short-term contract with The Sweet Life, down on Main Street, and have them supply us with pastries from their bakery. Bellamy should be able to supplement with our specialty items, and one of the line cooks might be able to move to *garde manger* to fill in the gaps. It'll take a little doing, but we'll work it out."

"Okay, but I could still do something," Adrian argued, digging his heels in hard. "You shouldn't be working doubles. That can't be good for you, right?" He dropped his eyes to her midsection, which looked the same as it always did. But holy crap, there was a *kid* in there.

The normalcy of yesterday hurtled even further away.

Carly smiled reassuringly. "My doctor says I'm fine to

work for now, and now that the morning sickness is gone, I feel pretty good. I think you're the one who needs to rest."

He bit back an exasperated breath. No way was he going to let her down now. There had to be *something* he could do, for both their sakes. "I get that working the line is out for a little while. But in a few days when this sling comes off, who knows, maybe—"

"No." Carly's tone brooked no argument. "I'm not talking about resting for a couple of days or weeks for your body to heal, although you need that, too. I'm talking about this." She reached out, gently flipping his uninjured palm up to reveal the dark lettering tattooed on his right forearm, and Adrian's hand tightened in hers. "You made a promise to your *nonna* that you're not making good on, Adrian. It's time you started."

His heart punched in his chest. "Carly, don't."

"Don't what?" Her eyes glittered over his, but she'd never been one to hold back. "Look, I'm grateful as hell that you ran La Dolce Vita while I was gone, but you were clearly on ten this morning, and that was before this even happened." She nodded down at the sling hugging his body, and fuck, the thing suddenly felt like a noose. "So do you want to tell me what's really going on with you?"

"What's going on with me?" he repeated, stiffening against the scuffed wood of the bar stool.

But Carly didn't let up. "You're working nonstop seventy-hour weeks, you nearly cleaned my clock this morning before checking to see who I was, and you don't even want to take six hours off after breaking your arm. What are you trying to hide from?"

"Nothing. I just needed a little sleep this morning, like you said," he argued, hating where this was going with every fiber in his worn-out body.

"And what about last week, or last month? This go-hard

routine isn't going to get rid of your ghosts, Ade. I'm going on an extended leave of absence next year, but before I do, I need to know you're straight. And right now . . ."

Adrian's head snapped up. "I can run the kitchen just fine."

Her expression softened, and damn it, he'd rather she cuss him up one side and down the other than give him the sympathy eyes. "I know you can. It's the rest of you I'm worried about. For the last couple of months, you haven't been *you*. Damn it, Adrian, we've been in Pine Mountain for over a year now and you don't even have furniture. It's like you're here, but you're empty. You're not keeping your promise."

Fear, frustration, and anger merged into a trifecta of crappy emotions in his chest. "I'm doing exactly what I said I'd do. I belong in the kitchen. It's all I have."

"No, it's not. You can't live without regrets if you never leave the kitchen, no matter how much you think you need to be there." Carly leaned in, squeezing his good arm right over his thickly lettered tattoo before moving toward the door. "Look, you've been through a lot today. Try to get some rest. I'll come back tomorrow to check on you and bring you some food. We can talk some more then if you want."

But Adrian knew better. "You're not going to let me back into the restaurant, are you?"

"No, *gnoccone*. Not until you heal. Both your arm and the rest of you."

Teagan made her way through the front door at the Double Shot just in time to catch a thick string of curse words flowing from behind the bar. Despite the exhaustion threatening the rest of her, a smile poked at the corners of her mouth. Her father's Irish accent was deceptively melodic, even as it curled around the harsh profanity directed at the case of beer in front of him.

"Trouble in paradise, Da?" Teagan's purposeful stride made quick work of the dining room's battle-tested hardwood floor. She slipped behind the mahogany bar lining the entire back wall, dodging a half keg of Budweiser and a rolling cart full of clean pint glasses. Her father's russet hair was graying more at the temples with each passing day, but his troubled scowl brightened to a smile as she approached.

"Ah! There's my pretty girl. I was just wrestlin' with these boxes, gettin' ready for the night before I prep the kitchen. Don't pay me no mind." He turned to let her plant a peck on his weathered cheek, and her gut twisted hard at the deep shadows painted under his eyes. A sheen of exertion seeded his brow, and his slower-than-usual movements weren't lost on her.

"This is a lot of work. Why don't you let Tommy do the heavy lifting?" Teagan's gaze roamed over the cases of beer stacked in a haphazard tower by the cooler at midbar, hating every inch of how hard her father had to work. Sure, this season had been slow out of the gate, but with decent traffic from college kids skiing on the weekends and a healthy cast of regulars from town, the place was successful enough. And all those late nights added up after a while.

Especially when you'd been at them for twenty-five years, and single-parented a daughter on top of that.

"Can't," her father grunted, thrusting two longneck bottles into the cooler hard enough to send ice skittering onto the rubber mat beneath his feet. "I gave Tommy the night off."

"You want to do a Friday night with no barback?" Her brows popped toward her hairline. Tommy was the only runner they had on payroll right now, and even though their

Friday nights had been leaner than usual lately, it was still a long way to last call. Hauling your own barware and beer gave those nonstop hours on your feet a whole new level of *ugh,* busy or not.

Her father mopped his brow with a flannel sleeve. "Brennan'll be at the door. He can help out when things get quiet."

Well, at least they weren't going without a bouncer, too. Teagan plucked a clean bar towel off the stack in front of her, snapping it at her father before putting it to good use on the time-buffed wood. "You need to stop being so nice. Next time Tommy asks for a weekend night off, tell him no." She scrubbed at a particularly difficult spot on the bar for a minute before the silence revealed her father's stare. "What?" she asked, staring back.

A slow beat passed before he returned his attention to the beer cooler with a wistful smile. "You're a stubborn one, just like . . ." He trailed off, the smile disappearing. "Well. You draw more flies with honey than vinegar, love."

Teagan froze at her father's unspoken déjà vu, but she checked her feelings in favor of some good, old-fashioned cynicism. He was nice enough to give a stranger the shirt right off his back. Never mind that he'd only end up cold for his trouble.

"I don't know. Last time I checked, vinegar gets the job done, and without the mess, too." Okay, so maybe she was a little rough around the edges, while her father had more inherent charm. Still, she managed to get by, and without being a doormat on top of it. She didn't need to be all touchy-feely to take care of business, so honestly, what good would it do to change her colors?

Her father's low chuckle cut through her thoughts. "One day, someone will have you singing a different tune. Wait and see."

Teagan's thoughts zeroed in on a pair of stormy hazel eyes, and her hand flew to her lips before she could pull back on the thought *or* the sizzling hot bolt of attraction that went with it.

Oh yeah, no. The memory of Adrian's ill-fated kiss, along with the ridiculous ice-cream craving she'd been having all damned day, could take a freaking hike. The last thing she needed was someone to change her tune. The one and only time she'd let anyone take care of her had ended in disaster, and it wasn't something she was eager to repeat.

Ever.

Teagan took another swipe at the bar, the towel knotted around her fingers tight enough to make them smart. "I don't think so, Da. Honey's not exactly my thing." She paused just long enough to snare the word with air quotes. "And anyway, I'm happy here, working the bar with you."

Her father stood abruptly from his crouched position behind the bar, turning to put the last of the beer in the cooler. "You know, about that. I think it's time we—"

But the rest of his response fell prey to the sound of the bottle tumbling from his hand, smashing into bits as it hit the lip of the chill chest on its way to the floor.

"Da!" Adrenaline skidded through Teagan's veins, and she deftly maneuvered around the tower of boxes to arrive at her father's side. He sagged against the bar, his breath rattling like an old storm door as he tried—unsuccessfully—to wave her off.

"I'm fine," he rumbled, but his wince betrayed the lie. Damn it, had he been this pale a few minutes ago? "Musta found my feet too quickly. Just let it pass."

"I don't think so." Teagan hammered her focus into place despite the fact that her heartbeat had gone haywire, dropping down to brace an arm around her father. Thankfully, he stopped trying to fight her, and she lowered him to sit on the floorboards by the cash register, outside the circumference of broken glass and spattered beer foam.

"Here. Look at me." Teagan mashed down the cold fear spearing through her chest, wrapping her fingers around her father's wrist. *Jeez, when did he get so thin?* "Do you have any pain in your chest or your arm?" She flipped her free wrist upward, counting meticulously, not pleased with the thready staccato of his pulse.

"You're not gettin' rid of me just yet, darlin'," he wheezed out, mustering a weak smile. "There's nothing wrong with my chest. My ticker's right as rain."

She snapped up his left hand, unconvinced. "Squeeze."

He did, with enough pressure that she was momentarily satisfied. "Told you. Fine."

"You almost passed out just standing still. That hardly counts as fine." Teagan ran through the checklist of possibilities in her head. "Numbness? Any tingling or weakness on this side?"

"It's a little dizzy spell. Give an old man a break."

She didn't budge a fraction of an inch, checking his pupils as best she could in the low light. "When was the last time you ate something?"

Her father paused, guilt flashing in his amber eyes. "I don't remember."

She shifted to her feet, watching him the whole way as she grabbed a carton of orange juice from the cooler next to the beer fridge. After a few sips, his pulse evened out a little, but Teagan's mind was made up.

"I'm calling the station. I want you to go to Riverside for a workup." Nick Brennan, their bouncer and backup bartender, would be here in a few minutes. He and Lou could at least get the rest of the afternoon prep done and call Tommy in while she got her father squared away.

"I'm not goin' back ta Riverside." Her father clipped out each word, precise and hard. "I don't need any more tests."

Teagan stared, her movements grinding to a graceless halt. "What did you say?"

Her father frowned, but didn't stand down. "I don't need any more tests. I've already been poked, prodded, and turned into a pincushion a coupla months ago."

"And you didn't tell me?" It wasn't like forgetting to deliver a phone message or blanking on which days he'd scheduled her to work. This was huge, and he'd kept it from her on purpose.

"I'm in good hands. I've got a pretty lady doctor in charge of me now, Dr. Riley."

"I know her." Teagan's knees shook and threatened to give way, so she parked it next to her father on the floor behind the bar. Michelle Riley was an endocrinologist at Riverside. They called her down from time to time for consults on patients who'd been brought in with complications from things like Type 2 diabetes and renal failure.

Oh God.

Teagan grabbed her father's hand, hating with all her might how hers trembled. She was supposed to be taking care of *him,* for Chrissake. How could she have missed something so utterly major?

"Da." Teagan dragged in a pathetic excuse for a breath. "Why have you been seeing Dr. Riley?"

Her father dropped his gaze to the carton of juice in his shaking fingers. "The regular doc at the hospital told me I needed a specialist. He sent me to her for all those tests, and she told me I'm diabetic. She's treating me for it, and a coupla other things. I go see her at Riverside every few weeks." He paused over a laborious breath before continuing. "But don't go gettin' all twisted up on it, now."

Her jaw tightened enough to make her molars beg for mercy. "You hid this from me!"

"Only because I knew you'd worry, and you've got enough on your plate without thinkin' of your old man."

Teagan barked out a humorless laugh and pinched the bridge of her nose. She had to fix this, one step at a time. "Okay. First things first. Where's your blood glucose meter?"

"I don't need—"

"Where?" she repeated, soft yet deadly serious.

"Behind you." He nodded to a small, nondescript box beneath the bar, the kind that usually housed cocktail napkins. Even though it sat far apart from the other inventory, Teagan must've passed over it a thousand times in the last few months, too caught up in the crush of helping customers or stocking the bar to give it a second thought.

She unearthed the meter, giving her father's ring finger a vigorous rub before placing the lancet into position as she'd done no less than a thousand times for various patients.

But this was no ordinary patient. No way could her father keep up with everything at the bar like this.

"What else?" Teagan bit out, forcing her focus into the task.

"What do you mean, 'what else?'"

"What else is Dr. Riley treating you for? And don't tell me not to worry about it. It's too late for that."

Her father nodded, resigned. "High blood pressure and high cholesterol. I got all kinds of colorful pills for my troubles. Of course, they gave me a whole new set of troubles."

"What are you talking about?" Teagan checked the digital readout on the meter with a frown. Her father's color was the rough equivalent of Elmer's paste, and he looked like he'd been awake for about a week straight.

Color first. She reached behind her for a package of cocktail mix, tearing open the bag of pretzels and peanuts and putting a healthy dose in her father's free hand.

He sighed, but followed the unspoken order. After a few bites, he said, "I didn't give Tommy the night off, love. I had to let him go. The day cook and that waitress, too. Things have just been too tight, but the work still needs to be done. It's just . . . not easy to pay for all the medicine." His voice coalesced into silence, and understanding trickled into Teagan's brain.

Owning a bar and grill gave you lots of things over the years. Health insurance wasn't one of them. Still, they did well enough that it shouldn't be *that* bad.

Unless she'd missed the memo on that, too.

Teagan's last thread of control unraveled in a hard snap. "When were you going to tell me about this? I could've helped more! I could've—"

"What?" her father interrupted, pinning her with a steely stare that reminded her that she came by her fire honestly. "Worked more shifts? Lord, girl, you're here more often than not as it is. I'm not havin' you work your fingers to the bone for me. You've got a life to live."

"Taking care of you is more important." Fear swirled into anger and then slid back into fear, but Teagan slammed a lid over all of it. She'd failed monumentally by missing all of this, but she'd be goddamned if she wasn't going to take care of it now, no matter what it took. "Your glucose level sucks, and I'm assuming from the way you wanted to let it pass that this isn't your first dizzy spell. If you've been skipping meds to try to conserve, or if your symptoms are getting worse, you need to be seen. You can't keep working like this." Teagan pulled her cell phone from the back pocket of her jeans, flicking it to life.

"I'm not goin' to the hospital. Friday's our busiest night, and we need the cash comin' in."

Nope. No way was her father going to outmuscle her on this one. Not even if she had to sedate him to get him out the door. She pulled up the number for Riverside Hospital, her finger hovering over the *send* button. "I don't care. Hypoglycemic shock isn't a joke, and neither is renal failure. You need IV fluids and insulin. Dr. Riley will probably want to monitor you overnight, just as a precaution."

"I skipped a meal and a pill or two, and I worked a little too hard, is all. Some of this juice and a coupla more minutes, and I'll be on my feet."

"You don't understand. This isn't about one night, Da. Dr. Riley should've been more clear about you taking it easy. Seventy-hour workweeks in a high-stress environment aren't part of a healthy regimen. You can't keep up a work schedule like this if your diabetes and blood pressure are out of control." Teagan turned to make the phone call, but the look of stark vulnerability crossing her father's face glued the argument to her throat.

"Dr. Riley was perfectly clear, darlin', but she just told me what I already know. This place is goin' ta be the end of me. But I'm not goin' ta let it be the end of you, too."

Chapter Six

Adrian stared absently at the ceiling, wondering how many more minutes would drop from the clock before he went clinically insane. Since only forty-seven had passed between when he'd woken from his painkiller-induced nap and now, making it to a triple-digit time count looked pretty bleak.

The next six weeks were going to take for freaking *ever*.

Adrian blew out a hard breath, ignoring the thudding pain that radiated from shoulder to cast as he pushed up from his rumpled bed. His stomach let loose a toothy growl, one that told him he needed to either fill it or face some barbarous consequences. He padded over the worn hardwood to the kitchen, hitting the light switch with his good hand.

Illumination didn't do much for the state of his pantry, other than to highlight the fact that the space inside was about as naked as the day he'd moved in. But he was never here long enough to use anything other than the bed or the shower, so keeping a stocked pantry seemed kind of stupid, even though his profession suggested otherwise. Not that it helped with the nausea currently making a playground out of his belly.

The sling grated uncomfortably across the back of Adrian's neck as he rummaged one-handed through the few items on the white plastic shelves. He pulled out some crackers he knew were past their prime, but since it was that or a jar of molasses, they'd have to do until he could hit the grocery store.

He shifted awkwardly against the sling, grappling with the plastic sleeve sealed around the crackers to no avail. How ironic that he'd managed to survive nine months in one of the nastiest penitentiaries in New York City, yet he was about to be bested by a package of fucking saltines. Frustration welled in his chest, hot and unrepentant, and Adrian twisted his arm up, sling and all, to rip open the package with both hands.

Big mistake.

Pain shot from his shoulder to his fingertips and back again on a continuous circuit of *holy shit,* barging out of his lungs on a groan. Okay, so maybe he needed the sling for a couple of days. He dropped his arm back into place and focused on breathing for a few minutes before graduating to eating, which thankfully replaced some of his waning strength.

Before he'd crashed into bed, he'd made arrangements to have his Harley towed from the impound to Grady's Garage. Bellamy's husband, Shane, ran the place, and he'd promised to take a look at it even though bikes weren't his thing. Regardless of where it was, though, the thing was as undrivable as Adrian was unable to drive it. He'd have to hit up Plan B if he wanted to get past the four walls that were crushing him like strawberries for jam.

Adrian froze in the dimly lit kitchen, the memory of Teagan's mouth over his making a permanent imprint on his libido. How on earth a woman could manage to broadcast *dare me* and *don't touch* at the same time, he had no clue, but Christ. Daring her had felt recklessly good, and kissing her had felt even better.

"Plan B," he muttered, shaking off the thought of her. He needed food, and anyway, his track record with being impulsive sucked. Better to just forget Teagan O'Malley, no matter how mouthwatering she smelled. Or tasted.

He needed to get out of here.

Adrian shoved the partially eaten sleeve of crackers aside, jamming his feet into the black work boots he'd kicked off before face-planting on his bed. He got his leather jacket halfway on before realizing it wasn't going any further, and he bit back a frown as he grabbed the keys hanging on a hook by the front door.

As much as he preferred the Harley to any other mode of transportation, having no fallback plan for Pine Mountain's notoriously snowy winters was just plain idiotic. The nothing-special pickup truck he'd bought last year ensured he'd get to work in snow, sleet, hail, or whatever else Mother Nature wanted to curveball his way, and he yanked the door to his apartment shut before making a beeline for the thing. It took a little doing to get situated behind the wheel—definitely weird to one-hand the seat belt into place over the pain-in-the-ass sling—but he managed.

Joe's Grocery was only three miles up the road, and by the time Adrian got to the sign marking the turnoff, he'd gotten the hang of one-handed driving. His nausea had subsided, but his nearly empty stomach still churned like it was on the spin cycle.

Which became infinitely more problematic when he realized Joe's parking lot was empty and the only lights on were the overheads brightening the asphalt.

"Shit." Between the accident and the groggy nap, Adrian had lost all track of time. Of course Joe's wasn't open at . . .

He paused to let the soft glow of the digital clock in his truck register.

Nine thirty on a Friday night.

Adrian's gut dropped to his knees. He might have lived here for a little over a year, but the only path he'd taken since landing in Pine Mountain was from his apartment to the resort and back. Hell, the only reason he knew the location of the grocery store in the first place was because it lay between the two.

But he couldn't go to the resort, not even in the name of a hot meal he desperately needed. Carly had made it clear she didn't want him there, and his showing up, even just to eat, would reek of awkward. He threw the truck into *drive* and pointed it back at his apartment. He'd have to settle for the rest of those saltines, although he knew he'd be starving again an hour after he downed them.

And then it would be just him, the four walls, and the molasses until morning.

Jerking his knee up to steady the wheel, he jammed the window control to the *down* position until lush spring air replaced the glass. Christ, how was he going to manage six weeks of this when the thought of even one night was enough to suffocate him?

And wait. Where the hell was he?

Adrian scanned the road in front of him with a disgruntled curse. The hunger tangling his belly, coupled with the realization that Carly really wasn't going to change her mind, must've distracted him into missing his turn. He guided the truck into the next turnoff, which opened directly into a wide, rectangular parking lot, and he took stock of his new surroundings to regain his bearings.

A decent handful of cars littered the spaces, and even though the gray and white clapboard building beyond wasn't much to speak of, it was brightly lit. A couple of giggling women made their way past his idling truck, allowing a blast of loud music to escape from within the building as they moved through the front door, and Adrian squinted at the weathered sign over the entryway where they'd disappeared.

THE DOUBLE SHOT BAR AND GRILL

This is a bad idea, came the ingrained survival instinct from the back of his mind, and Adrian knew it was spot-on. Keeping his nose spic and span meant giving places like bars a very wide berth when he was in a bad mood, even if they did have food inside. He tightened his grip over the grooves on his steering wheel, bypassing the front of the building with every intention of making a full circle around the place.

But the strained overtones of an argument, coupled with a glimpse of flame-red hair from beneath the light over the side entrance to the building, had him jamming his foot on the brake.

Teagan folded her bottom lip between her teeth and tried with all her might not to scream as her only cook walked out the Double Shot's side door and into the night.

"Lou, wait!" She scrambled after him, both shocked and relieved that he'd stopped a few paces into the parking lot. "You've got to help me out here. I've got a bar full of hungry people and it's Friday night. You can't walk, not right now."

But the expression on the cook's scruffy face and his cross-armed stance said otherwise. "I'm not working for free,

Teagan. One bounced paycheck, I can forgive. But today's was the third one, and you can't give me any answers."

"My dad does all the payroll," she said, genuinely apologetic. For as many tasks as Teagan juggled behind the bar, the books had always been her father's job, through and through. "I'm sure it's a mistake."

"One he's not around to rectify."

"He's . . . not feeling well." Teagan swallowed past the softball in her throat. She hadn't told any of the staff that her father was likely going to have to take a leave of absence. It had been bad enough getting him to go home and call Dr. Riley's office to at least get advice on stabilizing the episode he'd had earlier. Telling him they needed to figure out a way to run the bar until he was well enough to come back full-time was an argument that would have to wait until later, but she couldn't run anything without a cook.

She tried again, desperate. "I'll talk to him about it tomorrow, first thing. I'm sure he can clear it right up, but until then, I really need you, Lou. The only other person in the kitchen tonight is Jesse, and he can't cook any more than I can."

Lou didn't budge. "Jesse's check bounced too, and I've got to be honest. If your father can't even cover the dishwasher's pay, that ain't a good sign." He took a step closer, his age-creased eyes sweeping from side to side as he met her under the halo of the overhead light. "Look, I like your father, I really do. But I've got a family to think about."

"We'll get your check straightened out, I swear, if you just—"

"I'm not talking about just my check, Teagan. I need to keep my kneecaps intact, you know?"

She yanked her brows inward, straightening her spine in a blend of shock and confusion. "What are you talking about?"

Lou examined her with apparent surprise of his own. "You don't know?"

"Know what?" Fear flooded Teagan's belly. Seriously, she couldn't handle one more thing going wrong tonight. As it was, they were probably weeded to no end in both the kitchen and at the bar from this little tête-à-tête. "God, Lou. What is going on?"

But he just shook his head. "You need to have a long talk with your father, that's what. I'm not getting mixed up in this." He took a step back, then another, each one causing Teagan's heart to lurch. "I'm sorry. But I didn't sign on for trouble."

"Lou, wait!" She stumbled after him, calling again to no avail.

He was gone.

Teagan scraped in a deep breath, squinting her eyes closed against the swing of blazing headlights from a pickup truck doing a U-turn in the parking lot beyond. A million questions bubbled up in her head, but she had more pressing issues right now. Namely figuring out how to survive the night with a staff of five people rather than seven none of whom knew how to cook.

At all.

Teagan dropped her chin toward her chest, trying like hell to come up with a plan. She could no more run the kitchen than she could sprout wings and fly. There were *reasons* she stayed as far from the food as possible, reasons she didn't want to contemplate.

But thinking about that was a luxury she couldn't afford, so Teagan turned on her heel and marched back inside. She could take care of this. She *would* take care of this, even if it was a disaster.

There were no other options.

"Jesse!" she barked out, rounding the corner with haste.

Please God, let this guy have some kitchen skills. He'd only been back home in Pine Mountain for a couple of months, and even though she'd known him since grade school, Teagan had been so busy working one job or another lately that she hadn't gotten past basic pleasantries with him.

"Yes, ma'am?" Jesse poked his head out of the dishwashing station set up adjacent to the main kitchen, his blond hair cropped so close to his skull it was barely a step from shaved clean.

"It's you and me in the kitchen for the rest of the night." She whipped a clean apron from the neat stack on the wooden shelf by the door, knotting it around her waist. "And I respect that you've been in the military for the last six years, but I'm only thirty. If you ma'am me again, we're gonna have a go. Got it?"

"Yes . . ." He faltered, blowing out a breath in place of the newly missing word. "But I'm just a dishwasher. I don't know how to cook."

"That makes two of us." She snatched the tickets from the tiny box networked to the computerized register behind the bar, slightly woozy at how many there were. "Okay, these first two look pretty easy. Lou makes the sauce for the wings in batches, and I think it's all right here." She flipped a couple of stainless steel lids from the containers built into the workstation, guessing blindly. "Throw some of those wings in the fryer, then get to work on the next orders as best you can. I'm going to pull Brennan from the door to run the bar."

"Okay."

Teagan propped the two tickets in the metallic slots above Lou's workstation across from the grill, leaving Jesse to his own devices as she elbowed her way through the door to the main bar area. She blinked hard as her eyes struggled to adjust to the much dimmer lighting, and she caught a passing waitress to cover the outstanding drink orders at the bar. She zeroed in on a tall, deceptively unremarkable figure standing sentry in the alcove by the front door, her rushed steps eating up the space between them in about two seconds flat.

Nick Brennan had none of the typical big-and-mean of other bouncers—in fact, with his lean, lanky build and classic dark-haired, darker-eyed good looks, at first Teagan had pegged him for a nice, average guy with a nice, average job having a nice, average life.

And then she saw him handle himself, along with two drunk, mouthy college students, in the bar, and that impression disappeared faster than she could say Muhammad Ali. In the year and a half Brennan had worked at the Double Shot, Teagan had seen him hold his own in just about every scuffle, even when it was two on one.

Perfect, really, considering she was about to ask him to serve copious amounts of liquor to everyone in a fifty-foot radius.

"Brennan, I've got to put you behind the wood tonight, starting now. We're also cutting the menu to apps only for the rest of the night. Can you grab both waitresses on your way back and let them know?" They usually served their full menu until eleven on Friday nights, but it was going to be hard enough to get by as it was. They might take a little cut in cash-in for the night, but so be it. Right now, Teagan just needed to survive.

Brennan's eyes glittered black with surprise, and he pushed off from his wooden stool to move with her toward the back of the room. "I can do the bar, no problem, but the food thing's gonna be an issue."

A frustrated sound emerged from her throat. The food

thing was *already* an issue, for God's sake. How much worse could it get than the dishwasher and the kitchen-phobe trying to cook their way out of a paper bag during the busiest shift of the week?

"If anyone gets pissy about it, just come get me." Teagan turned to race back to the kitchen to make sure poor Jesse had at least figured out how to drop those wings into the fryer when Brennan's words stopped her cold.

"Okay, but you might want to save yourself some time and check out six and fourteen." He jutted his chin toward the heart of the dining room, and what was left of Teagan's composure did a triple-pretzel. Tables six and fourteen were their two biggest, each one seating up to ten people.

And both of them were freshly filled to maximum capacity. With big guys, each of whom looked like he could eat a rhinoceros for breakfast.

Teagan looked up just in time to overhear the only wait-ress currently on the floor say, "Wow, y'all look hungry! I highly recommend Lou's burgers. They're the best in two counties."

"Oh God." She was toast.

"They came in a couple of minutes ago, from the base-ball game in Riverside. Thought you'd be happy to see the business since we've been pretty slow lately." Brennan slid her a sympathetic look before narrowing his glance in obvious concern. "Is there some kind of problem in the kitchen?"

"Well, that all depends." She jammed her eyes shut over the hot tears threatening to form there. She hadn't cried in *years,* damn it. "You wouldn't happen to have secret cook-ing skills I don't know about, would you?"

Brennan stared at her through the soft, gold light spilling down from the brass lantern fixtures, music pulsing around them in an ironically business-as-usual manner. "Hell, Teagan. What happened to Lou?"

"He quit. And before you ask, the day cook's gone too, and my father's sick. I don't have anybody to call in, and I don't know anyone who can cook." Her voice wavered at the gravity of saying it out loud. "So if you have any brilliant ideas, now's the time to trot them out, Brennan."

But the response didn't come from the shell-shocked-looking bouncer. It came from the shadows behind him.

"I know how you can fix your problem, Red. But you aren't going to like it."

Chapter Seven

Even though every fiber of his better judgment screamed at him to shut up, Adrian shoved it aside. There were conservatively a million reasons he should haul himself right back out the door, but as he looked at Teagan, her wide, whiskey-colored stare so utterly desperate, those reasons took a backseat to one simple truth.

She had a kitchen that needed a chef. And he was a chef who needed a kitchen. The sanity-sucking walls of his apartment would be there tomorrow, and he'd have plenty of time to stare at them and heal, or whatever it was he was supposed to be doing. But for tonight, he could escape, and help Teagan while he was at it.

If she'd let him.

"You know this guy?" The wiry, dark-haired bouncer next to Teagan gave him a lingering up-and-down that broadcast his disdain, but Adrian didn't flinch.

"Uh, yeah." Teagan blinked as if she'd just arrived in the conversation, nodding quickly. "Long story. Look, I appreciate your offer, but your arm is in a couple pieces too many to run a kitchen, isn't it?"

His muscles tightened against the canvas sling holding his livelihood captive, but he still didn't back down. "No more than your kitchen is short a couple of people to make it run, from the sound of things. I might be a little worse for wear, but it looks like I'm the only chef you've got."

The bouncer's brow popped into a shadowy arc. "You're a chef?"

Adrian answered in a singular nod before swinging his gaze to Teagan, whose matching nod confirmed what he'd said.

"Still. With that injury, you can't cook," she said, her voice layered over with both finality and regret.

"No. But I know how to run a kitchen, and your arms work perfectly fine, don't they?"

Her lips parted, marking her shock. As much as he hated it, he couldn't help her by cooking. But he wasn't useless, either.

He needed to stay busy. He needed a kitchen.

"Okay," Teagan agreed, her surprise replaced by cool, calculated focus. "Here's what we're going to do. Brennan, Annabelle is covering the bar right now, but she's got tables waiting for her, and we're about to be slammed. I need you to take care of the bar and anything going down in the front of the house. Fake it if you have to. I'll take the kitchen with Jesse and Adrian."

The guy flicked a hard glance at Adrian, eyes full of doubt as they landed on his cast. "You serious with this, Teagan? It seems like a pretty big liability."

Adrian shifted his body just enough to make his irritation clear—he could do more with one finger than this guy could do unimpaired, for Chrissake—and Teagan's hand shot out to press against the center of his upper chest.

"Not the way we're going to do it." She pinned each of them with a look that mentally tacked on *so knock it off* before kicking herself into motion. She headed to the back of the dining room, giving them both no choice but to shut up and follow, and damn, her walk was full of purpose.

And her ass was sheer perfection in those low-slung jeans.

The bouncer shook his head as they reached the bar, muttering something that sounded suspiciously like "I hope you know what you're doing" before leaning in to take a drink order from a curvy blonde. Teagan didn't waste any time before aiming herself at the wood-paneled swinging door leading to what had to be the kitchen, and Adrian kept up with her, stride for stride.

"Thanks." The word spilled out with the breath he just realized he'd been clutching in his lungs, and hell if that didn't make him sound totally desperate.

She tossed her next words over her shoulder, auburn ponytail snapping around her face as she crossed the slick kitchen tiles beneath their feet. "Don't thank me yet. Brennan's right. The fact that you're off the books is a liability enough. Add that injury to the equation, and I'm earning health and labor violations like merit badges if you so much as boil water."

Unease flared deep in his belly. "I can still help you."

Teagan jammed to a halt at the mouth of a rectangular galley-style kitchen, where two six-burner cooktops flanked a large, open grill along the far wall. A long, double-sided workstation bisected the narrow room lengthwise, and it looked for all the world like the entire place had exploded. Tickets curled from the printer over the stainless steel workstation in a foot-long coil, and a guy wearing a high and tight crew cut and a stone-cold expression raced between the walk-in at the opposite end of the room and the grill currently belching up an ominous cloud of black smoke.

"I sure as hell hope so," Teagan said with a frown.

"Because I'll be honest. You don't have much to work with."

Adrian's unease switched over to full-on doubt as Crew Cut jumped to avoid getting roasted by a flare-up on the grill, and the motion sent one of the burgers he'd been trying to flip skittering to the floor.

Teagan winced, but gave the guy a tiny, reassuring nod before turning back Adrian's way. "Are you still in?"

He opened his mouth to argue with her, to tell her he could at least manage *something* other than the sidelines, but the vibrating pain running the length of his arm snagged his attention. He couldn't even open a package of crackers without agonizing fanfare. As much as he despised it, Teagan was right.

Walking her through this was the best option, and from the look on her face, it was the only way she wasn't going to show him the door.

"Yeah, I'm in. But you're going to have to do what I tell you, no questions asked, if you want this to work. Be sure you're good with it."

She didn't even blink, and God, her tenacity was hot as hell. "I am."

His eyes landed on the guy running in circles by the grill, trying to coax burgers from briquettes. "You, too?"

He nodded. "Yes, sir."

Well, that was a new one. "What's your name, slick?"

The guy practically stood at attention, straightening to an impressive six-foot-one. "Jesse Oliver."

Adrian narrowed his eyes on the darkly smoldering grates, shaking his head. "Okay, Jesse. Start with the tickets, in order. Let's see what we're dealing with."

Jesse rattled off the string of orders with efficiency, but man, it was a hell of a list. Adrian took two steps toward the grill on autopilot before jerking his feet to a halt. Oh hell, this really was going to take everything he had.

"Okay. Pass that spatula over to Red here and grab me a copy of your menu. I'm a chef, not a mind reader. You got someone on dishes in the back?" He craned his neck toward the open-air dry racks of various pots and pans marking the alcove at the rear of the room next to the walk-in. A good dishwasher was worth his weight in gold, especially when things got slammed.

"That would be Jesse," Teagan said, putting a death grip on the spatula as she took the offered utensil from the guy's hand.

"Of course it would." How ironic that his sanity would be saved for the night by such an epic train wreck. "Jesse, go back and give me a baseline on the dishes. We can't plate on nothing. Run whatever you can in thirty seconds and get back up here with that menu."

Adrian jerked his chin at the grill, his brain pulling priorities into place and searching for order in all the chaos. First things first. "Okay, Red, go ahead and waste those hockey pucks and get new burgers fired on the fly."

Teagan hitched into motion, awkwardly scraping the char-grilled offenders to the trash and scooping their floor-bound counterpart from the thick black floor mats to join them. "Now what?"

Adrian bit back his frustration and shifted against his pain-in-the-ass sling. He could've had new burgers on those grates twice by now, and he prickled with the desire to set his hands . . . hand . . . whatever would do the trick without making him scream . . . into gear and just *do* it.

But the look on Teagan's face reminded him that was a one-way ticket home, so he gritted out, "Just what I said. New burgers, ASAP. If the guy who left you in this jam has more than half a brain, they're premade and labeled. Check your lowboy."

"My what?"

"The refrigerator at your knees. And wear gloves, unless you want to get up close and personal with E. coli."

Jesse reappeared in the kitchen with the menu, and Adrian gave it a quick skim as he put the guy on fryer duty. The kitchen was as well-stocked as could be expected for a Friday night, although they'd likely cut it close with those two ten-tops about to put orders in. At least the menu was fairly straightforward. It'd been a while since Adrian had gone the greasy spoon route, but as long as no one ordered anything totally off the wall, they'd manage.

"Aha!" Teagan popped up from the lowboy with a half-sheet pan of premade burger patties in her hands. "These, right?"

Lord. It was a wonder this woman didn't starve to death. "Yeah. Go." He watched as she wrestled with the plastic wrap, finally managing to get all three burgers on the hissing grill. She peeled off both gloves with a well-practiced yank before white-knuckling the oversized spatula and setting her unwavering gaze on the grates.

"They're not gonna break into a dance routine, so go ahead and make yourself useful while they cook." He blew out a breath. Doing six things at once was Cooking 101, for God's sake, and they were way too jammed up for her to do one thing at a time.

But she hesitated. "You want me to just . . . leave them here?"

"It's called multitasking, sweetheart. Make it your friend." Adrian paused to bark a couple directives at Jesse as the guy brought up a basket full of wings, golden-brown and sizzling from the fryer.

Teagan set her mouth into a mulish line. "I know how to multitask."

"Then put your money where your mouth is and show me," he said, firmly in kitchen-mode. "You can start by getting that tray covered up and back into the lowboy. I wasn't kidding about E. coli."

For a second, she looked like she was about to light him up like the Fourth of July, and under other circumstances, he might deserve it. But that old adage about not being able to stand the heat rang true. Taking things personally in the kitchen would only nail up your coffin nice and tight.

Teagan bit her bottom lip hard enough to leave a crescent-shaped indentation on the soft, pink skin as she rewrapped the half sheet and replaced it in the lowboy. "Look, where I come from, if I turn my back on something, it usually codes. Or performs an unassisted shoulder reduction." She leveled an obvious stare at his sling, and yeah, touché. "So I'll do what you tell me to if it'll get me through this, but you're going to have to tell me *everything*. Unless that's too much for you."

The challenge in her eyes, coupled with the determination to take care of things no matter the cost, gave him an instant hard-on. He cocked his head at her, working up a slow grin. "You're going to get what you want. Just be sure you want what you're going to get."

Her grip on the spatula went thermonuclear, and she met his stare head-on. "Ready when you are, Superman."

The printout box on the shelf above her station whirred to life, spitting out a fat ribbon of paper without pause, and despite the total insanity of it, a hard shot of energy zinged through his veins.

"Well, then, flip those burgers so we can get to it. You've got a lot of multitasking to do."

The next hour and a half ran by in a blurry series of slow

and awkward prep to plate, but other than a couple of scrapped orders and dropped items, they didn't run into anything disastrous enough to sink them. Teagan's kitchen skills were pretty freaking abysmal, all elbows and stress and wasted movement, and he'd had to fight that overwhelming urge to relieve her of her spatula more than once.

But besides the fact that all that movement would've reduced his torso to Silly Putty, it also would've earned him a one-way ticket out of Dodge. Spending these few hours in Teagan's kitchen, while unorthodox as hell, really had saved him from losing his marbles tonight. She'd let him stay even though she probably shouldn't have, and he'd owed it to her to keep his word and stay on the sidelines.

Man, he *hated* the sidelines.

"Please tell me that was the last order for the night." Teagan groaned, her eyes trailing the waitress who'd just snapped up two plates from the hot window. Even Jesse, whose emotions seemed to run from poker-faced to impassive, let some hope flicker across his face at her words, and Adrian had to admit, he, too, was glad they were finally on the downswing.

"You tell me, Red." His arm smarted like a sonofabitch, and the rest of him wasn't far behind. Still, whether or not they were done wasn't his call to make.

Her brows snapped together, and the coppery wisps of hair that had jogged free of her ponytail fluttered over her confused stare. "Huh?"

"Chef decides when the kitchen's closed."

"Okay." Teagan extended the word as if it were a question. "You're the chef."

He shook his head. "Not tonight, I'm not. You were on the grill. It's your call."

"Oh." She split a startled look between him and Jesse.

"Well, I guess if there are no more orders in, then yeah. The kitchen's, um, closed."

Good thing, because the place looked like a culinary Jackson Pollock. On crack.

Adrian exhaled, long and slow. "You ever break down the back of the house before?"

"Not really, no. Lou and my father usually do it."

Jesse stepped up, speaking for the first time in easily an hour. "I've seen them break it down. And I can start running the dishes, which is half of it."

"That's definitely a start," Adrian said, watching the guy head toward the back of the kitchen. Without warning, his stomach let out a wail, reminding him that he'd been long overdue for sustenance when he'd walked in here two hours ago. The thought of eating had quickly been pushed to the back burner at the prospect of helping Teagan in the kitchen, but rather than idling at overdue, now his hunger had reached total foreclosure.

And it was enough to make his legs unsteady.

Teagan's eyes narrowed on him, and he braced for impact. "You must be exhausted. And starving. Did they give you a 'script for pain?"

He got halfway through his shrug before he remembered the gesture was a bad idea. "Yeah, but I haven't taken it in a while."

She took a step toward him, missing nothing as she did a critical once-over from head to toe. She shook her head, muttering something about low blood sugar being an epidemic lately. "You look pale. Come here."

"I'm good." Dark spots danced across his vision, threatening to out him. "Maybe a little hungry."

"Mmm-hmm." In a flash, Teagan was next to him, his good hand flipped up in the circle of her fingers while she called Jesse back up from the alcove.

"I told you I'm fine." Jeez, she was sneaky! Usually he was pretty aware of stuff like that—you tended to learn decent evasion tactics in prison—but between his lack of sleep the last two weeks, this morning's accident, and his negative food count, he was just out of sync.

"What's up? Everything okay?" Jesse asked, forehead creasing as he caught sight of Teagan doing her little look-see.

"It's going to be. Can you please tell Brennan I'll be upstairs for a minute? I have something to take care of."

The guy nodded and disappeared, leaving Teagan to hit him with a high-level frown. "Come on."

"Where are we going?" And more importantly, why were his traitorous feet following her without getting the pertinent information? Damn, his body ached, and those black spots were getting bigger and kind of swirly.

"To the office. I want you to sit down."

"I don't want to sit down." The argument lost its steam somewhere between concept and execution, and it fell from his lips more like a plea than anything else. Fuck. When did he get so tired?

Teagan gently prodded him toward the door between the dishwashing alcove and the walk-in, and up a set of dimly lit stairs. "Too bad. If you pass out on me, we're right back to liability territory. And anyway, you just took care of my kitchen. The least I can do is take care of you."

"I can . . . take care of myself." Adrian's feet felt sloppy beneath him as he followed her into a shadowy room at the top of the steps.

"Uh-huh. You sound like it." She hit the light switch with the flat of her hand, the soft illumination revealing a small, appropriately cluttered desk and office chair combo, along with the most unsightly couch he'd ever laid eyes on.

"Whoa. That's, ah. Orange, huh?" The thing was a Muppet, only slightly less subdued.

"Do not mock my office couch. What it lacks in style, it makes up for in comfort." She nudged him to sit, and he was vaguely aware of Jesse poking his head through the door. He murmured something to Teagan, who answered him in hushed tones before he disappeared back through the entryway.

"Okay. Here we go." She grabbed a bottle of water from a dorm-sized fridge next to the desk, cracking the cap as she maneuvered back to the orange monstrosity. Rather than sitting down at his side, she knelt in front of him, propping one elbow on the nicked-up coffee table. "Drink this."

Adrian was shocked to discover he was actually parched, and the ice-cold water slid down his throat as he took a long sip, then another. "You don't have to sit on the floor." He might be rough around the edges, but even exhausted, he could call up a little decency. Teaching him good manners had been his *nonna*'s first order of business when he'd gone to live with her at the ripe old age of ten, followed closely by teaching him how to cook.

God, he missed her.

"Thank you," Teagan said, looking genuinely surprised at his niceness. "But I'm okay right here."

Realization hit him slowly, but with surety. "It's easier for you to watch me this way, isn't it? Make sure I don't keel over, and all that rot?"

A smile eked past her heart-shaped mouth, and she motioned for him to keep drinking. "Maybe." She took a deep, audible breath before coming out with, "You saved my ass tonight. I really don't know how to thank you."

"You just did." He wasn't about to tell her the feeling

was mutual. She'd probably think he was a total freaking wing nut. "But I really should be downstairs telling Jesse how to break down your kitchen." Of course, every one of his limbs blackballed the idea, and the bone-weary exhaustion kept him pinned into place on the cushy, extra-wide couch.

"Jesse knows how to run dishes, and I have to stick around and help Brennan until last call anyway, so I'll make sure everything gets cleaned and put away." She took the empty water bottle from his hand, getting up to replace it with another.

"Yeah, but you need to prep for tomorrow."

"And you need to eat something and take your medicine. If the hunger doesn't get you, the pain will. Trust me when I tell you, you don't want both of them to gang up on you now that you've stopped moving."

A knock on the door punctuated her words, and before he could argue, Jesse materialized with a plate in one hand and Adrian's leather jacket in the other.

He held up the plate, looking uncertain. "I made this. It's, uh, ham and cheese. Nothing special, but I figured protein would be good if you're feeling out of it. The fries are hot, so be careful. And thanks for all your help tonight." He hung the jacket by the door and put the plate on the coffee table in front of Adrian before retracing his steps toward the exit.

"No problem, man. Thanks for the food," he said as Jesse disappeared for the second time in ten minutes. Adrian eyed the sandwich, then Teagan. "You're not going to get up from the floor until I eat all of this, are you?"

This time, she couldn't catch her smile before it flashed out. "Only to get you something to manage that arm." Her eyes flitted to his jacket, outlining her unspoken question.

Adrian gave in, too tired to argue. "Inside left-hand pocket."

Teagan produced the orange bottle and doled out two pills big enough to choke a grizzly bear. "These first, food on top."

He obliged, mostly because he'd bet she was serious about growing roots in the area rug until he did. The sandwich was a little dry and definitely plain, but it was the best thing Adrian had tasted in weeks, and it took all he had not to hoover it *and* the fries in about three seconds. Teagan waited patiently for him to eat, not breaking the comfortable silence between them until he was nearly done.

"Why didn't you say anything about being hungry?" she asked, and he swallowed his last bite before answering.

"Kitchen's more important." It was easier than trying to explain the weird dead-zone focus he felt when doing his job. He'd been surrounded by food for the last two hours, yet the angry pangs of hunger had hit the skids as soon as he'd seen those tickets needing to be filled.

Teagan nodded, tucking a strand of disobedient hair back into her crooked ponytail. "It sounds kind of crazy, but when I'm on a call, I forget I'm hungry. Or tired, or mad at someone, or whatever. I've done twenty-four-hour tours at the station where I barely ate a crumb, but I didn't notice until after they were over."

Surprise ribboned through him at how well she'd just summed up the thoughts he hadn't shared, but his head suddenly felt too heavy to even nod in agreement. "Yeah. I've done that."

"They say it has to do with the adrenaline. Me, I think it has more to do with the adrenaline junkies doing the job."

Man, her eyes were pretty in the low light filtering over from the desk lamp, all glittery and golden-brown, like sunlight shining through a stained-glass window. He wanted to keep looking at them, but his own eyes were so leaden, they just kept blinking.

"Adrian?" Teagan's voice was right there, but detached, like he was above her. "Oh hell. I should've known this would happen."

"Hmm?" He really had to keep his wits about him. He had to focus. Keeping his eyes open would be a good start.

"You're exhausted," she said, and somehow he managed to start floating as she spoke, which would be kind of creepy if it didn't feel so good. "And after your reaction to the Fentanyl earlier, I . . . God, I never should've let you do this."

"No." Okay, so at least that one made it out of his mouth. "I'm just . . . I only need a minute." One minute. Then he'd get up and go back to his quiet apartment with its even quieter walls. The woodsy scent of rosemary layered in with more familiar kitchen smells covered him like a blanket.

Wait, that was a blanket. Hold on . . .

"Get some rest, Adrian." A hand skated over his face, the sensation lulling him even further into oblivion until everything went completely, blissfully dark.

Chapter Eight

Teagan woke all at once, painfully aware of several things. A) Using a balled-up sweatshirt in lieu of a pillow was a really bad idea if you wanted to get some semblance of a decent night's sleep, and B) Dear God in heaven, what was that mouthwatering smell? She cracked her eyes open to investigate, barely resisting the urge to flail four feet into the air at the sight of Adrian's sexy-as-sin stare pinning her down from the center of the office couch.

"You let me sleep here all night." His gaze was unflinching, and the last twenty-four hours came crashing back to her in short order. Responding to the accident on Rural Route Four, finding out her father was sick, Lou walking out midshift, Adrian saving her ass.

Don't forget being kissed. That happened, too.

Teagan sat up quickly and yanked a hand through the rat's nest masquerading as her hair, the sweatshirt-pillow tumbling to the floor in a sloppy heap. "Uh, well, yeah. You were in no shape to drive, and by the time I got done downstairs, I kind of wasn't either. Plus, I was a little worried about your arm, so I just . . ." She capped off her words with a shrug, and okay, ow. Sleeping in that chair had bent her vertebrae like an accordion gone awry. "What time is it?"

"Eight thirty."

She blinked back her groggy surprise and swung her gaze toward the window. Sure enough, insistent sunlight was doing its best to poke past the tightly slatted blinds. "Oh." Damn, how had she slept so late? She had to get up, get moving, at the very least get a cup of . . .

"I made some coffee." Adrian pushed a mug full of dark, steaming morning goodness across the scarred surface of the coffee table.

"You're not supposed to cook." Teagan hesitated, despite the gimme vibes her brain was steadily pumping out. Oh Lordy, it was the most perfect shade of mahogany brown, like he'd brewed it just right and added a bare splash of milk but nothing more.

His voice rolled over her like a lazy Sunday morning, husky and slow, and okay, *some* parts of her were definitely awake. "Making coffee isn't cooking. It's self-preservation. Plus, it's done. You might as well have some."

Teagan shook off the ridiculous prickle of heat rolling up her spine and eyed the mug. There wasn't even a hint of anything frothy or frilly in it. Just a nice, hot cup of coffee, exactly the way she liked it.

"You may be right," she said, trying not to lunge out-right. The coffee tasted as bold and incredible as it smelled, and she drank deeply as she unsnarled her thoughts one strand at a time.

She'd averted disaster last night by a microscopic margin, and that had only been with serious help and even more serious luck. But today was going to be a whole new brand of difficult. Aside from getting her father taken care of at home, which wasn't going to be a bowl of cherries, she had to iron out this payroll kink if she was going to have a prayer of keeping what little staff they still had. They usually opened at two on the weekends, so at least she had a few hours, but Teagan didn't have a clue about the Double Shot's books. For all she knew, it would take half the damned day just to find them, let alone figure out what she was looking at. And then there was the not-so-small matter of not having a cook. God, this had all the makings of a grade-A nightmare.

But no way was she going to let her father come in and deal with this. He'd disregarded Dr. Riley's warning to rest more and take his meds long enough. His life depended on her finding a longer-term solution until his health was under control, and so she would.

But first she needed to address Pressing Issue Number One, which was currently leveling her with a very smoldering, very piercing, very unreadable stare.

"I suppose I owe you a bit of an explanation about last night. Things don't usually get that . . . hectic," Teagan said, but he cut her off with a curt shake of his head.

"You don't owe me anything."

The laugh that popped from her lips was involuntary. "Seriously? You helped me through a dinner shift the same day you got flattened by a minivan. I probably owe you my firstborn. Or I would if I had one."

A flicker of something Teagan couldn't quite pin down colored his eyes a stormy gray green, but he lifted one corner of his mouth in a half smile to temper it. "I wouldn't say I got flattened."

"No?" She lifted a brow at the cast-and-sling combo covering his left side.

"Clipped, maybe. But it was more like a love tap than a leveling. Let's not get crazy."

She dropped her chin with an ironic exhale. "My life is so far past crazy right now, it hurts."

"You want to talk about it?"

Her head sprang up. "You want to listen to my problems?"

"Polite conversation is for amateurs, remember? And anyway, I've got nowhere else to be."

Whether it was fear for her father, or the time she'd spent being thrust unexpectedly into a kitchen she hated, or the heated, penetrating way Adrian was looking at her right this very second, she couldn't be sure, but the words crowded out of her so fast, she was helpless to do anything other than listen to her own voice.

"The thing is, I just found out the not-so-easy way that my father is diabetic. Which wouldn't be the end of the world, really, except the disease is completely out of control, and the late nights and hard labor of running a bar and grill have made it pretty much impossible to manage. He needs to scale back on his hours to rest, and obviously, we're short-staffed. Until I can figure out a way to get someone in here to help for a while, this place is stuck with me, I guess."

"You seem pretty comfortable running the place, other than the kitchen." A tiny hitch in Adrian's shoulders served as his only apology for his last words, and what could she say? They were true. "Does he have you on the books as a manager?"

"On paper, yes. I'm second in command. But my father has run the place from door to door since I was in elementary school. He's got a solid staff. Or he did until recently, anyhow." Teagan's stomach gave a deep yank. Without Lou, she was well and truly screwed. "I have the authority to run things when he's not here—write the schedules, authorize orders for inventory, pay the bills, that kind of thing. But it's more theory than practice."

She'd seen the power of attorney papers he'd drawn up five or six years ago and put in the safe, although in the time that had passed between then and now, Teagan had run the Double Shot exactly once, for two days while her father had gone to her great-aunt's funeral. Even then, he'd left her detailed hand-written guidelines and done the weekly food and liquor orders before he'd left. "So even though my father is going to hate handing over the reins for a while, that's what's going to happen."

"Running a restaurant is a full-time gig. But I'm guessing from how things went last night that you know that." Adrian's voice was calm and quiet, and the lack of poor-you sympathy made her even more uncharacteristically inclined to share.

"I do. I'm planning to take a temporary leave of absence from work."

It was a reality she'd come to terms with in the bone-weary hours between closing the kitchen and closing the bar last night. Running the Double Shot while holding down her day job would require either a time machine or a body double, maybe both. Her savings were small but sturdy, and she could get by on a leave of absence for a little while. Convincing her father to let her do it for more than a night was going to be the hard part, but she'd get to that soon enough.

Teagan shook her head, her thoughts threatening to overwhelm her. "But not working the squad seems kind of like the least of my worries right now, you know? I'm down two cooks, a waitress, and a bookkeeper, and another manager wouldn't hurt this place either. I can figure out what needs to be done and delegate tasks just fine. It's finding people to delegate *to* that's biting me on the ass right now."

Stubble-covered muscles tightened over Adrian's jaw, and his voice went to gravel. "It might not be as difficult as you think."

"I'm not sure your definition of difficult is all that spot-on." Between her and Brennan and Jesse, she had a painfully short list.

He shot her a look that found her center in a direct hit. "Try looking right in front of you, Red."

Teagan's eyes flew wide, and it took all she had not to drop her coffee mug into her lap. Having Adrian in the kitchen last night had been an *emergency,* not a precedent. "You want to help me run this place?"

"Why not?"

"For starters, you already have a job, don't you?"

His stare shifted to a cool gray. "Let's just say I'm also taking a leave of absence, and mine isn't exactly voluntary, either."

"But you're on leave because you're injured, Adrian. You can't cook for me any more than you can cook for the resort."

"No, but I can teach you to do it."

Teagan's heart log-jammed in her esophagus. "I can't cook." The books, she could figure out. The management, no problem.

The kitchen? No chance in hell. Last night had been an exception, and she'd hated every burger-flipping second.

"You did well enough to survive last night, and I can show you how to get better." Adrian's expression sent a shot of ninety-proof heat down her spine. "The guy from the bar last night, Brennan. Is he in? To help you through this, I mean."

"I, uh . . . yes." There might be only a handful of things she could count on for certain, but Brennan's loyalty was on the list.

"Good. I can teach him enough management to get by in less than a week, at least until you find someone with experience to help out. He's already got the front of the house down well enough. By the end of the month, he'll be money with inventory and scheduling. Your books will be more complicated, but like I said, I've got time to kill, so I can make it work. The only thing I can't do is cook. Not until this thing comes off, anyway."

Which meant she would have to do it. Not just for a night, but indefinitely.

Teagan opened her mouth, the word *no* perfectly formed on her tongue, just begging to roll off.

But instead she said, "And you *want* to do this?"

"Absolutely."

A thought popped into Teagan's head, and even though it forced a wash of heat over her cheeks, she had no choice but to give it voice. "I don't know how much I'd be able to pay you." God, whatever she could scrape together would probably be a mere pittance in comparison to what Adrian made at La Dolce Vita. The place had a monthlong wait for reservations, for God's sake.

"I'm not asking you to pay me. In fact, I don't want to be on your books at all."

Teagan jerked back, her shoulders bumping the time-worn cushion of her chair. "You want to run the kitchen for nothing?"

"Doesn't look like nothing from where I sit," he said, but oh no. No way was she letting him skate by without answers.

"Why do you want to help me so much?"

The question seemed to throw Adrian, and he paused, long and hard. "Because it makes sense. Because you need the help. And because . . . I need it, too. Look, six weeks off might sound like paradise to some people, but to me it's hell on earth. I need to be in a kitchen, even if it's a little unconventional, until I can get back to work for real at La Dolce Vita." He shifted forward, locking his gaze with hers. "The only thing I need to be clear on is that everything here is on the up-and-up."

Her skin prickled as the words registered. "Everything

that goes on here is perfectly legal, if that's what you're asking. My father's not stupid." Keeping the frost from her tone was impossible, so Teagan didn't even try. Just because they ran an establishment that was as much bar as it was grill didn't mean they were delinquents, for God's sake.

Adrian nodded, an expression she'd swear was relief flicking over his face before disappearing into his gruff demeanor. "Then we're square. I can help you run the place. But you're going to have to let me. What do you say?"

Her mind's eye whirled backward, landing on the hazy image of a woman with rich, auburn hair, an apron tied tight around her trim waist as she watched her seven-year-old daughter roll out scraps of pastry dough.

One day, you'll be a famous chef like your mama. You can go anywhere you want, my sweet. Paris, New York, anywhere you please . . .

A year later, her mother had walked out the door, and Teagan had sworn on the spot she'd never cook another thing for the rest of her life.

But Adrian was right. Letting him teach her to cook made sense, and what's more, it was the only option she was going to get to save the man who'd raised her when her mother had chosen greener pastures over her own family.

"You've got yourself a deal, Superman. But trust me when I say teaching me to cook is going to take every ounce of what you've got."

Adrian's smile was dark and sexy and oh-so-good, and it arrowed all the way through her as he said, "Oh, trust me, sweetheart. I'm counting on it."

Teagan parked her seen-better-days Toyota Corolla in the gravel driveway outside her father's lakeside cottage and got out of the car. The late-morning sunlight threw tree-dappled patterns on the fresh carpet of spring grass surrounding her childhood home, conjuring a postcard-perfect scene that would put even the most ill-tempered mind at ease.

This conversation was going to suck.

She palmed the handles of the three grocery bags in the back of her car, steeling her resolve as she stared down the warm pine panels of her father's front door. As much as she hated it, this had to happen, and fast. Teagan checked her sturdy Timex, calculating her words as she mounted the steps to the tiny stone porch and gave the front door a solid rap.

"And just what d'ya think yer doin'?" Her father's good-natured tone made the words more teasing than heated, but they didn't come from the front door. Teagan swung around, a sharp bolt of irritation panging through her at the sight of her father in his work clothes, carrying a hefty arm-load of firewood from the side yard.

"I should ask the same of you. Are you out of your mind?" Teagan asked, leaving the groceries unattended to march through the yard. "You're supposed to be resting! As in, not exerting yourself, and certainly not doing yard work. What the hell are you doing hauling firewood in late April, anyway?"

"We're supposed ta have a cold snap tonight. You never can be too careful about the weather in the mountains." He paused, eyes sweeping over her wicked frown. "Ah, don't make that face. It's an armful'a firewood, pretty girl. It ain't goin' ta kill me."

She swept her fingers in a tight motion, trying not to lose her cool. "No, but I might. Hand it over."

Her father chuckled before doling out half the logs, keeping the rest nestled firmly in his grip. "Still haven't taken my advice about honey seriously, I see," he said over his flannel-clad shoulder, and damn it, she couldn't help feeling the warmth of his charm.

"I will when you take my advice about slowing down. I mean it, Da, this isn't good for you." Her tone slid lower, voice going soft as they reached the steps. "Your health issues are a big deal. I'm . . . worried."

"Well." Her father froze for just a second before lowering his logs to the nearly gone stack on the far end of the porch. "I suppose you'll be wantin' me to take it easy on a permanent basis, then? Stay at home and whittle me days off like an old man should."

Teagan huffed out a breath, measuring her words with extreme care. "No. I know that would make you miserable. But you do need to rest until Monday, when I can go with you to see Dr. Riley and we can get a long-term plan together. And we both already know that she's going to tell you that you need to cut back. You're working too hard."

"And not hard enough," her father murmured, so soft she nearly missed it. "There's things that need takin' care of. Things that don't involve you."

She dropped her logs to the pile with an unceremonious clatter, her face falling along with the firewood. "I can take care of you."

"Oh, darlin'." Her father's dark brown eyes crinkled at the edges, a look of pride canceling out whatever had been there seconds before. "I just meant . . . bah. It doesn't matter. You shouldn't be takin' care of my problems. You've got a job of yer own, one yer good at."

"And one that's not nearly as important as this. I talked to my battalion chief about an hour ago. He granted my request for temporary family leave, effective immediately."

Actually, he'd been more understanding than Teagan could've hoped, offering to transfer a fill-in paramedic from Riverside's larger crew until she could get her father back on his feet, both literally and figuratively.

Her father stopped short on the stone, halfway to the threshold of the cottage. "So you mean ta do this, then? Run the Double Shot without me for a bit?" His face was grave, more serious than she'd seen it in a long time.

Twenty-two years, in fact.

His expression tore at her, hot tears involuntarily pricking behind her eyelids. "I do. Just until we can get you well-rested and find someone to help out more."

Her father looked at her, his trademark charm spilling over in his gaze as he gave a bare hint of a smile. "Shoulda known you wouldn't give up on that vinegar, not even for your old man."

"I'd say I'm sorry, but . . ."

"But yer not. And anyway, I didn't raise you to apologize for who ya are." He kept his smile in place, but something serious sparked in his eyes. "I'll give you the bar for a spell, if that's what needs ta be done. But you need to leave me the books."

Damn it, she should've known he'd try to compromise. "I'm not negotiating with you. You need to rest, and that means no work."

"And I'm not negotiatin' with you, pretty girl. If you want me out of the bar ta rest up, you'll leave me the books. I'll do 'em from here, no heavy liftin'. I promise. But I *will* do 'em."

"Does this have to do with the paychecks?" Shit. *Shit.* Good conscience dictated that she should tell her father about Lou, she knew. But if she let it spill that she was out a cook, her father would barge back into the place no matter what she and Dr. Riley said.

Her father froze for just a breath, the movement gone as fast as it had arrived. "Ah, that's just an accountin' error. I'll fix it up right quick, no harm. Don't you worry your pretty head over it."

Teagan's gut pinched, but she maneuvered around the percolating emotion. "Whatever it is, I can—"

"No." Her father squeezed her shoulders with enough tension to stop her words midflow, but his eyes remained warm. "I'll do everything else ya want without a fuss, but you'll not have this. Sometimes a man's got business only he can take care of."

She opened her mouth to fight him, but the look on his face snapped her argument in half.

He wasn't going to back down.

"That is the most sexist thing I have ever heard," Teagan finally said, giving in to her father's good-natured expression with a wry twist of her lips.

He stepped toward her, arms outstretched. "Take it however ya like. But do take it."

Teagan wrapped herself in his embrace, exhaling with the first true relief she'd felt in over a day. Her father felt thinner, more brittle than usual, but she was going to make him better. She had a plan.

"All right, you win. For now, anyway." Teagan waited an extra second before letting him go, bending to scoop up the groceries she'd left on the doorstep. "Now get the door for a lady, would you? I want to get these put away before your guest arrives."

Her father pushed the door from ajar to open, brows upturned. "I'm not expectin' a guest."

Teagan pressed a cat-in-cream smile between her lips and headed for the kitchen. "Ah, but you are. Mrs. Teasdale is coming over to keep you company both today and tomorrow while I'm at the restaurant. Did you know her brother is diabetic?"

Her father's eyes narrowed by a scant degree, and he followed her into the cozy but neat space. "Is that so?"

"Yup. So she knows all about how to test blood sugar, and how often. She was more than happy to offer to come over and help you with yours. Isn't that the nicest?"

"Mrs. Teasdale is a nice woman. How is it again that you ran in'ta her?"

Teagan dialed her smile up to its brightest setting and held up one of the grocery bags. "I saw her at Joe's." Otherwise known as Pine Mountain's social center, where Teagan had known full well the woman would be.

"Ah. What a coincidence." The doubt in his voice was plain, but not angry. Patrick O'Malley might dig in his heels when it came to work, but his polite and charming side was way more norm than exception. Of course, Teagan had been counting on that when she scoped out Mrs. Teasdale in the produce department in the first place.

She hid her expression in the cupboards, unloading groceries just a little too fast to be natural even though her father was clearly onto her. "I thought so, too. She'll be here in five minutes."

Her father burst out with a laugh. "Minx. You did that on purpose."

Teagan gave up, her own laughter spilling out to mix with his. "I love you, Da. But I sure did."

The sudden emotion in her father's eyes caught her right in the chest. "I take it back, love."

"Take what back?" she whispered, her throat going tight.

But he just smiled and shook his head like he was stuck in a faraway memory.

"Yer not so bad at honey after all."

Chapter Nine

Adrian wrapped his cast in a couple of plastic bags, snapping a rubber band tightly around the edges before stepping into the hot, welcome spray of the shower. His joints and muscles throbbed from both yesterday's impact and last night's overuse, but it was familiar territory, same song, second verse. A spectacular display of purples and blues marred his left shoulder, but he did his best to ignore the Technicolor bruise as he clumsily ran the soap over his skin.

Christ, he was grateful to be rid of the sling, even if it was only long enough to bathe. Lifting his arm more than a few inches without ripping pain was still out of the question, but it didn't matter. Being able to strip the sling from his body along with his clothes was liberating, like he was on his way back to normal.

He'd found a kitchen, a purpose. Maybe, just maybe, this whole broken-arm thing wouldn't be as bad as he'd thought. Even if he couldn't cook, being in the kitchen with Teagan was sure to keep him occupied.

Damn, he hadn't been *occupied* in far too long.

Adrian froze, but apparently his cock missed the memo,

stirring to life at the thought of Teagan's fiery mouth and attitude to match. Okay, so technically, they weren't co-workers, and yeah, she had soft curves and tight angles in all the right places. Still, getting involved would only make helping her in the kitchen a lot more complicated, and it was his number one priority to avoid complications like a gaping pothole.

Which meant that much to his dick's chagrin, Teagan was off-limits.

Adrian gave the shower knob a healthy turn toward *cold* and ran through the rest of his scrub-down as best he could with one arm. Getting toweled off and dressed threatened to reduce his patience to fumes, but he managed eventually. The pain in his arm had simmered down to a steady but manageable ache, and Adrian opted for a couple of ibupro-fen to wash down the rest of the sleeve of saltines. Even money said Teagan would ask him point-blank what he'd eaten this morning, and even though his answer was bound to raise one of those feisty, red eyebrows of hers, at least he wouldn't have to tell her "nothing."

Off-limits, remember?

The sound of Adrian's landline startled him halfway off the linoleum, and he stared at the thing where it sat, a few feet away on the counter. Only two people had this number—the two people who insisted he have a landline at all—and right about now, Adrian didn't want to talk to either of them.

Of course, one could fire him permanently and the other wanted his ass back in jail, and both would come knocking down his door if he dodged their phone calls long enough.

Guess he should put his chatty pants on.

"Hello?" Adrian wedged the phone to his ear, and the scrape of it against his cheek reminded him that at some point he was going to have to master the art of one-handed shaving.

The voice at the other end sounded even crankier than he felt, sarcasm flowing like bad tequila at a bachelor party. "Good of you to finally answer, Holt. I was starting to take it personally."

Shit. Of course Big Ed had probably tried to call already. "Sorry. I was a little busy."

"Busy getting into trouble, I see. Went and banged yourself up real good, according to this police report on my desk."

"I'm sure it makes it sound worse than it is."

Disdain seeped into Big Ed's sarcasm, hardening his thick New York accent another layer. "Says you went and played chicken with a minivan. I always knew that bike was bad news."

"I got rear-ended by a lady on her cell phone. I wasn't even issued a citation." Adrian gritted his teeth hard enough to make dust. Forty-six days. In forty-six days, he would never have to deal with Big Ed again.

As long as the cantankerous bastard didn't find a reason to have him incarcerated, anyway.

"Yeah, yeah, I verified everything with the police down there. I talked to your boss-lady, too. Sounds like you've got a little time on your hands now that you've got your ass in a sling."

"It's my arm." Seriously, there wasn't enough patience on the earth's surface for this.

Big Ed snorted, clearly enjoying himself. "You say potato, I say ass in a sling. Anyway, since your hotshot boss vouched for you yet again, you're off the hook with work release. For now."

"Great," Adrian said, working up some sarcasm of his own. God, he hated how much Carly put on the line for him. Screwing up his own reputation was one thing. Taking his best friend down with him? Not gonna happen.

"Yeah well, just 'cause you're straight with them doesn't mean you're straight with me. We both know how you get when you've got nothing better to do, and I ain't a snot-nosed rookie. You may have weaseled your way out of the state all special on your fancy boss's name, but you're still a fuck-up waiting to happen. Don't think just because I'm not right there on you, I ain't watching. You so much as gulp the same air as anyone with a misdemeanor, and I'll have you *and* that superstar boss of yours dragged back here on parole violations. You feel me?"

Adrian's pulse was nothing but white noise and black anger in his veins. "Yeah. I feel you."

"Good. And next time I call you, answer the damn phone."

It took five minutes of solid breathing and the most imaginative curse words Adrian could conjure up before he was calm enough to consider driving, but once he managed to get on the road, he gathered his thoughts as rationally as he could.

As much as Adrian had hated every second of the exchange with the guy, at the very least, the conversation proved that Big Ed couldn't do anything with that police report other than file it. He wasn't the kind of guy to hold his cards, and if he'd managed to drum up some way to make the accident work against Adrian, he'd have done it. Not that he probably hadn't given it the old college try.

Still, Adrian was going to have to keep himself clean enough to make *squeaky* spit with envy if he wanted to get through the next forty-six days.

He pulled into the Double Shot's deserted lot and parked, taking in the details that had gone unnoticed in the dark of last night. The clapboard was comfortably weathered, as if it had been allowed to stay that way rather than being neglected, and the glossy black shutters made favorable companions to the wide, thickly paned windows. Brass lanternlike light fixtures hung at regular intervals along the overhang of the porch, with two matching sconces on either side of the oversized front door.

It was a far cry from many of the bars in New York, with their dank, underground smells and even danker underground activities. Although some of the upscale places were still worse, with drugs and money and who knew what else moving in and out the door.

Adrian's feet jerked to a halt on the strip of pavement separating his parking spot from the building. Was he out of his mind when he'd all but begged Teagan to let him work here? Sure, the place looked decent enough, but he knew from experience that appearances weren't always an accurate barometer. He'd asked to make sure, but of course she'd said everything was legit—who the hell came right out and admitted that shady things happened behind the scenes? And as much Adrian needed to stay busy, he needed to stay out of trouble more.

But when Teagan had told him in that dead-serious tone that everything here was legit, he'd believed her. And considering his bullshit meter had been raised on a steady diet of foster care, rough neighborhoods, and nine months of gen pop at Rikers, when Adrian believed somebody, it was a very big deal. Still, he'd have to keep his eyes wide open. Innocent until proven guilty didn't mean innocent no matter what. And as streetwise as Teagan seemed, he'd learned the hard way that sometimes owners don't know everything.

Adrian walked up to the building, but skipped the formality of the front door, heading instead for the side entrance where he'd first seen Teagan last night. The aging dark blue Corolla she'd driven away in a few hours ago was parked in the back lot, and Adrian put a solid knock on the door with his good hand. After a minute of stand-and-whistle, he tried again, with the same results. A test of the door shocked him by proving it unlocked, with a quiet kitchen beyond.

Adrian stood still on the industrial, flat brown tile, taking in the nearly noiseless hum of the walk-in and the shadows cast by the emergency lighting overhead. The kitchen was filled with rare calm, and he took in the sounds of the space's normalcy out of deeply ingrained habit. Once you knew what business as usual sounded like, it was a hell of a lot easier to pick out when things weren't quite right.

He moved past the open-air metal racks in the dishwashing alcove, noting that Jesse had been true to his word about getting everything prepped for today. Flat-sided trays of pint glasses stood stacked and at the ready on a rolling cart, and stainless steel pots and pans of various sizes dangled from drying hooks, silently begging to be called into action. All in good time, Adrian thought, though his chest panged at the delayed realization that it wouldn't be *him* cooking at all. It would be Teagan.

If he could figure out where the hell she was.

A handful of steps brought him to the pass-through dividing the front of the house from the back, and he peered through the large, circular window set in the swinging door. Although the darkened vantage point of the kitchen gave him a perfect view of things on the other side of the glass, he was wholly unprepared for what he saw.

Teagan sat directly in front of him on the customer side of the glossy, mahogany bar, the overhead light mingling with strains of sunshine from the far window to brighten her hair to a coppery gold. Head dipped down low, she pored over a thick sheaf of computer printouts, a tiny crease forming between her brows as she punched the numbers on the calculator topping the stack. Concentration stamped her pretty features, and she shook her head, pulling her lower lip between her teeth in thought.

Adrian's pulse heated in his veins, and although he knew he was ripping past the bounds of propriety by standing there staring, he was incapable of doing anything but exactly that. She looked serious, yet open, as if all her guarded toughness had been swept aside to reveal the unvarnished version underneath. She propped one elbow on the bar, leaning in so her forearm edged the swell of her breasts into the danger zone of visible skin in the deep V of her shirt, and the heat in Adrian's blood threatened full-on spontaneous combustion.

Christ above, this woman was stunning. And he realized, too late, that she was also staring right back at him.

Even stone-cold busted, he couldn't take his eyes off her.

"Hey," he said, not trusting his idiot voice with anything more as he blanked his expression, moving through the door to stand behind the bar. Nothing like a few feet of solid mahogany to hide a raging hard-on. "I didn't mean to barge in on you. I knocked, but . . ." Adrian gestured to the stack of papers in front of her.

Teagan shook her head, apology painting her expression. "Oh, I'm sorry. I'm just trying to get a handle on the, ah, ordering. I must've been too preoccupied to hear you."

"You really shouldn't leave your side door unlocked. It's dangerous, especially when you're here by yourself." His eyes did a methodical sweep of the interior of the bar, another habit he'd likely never break.

"Pine Mountain is a small town." The corners of her lush, red mouth tugged up in the suggestion of a smile, although her demeanor had regained its tough outer layer. "Plus, I'm not exactly a wallflower. I can handle myself just fine."

Something dark crackled to life in his chest, replacing the heat that had been under his skin just seconds ago. "Yeah? You bulletproof?" Savvy or not, she really shouldn't be here by herself, period.

She lowered her pencil, but not her guard. "Something like that."

"It's a safety issue, Red. It's not smart to invite trouble."

Adrian's mind tilted back to the night, nearly a year ago, when Teagan had jumped between him and Carly's now-husband, Jackson. The circumstances had been extreme—enough so that Adrian had shattered every one of his cardinal rules to go after Jackson without remorse. And yet Teagan had barged out of that ambulance and planted herself chin-up and attitude blazing, right in the thick of things, to the point that she'd actually defused the fight.

She'd been lucky he wasn't some strung-out junkie, or some lunatic. Or something worse.

"I'll take it under advisement." She gathered the papers from the bar with quick hands and hopped off her bar stool with ease that said she'd done it thousands of times before. "How's your arm feeling?"

He made a mental note to revisit the side door issue later. Maybe if he did it with Brennan or Jesse around, he could get one of them to sway her a little. "A step up from yesterday."

"Mmm. A step up from hurts-like-a-bitch still hurts. Did you eat anything this morning?"

His lips twitched with a smile at how well he'd pegged her, and what the hell, he let it loose. "Half a sleeve of saltines and some ibuprofen. You?"

"Plain low-fat yogurt and nine-grain granola." The words came out like a translation of *old rubber cement with a side of chunky sawdust*.

"My condolences. You got something against real

food?" He eyed her carefully. She seemed too tough to be one of those chicks who freaked out and ran a goddamn marathon out of guilt every time she threw the occasional Snickers bar down the hatch.

Teagan shook her head, putting the paperwork behind the bar before moving toward the kitchen. "I had breakfast with my father."

Understanding dawned, and Adrian followed her through the swinging door, flipping the light switch with his good hand. "Ah. So how did he take your plan?"

"About as well as he enjoyed breakfast. But even though both were tough to swallow, he knows there's no other way to do this until he gets better." She cast her eyes back toward the door to the bar. "Most of it, anyway."

Talk about something Adrian could relate to. "I can show you some things to make for him that'll go over better than twigs and berries, if you want."

Teagan's hands screeched to a stop under the hand-washing sink by the door, her gaze flashing over him with unflinching certainty. "I don't cook for my dad."

The *don't touch* vibe pouring off her was so strong, Adrian didn't push. "Okay. Just trying to help."

Her shoulders dipped slightly before she righted herself, giving a tiny, apologetic smile. "Thank you. But you've got your work cut out for you here as it is, so why don't we stick with that?"

"Sure." Adrian's mind switched gears, clicking seamlessly to the menu he'd been mulling over since last night. "I'm going to get you started on some of the basics while I check inventory and see what's what in your walk-in. The key to a well-run kitchen is being prepared, which unfortunately means a lot of grunt work. But you've got to get it right, otherwise nothing else will happen. Think of it like the foundation for your house."

She stood at rigid attention, hands in lockdown at her sides as she stood by the workstation opposite the grill. "Okay. What do I do first?"

"Relax."

Although he'd thought it impossible, her body coiled even tighter. "What?"

Jesus, this was going to be more than he bargained for. "Being tense sucks the energy right out of you, sweetheart. If you don't want to burn out before you even start, you have to relax."

She faced the counter with military precision, both palms on the scuffed white cutting board covering half of the work surface. "But I am relaxed. Just give me a job. Tell me what to do."

Whether it was the look he'd seen on her face just moments ago or the bossy *dare me* demand coming from her mouth, Adrian couldn't be sure, but something dark and hot propelled him right past reason and into her space, eliminating the no-man's-land of empty air between them until his chest pressed against the slim line of the back of her shoulders. She was probably going to deck him for this—hell, he might even deck himself—but he had to do *something* to get her to breathe.

"You're not relaxed. See this line of tension, right here?" He traced a path from behind her ear all the way down her neck, fingers gliding from warm skin to soft cotton to land on the ridge of her shoulder. "You need to let it go if you want to be able to move in the kitchen."

To his absolute shock, her muscles unfolded against his hand. "Like that?" Her voice, all husky and low, shot through him, and walking away was as impossible as moving the moon.

"Mmm." He pressed his palm against the outline of her

shoulder, and bit back the groan building in his throat.
"Like that."

"Where . . . where else?" Teagan whispered, and holy
shit, this was going to go south really fast if she didn't stop
sighing like that. She leaned her head back just slightly, but
it was enough to brush his pounding chest and resurrect
that earlier hard-on he'd done his best to dismiss.

"Wherever you need it." He dropped his mouth to her
neck, the heat of her skin pushing him to take a taste, and
for a second, he resisted. But then she arched into his hand,
sliding her body so his fingers rested in the curve of her
shoulder blade by the center of her back, and he gave in.

"There." The word was barely audible as it spilled from
her lips, but he answered as if she'd shouted, running the
edge of his tongue along her delicate neck. He slipped his
hand low against her back, sifting his fingers over her spine
as he set his mouth to the spot where her hair met her neck.
Her ponytail tickled against his cheek, but the heady scent
of rosemary and the silky heat of the spot under his tongue
had him so hard, he dove in without thinking. He tasted her
in slow circles, working his hand over her back in tight,
even strokes as he went.

"Oh God. *There*." Teagan arced into him from the slope
of her shoulders to the sweet swell of her ass, destroying his
last shred of reason. He ground against the press of her hips
just once, and the friction of her lush curves and the rough
denim between them was enough to lift a groan from his
chest.

More.

Adrian's free arm darted around her, latching on to the
belt loops on her jeans as he swung her to face him. Their
mouths came together in a rush of raw want, lips parting,
tongues sliding together, and god*damn,* he'd never wanted
anything so much, so fast, right now.

Maneuvering around the arm pinned between them by his sling, he angled his body against her, moving her backward toward the dishwashing alcove until her shoulders pressed against the wall. Using the leverage to his advantage, Adrian pushed beneath the hem of her thin T-shirt, fighting his knees for control as he reached the even thinner satin cradling her breasts.

More wasn't going to be enough.

"Don't stop," Teagan said, and the throaty command had him pushing the material aside to bare one perfect, tightly drawn nipple, blush red and begging to be plucked, just like her mouth.

Adrian uttered a low oath, holding her fast as she braced her hands overhead, gripping the edge of the open-aired shelf above to allow him unfettered access.

"Careful what you wish for, Red." His thumb lingered over her nipple, wicked satisfaction pulsing through him as he watched her tighten even more. "I could taste you for hours."

She answered with a frustrated whimper, snapping his control. He lowered his mouth to her breast, taking her in with one slick parting of his lips, and his moan twined with hers at the intimate contact. Teagan dropped a hand from above, lowering it toward her body before letting it veer off at the last second, and the move struck him with swift realization.

Adrian parted from her nipple, his breath coming in short bursts as he cast his eyes to her hand before locking his gaze on hers.

"Show me where you need it."

She took the dare without hesitation this time, replacing his palm beneath her breast with her own while she used her other hand to guide his fingers to the hot seam of her jeans. Her boldness had him within inches of wanting to come, fully clothed and all. But his want was nothing compared to the decadent tension thrumming beneath Teagan's skin, as if she didn't just want to break apart, but *needed* the release, like food or water or breath.

And no way was he going to deny her.

Adrian curled his fingers against her sex, sliding them over her jeans with intention until he reached the indent between her thighs that told him he'd hit home. Keeping them pressed there, he lifted his thumb against the midline between her legs until she sucked in a breath, then he lowered his mouth back to her breast.

Teagan choked out his name on a sob. "There. There. I need it right *there.*"

Oh. Hell. Yes.

Finding a rhythm between the steady swirl of his tongue above and the purposeful glide of his fingers below, he worked her jeans open, sliding them from her hips just enough to reveal the top edge of her pale pink underwear. Her fingers went taut beneath her upturned breast, the wordless encouragement sending his fingers back into play, only this time without barriers.

He sank into her, letting his thumb discover the tight bundle of nerves hidden above her core while he returned his mouth to her flushed, straining nipple. The harder she thrust against him, the more he coaxed her to come undone, using his tongue, his fingers, the edge of his teeth. He buried his thumb more tightly at the apex of her thighs, pressing into her folds as he felt her muscles quicken around his fingers, threatening release. Although his cock was unbearably hard, screaming with the need for release of its own, Adrian refused to give in to his own base desire.

"Take what you need, sweetheart. Take it."

With one last thrust of his fingers, she unraveled around him, clutching his shoulders with hot fists. The heat of her

climax vibrated deep inside of him, wrapping them together
in delicious tension before she went loose against his body.
Adrian slowed his movements, lessening the contact between them but not the space, until he slipped his hand from
the cradle of her hips to gently right her clothes.

Teagan looked at him, confusion covering the residual
blush still on her face. "But you didn't, ah . . ." She gestured
downward, sliding her hand over his abdomen with a glint
in her eyes. "Let me take care of you."

"And would it be so bad if someone just took care of you
for a change?"

He'd meant to tease her with the words, but the way her
body jerked to stillness had him tensing right alongside her.

"I don't need anyone to take care of me." She pulled
back, and just like that, her guard snapped right back into
place, stamping out the sweet abandon of just moments ago.

"You sure about that?" He let his eyes linger on hers, just
long enough to watch them go dark with heat, like liquid
copper.

"Is that was this was about? You trying to 'relax' me?"
She slashed air quotes around the word, but didn't budge
otherwise.

Adrian gave an involuntary flinch. He might be a lot of
things, but *that* guy wasn't one of them. "No."

Teagan smoothed a hand over her T-shirt even though it
was perfectly in place, repeating the process twice before
continuing in a crisp tone, "I owe you an apology. You came
here to help me in the kitchen, and clearly, I got carried
away. It won't happen again."

He opened his mouth to call bullshit—it wasn't as if he
was an innocent bystander, for God's sake, and he didn't
have any regrets. The last thing he wanted was an apology
for what had just happened between them. But reality kept

his jaw hinged shut, the sharp edges of truth like vicious bits of glass between his teeth.

He'd gotten carried away too, and that only led to bad things in the long run. Had he learned *nothing* five years ago?

"No big deal," Adrian said, and yeah, that one burned coming out. "I'm square if you are." As much as he hated it, snuffing out anything other than business between them was the best plan.

"I'm square." Teagan's voice softened just slightly as she spoke, but she cleared her throat, her next words infused with familiar resolve. "Now how do I get this kitchen ready for lunch service?"

Chapter Ten

"Orders in, last of the night! Two bacon-Swiss burgers, both medium rare, one barbecue chicken sandwich, two large orders of wings, one hot, one mild, and another bacon-Swiss burger with a side of fried onions to make three all day!"

No two ways about it. This dinner shift wasn't going to stop until Teagan was dead.

"Tell me where to start!" she hollered back at Adrian, who stood opposite her workstation, barking out gruff directives just as he'd done for the last three days straight.

"One ticket at a time, Red. Plate what's in front of you first and get it out the door. Jesse!" He tossed the word over his thickly muscled shoulder, readjusting his Harley-Davidson baseball hat over the hard-edged platinum hair slipping out from beneath the brim. "Drop the fries for the two coming up, then the wings as soon as those new burgers get fired. Go!"

Teagan's eyes stung from the one-two punch of smoke and heat coming off the grill, and she swiped an arm across her forehead in a sad attempt to keep her perspiration at least manageable. She gave the burger currently laid out on the plate in front of her an unsure glance and an even more unsure poke. How the hell Adrian knew if it was properly cooked with just one touch was a total flipping mystery.

But not half as magical as the *other* things he could do with just a few touches. Not to mention his mouth.

"Shit." Teagan watched helplessly as the top of the perfectly split, perfectly toasted burger roll tumbled from her shaking grasp to the floor, sadly not the first food-victim of her wandering, lust-addled mind. Frowning, she whirled to grab another roll from the shelf above her station, shoving it into the wide-mouthed industrial toaster with a firm *clank*.

Adrian shot a stare at the digital display on the fryer before sending his focus onto her station without so much as a hint of emotion, either good or bad. "Those fries are coming up in sixty. Let's get those burgers on the floor in sixty-five."

Things had been all business between them ever since the reality check of his comment the other day had re-minded her that her number one focus—her *only* focus—should be on taking care of things, not being taken care *of*. She needed him to help her in the kitchen, not the bedroom, and she'd do well to keep that thought front and center.

Damn it, how had she dropped two rolls in a row?

Teagan kicked the latest offender into the pile beneath her workstation and focused on her remaining tickets. While being in the kitchen still sent unease rippling under her skin, at least she was starting to get the hang of things. Adrian might be brusque, but he sure as hell knew his stuff. For the third night in a row, nothing massive had cropped up to sink them, although tonight's dinner rush had done its best to try. Teagan suspected it was more Adrian's skill and anticipation than anything she or Jesse had done, although Jesse had gone nose to grindstone with impressive dedica-tion. She really owed him—and Brennan, and everyone else left on her skeletal payroll—answers about those glitchy paychecks.

Problem was, as far as she could tell, there weren't any.

Teagan had genuinely meant to honor her father's request to handle the accounting on his own. She couldn't deny that the Double Shot was his business, one he'd built from a pile of fresh dirt and a dream of something more. And after twenty-five years, he could run the books in his sleep.

Which was exactly why she'd printed out the records the minute she'd crossed the threshold the other day. Her father hadn't made an accounting error since she was in the eighth grade, and something about this didn't pass the smell test.

"Your fries are up, unless you're waiting for them to invite themselves onto the plates."

Even though Adrian had notched his voice one level lower than normal as he approached her from behind, she still jumped halfway to the giant stainless steel updraft hood positioned over the grill.

"Oh!" Thankfully, she'd already put the replacement roll on the plate awaiting the fries and garnish, otherwise it would've likely joined its buddies in the reject pile spilling out from beneath her station. "Right. Sorry." She turned to finish plating the burgers in front of her, waiting for Adrian's nod of approval before sending them to the hot window and focusing on the next orders. As little as she liked it, her niggling worries over the books were going to have to stay pretty low on the priority totem pole until she could press more answers from her father. She had bigger fish to fry. Along with two batches of wings and some onions.

Twenty minutes later, she finally, *blessedly,* made the call to close the kitchen. Jesse headed back to the dish-washing station to work with the new guy, who had thankfully been eager enough for a job that he'd offered to work for peanuts and start today. Teagan braced both hands on the cool surface of the countertop, letting her chin loll onto her chest with a slow, exhausted exhale. The iron fingers of pain gripping her lower back didn't even consider relenting, although the rest of her was sorely tempted.

Working with food was sucking the life out of her.

"Just because the kitchen's closed doesn't mean you're off the hook, Red. We've got breakdown to do, and not a little bit." Adrian fixed her with his standard-issue smoky stare, and the nickname slid over her awareness to land smack in her libido's lap.

"You don't have to call me that," she said, hating the irritation seeping into her tone at his low-level teasing. But to her surprise, rather than pop a brow or get indignant, Adrian cracked a dark, sexy, holy-hell grin.

"I know. Now check your lowboy and tell me what you've got left. As much as it sucks, tomorrow's garnish vegetables aren't going to slice themselves."

Teagan consolidated what she had left from her line containers before starting in on the tomatoes they'd surely go through in tomorrow's lunch rush. Assembling already-prepped ingredients in the surging insanity of a shift felt somehow different from putting her hands on food with nothing but time, and the knots in her shoulders went for the full corkscrew.

"So do you want to tell me why you hate food so much?" The lack of judgment in Adrian's rough voice tripped up both her brain and her hands, and Teagan fumbled her tomato halfway across the cutting board, following the gaffe with an unladylike swear.

"I don't hate food," she said, but the words had none of

the conviction she'd wanted to pin them with, so she added, "I'm just not crazy about cooking."

"Mmm. It shows."

"Thanks. I hadn't noticed." She reset her grip on the smooth knife handle, focusing even harder on slicing the tomato. How the hell did some people find this relaxing?

"Here." Adrian took a step toward her, the corded muscles in his forearm flexing tight over the scrolled letters inked there as he gestured to her body. "You're losing all your energy to wasted movement. Keep your arms close to you, otherwise you'll burn out *and* get burned."

"Sounds fun." Despite her sarcasm, she let her elbows list in toward her rib cage as she continued to slice, and damn if Adrian wasn't right.

"It's not. How come you don't like to cook?"

Teagan's gut doubled down, but she didn't flinch. "I'm not good at it. What's your tattoo mean?"

"You're not bad at it. And nice try with the bait and switch. What's the real reason?"

For a split second, the words almost surfaced, begging to come up for air. "I . . . ouch!" Pain streaked across the pad of her finger, making her drop the knife with a clatter.

"Whoa, let's see it." Adrian snapped up her hand with surprising gentleness.

"It's fine." The default response pressed past her lips, as involuntary as her heartbeat, but he didn't let go.

"Ahh, you got yourself pretty good." He had a clean kitchen towel over the cut before she could see it, a tiny crimson stain blooming on the white cloth as he held her hand with pressure that was both firm and full of care.

"I'll be fine." Teagan made a move to extricate her fingers from his grip, but he didn't let go.

"I know. But if it doesn't stop bleeding, you're going to

have to redo all this prep work. So give it a minute. Where's your first-aid kit?"

The question was so methodical and straightforward that she gave in to it. "On the wall, by the pantry."

Adrian nodded, but didn't move. With his eyes focused on her hand in his, he quietly said, "Live with no regrets."

She blinked. "I'm sorry?"

"My tattoo. It means live with no regrets." He cradled her fingers just a fraction tighter. "It's something my *nonna* used to say all the time."

"Oh." Teagan was so stunned by the revelation that she couldn't come up with anything else for a long minute. "So, um, that's your grandmother?"

Adrian nodded, his unreadable gaze still fixed on their hands as he spoke. "It's Italian for grandmother, but we weren't actually related by blood. *Nonna* was my legal guardian. She adopted me from foster care when I was ten."

"So how come you called her *Nonna* and not Mom, then?" Teagan winced, inwardly cursing the nosy question, but to her surprise, he answered without pause.

"She always said that even though I didn't know the woman who gave birth to me, that person was still my mother. *Nonna* was in her fifties when she took me in, so the name just seemed to fit. She passed away not long after I finished culinary school."

The residual heat from the kitchen coupled with the closeness of Adrian's body, and it hummed over her skin where he cradled her from forearm to fingertips.

"I'm sorry. It sounds like you were close." Before she could cut the move short, Teagan lifted her right hand to cover their already-twined fingers.

"Mmm-hmm." He leveled her with a no-nonsense gaze as he fell quiet, and something about it loosened the words from deep in her chest.

"I don't like to cook because my mother was a chef." Her heart pounded with the admission she'd held inside for so long, and suddenly she couldn't stop herself from letting the whole story spill out.

"She was classically trained at a crazy young age—New York, Paris, you name it. She'd been everywhere before she was even twenty-five. Food was her whole life. But then she met my father in Dublin. They had this whirlwind romance, love at first sight and all that." Teagan couldn't squash the sardonic eye-roll that welled up every time she thought of it, but she continued, unable to rein the story in now that she'd popped the cork on the long-buried words.

"All my father ever wanted, besides her, was to run his own pub. Cheap land and amazing opportunity brought them here to the States, and in hindsight, I think my mother thought it would be an adventure, just like the rest of her life. But they had me by then, and things got harder."

Teagan paused, waiting for her survival instincts to catch up to her impulsive mouth. But there was no pity in Adrian's hazel stare, and the urge to stop talking didn't come.

So she didn't.

"It takes a lot of elbow grease to open a bar, and Pine Mountain is a far cry from big-city glamour, you know? My mother began to resent coming to the States, and she missed the life she had before she came here with my father. Before they had me. But by then, it was too late."

Adrian's hand remained steady over hers. "Sounds tough."

"Not too tough." Teagan shrugged, her lips feeling like sandpaper as they scraped over the rest. "A week before my eighth birthday, she walked out the door and never looked back."

His steady hand flinched just slightly before going even tighter. "I'm sorry."

She'd always hated when people went the sympathy route over her mother's departure, even though she knew the sentiment was usually well-intentioned. But pity was like pouring alcohol on an open wound. Sure, the person offering it up thought it would help. But really, all it did was end up stinging like a sonofabitch.

So how come she didn't want Adrian to let go?

"Yeah." Teagan snapped herself back to the kitchen with a hard blink. "My father was devastated, but he raised me by himself regardless. So now it's just me and him."

"And that's why you hate to cook."

Teagan nodded, the loss of the story she'd kept on lockdown making her shoulders strangely light. "My mother wanted me to be a chef, just like her, to live the dream she gave up. But I'm *not* like her. I chose to stay. I chose my family."

"You can have both, you know." Adrian unwound the towel from her injured finger, testing the cut with a gentle touch. It was shallow, the bleeding all but stopped now, although it stung with all the force of a small wound in a well-used place.

"I guess I'm going to find out, whether I want to or not."

She gathered her thoughts while Adrian went and got the first-aid kit, centering herself while she cleaned the cut and wrapped it in a thick dressing of gauze and waterproof bandages. They worked side by side in comfortable quiet as they finished breaking down the kitchen, and Teagan felt oddly energized despite the fatigue she knew should be invading her bones. When Adrian went to check in with Jesse, she headed to the bar, zeroing in on the spot where Brennan leaned heavily against the burnished wood.

"Hey. You okay?" Her brow pulled in concern as he

shifted his weight with a grimace, but the expression was gone just as fast as it appeared.

"Yup. It's getting pretty quiet now that it's after midnight. Well, more quiet, I guess." Brennan tipped his head toward the thinner-than-usual crowd dotting the bar, and Teagan took advantage of the lull.

"Brennan, I really appreciate all you've done over the past few days, and I'm grateful for your understanding over the paychecks. I promise to have it figured out really soon."

"No big deal on the hours. And your father beat you to it on the paycheck thing."

Teagan's head whipped up. "He . . . what?"

Brennan nodded and wiped down the bar, easygoing as ever. "He dropped a check by my place before I came in today. Said the bank made an error or something. He didn't tell you?"

"No," she said, and everything about this felt dead wrong. She'd seen her father this morning when she'd dropped off more test strips for his glucose meter. Why wouldn't he have said anything? "I must've missed that."

"Yeah, he said you were up to your eye teeth with the other stuff, so he was going to handle paychecks and all that from home to help you out." Brennan paused to shift his weight again, probably just as dead on his feet as she was. "I hope I'm not out of line for saying so, but he seemed kind of worried about you."

Teagan released a nerve-jangled breath. "My favorite two-way street."

Okay, so maybe all this kitchen work was getting to her. Accounting errors were uncommon, sure, but not unheard of, and it must've been something simple if her father had gotten it taken care of so quickly. Plus, if he was worried about her handling everything else, he probably wouldn't have wanted to bother her with the details. She wasn't prone to overreacting, but with everything that had gone down in the last few days, it was possible she'd just gotten caught up in a force field of all this think-the-worst crap.

She relaxed a notch at the thought, leaning back against the dark wood paneling opposite the bar. "I'm sure it'll all be fine once we get things settled. Thanks for being flexible until we figure it out."

"No problem. I don't mind helping with the management stuff." He tossed a nod to the door leading to the kitchen, serving up a crooked smile. "How's it going in the kitchen with Gigantor?"

Teagan laughed, the first burst of true goodness she'd felt in days. "Okay, I guess. He knows what he's doing, and it's keeping us afloat for now."

She busied herself with restocking the cocktail napkins on the bar, even though the holders were already full to brimming. Brennan was too perceptive for his own damned good, and the last thing she needed was for him to make a big deal out of things that weren't there.

Namely the totally weird sense of security she felt confiding her deepest, darkest secrets to her deeper, darker kitchen savior.

"Just let me know if that changes," Brennan said, the intention in his nearly black eyes clear as he finished wiping down the bar in front of him.

"Sure. Why don't you get out of here and catch up on your sleep? I can cover the bar for the rest of the night."

"Your father would be pissed purple if he knew I let you close by yourself. I'll stick around, just in case. It's not even two hours."

Teagan cranked up her smile to maximum wattage and looked Brennan dead in the eye. "There won't be more than five people here by the time we close, most of whom I've probably known since birth and all of whom would be thrilled to walk me to my car, *if* I needed that sort of chaperone. Which I don't. Now get out of this bar and get some decent sleep. I'm not asking."

For a second, Brennan looked like he was thinking about arguing, and she geared up to match him. But then he shot a glance down at his legs as if he'd wanted to get off them hours ago, and he relented. "Only if you text me when you leave, then again when you get home."

"Seriously?" Jeez. One XX chromosome, and the male population thought you couldn't take care of yourself. Or anyone else.

But on this, Brennan didn't budge. "Take it or leave it, O'Malley."

"Fine. Whatever rocks your cradle," she said, tucking her smile between her lips as she scanned the sparse crowd in the softly lit bar. "But fifty bucks says it'll be the quietest night we've had in ages."

Chapter Eleven

Adrian's arm throbbed with the kind of pain that made ibuprofen cackle 'til it ran out of breath, but he popped two anyway, just for grins. Those other painkillers turned him into a walking whack job, and he had to get home somehow. Spending another night on the office couch wasn't part of his game plan, no matter how weirdly comfortable the damned thing had been a few days ago.

Or how enticing the view when he woke up. Christ, he was straddling the line between stupid and extremely stupid by going all touchy-feely on Teagan, telling her about his *nonna* like that. But the only way he could get past the *don't touch* was to dare her, and that meant spilling his own stuff first. He hadn't meant to manipulate her, only to help ease the tension any idiot could see was swallowing her whole in the kitchen.

He hadn't been expecting to have it unthread some of his own tension, too.

Thankfully, the dull *thunk* of the door dividing the kitchen from the bar interrupted Adrian's thoughts, and he swung toward it to find Brennan limping slightly toward the stairs to the office.

The guy took a stutter step when he caught sight of Adrian, his surprise obvious. "You're still here?"

Adrian acknowledged that with raised brows. "Looks that way. Rough night on your feet?" He popped his chin at Brennan, letting his eyes flick toward the bartender's lower body.

Brennan paused, then gave a shrug, loose and easy. "No more than usual, but it's getting pretty dead out there." His dark-eyed gaze took a tour around the now-quiet kitchen space. "Where's Jesse?"

"I sent him and the new guy home. Kitchen's broken down." Adrian waited. While the guy's voice matched his normally laid-back nature, something small and unspoken lurked beneath the surface of his demeanor.

He measured Adrian with a more serious glance, and bingo, out came the question. "Are you sticking around?"

Huh. He hadn't really taken the guy for that territorial. Then again, Brennan seemed more concerned than pissed. Adrian decided to proceed with caution regardless. "I've got some inventory to check."

Brennan took a turn at raising his brows. "That doesn't really answer the question."

Damn, this guy wasn't half-bad. Adrian allowed a crooked smile to eke out. "I might stick around for a few. You got a problem at the bar?" Not that he'd be much help if Brennan did. Christ, this broken arm was a monumental pain in the ass.

"Teagan just kicked me out so she could close. I already broke down what I could while we're still open, but . . ."

"She shouldn't be here by herself at two A.M." Seriously, this woman took survival of the fittest as a personal freaking challenge. Was it really so bad to ask for a little help?

Brennan leaned back against the stainless steel counter,

his expression one of agreement. "Try telling her that. She's stubborn as hell."

"Yeah, I got the memo. I'll make sure she gets out of here safely."

Okay, yeah. Maybe there was a kernel of caveman instinct propelling him to keep his weary ass on the premises so Teagan wouldn't be alone in the bar with the night's earnings in the register. But the buddy system wasn't just for swimming, as far as Adrian was concerned.

"Thanks, man." Brennan pushed back to straighten up. "I guess I'll see you tomorrow."

"Sure. Go home and get some sleep."

Adrian watched the guy head up to the office to clock out, palming the clipboard with his uninjured hand. There was no shortage of things to keep him busy, although he knew Teagan wouldn't buy that as his reason for staying until closing time. It was only another hour and a half, anyway.

He slipped through the door leading to the bar, giving his eyes a minute to adjust to the dusky lighting. The booths and tables in the dining room proper all stood clean and empty, and only a small handful of people lingered at the bar. Teagan was at the opposite end of the service area, popping the cap off a Rolling Rock with a laugh as she chatted up its recipient. Her movements were simple and fluid, not at all like the simmering tension she carried around in the kitchen, and Adrian took them in for a minute before heading to the other side of the polished wood. The cushioned black leather of the bar stool felt way better than it should under his frame, and he sank into it with relief, getting situated at the end of the bar.

Teagan appeared in front of him barely a minute later, confusion in her expression. "Kitchen's way past closed. Don't you want to head home and rest?"

"And miss out on this inventory?" Adrian tapped the clipboard in front of him, lifting one corner of his mouth in an approximation of a smile. "No way."

She crossed her arms under her breasts, and he cursed the very nature of low-cut T-shirts. "You're off the clock," she said.

Hold on, here we go. "To be fair, I was never on the clock."

Other than knowing the Double Shot was being run cleanly, being off the books was the only thing Adrian had cared about when he and Teagan had hashed out the finer details of his helping in the kitchen. He had enough money stuffed away to get by, and on the off chance that Big Ed sniffed out the paperwork, Adrian would be screwed with unapproved work release. Plus, he wasn't so much working for her as he was just standing in the kitchen and offering his opinion. It didn't really count. Not in terms of getting paid, anyway.

Teagan cocked her head, her ponytail glinting auburn in the muted light spilling down from over the bar. "Okay. But liquor orders don't go in until Monday, meat and produce on Tuesday. So that can wait."

"What can I say? I like to be prepared." He turned his eyes toward the numbers on the clipboard, not about to let on that his left hand was about as useful as a tree stump. He didn't need both hands in order to get a handle on the numbers, and anyway, he wasn't leaving her here alone.

"Fine," she said, shocking the hell out of him even further by pouring a glass of iced tea and putting it on the bar next to the inventory. "Just do me a favor and stay hydrated, would you? It's hotter than hell's waiting room in that kitchen, and you've still got a long way to go healing up that arm."

Adrian laughed, unable to help it. "Fair enough, Red."

"Are you going to call me that just to try to annoy me?"

Good Christ, she was pretty when she was trying to hide being irritated. "That depends. Is it working?"

"No." The answer came too fast, and she covered up the rushed cadence with a smooth smile that made his blood spark through his veins. "Now drink up."

Adrian took a long draw from his glass, grateful for the cold jolt to bring him back to the land of the mentally stable. Flirting with Teagan was far too easy, and he knew there were a variety of reasons he shouldn't.

Trouble was, it felt far too good not to dare her into it every time she so much as shot him a warm-whiskey glance.

The soundtrack on the overhead speakers looped around for the nth time, the volume comfortably leveled off to match the quiet chatter of the few customers left. Adrian settled into his spot, checking the inventory numbers and making crude tick marks in the margins to delineate ordering patterns. While some people found numbers and inventory to be the most dreaded part of the job, he never really minded it. Food was food, and he loved it from concept to execution.

Adrian lost himself in the rhythm of the work, cross-checking the tally of menu items with the record of what they'd ordered in the past month and what was still left in the kitchen. He compiled a detailed list in his head, although what hit the paper was a lot rougher with the chicken scratch factor. Maybe he could come up with some kind of form like they used at La Dolce Vita, something online that would track inventory automatically. It never hurt to look at your trends and see where you could manage costs. In the long run, it might—

"Are you happy now?"

Teagan's throaty tone caught him completely off guard,

and he blinked up at her, caught smack between what-the-hell and hellllloooo-sexy-woman.

"Am I . . . what?"

"Whatever plan you and Brennan cooked up worked. We are officially the last two people in the restaurant." She sauntered around to the customer side of the bar, swinging the bar stools up to the mahogany with what looked like a well-practiced flip. When the hell had it gotten so late?

"Oh, right. Well, inventory should be a slam dunk. Your father actually keeps pretty detailed records, even though they're mostly by hand. I can go over it with you, if you want."

Teagan laughed, putting up the bar stool next to his. "The only thing I want to go over right now is my bed."

Adrian's mind zeroed in on the memory of her face, caught up in passionate release, and heat tore through his veins. "Really?"

Her eyes rounded, landing on his with a mixture of embarrassment and something he couldn't quite nail down. "Oh shit. I mean to sleep. In my bed, all alone. You know, just . . . God, sleep deprivation is not my friend."

Oh hell, he had to let her off the hook. "I get it. I was just giving you a hard time."

A small groan escaped her ample mouth, and Christ, he wanted to spend a week just tasting her. "Your unintentional innuendo is just as bad as mine."

He rewound his words, giving a chuckle as he pushed off from his bar stool and lifted it for her to flip. "Sorry," he said, although it was mostly untrue.

Teagan paused, fingers still laced through the wood back of the stool now resting on the bar. "Adrian, listen, maybe we should—"

"Well, well, well! Lookie what we have here!" The interrupting voice coming from the kitchen entrance needled Adrian's ears and nerves all at the same time, and he swung to instinctively put himself between Teagan and the stranger moving toward them. The guy was dressed like every other regular in the Blue Ridge, although the hard-edged menace he wore along with his Levi's and flannel shirt sent Adrian's heartbeat into fifth gear and his hackles into overdrive.

"The restaurant's closed. And since you're not an employee, you can get out from behind my bar." Teagan brushed a hard squeeze over Adrian's unhurt forearm as she moved past, and damn it, every last one of his deep-seated inclinations screamed to get her back behind him.

The man laughed, a raspy, gravel-laden smoker's hack, before taking a long look over the place that made Adrian want to wipe down everything the guy had laid eyes on. "No need to get uppity now, darlin'. And if you don't want nobody behind your bar after hours, you might think about lockin' that side door'a yours."

Fuck. He *knew* that damned door was an open invite for trouble. This was going straight from bad to hell in a handbasket. "I'm pretty sure the lady told you to get out from behind her bar." Adrian shifted forward, cursing both his sling and his situation with renewed vigor. How could he have thought to avoid this kind of thing in a god-damned *bar?*

The man's beady eyes screeched to a halt on Adrian, giving him a quick once-over. He moved coolly from his spot in the doorframe to the pass-through between the bar and the restaurant, keeping just enough distance between himself and Adrian to be out of arm's reach.

"Well, your daddy ain't stupid, is he, sugar britches? I shoulda known he wouldn't leave you be in this place all by your lonesome. But that's okay. See, me and Trigger just came here for a little look-see, now that we're business partners and all."

"Excuse me?" Teagan's words took on the tone of a different two-word directive, but her movement forward was cut short by the appearance of an absolute mountain of a man in the doorframe.

"Oh shit," Teagan whispered, echoing the sentiment slingshotting through Adrian's brain. The guy ducked past the threshold, the seams on his black muscle shirt threatening to surrender as he crossed his heavily tattooed arms over his chest.

This time, when Adrian stepped up next to her, she actually let him.

"Now you see how my brother got his nickname." Asshole Number One grinned, showcasing a mouth full of crooked teeth. "A trigger causes somethin' to happen. In our case, it's usually somebody crappin' their pants." The grin got bigger and more lascivious, and the guy strolled past her to run a hand down the rounded edge of the bar. "But you don't have to be scared, darlin'. Trigger ain't gonna bite 'cha. Not unless I tell him to."

"What do you want?" Teagan asked, crisp frost on every word in spite of the six-foot-seven pro wrestler knockoff eyeballing her from the doorframe. Adrian stood, firm but quiet at her side, hating every inch of where this conversation was headed.

The mouthy guy turned on one cowboy-booted heel, assessing the dining room as his eyes returned to Teagan's spot. "My apologies. I do believe we got off on the wrong foot. Name's Lonnie Armstrong. Your daddy and I do business together on the side."

"Bullshit," Teagan countered, chin up, and Christ, she was going to make getting out of this difficult. "My father does all his business here."

"Does he now?" Lonnie's eyes glinted, cold and steely, matching the snakelike smile pulling at his thin lips. "Well, that's gonna make two of us, then. See, your daddy came to me 'bout a month ago, lookin' for a little money to tide him over. Bank done turned him down for a loan, and he was real desperate. Awful hard to run a quality establishment like this *and* pay for doctor's bills."

"You know about my father's medical bills?" Despite her rigid stance, Teagan's voice pitched upward, and Adrian's pulse went for broke in his veins.

The one place in the entire Blue Ridge where he'd been able to find solace was overrun by redneck loan sharks fleecing sick old men for shits and giggles.

Fucking priceless.

Lonnie smiled, although there was no warmth or humor in the gesture. "I know about lots of things. Not the least of which is that your old man is into me for an awful lot of money, honey. I fixed his payroll problems up real good today, though. Don't you worry about that."

Teagan's shoulders gave a slight sag, one Adrian might not have even noticed if he hadn't been standing close enough to touch her. "The bounced paychecks weren't an accounting error."

Lonnie's scoff was answer enough. "'Course, that came with a price, namely the need for bigger collateral than normal since he already owed me. Deed to this here fine bar and grill sounded good enough, and your daddy agreed. He's got one month to pay me back, but 'til he does, I reckon I own a little piece of this place. And I intend to make a little money off it for my trouble."

Teagan's head whipped up, her ponytail slapping against her shoulder as she nailed Lonnie with a death glare. "You're not running anything illegal out of here. No drugs. Period."

Apparently, priceless had been an understatement. Adrian couldn't write his ticket back to Rikers better if he was standing over a dead body with a smoking gun and a big, fat *who-me* look plastered to his kisser. He needed to get out of here, the faster the better.

Lonnie shook his head, circling back through the empty space with a look of mock hurt. "I am wounded that you would think so little of me. I don't dabble in illegal substances. Too much risk. I prefer to stay on the security side'a things."

A cold sweat formed between Adrian's shoulder blades, sending a trickle of moisture and foreboding down his back. "You're running guns." Moving weapons had become exponentially more challenging in the last five years. He'd heard plenty about it when he'd had nothing but nine months' worth of time to listen.

Lonnie clapped his hands, looking at Adrian with a smug stare. "It seems your boyfriend has been around the block a time or two, honey. Matter of fact, he's got kind of a felonious look about him." He took a step closer, then another, his shiny black cowboy boots sending an echoing *clack* over the hardwood as his implication thickened the air.

Teagan swung her eyes up at Adrian in disbelief, and seriously, he wanted to beat the crap out of this guy. "I'm not interested in anything felonious."

"Well, then. I stand corrected." Lonnie returned his ratlike gaze to Teagan as he continued his prowl around the empty dining room. "You don't have to worry about my outside business endeavors creepin' into your space, darlin'. I ain't stupid enough to shit where I eat. See, what I need is a bookkeeper a sorts. And the books for this place are so nice and legal-lookin', what with it bein' such a fine establishment."

Adrian's heart locked in his throat as he added money

laundering to the top of the pile. Jesus, Big Ed could have
him arrested six ways to Sunday for just standing here.

"My father would never agree to this," Teagan said, as if
she was trying to convince herself. "You have to leave him
alone. He's sick. He's—"

Lonnie cut her off. "We're past that, darlin'. Your daddy
owes me too much. 'Course he was real insistent I not
come 'round here and let you in on our little deal. But what
kind of business partner would I be if I didn't introduce
myself?"

"You can't do this to him. There has to be something
else." Teagan didn't even try to mask the panic in her voice,
and it ripped through Adrian despite all the other emotions
vying for attention in his chest.

"There's always somethin' else," Lonnie said, the words
slithering out. "He pays me back in full, with interest, of
course, and I don't have to mess with nothin'."

"How much?" Adrian watched Lonnie very carefully as
he spoke, and saw exactly the hitch in movement he was
looking for when the words hit their target.

"Fifteen large, with yesterday's boost."

"My father owes you fifteen *thousand* dollars?" Teagan
half yelled, and it was the last nail in the self-preservation
coffin. Adrian had to end this conversation and get her out
of here, now.

"All right, Lonnie. You made your point," Adrian said,
sending a pointed glance to the door. Teagan opened her
mouth, presumably to argue, but Adrian kept talking. "In-
troductions are done. The bar's closed."

For a second, he thought Lonnie was going to argue, and
damn it, this was so not how Adrian wanted things to go
down. But then the sleazebag eased back to the doorway,
nodding to his brother as they both turned to leave.

"Fifteen grand, sweet pea. You got four weeks to scrape

it together better'n your old man did." His eyes narrowed to a suggestive stare. "I'm lookin' forward to workin' with you as my . . . *bookkeeper*."

Okay, yeah. Adrian had had enough. He took a step forward at the same time Teagan's spine snapped into place beside him, and Lonnie let out a cackle as he retreated.

"Y'all be safe, now. You never know who's just outside your door."

A minute later, the side door closed with an audible slam, and Teagan's shoulders slumped at the sound.

"Adrian, I can explain . . ."

But he just shook his head as he looked at her, a splash of hot anger replacing the cold fear of a moment ago. "Nothing to explain, Red. I think we're done here."

Chapter Twelve

Teagan's heart beat in a frantic game of tag-you're-it with her sternum, and it took every ounce of willpower for her not to throw up on her shoes. She'd been horrified at not figuring out her father was sick enough to need extended medical care. But not realizing he was in enough financial distress to borrow fifteen thousand dollars from a pair of menacing backwoods loan sharks? This was just too much.

And now, to top things off, her only semblance of hope for running this restaurant while she came up with a long-term plan stood across from her, looking furious. Not that she blamed him.

After all, Adrian had flat-out asked her if the Double Shot was on the up-and-up. And she'd flat-out told him yes.

"Right." Teagan nodded woodenly, her head feeling like it was attached by a spring that had seen one too many upward stretches. Stringing together any passable thoughts, let alone decent sentences, was just a no-go right now, so she didn't even bother trying. Her eyes landed on the door to the kitchen, but the way the legs of the bar stools protruded from their upside-down perches on the thick expanse of wood made her feel closed in, helpless.

No, no, no, no, no. She was going to fix this. She was going to find a way to make this work, just like she'd made the kitchen work all week. She was going to . . .

Throw up. Yeah, she needed to get out of here. *Now*.

"Thanks for sticking around tonight. I . . . I have to go." Fear and anger and every other negative emotion on the planet balled up in the lowest part of Teagan's belly, prompting her to bolt through the door to the kitchen. She smacked the light switches to the *off* position out of pure habit, plunging the space into shadowy darkness. The emergency lights flickered overhead, giving just enough illumination for her to snatch her coat and keys from the pegs in the alcove leading to the side door.

"You didn't know, did you?" Adrian stared at her, completely unmoving, framed by the industrial white tile and aged wood doorframe of the entryway to the alcove.

"No. I . . . no. I'm sorry." Lame, yes, but it was the only thing she could think of to say, and plus, he deserved it. Just because she hadn't misled him on purpose didn't mean she hadn't misled him.

And she knew just how it felt. God, how could she have failed so spectacularly at taking care of her father?

Adrian nodded, a tiny jerk of his darkly stubbled chin. "This is dangerous stuff. The kind of stuff I can't . . . be around." His voice pulled tight over the words even though they were barely a whisper.

Teagan shook her head, her emotions threatening to boil over and spill right out of her onto the floor. "It's okay. I'll take care of this. I don't expect you to help me." Self-preservation clung tight to her tone, and while she hadn't intended the words to be so defensive, they came out more serrated than sincere.

Adrian moved forward, so fast she didn't realize her corresponding step back would be interrupted by the cold steel of the door behind her until her shoulders bumped against it.

"You don't get it, do you? This isn't the same as break-ing up some bar fight, or doing a balancing act in the kitchen for a couple of weeks. These guys are the real deal, and they won't hesitate to take you down. Permanently."

Teagan's anger elbowed its way to the forefront, hot and bitter in her mouth as she pushed forward to regain her original position, even though it meant standing so close to Adrian, her chest brushed against his sling.

"And I thought Lonnie just dropped by to play checkers. Believe me, Adrian, I get it. But I have to fix it, okay? I can't just walk away from this. He's my father."

This time, Adrian flinched. "Lonnie wasn't wrong."

"I know my father probably borrowed money from him, but—"

"Not about your old man. About me."

The words trickled in, but Teagan still couldn't connect them to the conversation. "What are you talking about?"

He shifted, his eyes the turbulent green gray of Big Gap Lake after a huge storm. "I have forty-three days left on parole. When I said I can't be around stuff like this, I wasn't kidding."

Shock streaked through her with surgical precision, cut-ting deep. "You're on parole?"

Adrian met the question head-on. "Five years ago, I did a nine-month stint in Rikers."

Holy shit, her night officially couldn't get any worse. "For what?"

"For being stupid," he grated, his expression all remorse. "I made a bad choice and I paid for it. But my parole offi-cer is a crusty old bastard who wants nothing more than to toss me back in the clink and swallow the key."

Oh God. No wonder he'd been so adamant about the bar

being on the straight and narrow. "Is that why you didn't want me to pay you?"

"It's part of it, yeah."

Teagan's mind spun like a blender set to *triple scramble*. He'd only served nine months, and no way in hell could she see Adrian doing something truly malicious. But still . . .

"Did you steal anything?"

"No."

She exhaled shakily. "Have a drug problem?"

"No."

Her gut dropped down to her knees. "You didn't . . . kill anybody, did you?"

"No." Adrian pressed his mouth into a thin line, and he jammed his free hand into the pocket of his jeans. "Look, I think you need to have a really long talk with your old man. If the two of you can figure out a way to pay Lonnie off before he gets his claws into the books here, the dirtbag will have no choice but to go away."

Teagan blinked, switching gears at a dizzying pace. No way could it be that easy. "You really think Lonnie will just go away if we pay him back?"

"I know it. Guys like that are bullies. All that cheesy bravado only works because he has something on you, namely the cash. Once you take away his leverage, he won't have anything to hold over your heads, and he'll move on to the next guy who owes him. I'm sure he's got several to pick from, and in the end, all that keeps guys like Lonnie afloat is money and not getting caught."

"And what if I can't come up with the money fast enough?" God, she hated the wavering edge in her voice. The least she could do was stay strong enough to deal with this.

"Then Lonnie will use it against you, like he said. A restaurant is the perfect front for dirty funds. If he's running guns, he's probably got more illegal cash flow than he can handle." Adrian paused. "Look, I know he said he wouldn't mess with the actual restaurant for now, but you're going to need to be straight with Brennan and Jesse about this. You might think you're ten feet tall and bulletproof, but until you get this nailed down, it's not safe for anyone to be here alone."

Realization hit her in a swift stroke. "But you're not staying."

Adrian's jaw went tight, and the step he took to close the space between them this time wasn't predatory. "Teagan, I . . ."

She reached up and brushed her fingers over his lips, just a brief touch to stop the words from coming. "It must be serious if you're actually using my name." The awkward attempt at humor thudded like a ten-ton brick between them, but God, she was seriously at the tipping point here. Of course Adrian couldn't stick around. Who in his right mind would in the face of what had just happened, past or no past?

"It's serious," he agreed, his expression matching his ragged voice. "My parole officer won't care that I had nothing to do with this, or that I'm only trying to help you. And it's not just me who goes down if I screw this up. My boss vouched for me when we left New York, so her name's on the line, too. I want to help you." He lifted his hand as if he intended to touch her face, but then pulled back at the last second. "But I don't know how."

"I understand," Teagan said, and she did. This was her problem to fix, and anyway, she couldn't ask Adrian to risk going back to jail, no matter how weirdly right he made the kitchen feel to her. "I'll talk to Brennan and Jesse first thing tomorrow. We'll figure something out. And of course, I'll have a nice, long chat with my dad." Her anger made a repeat performance in her chest, but she tamped it down. She'd have plenty of time for fire and brimstone in the morning. Right now, she was just spent.

"Let me walk you to your car."

Teagan noticed it wasn't a question, but in truth, she was too tired to argue. Plus, while she could hold her own in lots of situations, the thought of having to square off against Lonnie again, or worse yet, his gargantuan brother, Trigger, made her skin crawl. "Okay, yeah. Thanks."

For a second, neither of them moved, and they stood there, as close as they could be to touching without actually taking the plunge.

"I'm sorry," Adrian whispered, the words so laced with emotion, Teagan's throat knotted over the *it's okay* brewing there. Unable to speak, she just nodded, then turned to move through the side door and into the cool, spring night.

She took four steps through the side service lot before realizing something was off. The overhead light that normally spilled illumination over the Dumpster and the area beyond was strangely dark, leaving the moon to cast only murky shadows over the entire section of asphalt. Something hard and small crunched under her boots, and she pulled to a stop in confusion at the same exact moment Adrian reached out with his uninjured arm to hold her in place.

"Jesus." He moved in front of her, head shifting from side to side in a quick scan of the narrow lot. Although her heart slammed in her chest, she at least had the wherewithal to turn her back to Adrian's to do the same behind them.

"I think it's empty," she said after a minute, and the waver in her voice felt vulnerable and permanent.

Adrian hissed out a low oath, then another as he pulled his back from hers. "I don't see anybody, either."

Teagan stepped around him, gut clenching like an industrial vise as she saw the smashed-out window and slashed back tire on the Corolla. Bits of shattered safety glass crackled and popped under her feet as she moved toward the car, and it took every ounce of her ironclad resolve not to let the tears burning her eyes tumble down her face.

"I guess Lonnie's more serious than I thought," she managed, and oh God, she'd need a bloody miracle to fix this.

Adrian nodded, eyes glittering in the moonlight. "Come on. Let's get your tire changed, then I'll follow you home."

All things considered, the Harley didn't look as bad as Adrian had thought it would.

His life, on the other hand? Definitely as fucked up as it appeared.

"So what do you want first, the good news or the bad?" Shane Griffin leaned back against the garage workbench adjacent to where Adrian stood, trying like hell to focus on what was in front of him instead of what he'd left behind last night. Shane had been cool enough to meet him early even though Grady's Garage wasn't normally open until nine, so he'd have to deal with thoughts of his shitastic night and even more shitastic situation later.

"Let's get the bad over with."

Shane winced slightly, jamming his thumbs through the belt loops on his well-aged Levi's. "I might not be right about this, so take it for what it's worth. But I don't think there's any way you can get around replacing your gas tank."

Adrian knew he should be more disgruntled—after all, the bike was the closest thing to a prized possession he'd ever owned, and the gas tank was one of the most expensive parts outside of the engine. Somehow, though, he just couldn't muster the appropriate piss and vinegar. "Okay."

He closed his eyes, like maybe when he opened them he'd be somewhere else.

Shane continued, his tone as apologetic as if he'd crashed the bike himself. "Like I said, I might not be right. My expertise is more in the four-wheel department. But if I had to guess . . ."

Right. The gas tank was history. "You said there was good news?"

"Oh yeah." Shane nodded, coming over to crouch down by the laid-out Harley. "Some of the damage is small, easy enough to fix with a couple parts from a distributor. Like the rearview and stuff. I can order them from my guy and swap them out at cost, no problem."

"I'll pay you for labor," Adrian said, his brow pulling in, but Shane waved him off.

"Consider us even for the crappy news about the gas tank." The guy paused, letting out a slow breath as he stood. "Look, I kind of suck at this, so I'm just going to say it. Bellamy and Carly are worried about you."

If there was one thing on the planet he needed less than redneck loan sharks, it was his friends' pity. But Carly's no-coming-back-until-you've-healed edict had left zero ambiguity. Despite his flat-out admission that he needed the kitchen, she'd kicked him out.

She couldn't have her cannoli and eat it, too.

"I know," Adrian said, since it was the only thing he could manage without sounding bitter or getting mad, neither of which would accomplish anything right now. "I got their messages."

"Personally, I get that you probably operate a lot differently than they do, and I have a hunch you don't want to talk about it. But if something's upsetting my wife and I can do anything about it . . . let's just say I'm going to give it my all. For her and for you."

Damn. It was hard to argue with that. "Understood."

Shane stood to lean against the wooden workbench behind them, tacking on a self-deprecating shrug. "So do you think, in the interest of your personal peace and mine, you could maybe throw me a bone here? Because I gotta tell you, man. You're looking rough, and they *are* gonna ask me."

Of course the guy had to go and make sense on top of it all. "I'm cool," Adrian said, choosing his words with care. "It's just kind of complicated."

Which was just *kind of* the biggest understatement he'd ever uttered. He'd resigned himself to not being able to help Teagan last night—how the hell could he stay out of trouble when she was up to her ears in it? But getting the image of the broken glass and slashed tire out of his head had been impossible, to the point that he'd gotten a grand total of three hours' worth of shitty sleep.

Walking away just felt wrong.

"Yeah," Shane said, yanking him back down to the garage. "I've been there before. Life can twist you into double knots sometimes."

Adrian snorted. "You have no idea."

"Oh, I'm pretty sure I do." Shane laughed, although not with malice. "Everything you want to avoid starts staring you in the face, and no matter which way you turn, it's right there in front of you trying to shove you to the ground?"

What was this guy, a mind reader? "Sounds about right."

"Yeah. I'm not going to sugarcoat it for you. Figuring out the big stuff sucks. But there is a little good news."

Adrian waited for a second before asking, "Which is?"

Shane pegged him with a dark-eyed stare, and the guy's expression was so devoid of anything other than straight-up honesty, Adrian just listened.

"It might sound like a bunch of bullshit now—I sure as hell thought so when I first heard it—but most of the time, your answers are right in front of you. You've just got to look in the right place, and listen when you find 'em."

Adrian dropped his chin in disappointment. What had he been expecting anyway? Still, Shane had been decent enough to try and help.

"I'll keep it in mind, but in the meantime, you can tell Bellamy and Carly I'm fine." Adrian shifted to shake the guy's hand and at least thank him for his time, when his awareness caught up with what lay smack in his path of vision.

The tattoo on his right forearm glared back, as if it had been daring him to notice it all this time.

Promise me . . . promise me you'll live your life every day. Promise there won't be any regrets.

Vivere senza rimpianti. He needed to live without regrets.

Adrian's head jerked up, his eyes zeroing in on the door. "I've got to go." He stopped long enough to shake Shane's hand, but only just. Christ, this was crazy, but Adrian didn't care.

It was the first thing in months, hell, maybe *years,* that had actually felt right.

"Everything okay?" Shane watched him with a look that was equal parts question and understanding, but didn't argue as he followed Adrian to the door of the garage.

"Yeah, I just have something I've got to do. Thanks for all your help. I, ah . . . I really appreciate it."

"No problem. I'll keep you posted on the bike. And, Adrian?"

"Yeah?"

Shane lifted the corner of his mouth in a knowing smile. "Glad you figured it out."

Chapter Thirteen

"Well, now. If you're here ta make sure I eat that awful slop again for breakfast, me and you may be havin' some words. But if a cup of coffee's what you're after, then you're in the right place."

Teagan leaned against the doorframe of the cottage, grateful she still had the cover of her sunglasses to mask the shadows surely showing beneath her eyes. God, how she wished this were as easy as conning her father into eating a little low-fat yogurt.

"I'm not here for either, actually. You and I need to talk." Well, at least her voice was relatively steady, unlike the rest of her. In the last eight hours, Teagan had alternated so many times between being furious with her father and terrified for his safety, it'd been a crap shoot as to what might come out.

He waved her into the cottage, closing the front door behind her with a smile. "So it looks as if we're havin' some words anyway, then." Her father's eyes lost their trademark gleam as he registered her stony expression, and his graying brows creased inward over the streak of worry on his deeply lined face. "What's the matter?"

Oh hell. There was no point in prettying this up, and

she'd never been much for beating around the bush, anyway. "Why didn't you tell me you needed money?"

Her father jerked to a stop halfway across the tiny living room. "I don't know what—"

"Spare me the runaround, Da. Lonnie Armstrong showed up at the bar last night."

The words curdled her father's expression as he swore. "I told him to stay the hell away from the place." The look on his face shifted like a delayed reaction, his already-grim expression going pale. "He didn't . . . if that rotten bastard so much as laid a finger on you, so help me God, I will—"

Teagan shook her head, quick to cut off his line of thought. "I'm fine. See?" She swept a quick gesture over herself before crossing her arms tight. No way was she letting him off the hook. "So why didn't you tell me?"

Her father paused. "Lonnie's business is with me. He said we'd keep it that way."

Just like that, Teagan boiled over. "You used the bar for collateral on an illegal loan! His business is with all of us now. If you had just told me, I could've—"

"What?" The word came quietly, but with deadly precision. "What could you have done, hmm? Worked your fingers even harder? Focused even more of your life on your old man? It's no way ta live."

"So what, you thought you could just borrow the money under the table and have that be that? That's no way to live either."

"I didn't . . ." He broke off, his look of defeat ripping a hole through Teagan's chest. Her father drew in a breath, pulling himself to his full six feet even though it clearly took effort. "This isn't what I intended. At first it was just a little pick-me-up. The bills were gettin' harder ta pay, and it was only a few thousand. I tried ta borrow it against the bar like I did when we replaced the ovens a few years ago, but the bank said no. Too high risk in this economy, they said. As if I've not run the place at a profit for the last twenty years."

Her father slashed an angry hand through the air, his pride on full display, but Teagan was still unconvinced. "So how does Lonnie factor in to all of this?" It wasn't as if scuzzy loan sharks were their regular clientele and Teagan had never even seen Lonnie before last night, despite having lived in Pine Mountain since childhood.

"Lou knew someone in Bealetown. Turned out ta be Lonnie's cousin. Lou said it was off the books, but easy. He'd borrowed from Lonnie in a pinch before, no harm done."

Teagan hissed. No wonder the frickin' guy had tucked tail and run. "And none of this felt off to you?"

Her father stood firm on the living room floorboards. "Of course it did. I meant ta pay it back and be done. But business hasn't been what it used ta be. And then . . ."

"You got sick." Oh God. How could she have not realized he'd been in such trouble?

"I got sick," he said, his voice barely supporting the words before he halted them with a tight shake of his head. "Anyway, none of it matters now. I've got ta come back and make this right."

"No."

Her father's normally happy-go-lucky expression hardened to tempered steel, and damn it, she should've known he'd fight her on this. "I'll not have you in the place if Lonnie's about. He's . . . a nasty man." Remorse flickered in her father's eyes, and Teagan's heart stuttered as she stepped forward to take his hand.

"I know, Da. I'm going to figure it out. We've got Brennan and Jesse, and . . ." Teagan caught herself with Adrian's name on her tongue, ready to roll off as if it belonged there, and the realization did nothing to slow her skittering pulse. "And we've been doing okay for the last couple of days." She gave him the short-and-pretty version of how they'd stayed afloat with her in the kitchen and Brennan behind the bar. It got a little dicey when she admitted that Lou had taken the self-preservation path, but in the end, her father just shook his head.

"It wasn't supposed ta turn out this way, pretty girl. With you takin' care of me." His face was pale, etched with deep lines from both age and worry. "This is all my doin'. I can't have ya in the bar if it's not safe."

His concern was one Teagan had anticipated, and she was ready with her reply. "I can't have you there for the same reasons. Even without Lonnie, Dr. Riley said you're not well enough for the long shifts yet."

She curled an arm around his frail frame and led him to the sofa, knowing he'd probably wanted to sit ages ago but his pride wouldn't let him make the move. "Look, I'm not entirely reckless. I get that it's not a schoolyard. But what Lonnie said makes sense. If he hangs around the bar, especially doing anything illegal, it'll draw attention to the place. And for now, he doesn't want that."

"It's not worth the risk." Her father shook his head, unyielding, but she pressed on, the revelation she'd had in the throes of the early-morning hours making its way forward.

"It won't be a risk, because we're going to fix this. Remember that street fair that Main Street Diner did last year, to raise money for the new expansion?"

Her father's brows knit together, framing the confusion on his face, and he pushed back against the time-faded sofa cushions. "What's that got ta do with anything?"

Teagan fixed him with a confident look, praying to God he wouldn't see how precarious the idea beneath it was.

This had to work, because truly, there was nothing else. And she couldn't fail him again.

"We're going to do the same thing, only bigger. Plenty of businesses organize special events to raise money. Some do it for charity, others for something specific, like the diner. And we're going to do it at the Double Shot."

"I'm not lookin' for a handout," her father growled, knotting his arms over his rigid chest to turn himself into a life-sized embodiment of the word *no*. But no way was she going to let that baseball fly. This was their ticket out of this mess, and she sure as hell meant to punch it.

"It's not a handout. Believe me, we're going to work for whatever we raise. I'm talking about hosting an event, like a party. Everyone who attends will pay to eat and drink and enjoy the entertainment, but no donations, no charity. Now that it's getting warmer out, the timing is perfect."

Her father frowned. "We don't have the funds as it is. How're we goin' ta afford all of that?"

"Well, a lot of people owe you favors, for one, and now is the time to cash them in. Plus, I've got a little money saved. It's not much, but if we're smart about how we use it and we wrangle some really good deals on the food and beer, I think we can pull this off."

"I'm not takin' yer money," her father said, but Teagan shook her head, adamant.

"You have no choice, Da. Call it a loan if you like, but I'm not letting twenty-five years of hard work go down the drain. Trust me when I tell you, this is the only way." She leaned in to squeeze his forearm, and oh God, even over the thick cotton of his sleeve, he felt so thin. "Let me take care of this, Da. Please. Let me take care of you so you don't lose the bar, or worse."

For a second that felt more like an ice age, her father sat utterly silent next to her on the tiny sofa. Finally, he said, "There never was tellin' you no. Stubborn as ya are, you've probably got it half-planned by now. But know this. You'll be gettin' every penny back from me. I'm endin' up as even as when I started all of this, with everyone. You understand?"

Teagan exhaled, relief coursing through her hard enough to threaten her vision. "I understand."

"So tell me, then. How d'ya plan to do this?"

Teagan scooped in the first deep breath she'd been able to take all morning. "The key is getting as many people to attend as possible for as little money as we can spend. Pine Mountain has a grapevine that could survive a nuclear blast. It's the best free advertising on the planet. We can start there to get the word out. Then we can work on our distributors and staff to see who's willing to cut us a deal on food and drinks in exchange for the advertising. Hopefully, all those favors you've done for people over the years will really pay off. It'll help us net a higher overall profit without asking for money straight out, the way a company would for charity."

The preliminary research on how to maximize a fund-raising event had been the only good thing to come from Teagan's insomnia, but right now, it was worth its weight in gold. Especially since her father seemed to be on board with the idea.

"There are a few people I could call on who might be willing ta help," he agreed. "I can make a list and start reachin' out. See what's what."

"Okay. I'll work up a list of what we'll need and get it to you. Then you can work your contacts from here and we'll plan this thing together."

"You mean ta let me help you, then?" Her father's russet-gray brows went up, but she met his surprise head-on.

"I might want to take care of you, but the Double Shot is your bar. Whatever you're well enough to do, you'll do.

We're going to need every ounce of manpower we can get on this project." Tempted as she was to get angry about her father's bad decisions, it would waste energy Teagan simply couldn't spare. But helping him take care of this mess didn't equate to him not being a part of the solution, either. After all, he'd gotten himself into this. "We've got a lot of work ahead of us, especially since we have to pull it together pretty fast. But for now, Lonnie wants to keep a low profile. The busier we are, the better the chances that he'll really stay out of our hair at the restaurant. And paying him back is the only way for us to turn this right-side up."

"And what of you, pretty girl?" her father asked, looking at her with an equal blend of curiosity and sadness. "Are you right-side up, bein' in the kitchen, then?"

The question was so unexpected that it leveled her, the resulting surprise pushing the truth past her lips before she could cage it. "I've had some help from a friend." Ah, damn it. Why couldn't she have just said *yes* and been done with it?

The weight of her father's stare was palpable, even though she couldn't meet his eyes. "Have you now? Anyone I know?"

Okay, at least this one she could answer with a straight face. "No. He just helped out until I got a handle on things, that's all. Made it better than I thought it would be. But now I'm good, and once we get this money part figured out, we can get you back on track. I'm okay in the kitchen, but I still don't want to be there forever."

Teagan squeezed her father's hand, trying on a tiny smile. For a minute, she was certain the nudge toward humor wouldn't work, that he'd fight her in spite of his normally level demeanor, and damn it, she didn't want to argue with him.

On the contrary, all she wanted was to take care of the

man, just like he'd taken care of her. And until now, she'd done a piss-poor job of it.

"I don't s'pose I should find it at all surprisin' that even your honey has a touch of vinegar in it. You've got yer head set on this, I can see, and it's a good plan."

Relief saturated her chest, spilling out to cover the rest of her as she exhaled. "We'll plan it together, all of us. It'll work, Da. You won't be sorry."

"Aye, but you may be. You're not to be in the bar alone, not even for a minute, and if Lonnie comes back, all this changes. I know you're grown, but you're still my girl. Are we clear, then?"

Teagan wanted to argue on principle—she could handle herself just fine. But the look on her father's face stopped the words in her throat.

If she wanted him to let her take care of him, she was going to have to return the favor.

"We're going to pay Lonnie the money before he even gets a chance to be dangerous. But until then, yes. Nobody's there alone, including me. I promise."

Teagan sat back against the nuclear orange couch cushions in the office, trying as hard as she could to talk herself into setting foot in the kitchen completely un-attended. She only had a few minutes before getting down there to start the necessary prep for the day, but the great, big slab of fear in her gut held her pinned in place.

She didn't want to go down there alone. Sure, Jesse and Caleb, the new guy on dishes, would be in the kitchen with her, and Brennan would run the bar and the front of the house with the waitstaff. That was all reassuring. But deep down, the thought of being one-on-one with the food, of getting up close and personal with the act of cooking without anyone to calm her down and keep her in line, scared the shit out of her.

She wanted Adrian. Not a little bit.

"Stupid." The whisper escaped on a bare hint of breath, but it echoed in her head all the same. Teagan had known the guy for all of a week. Yes, he knew what he was doing in the kitchen, and okay, she'd had a weak moment with him on top of that. But nothing about that should make her feel strangely comfortable around him, to the point that she didn't want to cook without him there.

Would it be so bad if someone just took care of you for a change?

"Hey, boss." Brennan's voice filtered into the office from the open doorway, making her jump clean out of her skin as she swung against the cushions to look at him. He gave her an apologetic smile, tipping his head toward the spot where Jesse stood next to him. "You needed to see us?"

Teagan's stomach tightened, threatening mutiny, but she drew in a breath to set herself to rights. "Yeah. Why don't you close the door."

"That doesn't sound good," Brennan said, although he did what she'd asked. "Is everything okay with your dad?"

"Not really." She gave them a condensed version of things, telling them only what she needed to in order to get them up to speed, but also giving them enough details to make things crystal clear. Both Brennan's and Jesse's faces went stone-cold and pissed off when she got to Lonnie's visit last night, and Brennan swore under his breath.

"Jesus, Teagan. I should've stayed." The look on his face swirled anger together with guilt, but she was quick to chase it off.

"I'm fine, Brennan. I know it could've gone differently, but . . ."

"We'll just have to stick together when we're here from now on, just in case. *All* of us." Jesse shot a glance at Brennan, who was already nodding in agreement.

Shock reverberated through Teagan's chest at the depth of their loyalty, and she split a stare between the two of them, her grip going tight over the armrest of the couch. "Look, I'm not going to lie to you. My father screwed up, and this guy Lonnie is dangerous. I don't think he'll come back in the bar itself, but I can't make any guarantees. If you think being here is too risky—"

"No riskier than your father taking a flyer on me a year and a half ago when I needed a job and had no experience," Brennan interrupted.

"Or me a couple of months ago when I came back home." Jesse stood firm next to Brennan, a sudden flicker of something dark showing beneath his quiet, even calm. "Whatever it takes to help him out of this, we're in."

"It's going to mean a lot of hard work. I don't . . ." She broke off, willing her voice to keep steady even though the rest of her felt as if it was made of unset Jell-O.

Brennan stepped in to sit next to her on the overstuffed orange cushions. "With the four of us, we'll get it done."

The tears she'd been fighting all morning burned hot beneath her eyelids, but Teagan refused to let them fall. She was going to have to say this sooner or later—better to go the Band-Aid route and do it all in one fast yank. "Actually, here's the thing. It's just going to be the three of us. Adrian can't, uh . . . stick around for this."

Jesse's dark blond eyebrows shot upward toward the shadow of his closely cropped hairline, his gaze glancing off Brennan's before landing on hers. "You might want to tell him that. He's been in the kitchen for the last half hour."

The words arrowed directly into her center, piercing deep. "I'm sorry?"

"He got here just after I did. Last I saw, he was in the walk-in, working on inventory."

Her legs moved without consulting her brain, heart rattling against her rib cage like a pinball going for broke as she hit the stairs as fast as her feet would allow. Somewhere in the back of her brain, Teagan realized this was ridiculous. In fact, it was beyond ridiculous. It was downright *crazy*.

But there he was in the kitchen, with that battered Harley-Davidson baseball hat on his head and a crooked old Sinatra song on his lips, standing behind the grill like his only purpose was to be there, and oh God, how could anything this crazy feel so freaking good?

"What are you doing?" She stepped in closer, her boots making muted thumps against the kitchen tile.

Adrian tipped his head toward the frying pan balanced over the low flame of the grill, rolling his free shoulder against his snug gray T-shirt. "I'm making scrambled eggs. My medical advisor gets pissy when I don't eat."

Her tiny laugh popped forward, unbidden. "You're not supposed to cook."

"I'm not supposed to lift anything. It's different."

"You just love to push things to see how far they'll go, don't you?"

Her words echoed between them, and his expression made it clear he knew she was talking about more than just the eggs. "Maybe."

"Is that why you came back?"

Adrian's grip on the spatula tightened, his knuckles showing white over the dark belly of the skillet. He slid the frying pan from the burner, dropping the spatula to the counter with a clatter as he turned to face her full-on. "No. I came back because I want to stay. I want to help you."

Teagan felt her eyes go wide. "But—"

"Shh." He placed a finger over the protest brewing on her lips. "I know you're going to say you don't need any help, but I don't care. I know what I told you last night about not being able to stay, but the truth is, I belong in the kitchen with no regrets, and right now that means I belong in here with you. I don't just want to be around the food. I want to help you. So while I'll do my best to steer clear of what happens out there"—he flicked a glance toward the dining room, returning his eyes to hers with a dead-serious stare—"you are stuck with me in here, Red."

For a second, she couldn't move, couldn't think, couldn't breathe. But then she dropped her eyes to Adrian's finger, still hot on her lips. She reached up to wrap her hand around his, moving it from her mouth as she stepped in close enough to erase any daylight between them.

"Did you just *shush* me so you could say your piece?"

Adrian paused, his body going rigid against hers even though his gaze didn't waver. "I guess I did."

"Mmm." Teagan pressed up on her toes, relishing the taste of his shock as she brushed her mouth over his. "I'll let you slide exactly once, but if you make a habit of it, you *will* be sorry."

He drew back, but only enough to pin her with a wide-eyed stare. "You're going to let me help you?"

Something that had no name loosened in her chest, and she felt her body slowly unwind against the strength of his frame as she tucked herself into his left side. Suddenly, it didn't matter that the words bubbling up from inside her were ones that would normally scare her to death. Right now, for the first time since she'd walked into the Double

Shot to find her father half-passed out behind the bar, Teagan wasn't scared at all.

"Yeah, Superman," she said, wrapping her arms around the broad expanse of Adrian's shoulders and holding on tight. "I'm going to let you help me."

Chapter Fourteen

Even though Lonnie had been true to his word about not reappearing at the Double Shot, Adrian triple-checked the side door before making his way back through the now-darkened kitchen. The dirtbag might've kept his distance this week, but Adrian knew it was just a matter of time before the guy oozed back into the place. The only thing criminals like Lonnie wanted more than leverage was money, and he would come looking for his soon enough.

And no matter how right Adrian felt in Teagan's kitchen, by the time that happened, he needed to be good and gone.

He shook off the thought, aiming himself at the door to the dining room. Like many small-town establishments, the Double Shot closed early on Sundays, and the last few hours of tonight's service had been slow at best. Despite the lull, Adrian knew he should feel tested at the seams, like an old shirt wrung out one time too many. His hands might not have been on the food itself, but orbiting around Teagan and Brennan and Jesse, making sure things were done properly or redone, keeping the meager line running smoothly . . . yeah. It was enough to exhaust anyone.

Christ, he felt more energized than ever.

"Hey." He swung through the door connecting the

kitchen to the dining room, eyes moving automatically to the spot where Teagan liked to sit on the customer side of the bar. Her auburn hair was twisted up in a sloppy knot on the back of her head, and a couple of decent-sized wisps had broken free to frame her face, with even more brushing over the shoulders of her snug-fitting button-down shirt. She pushed the rolled-up sleeves past her elbows, lifting her attention from the fat stack of papers in front of her to meet his gaze.

"Oh, hey. Did Brennan and Jesse go home?" She blinked a few times, as if readjusting from the time warp of coming out of deep concentration. The uncharacteristic softening at the edges he'd seen earlier this week as she'd told him she wanted his help was long gone, replaced by the armor-hard moxie that once again screamed *don't touch.* Adrian knew he should honor it, that getting involved with her now that they were working together was a bad idea of unrivaled proportions, and that what he really should do was walk her to her car.

Trouble was, he'd already seen the flip side of her, the one that screamed *dare me,* and he'd never been particularly good at keeping himself in check when those two words entered the equation. And while part of him knew he should walk away before he screwed things up, a darker part of him wanted to dare her until neither one of them could stand.

"Hello? You in there, Superman?" Teagan straightened against the time-softened leather of her bar stool, a fleeting look of relief floating over her face as she elongated her body into a stretch. The move sizzled through him with suggestion before the more general implication hit him without subtlety. As tough as she was, she had to be utterly spent from the grueling week they'd just had. And here he'd been, caught up in the provocative rise of her breasts beneath her shirt as she'd lengthened her arms overhead.

God, he really was an ass. It was all the more reason he should steer clear of her.

"Yeah, sorry. Brennan and Jesse are out, and everything in the back is prepped for tomorrow. You need anything done up here?" Maybe if his brain focused on work, his dick would man up and follow suit.

"Oh. No, thanks." Teagan's *don't touch* demeanor lifted just slightly around the edges. "The front of the house is set for tomorrow. I was just working on the plans for the street fair. My father and I put together some ideas when I checked in on him this morning."

Ah, right. Brennan had mentioned she'd spent the morning with the old man when Adrian had arrived for dinner shift. "How's he doing?"

She crossed her arms, and all of a sudden, *don't touch* made a screaming comeback. "Dr. Riley says he's holding up okay, but he's still doing a ton of work from home. He'd be better if he didn't push it so much."

Well, *that* apple had taken a nonstop trip under the tree, hadn't it? Teagan probably pushed the boundaries even in her sleep. For a hot second, Adrian was tempted to call her on it. She was going to burn out herself if she didn't take it easy. But pushing her meant she'd push back, and that road had a bad destination.

No matter how provocative the trip looked.

Adrian cleared his throat. "Looks as if you two got a lot done." He shot a glance at the gargantuan stack of papers covering the glossy wood in front of her, and she nodded.

"It's going to be really tight, but after looking at the logistics, I think we can swing doing this street fair three weeks from now."

Adrian let out a low whistle. He'd worked on enough

catered events in his career to know that even twice that many weeks would make for an insane time line. But three weeks was what they had, so he said, "It'll be tight, but not impossible. You put in for the permits?"

A frown pinched the edges of her mouth. "Yeah, but the fire code reads like an unabridged version of *War and Peace*. Making sure we're up to spec for an event this size is going to be a pain, but I might be able to call in a favor with some of the guys at the station."

Damn, Adrian hoped so. The last thing they needed was to get shut down before they started, and while he might know his way around everything from a Hibachi to a high-end kitchen, getting things up to code for an off-site catered event fell smack into Adrian's don't-look-at-me category. But maybe if he got her talking about the parts that were working, it would ease a little bit of the stress clearly marking her face.

"What about distributors?" he asked, aiming for his comfort zone, and bingo, Teagan's expression brightened a notch.

"My father's working the supply end pretty hard. It looks as if we might catch a break with that local brewery in Riverside. He's trying to charm them into a discount that fits our budget. Said he thinks we can cut a good deal on the beer. Knowing him, the deal's probably halfway done already."

"Sounds like a good start." With the stack of work at her elbow, he'd be willing to bet Teagan had put every waking hour—and maybe even some of her sleep time—into the plans she'd already made. God, she'd make most event coordinators in New York look like full-time slackers. But not even die-hard intentions would keep her going if she keeled over from exhaustion. "We can work on the food service part tomorrow now that you're rolling with the rest. I'll walk you to your car if you're ready to go home."

"Okay, sure," she said, although she didn't accompany the words with movement. He didn't mind the wait—hell, all he'd be going home to were his four plain white walls anyway—so he leaned back against the edge of the work space across from her.

"You look a lot happier without the sling." Teagan tipped her chin at his left arm, which was now thankfully free and clear of the constricting canvas nightmare, courtesy of a visit to the outpatient PT clinic in Riverside yesterday. Of course, the monstrosity of his cast was still present in all its fiberglass glory, stopping just shy of his elbow and holding his thumb prisoner. But at least he had his shoulder and decent use of all four fingers back.

"Yeah. The physical therapist said my rotator cuff looks good enough, and Dr. Russell agreed. Said he didn't want the joint to get too stiff from not moving. Something about the scar tissue, I guess."

"So you've dislocated it before?"

Shit. Of course she'd know that. "A time or two."

"Doing what?"

"Something I should've known better about." He shifted his weight uncomfortably against the service counter behind him, and damn if Teagan missed not one ounce of his unease.

"I'm sorry, that was really nosy. I didn't mean to put you on the spot." She dropped her pencil and bit her lip, and okay, yeah. That did nothing to assuage the dark, demanding urge to break ranks and kiss her senseless.

"No big deal," he said, and hell, even if they were only here for another five minutes, this was going to be a long night.

An apologetic smile flickered over her mouth, and she

sank against the wooden backrest of her bar stool. "I know I should be exhausted. I mean, I'm pretty sure my back went into complete lockdown a couple hours ago. But still, I can't get my brain to settle down."

"Being wired after a shift is pretty normal, even though it's late at night. Almost all chefs get that way."

Adrian had learned the hard way that twelve straight hours of unvarnished adrenaline jammed into a pressure cooker environment tended to do that to a person. Add in the off-the-wall hours that went with the restaurant industry, and voilà. Even the most stalwart circadian rhythms were toast.

Teagan shrugged, ghosting a palm over her lower back. "I'm definitely not a chef. And anyway, I'm used to weird hours. We do twenty-four on, forty-eight off at the station, and then I'm here most of the time I'm not there. This just feels different."

Adrian grabbed a clean bar towel from the neatly folded stack by the sink built into the back counter, cranking the hot water knob as high as it would go. "Let me guess. You feel like your mind could run a marathon even though your body's ready to give out?"

Teagan stiffened, just a slight shift of her spine that probably wouldn't have been noticeable if he hadn't been right across from her, and she pulled her chin up with that totally stubborn, totally sexy air that burned his resolve down to fumes. "My body's not ready to give out."

Jesus, she was difficult. It would drive him nuts if it didn't turn him on like a goddamn spotlight. "You don't have to be so tough all the time. Nobody here is going to think any less of you if you turn out to be human, you know."

That got her attention. She measured him with a look he couldn't quite decipher, caught somewhere smack in the no-man's-land between cautious and curious. "And how do you know what anyone here thinks of me?"

"Because I'm perceptive." He ran the bar towel beneath the jet of steaming water, leaving it there for a minute before letting it burn his fingers as he wrung it out as best he could with one hand. "Anyway, being wired just means your mind is adjusting to the way things work in the kitchen. You're actually getting used to it quicker than most people do."

"You think so?" Her expression clearly outlined her doubt, but he shook it off.

"Yup. It's an adrenaline thing, just like you said the other night. Not too different from being a paramedic, I'd assume. At least as far as the pace is concerned." Okay, so she was still pretty stiff and awkward when it came to the actual food. But at least that, he could teach her. The grace under pressure part? You either had it or you didn't.

"I didn't think you remembered that conversation," she said, catching the bar towel he'd folded tightly into a plastic storage bag. "What's this?"

"It's a heating pad. For your back. And I don't forget conversations."

Teagan's coppery lashes fanned up in surprise, but she shocked the hell out of him by lifting the edges of her mouth into a tiny smile. "Old school. Very nice." She tucked the bag around behind her, her expression collapsing into a moan of relief as she pressed it against her back.

Well, shit. Of course he hadn't thought she'd acquiesce over something little when she was so hardheaded about everything else.

Adrian selfishly let the sound of her sigh thread through him before battening down the sexual hatches yet again. He needed to cut this attraction off at the quick, before he didn't. "Glad you approve."

"So how do most chefs deal with it? You know, when your brain doesn't want to stop going?"

"The usual outlets, I guess. Some people drink too much. Others have sex."

"Oh." Matching pink spots crept high over Teagan's cheekbones, but she didn't budge. "And what do you do?"

"Neither." Not anymore, at least. His mind tilted backward, landing on a spot five years ago that he'd give just about anything to erase. *Not going there.* "I cook."

"If the idea is to find a way to unwind from the intensity of the kitchen, doesn't more cooking just perpetuate things?" Teagan asked, putting the makeshift heating pad on the bar in front of her and slipping off the smooth wood of her stool. She crossed the pass-through to the other side of the bar, her boots clacking against the hardwood before being swallowed by the buffer of the rubber mats as she approached the cooler.

"Not if you do it until your mind is straight."

She nodded. "Is that why you want to be in the kitchen no matter what? So it'll keep your mind straight?"

The question was so matter-of-fact, so free of judgment that Adrian's answer barged out before he could even think about cloaking it or swallowing it back. "It's one reason, yeah."

"Wow. And I thought I was a workaholic." Teagan palmed the handle of the cooler, sliding the frosted glass door on its track and propping it open with her lean forearm. She laced the fingers of her other hand comfortably around a bottle of water, barely looking at it as she uncapped the thing and passed it over with movements so practiced, he'd bet his one good arm she could do it in her sleep.

"You are a workaholic. What are you doing?"

"That kitchen is conservatively eight thousand degrees,

and even without that sling, you're still healing. You need to stay hydrated."

Adrian lifted a brow. "And what about you?"

"Well, since I'm not crazy about cooking even when I have to, I guess my only option for getting my mind straight is to have a beer," she said, reaching back into the cooler for an amber-colored bottle.

A not-so-tiny, definitely dark part of Adrian was tempted to point out she'd skipped the sex option. But hell, he was having a hard enough time keeping his hands over in his own camp as it was. If they started talking about sex, that beer was never going to make it to her lips.

And he couldn't afford to make the same mistake twice.

"Not too many women go for a straight-up beer after a hard day's work," he said, veering back into safe-topic territory.

Teagan shrugged, tilting her bottle upward. "I was raised in a small-town bar and grill. It's not as if there's an extensive wine list."

The laugh that sprang up from Adrian's chest felt rusty, as if it hadn't been used in far too long. "I spent half my life in a house so Italian, there was a wine list at breakfast. In fact, I'm pretty sure my *nonna* never had beer in the house the entire time we lived there."

"So do you speak Italian, then?" She paused to slide her fingertips over her right forearm while keeping her eyes fixed on his tattoo. "Or just a couple of phrases?"

"No, I'm fluent. *Nonna* was pretty adamant about me learning the language. We lived in a really Italian neighborhood in New York, and it was easy enough for me to learn."

"She adopted you when you were ten?" Teagan moved back around to the customer side of the bar, scooping up the makeshift heating pad and pressing it against the small of her back. Her curiosity, even in the face of exhaustion, was so wide-open and genuine that rather than cut the conversation off at the knees, Adrian just answered.

"Yup. She volunteered at the soup kitchen in the shelter where I'd been living between foster homes." He kicked his legs out in front of him, settling back against the workplace counter again. "I hung around the kitchen twenty-four seven because I was hungry. All the other volunteers shooed me away, but not *Nonna*."

"She fed you?" A streak of something Adrian couldn't catch flashed over Teagan's warm brown gaze, but he shook his head.

"Nah. She put me to work. At first, it was just easy stuff, like washing vegetables and counting out portions of bread. But then she let me move up to stirring onions in the stockpots and teaching me how to measure and slice. I was totally addicted."

"Did she get into trouble for letting you help?"

"Are you kidding?" he scoffed, but with a lot more endearment than edge. "*Nonna* ran that kitchen from stem to stern. Even after she adopted me, we worked at the shelter twice a week without fail. I guess teaching a moody ten-year-old foster kid how to cook was a little unorthodox. But she said she knew from the start where I belonged."

"Living with her, you mean?" Teagan asked, lifting her beer to take another sip.

Adrian paused, his words rattling through him like a heavy-bottomed saucepan being dropped from the top shelf. "In the kitchen, Red. I belong in the kitchen."

"My mother was the same way." Teagan's voice went low, but not soft, her eyes firm on the bottle in her hand. "So is that *really* why you're here? You need to be in the kitchen, and mine is the only one available?"

The question was laced with an obvious desire to know, but he dodged it anyway. "You need the help," he pointed out, but she blew right past the deflection just like she blew past his composure.

"And you're on parole. You're risking an awful lot to be here, Adrian. So what gives? Is the kitchen really more important to you than anything else? I . . ." Teagan hitched to a stop, but only for a second. "I need to know, okay?"

"Yeah. It is," he said, but the response he'd always counted as automatic somehow felt like a handful of stones in his mouth, hard and heavy and in the wrong place. "I know I have to lie low, but being in the kitchen is worth the risk."

"For now." Teagan lowered her beer to the polished mahogany bar with a *thunk*, tiny lines of worry bracketing her frown. "If things with Lonnie change—"

"Then I'll deal with it." Adrian knotted his arms over his chest despite the residual ache it sent through his still-pissed shoulder. "What about you?"

"What about me?"

He went for the full-throttle subject change. "Well, no offense, but you kind of suck at unwinding."

Her laughter sizzled through his veins, and shit. Maybe switching the topic and trying to get her to relax was a bad idea after all. "Point taken. I guess taking care of other people is my version of being in the kitchen. It might sound hokey, but it's where *I* belong."

"That makes sense," he allowed. "But you didn't answer the question."

"What question?" Teagan's red-gold brows drew downward, and even though Adrian knew he risked her snapping back or shutting down, he asked, "Who takes care of you?"

She paused, tracing the edge of her half-empty beer bottle with one long finger. "Who cooks for you?"

"What does that have to do with anything?" he asked,

pulling back in confusion, but of course, Teagan didn't budge.

"Humor me. Who cooks for you?"

"I'm a chef. I cook for myself."

"Do you?" Her tone lifted in accusation. "I mean, do you really? Or are you just putting together what you eat?"

A hard pang shot through Adrian's gut as he realized she wasn't just talking about the quick omelet he'd thrown on his plate for breakfast this morning. What she meant was deeper than that, past all the ingredients and the recipes and the dishes.

Teagan was talking about taking care of himself through cooking. And damn it, even though he'd made thousands of meals since landing in Pine Mountain last year, Adrian couldn't remember the last time he'd cooked purely for himself, for the out-and-out love of being around the food rather than the hard-driven desire to be in motion.

"I do enough to get by," he said, although his mouth burned with the aftertaste of the lie. Christ, how did this woman manage to turn the tables on him and turn him on so much all at the same freaking time?

Teagan slipped from her seat at the bar, closing the space between them until only a sliver remained. As if she'd crawled into his mind for the guided tour, she whispered, "Yeah, well, I'm not so great at taking care of myself, either. Guess we're a perfect match."

For just a second, the hard lines of her *don't touch* veneer disappeared under the low lights in the bar. Teagan looked up, her infuriatingly red lips only inches away from his mouth. She locked her gaze onto his with that rare openness that speared all the way through him, and in that moment, Adrian had never been so tempted to give in to impulse in his entire life.

But the kitchen where he belonged in the long run

wasn't here, and in less than five weeks, he wouldn't be here either.

"Right," Adrian said, angling his body away from her and toward the door. "It's kind of late. We should get going."

Teagan's eyes widened with surprise, and Adrian cursed himself with renewed vigor. But better to piss her off by being brusque than tangle them both in the alternative. Getting involved with Teagan, even in the short term, was a bad idea, and not just because they would be sharing space for the next month or so.

She deserved more than a felon with an expiration date, and he simply couldn't deliver.

"Oh." A flash of hurt backlit her expression, peppering Adrian's chest with holes before she slammed over it with one fluid step back toward the bar. "Yeah, you're right. We should definitely go."

But as she turned on her heel and walked away without so much as a hitch in her stride, Adrian's only thought was that he wanted her back.

Chapter Fifteen

Teagan stared at the screen of her laptop, shifting her weight in the ancient desk chair in the Double Shot's office for the ninetieth time this hour. Her back muscles gripped her spine with unforgiving tension, throbbing out a dare to surrender with every move, and she popped the lid off the bottle of ibuprofen at her elbow. This morning's dose had gotten her through a two-hour planning session with her father and the manager at the Cold Creek Brewery, as well as grueling kitchen prep and a liquor delivery. But they were coming up on the dinner shift, and even though Mondays were usually slow, she needed all the strength she could muster if she was going to run the kitchen with Adrian.

Adrian, who had seen right through every wall she'd ever cemented around herself in self-preservation. Adrian, who she'd essentially flung herself at last night in an attack of needy weakness.

Adrian, who'd all but run from the building the second she got close to him.

"Hey, boss. You got a second?" Brennan's voice tipped Teagan out of her reverie, and she bolted upright despite the screeching from her back at the movement.

"Absolutely," she said, pasting a smile over the grimace welling up on her face. "Is everything okay downstairs?"

A shot of panic clipped through Teagan's veins, but Brennan cut it off with a quick nod of his dark head.

"Oh yeah, everything's fine. Gigantor's actually pretty tight with the management stuff. You were right when you said he knows what he's talking about."

"Good." Although Brennan had never really been the type to buck authority and go territorial over the bar, Teagan had to admit a sense of relief at how seamlessly he and Adrian had fallen into rhythm. She'd even been able to put all the bar inventory in Brennan's now-capable hands, as well as the scheduling for the waitstaff. "So, what's up?"

"Nothing major. I just, ah . . . I know you're planning on doing most of the cooking for the street fair outside, right?"

She nodded. "The fire code limits how many people we can have inside the building at any given time, and we have room on the south side of the lot to set up some tents and tables to go with the entertainment. Hosting as much of the event as possible outside the actual building accommodates more people in the long run, so yes. That's probably what we'll do, once I figure out the insane regulations for the equipment." She'd tried to wade through the fire code, but the damn thing read more like secret code.

"Right." Brennan skated a palm over the back of his neck. "I can help you with the setup. You know, making sure all the cooking stations are up to code per the fire regs."

"That's a ton of research. And let's just say this thing isn't exactly user-friendly." Teagan gestured to the three inches of fire code manual sitting on her father's desk like the world's thickest doorstop. She'd already come to terms with the fact that she'd have to call in the mother of all favors with the guys at the station in order to make the logistics happen. Even then, she'd have to pray they had the time to go with their inclination, which she knew full well they likely didn't. "Don't get me wrong. I appreciate the offer, but even if you were lucky, it would take at least a week to learn all the ins and outs of the fire code for an event like this."

"It's a week you don't have to spare," Brennan countered. "And anyway, I, ah . . . already know it."

Surprise sent her shoulder blades against the back of her desk chair with a squeak. "You understand the technicalities in the Pennsylvania state fire code well enough to manage the permits for the entire street fair?"

"Yeah. I . . . yeah."

"Jeez, Brennan." Her shock grew roots and spread out. "Do you want to tell me how you gained all this knowledge?"

"No," he said, quickly tacking on, "but it's legit, Teagan, I swear. I wouldn't bullshit you about this. I know the fire code, and I can do all the paperwork for the permits and get everything set up the right way. I just . . . don't want to talk about the rest."

She measured the information for a long minute before meeting Brennan's nearly black stare with absolute surety. "Okay."

He took a step back toward the doorframe, staring as if he'd heard incorrectly. "Okay?"

"Look, I'm not going to lie and tell you I'm not curious as hell about how you know all this stuff. But I've got laundry in my closet that I don't like to put on the line, either. If you don't want to spill, I can respect that, and if you change your mind, I'm here. Until then, it would make my life exponentially easier to have you handle the permits and the setup for the street fair. You're part of the Double Shot, like me and my dad and Jesse. If you say you've got this, I trust you."

"Thanks." The rigid line of his mouth softened just a shade, and he took the stack of permits she extended across the cluttered desk. "So, what about Adrian?"

Teagan scooped in a breath to counter her accelerating heartbeat, and ugh, she really needed to forget about last night. "What about him?"

"How does he fit into all of this?"

It was time to forget everything but the facts, once and for all. "Adrian just needs to keep working, Brennan. He's not staying permanently. But it's not anything to worry about, if that's what you mean."

"Please." Brennan's mouth flattened back into a hard line. "If I thought I had to worry about him, we'd be having a very different conversation. I don't care *how* big the guy is." He paused to let Teagan eke out a thanks-for-having-my-back smile before continuing. "I guess what I'm asking is, even though he's temporary, do you trust him, too?"

"Yes." The word fired out of her mouth automatically, and even though it took her by no small amount of surprise, Teagan couldn't deny its truth. "He's only here for a little while until he goes back to the restaurant at the resort, but I still trust him."

"Good," Brennan said, his boots shuffling over the thinning carpet as he turned toward the door. "Because he just handed the kitchen over to Jesse and Caleb. It seems you have the night off, boss."

"Excuse me, Superman, but are you out of your freaking *mind*?"

Adrian looked up from where he and Jesse stood at the grill station just in time to get an eyeful of very pissed-off female. Okay, so he'd known full well that covering Teagan's shift for the night would infuriate her to no end, but still.

Did she have to look so damned pretty when she was mad?

"Not last time I checked," he said, tipping his head at Jesse in a wordless approximation of *you got this?* The guy gave a wide-eyed nod, and Adrian moved toward the entryway to the kitchen, bracing for impact.

Teagan didn't waste any time delivering. "I'm not taking the night off." She jammed her hands into the faded denim wrapped low on her hips, but Adrian was prepared for her ire.

"Monday's the slowest night of the week. Traditionally, whoever's in charge of the kitchen gets the night off."

"Guess that means you're off tonight, then. I'm not in charge of the kitchen."

"I took tonight off, too."

Well, that got her. "You what?" Teagan asked, her lips parting in surprise.

"I looked at the numbers from the last four Monday nights, and we should be able to stay out of the weeds with Brennan and Jesse and Caleb. If not"—He held up one hand to stave off the argument she was clearly locking into place in her mind—"then Brennan will call me, and as a last resort, I'll call you. But you need a night off."

"What about everyone else?" She shifted her weight from one brown leather boot to the other, but her eyes said she was still far from giving in. Too bad for her, Adrian had her pegged, lock, stock, and stubborn-to-the-core barrel.

"Brennan goes tomorrow. The night after that will be Jesse's turn. But Mondays are slowest, so tonight is yours."

"Even if we're slow on dinner service, there's still too

much to do with the street fair. I can't afford to take a night off."

Adrian stepped toward her, dropping his voice so the kitchen noises around them made their conversation private. "And you can't take care of anything if you collapse. This stuff will all be here tomorrow, and you'll be that much better equipped to handle it if you've had some decent sleep. But you've been here pretty much nonstop for over a week, and last night, your back was snarled up like rush-hour traffic in midtown. You're riding on fumes, and the rest of us are, too." He popped his chin at Brennan and Jesse as they slid trays of clean pint glasses from the dishwasher in the alcove. "You think they'll take a break if you don't?"

Teagan's slender shoulders hitched, her exhale of realization brushing over him in a warm rush that said he'd hit home. "Fine. You made your point. But you're the one with a broken arm. Why don't you go tonight, and I'll go tomorrow?"

The image of her face, streaked through with both need and hurt as he walked away from her last night, slapped into him without remorse, and Adrian didn't think twice as he said, "Because I don't trust you to take care of yourself, Red. So we're both off tonight, and I'm going to do it for you."

Chapter Sixteen

Adrian unlocked the door to his apartment, ushering Teagan inside the tiny, bare-bones foyer that matched the rest of the place before pulling the door shut behind them. He'd known when he came up with this idea that he was playing with fire, but her words from last night reverberated through him, pushing past his well-placed defenses in a way that was impossible to ignore.

He *hadn't* cooked for himself in far too long. And while he might not be ready to put his shit-kickers on that path yet, he could sure as hell cook for her. Even if it was just for tonight.

"You don't have to babysit me, you know," Teagan said, yanking him from his thoughts with her infuriatingly sexy frown. "Contrary to popular belief, I can manage a night off."

"Eating a frozen dinner while doing enough Internet research on street fairs to make your eyes bleed doesn't count as a night off." Adrian turned and took the five meager steps needed to reach his kitchen, forcing himself to focus on the food rather than the ripe curve of Teagan's pout. "So if it's all the same to you, why don't I cook some dinner so you can actually relax?"

Her frown intensified. "You're not supposed to cook."

"No, I'm not supposed to lift anything heavy, remember? But you've got medical training. I'm sure you'll keep me in line."

For a second, Adrian just watched her from his spot at the kitchen counter. Jesus, she was a work of art, all deep, sinful hips and sexy curves. She stared back at him, amber eyes unflinching, before she finally gave a nod.

"Suit yourself. But you try and pick up anything heavier than a glass of water and we're going to have a go."

Relief spread out in his chest, leaving a dark chuckle in its wake. "Fair enough. I'll even give you the best seat in the house." He canted his head toward the other side of the counter, where the small breakfast bar separated the kitchen from the rest of his paltry living space.

"This looks like the only seat in the house," she flipped back, hooking her fingers under the polished wood of the bar stool while swinging one impossibly long leg over the seat. "Do you have some kind of moral objection to furniture?"

"I'm not really ever here to use much of anything." Adrian grabbed the bag of potatoes he'd picked up earlier this morning at Joe's Grocery and one-handed the thing open. His place might not be all decked out, but he had the necessities. Most of them were in the kitchen cabinets.

Of course, Teagan didn't let up. "Well, yeah, but come on. No pictures on the walls, no curtains over the blinds. You don't even have a couch."

"I don't need a couch." He flipped the kitchen faucet with a shrug, testing the running water with the back of his free hand. "Having too much stuff just makes it harder when you move, anyway."

"If a couch is too much of a commitment, you could start small, you know," she said with a brassy smile that could stop crime. Christ above, he was never going to get used to the heat coming off of this woman.

"Small, huh?" He pulled back on the urge to clear his throat even though his voice sounded like forty-grit sandpaper. "Like just a throw pillow?"

"No offense, but you don't strike me as the throw pillow type. I'm thinking more along the lines of a house plant."

Adrian barked out a laugh. "Better make it a cactus unless you want me to kill the thing."

"Tough and prickly. Now that does seem more your speed." Teagan propped her elbows on the time-scuffed breakfast bar, her gaze flickering over the kitchen before landing on him with a hint of curiosity. "So, um, what are you cooking?"

She nodded down at the potato in his hand. It glistened under the steady stream of water from the sink, and Adrian cupped the vegetable in his palm, moving the fingers of his unhurt hand over the hard flesh in sure, even strokes to remove the residual dirt.

"Gnocchi. Have you ever had it before?" He finished with the potato in his grasp, admiring the imperfect texture and the heaviness of it before trading it for another one. Damn, the ten days he'd gone without food in his hands felt more like ten years.

And the time he'd gone without actually listening to the food as he cooked felt like pure eternity.

"No." Teagan fastened her steady stare over his hands, but the waver in her voice gave her away. "My mother did a lot of French cuisine, really old-school classical dishes. We had coq au vin up to our eye teeth, but Italian food, not so much. Is it complicated?"

"Are you kidding? Four ingredients, that's it." He finished with the potatoes and put them in a stockpot, barely covering them with water from the tap. "Gnocchi is a cross between pasta and potato dumplings. Total comfort food. My *nonna* used to make it all the time."

Teagan slid from her spot across from him at the counter, all swaying hips and *dare me* bravado as she moved next to him and curled her fingers around the handles of the stockpot. "I'm sure it's good then."

"It is. What are you doing?"

One fiery brow popped. "No lifting. Where do you want this?"

She was close enough for him to catch the warm scent of rosemary riding the air around her, and okay, this was going to be an exercise in self-restraint.

"Front burner's fine." Adrian stepped back as she slid the stockpot over the burner grate with a muted scrape. "Might as well do the other one now, too." He filled a second, larger stockpot with water from the sink before stepping back to let Teagan angle it over an adjacent burner. But as soon as the task was done, she retreated to her spot at the breakfast bar, clearly wanting no part of the kitchen unless it was absolutely necessary.

"It sounds like your *nonna* was a great lady," Teagan said, her voice soft yet serious. "You must miss her."

"Yeah."

Nonna's ancient kitchen in Brooklyn, with the harvest gold refrigerator circa 1972 and the lovingly worn Formica countertops, flashed through Adrian's mind's eye, the image fresh as loaves of bread on the windowsill. The pang in his chest told him to shut up, that he was supposed to be making her dinner, and revealing all his down-deep feelings like this wasn't part of the deal. But the look on Teagan's face, along with how much she seemed to hate cooking because of her mother, struck him with startling clarity.

She needed to believe something good could come out of the kitchen, and he had the power to show her.

"My biological mother left me on the front steps of a church in Queens when I was nine days old," Adrian said, the words surprisingly easy in his mouth. "Family Services tried to find her, but in a city like New York, it was wasted effort. Clearly, she didn't want to be found, so I became a ward of the state."

Teagan didn't say anything, but a flicker of understanding lit her expression, and it pulled more of the story right on out of him.

"I was almost adopted twice. The first time things fell through, I was still a baby, so I don't remember any of what happened, and nobody ever told me the details. But the second time was . . . different." He swallowed hard, bracing for the inevitable pity party that came whenever people heard a story like his.

But Teagan just said, "How old were you?"

"Six. I lived with the family for about a month. But I had trouble getting used to having a permanent home after all that time in the system."

"It must not be easy, being placed after six years of living in foster homes."

Damn, her matter-of-fact demeanor and see-everything eyes were going to upend him, they really were. "Yeah, but I wouldn't even unpack my clothes, let alone play with the other kids in the neighborhood or go to school. I kept thinking I'd wake up and Family Services would tell me I had to go somewhere else, so I just kept to myself, you know? Waiting."

"What happened?" Teagan asked.

"The couple eventually decided they wanted a kid with no 'adjustment issues,' so they sent me back into the system."

This time she flinched. "God, Adrian, I'm so sorry."

He stemmed her apology with a wave, twisting the thick

knobs on the cooktop. The telltale *click-click-click* of the gas burner popped against his nerves, but it was quickly followed by the *whoosh* of dancing blue flames that always calmed him.

"I'm not. If that stuff hadn't happened, I wouldn't have ended up living with my *nonna*. And if she hadn't adopted me, I never would've figured out where I really belong."

"She taught you how to make this?" Teagan pointed to the cooktop, leaning in close enough for Adrian to see the genuine interest playing over her features.

"My *nonna* could make gnocchi with her eyes closed, literally. She taught me how to do more than just taste food to know whether or not I'd gotten it right. For her, it was all about the feel of it under her hands, the smells . . . the whole experience mattered, start to finish."

"My mother used to be so serious about cooking. I mean, there was no doubt she loved it. But I think she took it as more of a personal challenge than a labor of actual love."

Ah. Well that explained where the stubborn came from. "*Nonna* took cooking seriously too, just in a different way. For her, it was about listening to the food. Really letting it nurture her *and* the people she cooked for."

"Yeah." Teagan's eyes went wide for a single breath before slamming shut, and when she reopened them, they were brimming over with *don't touch*. "That was a bit of a foreign concept in my house."

"You want a glass of wine?"

"What?" She blinked, but no way was he going to let go of distracting her now. Plus, if anything could divert her attention and make her relax it was a bottle of wine and a kickass meal.

"Call it an exercise in relaxation. Are you in?" He put just enough mustard on the words to make them a dare, knowing she'd bite. But her stress was going to swallow her whole if she didn't offload some of it. Teagan wouldn't last three days, let alone three more weeks, at the pace she'd been carving out.

She paused. "Wine's not really my thing, remember?"

"Mmm. You'll like this." Adrian watched the flare grow in her eyes as he slid a bottle of merlot from the adjacent pantry, returning to the work space to unearth a corkscrew from a drawer. "Come on, I'll even let you uncork it. What do you say?"

Teagan unfolded her curves-and-attitude frame from the bar stool, but she didn't hesitate to reenter the kitchen. Her movements challenged him right back as she curled her fingers around the bottle, easing the sharp, silver point of the corkscrew into the cork without looking.

"I say you're awfully presumptuous."

It didn't come out sounding like a compliment, and heat stirred low in Adrian's gut before heading south. He knew that daring her into the kitchen, even with good intentions, was a bad plan. Experience told him putting two volatile things too close together only meant they were bound to explode. But then she looked up at him with a slow and sexy smile on her decadent mouth, and damn it, part of him wanted to watch her ignite.

"If you want to insult me, you're going to have to do better than that. I've heard the presumptuous thing once or twice before." Adrian pulled the wineglasses he'd borrowed from the Double Shot from a cupboard, placing them just far enough away on the counter that Teagan would have to take a step closer to pour.

If he was going to get her into the kitchen, he might as well go all freaking in.

The cork gave a soft pop as she released it from the

mouth of the bottle, and she inclined her head at him in thought. "Okay. How does pompous ass suit you?"

Damn, he wanted this woman more than he wanted his next freaking breath. "Barely lukewarm, Red."

"Egotistical cretin?" Teagan asked, the words sounding strangely seductive in her throaty voice as she cut the space between them to pour.

"Ah, getting warmer."

Her hip brushed against his, ever so slightly as she leaned in to place the bottle on the counter, pulling back to return to the breakfast bar. Adrian let out a breath, sliding one of the glasses toward her before lifting the other to take a sip. The rich notes of the wine slid across his palate and lingered, heady and smooth on his tongue, and he edged closer to the counter, watching her.

"Getting warmer, huh? Hmm." Teagan tapped a finger against her lips in thought before brightening. "Narcissistic muttonhead," she offered, folding her hands in front of her with an angelic smile.

Adrian's laugh came from deep in his chest. "Well done. Now you're hot."

The corners of Teagan's strawberry-red mouth twitched upward into a smirk that sparked through his blood, and she nodded down at the stove. "And it looks like you're boiling."

Understatement. Of. The. Year.

"Okay, wine boy," Teagan said, holding on to her smile as she took the glass of merlot in her hand. "Do I need to do anything highbrow before I drink this?"

"Hold the glass up to your lips and breathe in first," Adrian said, moving to gather more ingredients from the narrow pantry by the refrigerator.

"You're always this bossy in the kitchen, aren't you?"

He didn't hesitate. "Yes." She scoffed softly, but he

continued before she could work up a smart comment. "In order to enjoy a good glass of wine, you have to do more than taste it. You've got to gather it in and make it a part of you."

Teagan made a face. "What if I hate it? Then I won't want to make it a part of me."

Adrian put the bag of flour he'd retrieved from the pantry on the counter and nudged the boiling pot, watching the potatoes gently rock and nestle together. "If you hate it, that's fine. But you should try it the right way before you decide."

She ran a finger around the base of the glass. "I guess I never thought of wine, or any food, really, as something to take my time with."

"Don't feel bad. A lot of people rush through what they eat and drink—they don't take time to smell it, to feel it in their mouths, to really *experience* it." He drew his wineglass up to his face, letting it brush against the rough stubble on his chin before inhaling. "Taste is the last sense you use on the things you eat and drink, although everyone thinks it's the only one."

Her expression softened, surprising him. "Okay, I'll humor you. You want me to just pretend I'm taking a sip, only smell it instead?"

"It's not milk with a questionable expiration date." He gave in to his satisfied smile and leaned in closer, until only a scant stretch of Formica countertop and his dwindling willpower separated their bodies. "Don't just smell it. Breathe it in. Experience it."

Teagan's laugh caught him like a sucker punch to the sternum, but she didn't pull back to reclaim the space between them. "'Experience it,'" she repeated, dropping her eyes seductively to the glass.

"Yeah," Adrian managed, trying to right himself. Damn

it, she was killing him with those endlessly long legs parted over the bar stool just wide enough to make him wonder what else she could do with them. "Let it take care of you a little." He motioned to her glass, knowing his words would hit home.

"Screw you," she muttered, but he caught the twist of her sardonic smile as she raised the rim of her wineglass and inhaled. Her eyes shuttered closed, cinnamon-colored lashes sweeping low over her face, and even though his self-protective instinct screamed at him not to, he impulsively moved closer.

"See? You can smell the flavors before they even hit your tongue. This merlot is rich, complex. And it tells you all about itself before you drink it."

Teagan kept her eyes closed and breathed in again, her bottom lip pressing slightly against the rim of her glass, and she gave a small nod and sigh combination that shot straight to his cock.

"Breathing it in enhances the experience. It makes you want it more." Adrian braced himself against the narrow stretch of countertop between them, palms hot on the cool surface. He leaned in close enough to feel the heat coming off of her, to smell the earthy scent of rosemary where her neck met her ear. The irony of it hit him full-on.

Just like the wine, when he breathed her in, it only made him want her more.

"So go ahead," Adrian said. "Drink."

She raised the glass, tipping the ruby liquid along its curve until it reached her lips. Adrian watched her, completely entranced by the newness of the experience on her face, as she took a sip and cradled the glass in her palm. A drop of wine lingered on her bottom lip, staining it a perfect, sensual red. God, Adrian wanted to have that bottom lip for breakfast, to trace it with his tongue and relish the flavor of her in his mouth. He didn't just want to kiss her, but to taste her, to savor her.

To *have* her.

But then her eyes blinked open and she lowered the glass.

"I'm not sure about the whole deep experience thing, but the wine is nice," she admitted, taking another sip.

"Told you." Adrian scooped the potatoes from the stockpot with a slotted spoon, letting the heat from the steam wash over his face. He'd been fighting the desire to kiss Teagan again ever since he'd botched things that stupid morning he'd first taught her to cook, only this time, he wanted to dive into her and never come up for air.

This time, if he kissed her, he wasn't going to stop.

Without fanfare, he scooped one of the potatoes into a tea towel on the counter. After a second's worth of awkward fumbling, he got a decent grip on it with his left fingers, although his incapacitated thumb itched to get in on the action. Keeping the towel-wrapped potato steady as best he could by cradling it between his fingers and chest, he started to peel it with quick precision. Long ribbons of light brown skin, thin enough to see through, snaked over the tea towel as he worked, and the task helped him focus.

"How come you didn't peel those before you boiled them? I mean, isn't it easier that way, so you don't burn your fingers?" Teagan leaned forward on her elbows, watching him start on the second potato with an inquisitive stare. Damn, she didn't miss anything.

"It changes the starch content if you boil them that way. Plus, when they're hot, the peels slide off easier. Pretty helpful when you've only got one and a half hands."

"Oh. That was probably a stupid question, huh?" Teagan didn't look sheepish very often, or, okay, ever, but hell, if it didn't light him up like the Fourth of July right now.

"No such thing as a stupid question."

Teagan eyed him over the rim of her wineglass and smirked. "Does this make me look fat?"

Adrian finished peeling the last potato, shooting her a disapproving look even though he knew it wouldn't stick. "Okay. *Almost* no such thing as a stupid question."

He scooped just enough flour into a soft mound on the counter, giving it a gentle roll with the backs of his knuckles to create a well. Going through the familiar motions, even without the full use of his left hand, sent another wave of calm through his chest.

"You don't measure anything," Teagan noted, more statement than question, and Adrian nodded in agreement.

"After a while, you start to recognize when things are right. A lot of it is by feel and taste. But I've made this enough to know it by heart."

Holding one of the still-steaming potatoes in the thinly textured weave of the tea towel, Adrian hooked his left fingers beneath the handle of a bell grater. Slowly, he worked the potato over the holes, watching as the cream-colored flesh left a trail of steam on the stainless steel. He moved in brisk, even strokes, watching the curls of yellow-white potato drop into the well like confetti. "So even though we don't have a whole lot of ingredients here, we still have to make sure that they play nicely together."

"Playing nicely doesn't seem to suit you."

"And yet that doesn't bother you," Adrian flipped back, working the second potato into fine shreds.

One red-gold brow lifted. "I don't play nicely either."

Right. Because just what he needed was another reason to want her.

"Well, you'd better learn quick, because you're up."

Teagan's shoulders lifted in a slim line of surprise, and

she pulled back from the counter to stare at him. "You can't be serious."

"When it comes to food, I'm always serious." Adrian tipped his head at the counter, dividing his expression between *trust me* and *I dare you*. Damn, she was full to the brim with tension and tired, and all he wanted was to get her to relax. "Come on. I can't do this part alone, and I'll walk you through it. I'm a chef. It's not like I'm going to steer you wrong."

For a second, she didn't move, and hell, maybe pushing her had been a bad plan. But then she gave a barely perceptible nod and slid from her bar stool to round the corner into the kitchen.

"Fine. Let's do this before I change my mind."

Adrian turned to get an egg and some butter out of the refrigerator, trapping his satisfied smile between his teeth. "The trick here is to get the ingredients incorporated just right, and the best way to do that is to go by feel."

Returning to the counter, he closed his fingers around the smooth contours of the egg, giving it a one-handed tap-and-break into the flour well.

Teagan scoffed. "Show-off."

But Adrian kept steady with the food, nice and easy so she would, too. "It's important to go slow—you don't want to maul it, or else the dough turns out too tough." He reached forward for a pinch of salt from the covered bowl on the counter, sprinkling it over the well before stepping back to gesture her into the space.

Her lips parted. "You want me to use my hands?"

"Yup. It's just like the wine, only instead of breathing it in, you're letting it talk to you by feeling it."

"I hope you have the pizza guy on speed dial, because I'm totally going to screw this up," she muttered, but she sank her fingers into the mixture anyway. Her brow tugged down in fierce concentration, but Adrian countered it by stepping in behind her.

"You're not going to screw this up." Caging her body gently with his own, he put his right hand over hers to guide her through the motions. He worked his hand—and hers— over the mixture, first one pass, then another. "Take a breath. Relax, and let the food do its thing."

"Like that?" Teagan asked, her back melting into his chest with each move of their hands. She tipped her chin toward her shoulder to look up at him in question, and he sucked in a breath full of rosemary and total, undiluted want.

"Yeah," he said. "Like that."

Slowly, the ingredients began to find their way together, and a ball of dough the color of spring sunshine began to take shape between Teagan's palms, smooth and pliable. Her shoulders rolled, low and easy against his body, her breath coming in soft pulls as she looked down at their entwined hands. "God, that's amazing."

Adrian threw every last shred of his focus into the food. "Isn't it? It's only a few ingredients, yet when you bring them together without forcing it, they just find their way to where they belong."

"So now what?"

"Now all we have to do is roll it out and cut it," he said, stepping back from her even though his body screamed in protest. He skimmed a thin layer of flour over the counter-top, reminding himself that this was about taking care of *her*. Without quite meeting her gaze—God, he was such a selfish bastard—Adrian gestured for her to place the dough on the flour-coated counter and pressed a rolling pin into her hands.

"Nice and even, Red. It's all about feel." He fixed his eyes on the dough as she rolled it out, her movements tentative yet efficient. "Good. Use your fingers to check for ripples in the surface. Missing them with your eyes is easy, but you'll catch them if you go by touch."

"Oh." The word rode out on a sigh as she skimmed the pale yellow disc of dough with one hand, then the other. "It really *is* all about feel."

"See? You're a natural."

Adrian palmed a dough cutter, the handle smooth in his palm, and he edged in next to her to begin cutting the dough with one-handed movements. Teagan watched as if in a trance, and he watched her face the same way, drinking her in as she stared.

"If you know how to listen, the food tells you everything." He ran the gleaming tines of a fork across each little bead of dough, imprinting the supple surface with the trademark triple slash of gnocchi.

"The way you do that is really incredible." Teagan swung her gaze upward to meet his, her face as open and pure as sunrise, and in that moment, Adrian knew the difference between just wanting someone and being hungry for someone.

He was fucking *starving* for her.

Chapter Seventeen

Heat pulsed through Teagan clear down to her bones as she watched Adrian's big, capable hands sweep over the pasta dough. Each of his movements showed such quiet power, such attention to detail, it was as if the dough simply belonged in his hands and his hands belonged in the kitchen. The natural way his fingers coaxed everything into place was pure, sensual magic, and she couldn't look away.

What could those hands do to a woman? To her?

Teagan flushed and clamped down on the thought, but not before she realized that Adrian wasn't looking at the pasta dough on the counter.

He was looking at her. And he was definitely hungry.

"You want to do the honors, then?" His raspy voice found the pit of her belly, low and deep. She'd hated the kitchen on principle for so long that her gut instinct was to shoot back a *no*. But cooking with Adrian was different, easy in a way that she'd never felt around food before, and instead of giving the *no* any airtime, she just nodded.

"Okay. What do I do?"

"Just scoop them up and lay them into the water, one batch at a time." Adrian handed her what looked like a wire mesh ladle, its intricate, spiny web branching out from the handle like a gaudy silver cloak.

Teagan narrowed her eyes on him. Okay, fine, so the dark-edged stare that most people would probably find arrogant was turning her on like Christmas lights, and yes, the more he did it, the more she wanted to do something wild like, say, rip his shirt off right here in the kitchen. But come on, she wasn't exactly wallflower material. She opened her mouth to give him a little attitude when it hit her.

He was pushing her on purpose just to watch her push back.

"Okay," she answered, and from the look on his face, she wasn't the only one surprised at the concession. Doing her best to keep a steady hand, Teagan filled the ladle thingy with gnocchi. She eyed the boiling pot and exhaled.

She could do this.

It might not have been the prettiest thing going, but Teagan managed to get all of the gnocchi into the pot without scalding herself or ruining the pasta.

"Now go ahead and grab the butter." Adrian looked at her, hazel eyes glittering in the golden overhead light of the kitchen, before he brought another burner to life and situated an empty saucepan on top of the grate with a faint clang.

The odd request distracted Teagan from her urge to balk, or at the very least, make him say *please*. "What's the butter for? Don't you normally put sauce on pasta?"

"Yup. Which is exactly why we're not doing it. Not tonight, anyway." Adrian took the butter from her and dropped it into the saucepan without elaborating, then skimmed the gnocchi from the steamy froth of the stockpot while it melted into slow swirls of yellow and white.

"Okay, so what *are* we doing?" Patience had never really been one of Teagan's virtues. Subtlety? Even less.

Adrian shrugged, his muscles rolling beneath the snug black cotton of his T-shirt as he popped open a cabinet. "Bucking tradition. You don't really strike me as a purist."

Oh, no way was she leaving that one alone. "Really? What do I strike you as?"

"Someone who wants to grab the sugar from the pantry."

Damn.

She took the few necessary steps to the pantry, examining its contents while trying to focus. No junk food for this cowboy, although it was hardly surprising. There were canned organic tomatoes, a half-empty box of saltines that looked as if it had seen better days, containers of chicken stock, something called Panko—which looked like plain old bread crumbs, but what did she know—all sorts of things lined the shelves and set Teagan's curiosity on fire. And instead of asking for a jar of pasta sauce, he'd asked her to get the sugar, of all things. Not that there was any jarred sauce in sight.

"I've got to admit, you've piqued my interest. What's with the sugar?" She slid it across the counter, studying his reaction.

"A lot of times, the best dishes are the ones we don't expect. Could we put this gnocchi in a red sauce and have a spectacular dish? Sure." Adrian paused to give the saucepan a shake, and the thick muscles in his forearms flexed under the inky black outline of the tattoo running from elbow to wrist.

"But lots of people can do that," he continued. "If you want to create something really memorable, you have to pay attention to the flavors. Think outside the box. You've gotta keep it fresh." The cockiness that seemed to surround him like an aura would've irritated the hell out of her if it didn't make her so hot.

"Okay. So how do you do that?"

"By giving people what they're least expecting, that's how."

Adrian pulled the saucepan from the burner, and Teagan leaned forward to watch the melted butter curl into golden eddies like a Picasso. He sight-measured some sugar into the pan, then handed her a wooden spoon. She started to protest, and he brushed a finger over her lips, so lightly that for a second, she couldn't be certain he'd done it.

"Stop panicking, Red. All I want you to do is stir."

Every one of her nerve endings wept with joy.

"O-okay." Teagan commanded herself to stir with rapt concentration so as not to spontaneously combust. The sugar began to melt into the warmth of the butter, the granules softly scraping against the bottom of the pan, and Adrian grabbed the small jar of whatever he'd pulled from the spice cabinet.

"So now all we need is one more ingredient." He flipped the shaker top on the container in his hand, and the familiar spice of something as wicked and good as sin itself wafted out to greet her.

"Cinnamon? Are you kidding me?" Teagan's lips fell into a tiny O as she caught a breath from the pan, then inhaled more deeply.

His grin one-upped the cinnamon in both the *wicked* and *good as sin* categories. "I don't kid about food, remember?"

Teagan couldn't do anything but stare as he measured enough cinnamon into the saucepan to darken the mixture, and the heady, almost forbidden scent wrapped around her as if it had bad intentions.

"And now we plate it. This dish has simple ingredients,

and the colors are warm, beautiful. So we want to show them off." He reached for the pot with the gnocchi, skimming them into the bowls with a series of little flips before adding the cinnamon mixture on top.

She frowned. "But the bowls are plain white."

"Exactly." Adrian gave each shallow bowl a gentle shake to coat the pasta, explaining as he went. "The dark cinnamon plays off the white dishes, and look. Under this light, with the sugar only partly melted, the gnocchi actually shines. With the way the pasta is ridged, it adds even more texture, depth."

Teagan didn't even try to rein in her surprise. "Oh my God. It really does. How did you even think of that?"

"I listened to the food." He scooped up both bowls and jerked his head at the breakfast bar, his eyes shining with a mischievous gleam. "You hungry?"

Her stomach jerked in an involuntary response that didn't have anything to do with eating. "Yeah, sure." She scooped up her wineglass from the counter, and took a sip more for courage than anything else. The flavor of the wine, bold and more lush than Teagan wanted to admit, lingered in the back of her throat, making the skin on her neck tingle. Adrian gestured to the bar stool, and she sat down, suddenly nervous.

It had been embarrassingly long since she'd been on a date. Not that this *was* one, mind you, but still. Adrian had cooked dinner for her, and now they were about to share a meal together. The odd intimacy of the scenario struck her, unexpectedly deep, and she shifted against the bar stool.

"You don't have anywhere to sit," she said, hitching forward to let him have the lone chair, but his glittering stare pinned her into place.

"You really don't ever take care of yourself, do you?"

Rather than dodge the question or lie outright, Teagan

opted for changing the subject. "So, uh, now what?" she asked, focusing on the dark brush of five o'clock shadow over his angular jaw. The quick, hot memory of how surprisingly soft it felt when he'd kissed her last week flooded her circuitry, and she knew her Irish coloring was broadcasting the flush on her face in Technicolor.

"Now we eat." Adrian dipped his gaze to her plate, but didn't move otherwise.

"But you're not eating," she protested, and his smile caught her off guard.

"I'm waiting for you."

Good God, she wanted him to kiss her again.

"Oh," she managed, her belly going tight with something far, far different from hunger. In an effort to distract herself from the simmering heat of his smile, she stabbed her fork into the pasta and took a bite.

And then everything changed.

Teagan closed her lips around the tines of the fork just as the deep, hypnotic flavors exploded on her tongue. "Oh!" The word escaped from her full mouth, and she pressed her fingers to her lips, but whether it was to cover her bad manners or hold the flavors in, she couldn't be sure.

The spicy cinnamon, heady and rich, hit her first, but the sweetness of the sugar and the hearty perfection of the pasta were there too, and it all felt so perfect and right on her taste buds. And oh God, it got even better as she chewed, moving the flavors around, as if they were exploring the best places to be in her mouth and then setting up camp there, blissfully refusing to leave.

"Oh my God," Teagan mumbled, fighting the urge to shovel as much in as possible as she scooped another bite into her mouth. More flavors, more texture, more *everything* filled her up, and she wanted desperately to both have the meal and save it for later, to be in the kitchen so she could eat it again and again and never stop.

Teagan covered her mouth with the back of her hand, unwilling to stop eating even to speak. Under any other circumstances, the way her voice came out on a breathy little moan would've probably made her ears burn, but as it stood right now, Teagan didn't care. Another forkful went in, heightening her awareness of every taste bud, and she tried to slow down to savor it, but she couldn't. She dug into the bowl again, inhaling the seductive scent of cinnamon over her ear-to-ear smile. "Really, Adrian. You should—"

Both her words and her movements jerked to a stop, and Teagan lowered her fork to the table. Adrian hadn't moved anything but his eyes since she'd sat down, the stormy green gray piercing right through her to penetrate every tough defense she'd ever cooked up in her life.

"I like it when you say my name." His gravelly voice rippled down the ladder of her spine in slow motion, teasing the base of her hips before settling in. Suddenly, the food, the kitchen, everything in the universe except for the two of them, was very far away.

"Adrian."

His eyes flared, pupils black and gleaming, and all Teagan could think about was daring him back. "What else do you like?" she asked.

"You sure you want to do this?" He'd been pushing her since she'd walked in the door, but as dark and suggestive as his expression was right now, Teagan still knew that if she said no, he'd let her walk away.

"Yes."

Adrian moved toward her in one decisive motion, and she rose to meet him, just as fast. Their bodies crashed together with force, stinging and hot and so good, Teagan wanted to cry.

"I like the way you taste," he rumbled, slanting his mouth over hers, brushing her lower lip with the softness of his tongue. "And I definitely like cooking with you. You're so beautiful with your hands on the food." He kissed her with surprising gentleness, and she arched up greedily, wanting more.

"Slow down and let me listen to you." Adrian smiled into her mouth, curving his lips over hers before he slid them to the angle of her jaw, nuzzling her neck with excruciating care. "I think you have a lot to say."

Her hands curled over the cotton on his hard shoulders, and she bit back a groan. "Aren't we past talking?" Oh God, if he slowed down, she wasn't going to make it.

Again, his lips parted over her skin, and his wicked smile sent heat flooding to the furrow between her legs.

"It's figurative." His tongue swept over her earlobe, and just the one tentative pass brought a moan from her chest, unbidden. "And lucky for you, I'm very observant."

Refusing to be completely outdone, Teagan dropped one hand to the tight space between them, running her hand up the corded muscles of his denim-covered thigh. "And lucky for *you,* two can play at that game."

Adrian exhaled a hard breath onto her neck, bending low to trail feather-soft kisses into the hollow of her throat. "Christ, you're beautiful." He lowered his free hand to her hip, cradling her with tight fingers, grasping her close before dipping his mouth to hers again, sampling, tasting. Her answer was bold, and she pressed her tongue against his, seeking more.

"And impatient." Adrian released her hip and slid his hand beneath the thin cotton of her T-shirt, pressing his fingers into the curve of her lower back. A current ran through Teagan's body, moving like a live wire under her skin.

"Oh God, that feels good," she murmured, the words spilling from her lips. Before she could even register his movements, Adrian had snaked one massive arm around her and used the other to swing her around. He fit his chest to her back, sliding the hard planes of his muscles against her with the friction of the clothes between them.

"Let me take my time with you, Teagan." He paused to sweep her hair over one shoulder and place just the breath of a kiss at the base of her neck. "Slow down and let me in."

Her heart pounded in her chest, fast and dangerous. "Okay," she whispered, her breath catching as he moved his hand back underneath the hem of her shirt.

"You like this, don't you?" Adrian asked, his voice a dark rasp. "When I touch you here." He curled his fingers around the lowest part of her rib cage, stroking her back with his thumb.

Teagan's nipples tightened into aching peaks, but it was the skin already under his hand that demanded more of his touch.

"Yes. Oh God, yes." She rounded her back toward him, greedily pulling her shoulder blades away from the column of her spine to offer him the sensitive skin there. Keeping his left arm firm around her waist, he slid her shirt up so she could pull it over her head.

"Your skin practically hums with it." Adrian guided her body into a gentle lean on the breakfast bar, giving himself unimpeded access to the now-bare skin of her back. Using his hands and mouth, Adrian traced his way from the small of her back upward, laving attention on every inch as if she were a four-course meal and he wanted to savor every taste of her. By the time he made his way to her shoulders, the juncture between Teagan's thighs was impossibly hot and aching with need. She arched her hips into him, giving a soft groan as he pressed his rock-hard cock into her back.

"You're just not going to slow down until you get what you want, are you?" Adrian rasped into her ear, and the words alone made her want to come. He slipped those able hands up over her bra to cup the weight of her breasts, and her nipples pebbled even harder beneath the dark silk.

"No. I don't want to slow down." Teagan swung around to face him, kissing him with ravenous need. Her hands found the edge of his T-shirt, and with one seamless yank, it was over his head, on the floor.

Her mouth found his again, craving his heat. "I want you *now*."

His laugh was a slow, sexy rumble that only seduced her closer to the edge. "You're tough to refuse, you know that?" Adrian nibbled her bottom lip with just enough pressure that Teagan wanted to scream. "But I have plans for you. And they're so much better slow."

Without another word, his hands shot to her shoulders, moving her backward through the empty living space as he kissed her long and deep. He expelled a hot breath against her collarbone when she slid her hand down low over the hard length behind his button fly, but it didn't deter his purpose. With a handful of even strides, they crossed the threshold of his bedroom, and Teagan inhaled the dark, spicy scent of his skin that lingered on the bedsheets as he lay her on top of them. Adrian dropped his mouth to her neck, shuttering his eyes closed and breathing in deeply.

"You smell like rosemary. Just a hint of sweetness right . . . here." He paused where her neck flared down into her shoulder, grazing his teeth along her collarbone, and the husky tenor of his voice sent a jolt of lust arrowing through her.

"And you taste even better." Again, Adrian curved his hand around her breast, and again, she sighed in pleasure, her nipple pearling under his movements. When he slipped the navy blue silk from her shoulders, the brush of his stubble against her sensitive skin ratcheted her sigh into a soft moan.

"Adrian," she said, dizzy with want.

"Say it again." He lowered his mouth to one nipple, sucking just hard enough to make her want to scream.

"*Adrian.*" Teagan barely recognized the throaty whisper as hers. She knotted her fingers in his hair, and he responded with hunger, teasing her into a frenzy with his mouth. The exquisite tension mounting between her legs crested higher, and she rocked against him in search of desperate release.

"You want me to touch you," he said, his voice like honey, and she nodded, capturing his stubbly face between her hands.

"I want to touch *you.*" Teagan drew him up so that he hovered over her, bracing his weight on his thickly muscled uninjured arm as she opened her knees around the strong angle of his jeans-clad hips. "You're not the only good listener around here, you know." So slowly she thought she'd lose her mind, she canted her hips up, brushing against his cock with the seam of her body.

Adrian breathed a curse that colored Teagan's face with want.

"Let me listen to you." She slid one hand between their bodies, and stroked him against her sex.

"Teagan," he grated out, his voice hoarse with want as he thrust against her in rhythm with her movements.

"Adrian," she answered, each syllable its own reverent call.

He shifted to his side, just enough to fit his hand over hers. "You have to stop doing that."

She tightened her fingers around him just slightly, and the groan that escaped from his lips told her all she needed to know. "I want you, Adrian." Teagan let go of him just long enough to replace her hand with the aching space between her thighs, sliding against him with electric friction.

Adrian's eyes flashed over her in a liquid stare, and he thrust against her, hard. "And I want to take care of you. Let me take care of you, Teagan."

His hands moved over her with singular purpose, unbuttoning her jeans with deft fingers while she returned the favor. The plane of his chest flexed and squeezed as he knelt between her hips and slipped her jeans from her body, and Teagan felt something hot and tight break free in her chest as Adrian stared at her with an expression she'd never seen on his face before.

"Sweet Jesus, you are perfect." He lowered himself to her side, running one hand over her skin from hip to shoulder and back again. "I could spend all night showing you how beautiful you are."

Teagan let out a moan as his hand drifted to the center of her belly, then lower to cup her through her panties, her legs starting to tremble with anticipation and want. "Don't stop."

He traced a slow circle over the triangle of silk between her legs before moving it aside to find her heat.

"I haven't even started," Adrian said, lowering his face to hers. He parted her mouth with his, swallowing her wanton cry as he slipped a finger into her folds. Every one of her muscles bore down with hot intensity.

"Oh my *God*." Teagan's hands curled into fists, her nails digging into the soft flesh of her palms as she rushed toward release, every part of her begging for him. He caressed her with sweet intention, circling and thrusting and daring her until she lost her breath on a broken cry.

"I've got you, Red. Let me take care of you."

With his words as the final trigger, Teagan tumbled right

over the edge, exploding into such an intense orgasm that it left her gasping for air. Adrian smiled into the column of her neck, lining her skin with soft kisses that pricked at her senses.

Something inside of her snapped free, rising up to meet his commanding demeanor with her own boldness.

"Now let's see if you can take it as well as you dish it out." With a swift maneuver, Teagan hooked one foot around the corded muscle of Adrian's leg, using it as leverage to push him to his back.

"Wait . . ." he started, but she put one finger on his lush lips, shushing him.

"No. No more waiting."

She freed him from the rest of his clothes as quickly as he'd undressed her, reveling in the sculpted muscles of his abs and the trail of dark hair that led from his belly button down to his strong, angular hips. Dauntless, she swung one leg over his waist, squeezing her thighs tightly enough to hover over the heat of his body.

"I want you inside me, Adrian." Teagan leaned forward, stroking him with light fingers, leaving no expanse of his shoulders or chest untouched. Driven by the glint of pure desire in his eyes as he watched her, and she stretched over him to press her lips to his ear. "I want to take care of you, too."

He was on her so fast that she barely registered his movements, the hard grip on her hips to remove her from his lap, the flurry of movement at his bedside table that yielded a condom. Within seconds, Adrian's body was back over hers, tantalizingly close.

"You're coming with me when I go."

He plunged into her with slow strength, and Teagan thought she would absolutely die from the pleasure of him inside her body, finding her and filling her up all at once.

Desire sparked in her core as they found a flawless rhythm, both deep and desperate, and he rocked against her again and again.

"So *beautiful*," he grated, his hot breath fanning over the bare skin of her neck and rushing over her collarbone. Her nipples tightened at the seductive stroke of his chest on her soft curves, and with every hard thrust, the delicious tension between her thighs increased, daring her to come.

"Oh God, so are you." Teagan reached low to wrap her arms around Adrian's hips, gathering him right into her center before she unraveled beneath him with a sharp cry. With nothing but dark, uncut intensity on his face, he lowered himself to cover her body, thrusting into her faster and harder until he finally shuddered out her name as he followed.

They lay together in the last fading strains of twilight for a while, and although Teagan knew time was passing, she had no concept of how much. Minutes were somehow different, altered slightly by Adrian's nearness, by the spicy-cinnamon smell of his skin on hers. He moved to her side without breaking contact, pulling her close and kissing her temple, her hair.

"I've got you, Red. I've got you."

As she drifted off to sleep, it was the first time she could remember when the darkness around her didn't threaten to swallow her whole.

Chapter Eighteen

Adrian shifted his weight against the warmth of the mattress beneath him, trying his damnedest not to wake Teagan even though the sun had started to poke past his bedroom blinds two hours ago. She lay nestled in the bedsheets, flame-colored hair tumbling down her bare back in waves, face sweet and lax in deep sleep. For the tenth time this hour, Adrian let his eyes drink their fill, skimming the taut angle where her shoulder blade met her spine, memorizing the spray of light brown freckles on the bridge of her nose.

He was utterly, completely, unequivocally out of his league with this woman.

Moving as covertly as his big frame would allow, Adrian edged from the covers and skinned into the jeans he'd discarded last night. Stopping shy of the top button, he decided to forgo rummaging for a shirt so as not to risk waking Teagan. He'd meant to let her get more sleep last night, but after they got up for seconds in the kitchen, all it had taken was one hot little *dare me* smile before they were having seconds in his bedroom, too.

Right. Out of his league didn't even touch this.

Padding into the kitchen, Adrian went through the motions of feeding the coffeepot with enough grounds to get a rise out of the dead. The comforting, earthy scent, combined with the simple task, reminded him how good it felt to be in the kitchen again, and the sense of purpose sent a thread of ease through his chest. He might not be able to really cook for another four weeks, but helping Teagan at the Double Shot wasn't such a bad way to spend that time. She already knew he couldn't stick around for good, and anyway, when her father got better, he'd surely want his kitchen back. But for now, just maybe, he could spend some time around her with no regrets.

As if to shoot the idea full of holes, his cell phone chirped from his jacket pocket, signaling a new message. Adrian crossed the kitchen, digging the thing out of his pocket as dread wormed its way back into his gut.

"*You might only have a month left on parole, Holt, but answering your phone ain't optional.*" Big Ed's voice grated over the line, and even recorded, it raked over Adrian's skin like bits of broken glass. "*Your hotshot boss says she hasn't heard a peep out of you for over a week, but I know better than to think that means you been keepin' clean. Just because you got off easy doesn't make you any less of a felon. Don't tempt me to haul my ass to the mountains to find you to prove it. Believe me, if I show up on your doorstep, it won't be a pleasure visit.*"

Fuck. *Fuck.* Adrian should've known better than to think he could hide from this, even for a few weeks.

"Wow. And I thought I looked rough in the morning."

Teagan's voice whipped him back to the reality of his kitchen, and he dropped his phone to the breakfast bar with a clatter.

"Hey," he said, battening down his emotional hatches one by one. Damn, she looked so pretty, even with her sleep-mussed hair and wrinkled version of yesterday's clothes. "Sorry. I didn't want to wake you."

"You didn't. Is everything okay at the Double Shot?" Her gaze locked on his cell phone for just a second before returning to his face.

"Yeah, everything's fine." Big Ed's diatribe was the only message on his phone, besides the six collective voice mails Carly and Bellamy had left over the course of the last week.

Just like that, the tension in his shoulders did a great, big loop-the-loop.

"Everything doesn't look fine," Teagan observed, sliding Adrian's only two coffee mugs down from the cupboard over the coffeepot. A seamless flick of her wrist had both cups filled within seconds, and she slid one across the counter in his direction before turning toward the fridge to take out the milk.

"Brennan texted me last night when he and Jesse left. Said it all went without a hitch." Adrian tapped his cell phone to life, jamming his thumb over the *delete* button to purge Big Ed's message from the queue before scrolling to Brennan's text. He'd deal with Big Ed later. Just as long as the guy didn't actually make good on his threat to take his crotchety old show on the road.

"Mmm." Teagan took the phone from his outstretched hand, the pads of her fingers brushing his palm, and yeah. Being this close to her shouldn't feel so easy or so good. "They're probably exhausted from closing shorthanded. I should have stayed."

The hard flash of guilt on her face had Adrian's feet in gear before he could even register the movement, and he covered the space between them to pull her in close. "Don't. You can't do all of this by yourself, and you needed a little breathing room. They'll get a chance to rest too, I promise."

To his absolute surprise, she softened, leaning her forehead against his bare chest. "I know. It's just . . . taking care of myself is difficult for me. I'm not trying to be a hard-ass. I'm just not very good at any of this."

"You've got a lot going on, Red." Adrian brushed at a tangled wisp of hair that had escaped from her low pony-tail, letting his fingers run the length of the strand before tucking it behind her ear. "Just take it one thing at a time."

"Is that what we're doing, me and you? Taking things one day at a time?" she asked, lifting her chin to serve him with a look so devoid of drama or pretense that the honesty just flew from his mouth.

"I don't have much more than that."

He wanted to give her more—hell, she *deserved* more. But one slip-up with Lonnie or Big Ed, and Adrian wouldn't just land in deep trouble.

He'd end up back in prison, and his pregnant best friend would be sanctioned up to her elbows for trusting him to be a decent guy.

"I'm okay with one day at a time, Adrian. I know this is temporary, but I want to be with you. In the kitchen and out." Teagan pressed up on her toes to slant her mouth against his, and suddenly everything else felt like an echo, fading out as it got further and further away.

"Hmm." Adrian slid his tongue over the curve of her lower lip, coaxing her mouth open for more. Which was crazy, really, because no way would he ever get enough of her mouth, so full and red and flawlessly perfect. He kissed her again, swinging her around with every intention of taking her right back to his bedroom for a proper good morning, when a loud rumble vibrated against his hips and stopped him midstride.

"Was that . . . are you hungry?"

"It can wait," she murmured into his neck, her hands

coasting lower toward the waistband of his jeans, but he pulled back.

"It can't wait." Despite the absolute tirade his cock leveled at his frontal lobe for the judgment call to put breakfast first, Adrian broke from her grasp. A cursory scan of the kitchen linoleum turned up his shirt from the night before, and he yanked it over his head before turning to pop open the fridge. He might not be able to give Teagan much, but at the very least, he could keep himself in check long enough to make her something to eat.

Teagan exhaled, pressing her eyes shut even though a smile tipped her lips upward. "You're taking this care-for-myself thing to the extreme, you know that?"

"Yup." He rifled through the refrigerator, grabbing a package of bacon and a half carton of eggs from the narrow shelf. "You helping?"

"Sure." When Adrian turned to fasten her with a brows-up stare, she added, "You're not going to let me get away without a food lesson, and anyway, I'm hungry."

"Fair enough."

For a few minutes, they gravitated around each other in the tight confines of his kitchen, with her getting situated on the left-side burner with the bacon, and him putting together the few simple ingredients for his secret-recipe scrambled eggs. She moved fluidly next to him, one hand giving the skillet in front of her a gentle shake while she plucked a wooden spatula from the utensil drawer at her side with the other, and he fell into a rhythm with her that felt as easy as breathing.

"So did you get some bad news this morning?" Teagan asked, her eyes darting back to his cell phone on the counter. So much for easy.

"Sort of."

"Anything I can help with?" She leaned one denim-wrapped hip against the kitchen counter, looking right into him with those warm brown eyes that managed to see freaking everything, and the words were out before Adrian could bite down on them.

"My parole officer called. He's kind of militant about keeping tabs on me, so he's a little pissed I didn't answer. He'll get over it."

"Sounds a little above and beyond for a parole officer," she said without pushing, and damn it, here came the landslide.

"Big Ed's not exactly the forgiving type. Which wouldn't suck so bad, except he thinks I got special treatment on top of being a felon, so he rides me pretty hard. And by pretty hard, I mean he'd rather find me in violation of my parole than win the goddamn lottery. I've learned to deal with it, but I'm not gonna lie. It's not easy."

"So did you?"

Confusion jerked his chin upward. "Did I what?"

"Get special treatment," Teagan said, nudging the sizzling bacon in the skillet without moving her eyes from his face.

"Oh. No." He shrugged. "Carly spoke at my hearing, then again when I petitioned to leave New York so I could take this job with her at the resort. I guess Big Ed felt like I got off too easy when the judge granted me permission to leave the state to come here to work with her. But everything was on the up-and-up."

"I don't get it. She's your boss, and you guys are friends, right? Why would her testimony be preferential?"

"Carly's made a hell of a name for herself, both here and in New York. She had a cooking show on local TV for a while, and we were always booked solid at Gracie's, where we used to work in the city. Anyone who knows food in New York knows her."

Teagan's face lit with understanding. "So your parole officer felt like it was celebrity bias."

"Yeah. He's always jawing about my hotshot boss getting me off the hook. I know Carly really put her reputation on the line by vouching for me, but no matter what Big Ed thinks, I never asked her to speak at those hearings. All I ever wanted was to do my time and get back to the kitchen where I belong."

As if to hammer the sentiment home, Adrian ground some white pepper over the egg mixture he'd assembled as they talked. He hooked his forearm around the bowl as best he could with the stupid frigging cast in the way, sending the whisk in his opposite hand through the eggs with a rapid-fire *tat-tat-tat*.

"You never said what you did that time for."

Teagan's statement was clearly a question, and one he knew he should answer. But his egregious lack of judgment five years ago wouldn't change with a good airing out, and anyway, he wasn't about to repeat his mistakes.

He'd learned the all-too-hard way about the damage of falling for the wrong woman.

"I did my time for a stupid mistake. But you don't have to worry. I'm not ever going to make it again."

"I'm not worried," Teagan said, her hard-edged demeanor making an appearance in her tone. "I'm just trying to help you."

Well, *hell*. Of course she'd go and be matter-of-fact about it. "I know," he said, blowing out a slow breath. "Look, it happened a long time ago, and I'm straight now. I just want the whole thing behind me."

For a second, Teagan looked like she'd throw on her armor and argue, but then her eyes softened with a warm-whiskey flicker. "Okay."

His expression must've betrayed the shock rebounding

through his system, because she continued with, "Look, I can sympathize with having things in your past that you want to let go of. As harsh as it sounds, I'd love to forget my mother even existed. So as much as I want to help, if you don't want to talk about it, believe me, I understand."

"Thanks." Adrian's shock gave way to something deeper, something that lodged in good and hard behind his sternum, and he lowered a skillet over the burner in front of him with a metal-on-metal clang. But instead of letting the conversation smother under a thick blanket of awkward, Teagan stayed true to her word and shifted the subject with ease.

"Your shoulder looks like it's healing nicely. To be honest, you have more mobility than I thought you might." She watched as he dropped some butter into the skillet, and he gave the joint in question a quick stretch and roll before following the butter with the eggs.

"It's still a little sore, but I'll live."

"With how much you love the kitchen, it must be hard for you to take a leave of absence," Teagan said, and even though her voice steered far clear of pity-party levels, it snapped a thread in Adrian's chest.

"Might've stung less if Carly hadn't kicked me out."

"Wait . . . she kicked you out? I thought you were on leave." The words slipped from Teagan's mouth on a shocked breath, and even though he knew he shouldn't give his emotions any room to move, he let them loose anyway.

"Okay, yeah, I probably could've stood a little bit of a rest after this." He nodded down at his cast with a tight jerk of his chin. "But clearly, I'm not a total waste of space. She could've let me come back to La Dolce Vita, at least to help, but instead, she kicked me out for the entire six weeks."

Teagan lifted a brow, her expression betraying nothing. "She give you a reason?"

The thread in his chest went for the full-on unravel. "Carly's in this happy-honeymoon phase of her life. Don't get me wrong—she's earned every second of being in a good place. But now she thinks anyone who puts work first is missing the bigger picture. She doesn't get that for me, the kitchen is always going to be the bigger picture."

"Yeah, I can sympathize." Teagan cracked a tiny grin as she flipped the bacon in her pan with an easy maneuver. "Well, not with the kitchen part. But not a lot of people get the whole workaholic thing. Da's always harping on how I need a life of my own, away from the station and away from the bar. But I don't mind the work, and he's my father. Helping him is where I belong."

"Between running the Double Shot and organizing this street fair, I'd say you're in your element, then." Adrian curled his fingers around the skillet handle to keep it steady, using his free hand to finish the scrambled eggs. All this blabbing should give him the shakes—hell, he hadn't opened up this much, not even with Carly, in years. But something about the one-two punch of being in the kitchen and being in the kitchen with *Teagan* made the whole thing seamless instead of stressful.

The weirdest part was, the more they talked, the more he wanted to keep letting the words just slide on out.

"Yeah," she agreed, dividing the bacon between two plates as he wordlessly did the same with the eggs. "But like you said, I'm not in it alone. Just like you're not in it alone while your arm heals."

Her wide-open expression hit him full-on, and holy hell. Even in her wrinkled T-shirt and haphazard ponytail, the truth on her face made her gorgeous.

"Nope." Adrian wrapped an arm around her, breathing

in the earthy scent of rosemary as he pulled her close. They might not have a whole lot of time, but he was going to make every minute of the here-and-now matter.

"We're in it together, Red. Now grab a fork, because I guarantee this is the best breakfast you'll ever have."

Chapter Nineteen

Teagan scanned the freshly printed schematic for the street fair, the feeling in her chest oscillating between shock and pure, unadulterated excitement.

"Jeez, Brennan. You did this in four days?" She lowered the detailed pages to the already-covered office desk in front of her, letting the excitement win out. "It's amazing."

Brennan shrugged, kicking back in the chair on the other side of the desk like no great shakes. "It wasn't so hard, once Adrian and I factored in how many tents we'll need for food service and the best setup for the prep stations. He's done some catering and stuff before."

"Yeah, but you thought of everything. Foot traffic, evacuation routes, a first-aid station. Not to mention exactly what equipment we'll need in each tent. I mean, it's . . ."

"It's up to code," Brennan said, his stare pinned firmly to the schematic. "It'll do. How's your dad?"

"Still doing too much." She closed her eyes, riding out her exhale before popping them open to continue. "Dr. Riley's got him on a pretty good regimen with monitoring and meds right now. As long as he keeps taking it easy, he'll be okay."

Not that she'd been able to get him to take it easy to begin with. Her father might not be putting in any grueling hours at the restaurant, proper, but he'd thrown himself into plans for the street fair, locking up the deal with the owner of the Cold Creek Brewery and doing tireless work to get the word out about the event. But all the easygoing charm on the planet couldn't erase the lines of fatigue that had been etched around his eyes just this morning, and damn if they hadn't torn at Teagan all day.

Her father wasn't getting any better. If anything, he was only getting worse.

"Listen." Brennan leaned forward, pushing up the sleeves of his gray Henley shirt to prop his forearms over his thighs and clearly choosing his words with care. "I don't mean to pry, and you can tell me to go screw if you want. But I've got to ask, have you got a long-term solution worked out here? I mean, I'm glad as hell your dad is able to take some time to rest. But Lou is out of the picture for good. Diabetes and high blood pressure are no joke, and we both know the hours and the labor involved in running this place aren't too kind. Are you sure your father is going to be able to come back for the long haul?"

"No."

Teagan's gut pitched toward her knees at the out-loud admission, and God, she'd never hated the word so much. But she was far from stupid, and denying the truth wouldn't take care of her father. "I'm not going to lie to you, Brennan. Even after we pull off this street fair and get things right with the bills, it's going to take a lot to get this place running smoothly again. I know you and I can figure out the bar, even once I go back to the station. But the kitchen . . ." She trailed off, unease burning a path through her chest, and Brennan lifted his chin in a quick nod of understanding.

"You need someone permanent. Someone who'll stay."

Teagan bit down on the *yes* forcing its way out of her mouth, snapping the sentiment in half. Sure, denial wouldn't serve her in the long run, but she wasn't about to let the bigger picture torpedo her efforts, either.

No matter how spot-on Brennan was about what she needed.

"I'll have to figure out the kitchen and hire someone new, yes. But first things first. I need to get through the next two weeks, and the only way I can do that is one step at a time."

"I'm sorry," Brennan said, his dark eyes flashing with honesty. "I know you're dealing with a lot. I didn't mean to make this harder for you."

"You didn't," she said, matching the truth in his words. "In fact, this work you did on the setup has been incredible. Thank you."

He waved her off. "No problem. I'm glad to be busy. Speaking of which, I've got to do bar inventory before we open. Just let me know what else I can do for the street fair."

He pushed up from the armchair adjacent to the desk, a momentary flicker that looked an awful lot like pain streaking across his face. The expression lasted barely a second, but it slapped Teagan to her feet anyway.

"Are you okay?" she asked, and Brennan froze into place across from her.

"I'm fine." The words flew from his mouth as if they were automatic. "A little hungry, but otherwise great."

"Oh." She slid a quick head-to-toe assessment over his frame, but everything appeared to be all systems go. Damn, all this worrying about her father and the bar had her seeing things. "Well, definitely eat before dinner shift starts. I'm hoping for a busy night."

"You got it, boss."

Teagan sank back down into the geriatric office chair behind the desk, shuffling through the mountain range of paperwork for the street fair. Now that the schematic was done and the permits had been approved, they could really dive into planning the food. Coiling her hair into a knot at the nape of her neck, she picked up the tentative menu ideas she'd worked out with their food service distributor, then started to fine-tune with Jesse and Adrian.

You need someone permanent. Someone who'll stay.

Okay, so she hadn't planned on falling into bed with Adrian, and she damn sure hadn't planned on it being the most mind-leveling experience she'd had since . . . well, ever. But the thing Teagan had expected least of all was repeating the process every night after that, to the point that being with Adrian, even one day at a time, had become her default.

And it felt deliciously good.

"No," she whispered, giving herself a stern shake. No matter how good he made her feel in both the kitchen and the bedroom, what was going on between her and Adrian was as temporary as everything else. The sooner she got the Double Shot back in the black, the sooner Adrian could get on with his life where he belonged. The kitchen was his lifeblood, and he was already risking too much by being here. Once the street fair was over and his arm healed completely, he'd go back to the resort and she'd take care of her father and find a new cook, just like they'd planned.

Damn it, her stomach hurt.

"You skipped lunch again, didn't you?" came the gravelly voice from the doorway, and Teagan shot halfway out of her seat, the pen in her hand clattering to the desktop.

"Jeez, you scared the crap out of me!" she chirped,

splaying her fingers over her slamming heart. "And how do you know I skipped lunch?"

"First of all, I've been in the building as long as you have, and you haven't left this office since we passed the threshold this morning. Secondly . . ." He crossed the room, his hazel stare full of hot intention as he stepped behind the desk to put a plate full of food down in front of her. "You always skip lunch."

Teagan went from startled to sexed-up in about two seconds flat, her heartbeat not slowing an inch. "What's this, then?" she asked, pointing to the plate with lifted brows.

"Call it an early dinner. You need to eat."

Oh God, the heat rolling off his body was intoxicating, and it shot straight through her as she stood up next to his muscle-wrapped frame. "Isn't that my line?" she asked, wordlessly daring him closer.

"Fair enough," Adrian said, surprising her with the concession. But then he pulled her in tight with a quick yank toward his chest, and her breath escaped on a heated gasp. "Then I need to cook for you. How about that?"

"Okay." The word collapsed from her lips on a whispered sigh, and she pressed up to brush her mouth over his in a long, indulgent stroke. Adrian's free hand uncurled against the back of her rib cage, locking them together from shoulder to hip, and the slide of rough denim and soft cotton sparked just enough friction on Teagan's aching skin to make her whimper.

"Christ, you're going to be the end of me, you know that?" His fingers drifted over her spine, ratcheting up her desire as he cupped the back of her neck to kiss her even harder. She parted her lips in wordless invitation, losing herself in the rasp of his calloused hands on the spot by her ear, the spicy cinnamon scent of his skin on her own. Suddenly, everything outside the room shrank backward, ceasing to exist. The only thing on the planet was this man, right in front of her in this moment.

And she was going to take him.

"But I've only just started with you," Teagan said, tightening her grip over the hard plane of Adrian's chest. She felt his mouth part into a dark smile against the column of her neck, his reply hot over the angle where it tapered into her shoulder.

"Be careful, Red."

She slid her hands outward over his chest, skimming a nipple through his shirt with the edge of one finger. "And why should I do that?"

His heart took up a fast, steady rhythm beneath her palm, his smile becoming downright wicked as he captured her wrist with his free hand and brought his mouth scant inches above her ear.

"Because I'm not too big on impulse control, which means if you're not careful, I'm going to lock that door, and you're going to end up naked and screaming right here on this desk."

Their mouths crashed together in a tangle of tongues and unmistakable intentions, and Teagan didn't resist. She arched to meet Adrian's kiss with equal intensity, only the deeper it got, the more she wanted. Rocking back on the balls of her feet, Teagan shifted to gain better access to the rest of Adrian's body, but the combination of halted footsteps and a blurted curse from the doorway had her jerking to a stop.

"Uh." Jesse jumped back in the doorframe and averted his eyes at the same instant Adrian swung Teagan in the other direction, shielding her from Jesse's view while still partly facing the door with instinctively curled fists.

"I'm really sorry," Jesse said, the words a tangled rush.

"The door was open, so I thought . . . I'll just catch you later."

"Jesse." Her voice wavered as she sidestepped around Adrian, sudden tension humming off his body in waves. "Is everything okay in the kitchen?"

"Oh. Yeah, absolutely." Jesse gave his boots a good, thorough examination before chancing a look in her direction. "I just wanted to let Adrian know I finished station prep, but we can work on the menu for the street fair, you know. Another time."

"Wait." The word rumbled over Teagan's shoulder, and Adrian ran a hand over his T-shirt before stepping all the way back. "We're straight, Jesse. I didn't realize what time it was, but I'll be down in a minute, yeah?"

"Sure." He ducked out of the doorframe with a nod, and as much as she wanted to pray for the ground to open wide and swallow her whole, Teagan lifted her eyes to Adrian's.

"God, Adrian, I'm sorry. I got carried away. I shouldn't have . . ." She trailed off, waving a hand between them rather than making an attempt to define the utterly magnetic kiss with words.

But rather than going all awkward or distant, Adrian reached up to cup her face, placing a soft, barely there kiss over her mouth. "You didn't, Red. This one's on me."

"But I—"

"Make sure you eat before you come down for dinner shift. Fridays are usually a killer."

Impulse had a protest springboarding to her mouth, but the words skidded to a stop before they could fully form. Adrian's expression wasn't his usual mask of hard lines and don't-mess-with-me bravado, nor was it full of a sexy dare just to watch her push back. The look on his face was so foreign, so at odds with anything else she'd ever seen there, it took her a minute to place it.

But by the time Teagan recognized the complete vulnerability glittering in Adrian's eyes, he'd already disappeared down the hall.

Adrian hit the stairs at the Double Shot with a curse under his breath and a belly full of unease. Being around Teagan was far too effortless, both in the restaurant and out, and damn it, he knew better than to get caught up in a woman. But something about Teagan pulled him in like a force of nature, too big and powerful and gut-wrenchingly beautiful to resist, and giving in was a foregone conclusion.

Jesus. He'd been milliseconds away from tearing off every stitch of her clothing, right there on her desk. It didn't matter how high-powered his attraction to her was. He needed to get this under control, and he needed to do it *yesterday*.

"Hey." Adrian jammed his thoughts into a mental drawer, slamming it tight as he rounded the corner to the main stretch of the Double Shot's kitchen. Jesse's nearly shaved head popped up in surprise, and he paused over the tidy pile of ingredients at the workstation in front of him.

"Hey. I didn't mean to bother you," Jesse said, his focus lasered in on the food.

"No worries." The unease in Adrian's belly made an encore performance, and hell. He might not be a share-your-feelings-by-the-campfire kind of guy, but Teagan was going to work with Jesse for the long term, and there wasn't any wiggle room in what the guy had seen. Time to man up and clear the air.

Adrian hauled in a breath. "So, about what happened up there . . ."

"You don't have to explain," Jesse said in quiet interruption. "To be honest, I kind of just assumed, anyway."

Shock filtered through Adrian's veins. "You did?"

Jesse's mouth ruffled in the smallest suggestion of a smile. "I'm back here in the kitchen with you two all the time. Just because I'm quiet doesn't mean I don't notice things."

"Oh." *Way to go, Holt. Real eloquent.* "Well, I don't want you to, you know. Think any less of her."

"Why would I do that?" Jesse dropped the whisk in his hand to the stainless steel counter with a *click*. "I mean, the way you two look at each other, it's pretty obvious things are mutual."

Adrian's brain flashed back over the last few weeks he'd spent at the restaurant, coupled with the last four nights he'd spent with Teagan in his bed, and yeah. *Mutual* about covered it. "As long as we're cool," he said, stepping in toward the counter.

But Jesse straightened up and stood his ground. "You tell me."

The unspoken question and everything that went with it hung heavy in the air between them, but Adrian didn't even hesitate.

"I might not be able to stick around forever, but I've still got her back, Jesse. Just like you."

"Good." Palming the whisk, Jesse dropped it, and his gaze, back to the bowl in front of him. "I tried making that new sauce we talked about for the Cajun chicken sandwiches. I'm not sure how it turned out, though."

Relief, and something deeper Adrian couldn't quite pin down, stole its way down his spine, and he reached for a tasting spoon.

"Let's find out."

The next few hours blurred by in a combination of dinner orders and on-the-fly menu planning for the street fair. Although they were still short-staffed on the line, both Teagan and Jesse had gotten the hang of running the kitchen better than Adrian had hoped, to the point that they worked efficiently together, even in a jam. By the time the dinner rush downshifted into a manageable trickle, Adrian was more than ready to start doling out breaks. He elbowed his way through the swinging door leading out to the bar, where Brennan stood in the small alcove by the sink, unloading a rack of clean pint glasses.

"Looks pretty quiet out here," Adrian diagnosed, tossing a clean bar towel over the shoulder of his light gray T-shirt, and Brennan nodded, his dark eyes giving the smattering of customers a careful once-over.

"Not so bad. In fact, it's been kind of slow all night." His frown mirrored the jab of disappointment tugging at Adrian's gut, but neither of them gave it a voice. Saying that business was slower than usual wouldn't bring in customers, no matter how badly the Double Shot needed the cash flow. "You closing down the kitchen?"

Adrian jerked his chin in the affirmative. "Yup. Go ahead and grab fifteen. I can cover the wood."

Brennan moved toward the pass-through, and Adrian origamied himself into the abandoned spot by the sink to finish putting away the pint glasses. While it took a distant second to being around food, picking up slack behind the bar had never bothered Adrian. Having a place, a purpose at the Double Shot sent his muscles into relaxation mode, and he turned toward the bar to check the status of everyone's orders.

"You Adrian Holt?" The guy at the end of the bar flashed him with a head-to-toe that had Adrian's hackles locked and loaded, but he dialed his expression down to its most bored setting.

Adrian swiped at the mahogany with a damp bar towel, purposely waiting a beat, then two before responding with, "Who's asking?"

"I'm a business associate of Lonnie Armstrong's." The man's weathered face cracked into an oily smile, and Adrian's breath log-jammed in his windpipe.

"In that case, we're closed," he managed, roughing up his delivery as much as possible. How the hell did this guy know his name?

"He said to give you a message," the guy persisted. "Wants you to know he's got his eye on y'all. Especially you and that leggy redhead. Said he's real excited about getting . . . *paid*." His smile hardened and turned lecherous around the edges, and it took all of Adrian's restraint not to vault the bar and turn the guy into paste.

"Door's that way," Adrian bit out, infusing each word with the anger brewing hot in his belly.

But the man laughed, not budging a millimeter. "Now, now. What would your parole officer say about those bad manners of yours, I wonder?"

Adrian's breath and blood completely seized under his skin, the adrenaline replacing both just begging to take a swing while the scissor-sharp dread that followed bolted him into place.

After a beat, the minion pushed off from the bar with a dirty smirk. "You and the cherry have got two weeks, Mr. Holt. Looking forward to helping Lonnie collect."

Even after the guy had slithered his way out the front door, Adrian's pulse still slammed through him like a wrecking ball at warp speed. Damn it, Pine Mountain was a small town where everyone knew everyone. How had he underestimated how easy it would be for Lonnie to figure out who he was? Hell, the arrest and conviction had been a matter of public record. Even Lonnie could do the math on the parole hearing and know Adrian wasn't in the clear.

And if Big Ed caught even a sniff of Adrian's setting foot in the Double Shot, he'd be back in a jumpsuit faster than any of them could say *prison orange*.

Desperate for something—anything—to put his hands on that would resemble the food that always calmed him, Adrian took an abrupt step toward the bar.

And ended up looking smack into the face of Carly's husband.

"Holy shit, Holt. What're you doing here?"

Jackson Carter's brows shot toward the edge of his dark blond crew cut, his eyes doing the round-and-wide routine as he froze to his spot at the bar, and really, Adrian couldn't have cooked up a worse nightmare if he'd been paid for the job. Thankfully, Shane, who stood right next to his buddy, swooped in to mop up some of the tension.

"I think what Jackson's trying to say is it's a surprise to see you behind the bar." Shane leaned a forearm against the glossy mahogany, dividing his gaze between Jackson and Adrian with equal face time. While he and Jackson had gotten over their active dislike for each other almost a year ago, Adrian had never gone all Kumbaya for the guy. The whole avoiding-Carly-like-an-active-strain-of-the-plague thing wasn't helping right now, either.

Could anything else possibly bite him on the ass tonight?

"Yeah." Adrian nodded, snapping the lid off a bottle of Corona for the guy two down who'd lifted his empty in a wordless request for another. "Gotta fill the time somehow, you know." He tried his level best to make his voice nice and easy, but damn it, pulling back on the hard edges was pretty much impossible.

Of course, Jackson matched him, tone for tone. "Thought the whole point of a leave of absence was to take it easy."

Adrian locked his molars with a *clack* and pulled in a deep lungful of air. While he could—and did—fault Carly for tossing him out of the kitchen when he needed to be there most, it was kind of hard to take issue with her husband for siding with her. But the last thing Adrian needed right now was to tangle with Jackson over this. Even if the guy was skirting the edges of asshattery.

"Arm's just fine. Clearly," Adrian said, serving up the Corona and clanking the empty bottle he'd traded it for into the recycling bin behind the bar with an easy toss.

"You might want to tell Carly that. Seeing as how she's been worried sick about you and you haven't returned her calls."

This time, Adrian had to wrestle for his inhale. He was all for trying to defuse a bad state of affairs, but there were two sides to this coin, and he was already on edge.

"She wasn't too worried to kick me out of the kitchen," he pointed out. "And she can't have it both ways, Carter."

"You guys—" Shane started, but Jackson cut him off with a frost-encrusted glare.

"Oh, *bullshit,*" Jackson hissed. "She lied to your parole officer yesterday, Adrian. Which, oh, by the way, is illegal in both Pennsylvania and New York."

Adrian's head snapped back in shock. "She what?"

Shane cranked his eyes shut in an expression chock-full of *hold on, here we go,* but it didn't stop Jackson.

"Oh, come on. Don't tell me you're surprised she bailed you out. The guy has been hounding her nonstop ever since you got into this mess. There were only so many times Carly could say she hadn't heard from you before he threatened to come down here and yank you back upstate for real. What'd you think she'd do?"

Adrian forced his jaw to work, but it took all the effort he could scratch together. "She lied and told him she'd seen me so he'd back off."

Hell, he should've known there was something behind the fact that Big Ed hadn't followed up after his last nasty message. Even the guy's ulterior motives had ulterior motives, for God's sake.

Jackson's knuckles went white over the bar top. "Of course she did, Einstein. But it's not just her reputation on the line this time. Your parole officer made it crystal clear that if her reports aren't on the straight and narrow and he finds out about it, he won't just sanction her. He'll have her brought up on charges."

Jesus. Adrian had always known Big Ed was a card-carrying member of Jackasses-R-Us, but he'd never thought the guy would use Carly so blatantly to get to him. Mad at her or not, Adrian had to put an end to Big Ed's threats once and for all.

And the only way to do it was to keep his nose, and the rest of him, one hundred and ten percent spic and span.

"I'll call Big Ed first thing in the morning. He *will* leave her alone," Adrian vowed, and Jackson pressed his palms against the bar, leaning in to peg Adrian with a stare like a box full of razor blades.

"That's mighty big of you, since it's your mess in the first place. And while you're in a chatty mood, do me a favor. You might be mad at Carly right now, but she's got reasons for putting you on a leave of absence, ones that don't have jack shit to do with your arm. So get your head out of your ass, stop dodging her calls, and talk to her. She really cares about you. Even if you don't fucking deserve it."

Before Adrian could react or move or even think, Jackson was gone.

Shane let out a slow breath, dropping his voice but not his guard. "Listen, Adrian. I get that this is complicated. But it's rough for him to see Carly upset. And I gotta be honest. I'm feeling it on my end too," he said, but Adrian shook his head to bring the conversation to a halt.

"I hear you. Both of you." He sent a look in Jackson's wake, his gut jangling like a hundred metal spoons set loose in a drawer. "I'll take care of Big Ed."

"Good," Shane said, stepping back from his spot at the bar. "Because if he comes after Carly, Jackson's coming after you."

Adrian swung toward the alcove, yanking out a tray of clean barware. But pint glasses and pitchers of Budweiser weren't going to cut it. He needed to sort this out, to loosen the vise grip splintering his rib cage, to *think*.

He needed the real deal, and he needed it right fucking now.

Cutting a path toward the swinging door, Adrian shouldered his way back into the brightly lit kitchen, his palms going slick as the feelings he'd done his best to knock back for the last two weeks ricocheted around in his head. Catching one of the waitresses on his way toward the pantry, he made sure the bar was covered until Brennan made it back from his break. But damn it, Adrian knew his churning emotions were scrawled all over his face, and he needed to get them in check, especially before he laid eyes on Teagan.

He was too close to losing control.

He burst into the pantry, stabbing his unhurt hand through his hair with an angry tug before riffling through a bunch of ingredients he barely saw. Yes, he'd been pissed that Carly would boot him from La Dolce Vita when she knew he belonged in the kitchen first and foremost, and yes again, that anger had morphed into a deeper ache he'd tried not to tag with a name. But his life wasn't supposed to turn out like this, with his best friend on the ropes and the impulsive feelings he'd sworn he'd never let himself have again boiling over hotter than ever. It was supposed to be nose to grindstone, ducks in a goddamn row just like the last few years. Fuck it all, he was *supposed* to ride out the rest of his parole keeping busy in the kitchen, with his hands on the food and everything else guarded tight.

He couldn't risk his livelihood. Not again. He needed the kitchen now more than ever.

"Adrian?"

The hushed half whisper hit him only a second before the scent of sweet, heady rosemary filled his senses, and Adrian wobbled from the impact of both.

"I'm looking for something. Give me a second." Gravel clung to the rough demand, but of course, that just made Teagan step closer.

"No."

Her soft-soled boots shushed over the tiles, one endlessly long denim-covered leg in front of the other, and God above, he wasn't going to make it with her standing just a breath away.

"I just . . . I need to . . ." But in the thick of the moment, Adrian couldn't think of a single dish he could put together that would make everything okay.

Instead of peppering him with a bunch of pushy questions, Teagan simply wrapped her fingers around his. "Come on."

"Where are we going?"

"Not here." Her eyes flashed, whiskey warm and wide-open, and she turned toward the door. "Come on."

In that moment, Adrian knew he was well and truly in the most bottomless trouble, because for the first time in his entire existence, he didn't want his hands on food to make things right.

He wanted them on Teagan instead.

Chapter Twenty

Teagan unlocked the door to her tiny cottage, stepping into the foyer in silence. She hadn't spoken since grabbing Jesse at the Double Shot and asking him to take care of the waning crowd at the bar with Brennan, which he'd agreed to without question. Teagan trusted them to call her if anything went south, and right now, no matter how deep her dedication to the place ran, she needed to be here.

With Adrian. In her kitchen.

"Come on in," she said, flipping on the lights and putting her keys in the chipped ceramic bowl on the side table by the door. Despite Adrian's lack of furniture, his place was closer to the bar, so they'd spent their nights together there. She led the way down the hall, pausing as he took in the framed photos on her walls with quiet austerity. He stopped between one of her with the guys at the station and her favorite, a shot Brennan had snapped last year of her with her father behind the bar. His eyes didn't leave the photographs as he finally spoke.

"Why did you bring me here?" Adrian asked, and although she should've known he'd get right to it, her heart kicked against her ribs anyway.

"Because something is clearly bothering you." Teagan

lifted a hand to squelch the protest brewing on the hard edges of his mouth, continuing before he could start. "We don't have to talk about it. But for the last two weeks, you've been there when I needed you. Right now I want to return the favor."

"You don't owe me anything, Red."

"Good," Teagan said, tipping her head toward the rear of her cottage and shifting her feet back into motion. "Because I've got about seven ingredients in the fridge, total, so this might turn out to be a disaster."

Adrian jerked to a halt on the threshold of her kitchen, realization sliding over his face. "You don't have to do this."

"It's just a meal, Adrian. Plus, you're a chef, remember? You won't steer me wrong."

The echo of his words from when he'd cajoled her into making gnocchi seemed to ground him a little, and she stepped in close, brushing a kiss over his stubbled jaw. "I want to do this. Let me take care of you a little. Please."

His shoulders unwound beneath her hands, and he bent down, leaning his forehead against hers with his eyes shut tight. "Yeah. Okay."

Teagan led the rest of the way into her kitchen, praying there wasn't a thick layer of dust on the appliances from their severe lack of use. Her stomach knotted over, sending a last-ditch appeal to her brain, but she took a deep inhale and palmed the handle of the fridge with a steady grip. Something about Adrian's expression sent a deep spear of knowledge through her, one that made cooking for him a foregone conclusion. Even if what they had was temporary, she could do this.

She needed it as much as he did.

Adrian pulled out one of the two ladder-backed farm-house chairs at her breakfast table, turning it to face the spot where she stood. Rather than jangling her nerves, his quiet presence bolstered her, her thoughts sliding into place and cementing her resolve.

"I know it's not homemade pasta, but I've always been partial to a good grilled cheese sandwich." She bent down low to grab a skillet from one of the whitewashed cabinets, letting the motion soothe her.

"Yeah. Sounds good." Adrian followed her movements with his eyes, his green-gray stare like the sky before a thunderstorm. She assembled the handful of necessary ingredients, pausing at the crisper drawer in the fridge for a long second. But Teagan couldn't deny that spending the last two weeks immersed in real food at the Double Shot had prompted her to look past the freezer section at Joe's, and what the hell. She'd already taken a huge risk in deciding to cook in the first place. Putting her own spin on a grilled cheese sandwich seemed pretty tame in comparison.

The rich, mellow scent of butter melting evenly over the black-bottomed skillet accompanied her movements as she pulled two slices of bread from the bag on her butcher block counter. Adrian watched her without judgment, and although her motions were probably painstakingly slow to his eyes, she managed to assemble the sandwich with decent competence.

"Poblanos, huh?" Adrian's gaze dropped to the cutting board, where she'd carefully sliced the mild chili pepper that had been hiding in her crisper, and she bit her lip with a nod.

"I don't have a tomato, so, you know . . ."

"So you stepped outside the box," he finished.

Teagan slipped a smile over her lips. "Maybe."

"Nice."

She placed the sandwich in the skillet, taking in the volume of the *hiss* and adjusting the flame on the burner accordingly. When both sides had turned golden-brown,

just firm to the touch, she nudged the sandwich to a plate
and brought it over to the table.

Adrian looked up at her, his eyes going dark. "Thank
you."

"Sure." Her cheeks heated as she sat down across from
him, but her built-in moxie refused to let her pull up her
gaze. Adrian turned his attention to the plate, the silence
between them surprisingly comfortable as he ate. The tension threading his shoulders into a tight knot around his
neck eased with each bite, smoothing the muscles beneath
his black Harley-Davidson T-shirt into long, strong lines.
The perpetual stubble shadowing his face outlined the
angle of his jaw with sexy precision, the obvious unease
he'd carried into the room with him turning into something
calmer, but no less intense as he finished the meal she'd
prepared.

Holy hell, Teagan wanted everything about him.

"I'm glad you ate." She forced herself to pick up the
now-empty plate, but Adrian reached out, stopping her
before she could take a step toward the sink.

"Lonnie sent someone to the bar tonight."

"What?" Teagan dropped the plate back to the pine
tabletop with a graceless clunk, fear catapulting through
her veins. "Oh my God, we have to tell Brennan. He and
Jesse—"

"I told Jesse before we left, and he called your father to
make sure he was safe. But it doesn't matter. The guy didn't
come in to start any trouble. Not tonight, anyway."

Anger tangled with the fear in Teagan's belly, pushing
hard at her seams. "I don't understand. Why would Lonnie
send someone, then?"

"For me."

Oh God. "But Lonnie doesn't know who you are."

Adrian exhaled, his jaw tightening as if his words were

strung with shards of glass. "He does now. And my parole officer threatened Carly. It's not going to take much for Big Ed to put two and two together if any of this goes south."

"It won't," Teagan said, the promise welling all the way up from her toes. "We're going to pay Lonnie back the fifteen thousand and make him go away, just like you said. I'm not going to let that knuckle-dragging bag of filth touch my father, and I'm sure as hell not going to let him touch you, either."

Adrian hesitated. "You don't know what you're up against, Red. If you don't come up with that money—"

"No." She leaned forward, her fingers impulsive on Adrian's mouth. "I will come up with the money. I said I would take care of this, and I meant it. I don't care what it takes."

For a second, Adrian moved nothing but his eyes, and oh God, they were so full of churning emotions that Teagan felt more of his stare than she saw. But then he reached up, clasping his strong, calloused hand around her fingers and said, "Did you just *shush* me so you could say your piece?"

Powerless against the instinctive, unbidden smile springing to her lips, she simply nodded. "I guess I did."

"Mmm." Adrian pulled her in close, surrounding her with the spicy, forbidden scent of cinnamon. "I suppose I had that coming."

"I know what's on the line for you, Adrian." Her chest constricted over all the emotions flying around her rib cage, but she forced herself to give them a voice. Money or no money, he could still lose everything by staying to help her at the Double Shot, especially if Lonnie knew he was on parole. "I meant what I said about paying Lonnie back. But if you need to leave now, I understand."

Every muscle in his body went rigid under her hands,

and he pulled back to look at her. "I can't . . . I mean, I don't . . ." Adrian broke off with a low oath, and Teagan parked herself in the chair across from him.

"It's okay," she said, although she'd never felt further from the word in her life. "I can take care of the restaurant."

"It's not about the restaurant." Adrian looked down at the plate in front of him, pulling in a breath before returning his gaze to her face. "Five years ago, I lost everything I had on an impulsive mistake. I can't do that again."

Teagan's head snapped up. "When you went to jail."

He nodded, his voice sinking to match the quiet of her cozy kitchen. "It started before that, but yes. About a year after I finished culinary school, my *nonna* had a stroke. One minute, we were standing in the kitchen making amaretti, the next, she'd collapsed in front of the oven."

The memory of her father getting dizzy behind the bar only a few weeks ago echoed through Teagan's mind, and it tore at her heart to think of Adrian going through something so much worse. "I'm so sorry," she whispered.

"I am, too," he said, raw honesty filling the words. "She was conscious when I called nine-one-one, but kind of altered. She just kept saying I'd find where I belonged, and that I needed to live my life, really *live* it, with no regrets. I think she knew something was really wrong, and I didn't want her to get worked up, so I swore to her that I would."

"I'm sure she felt comforted that you were there with her, Adrian."

His stare glittered, darkening under the soft kitchen light cutting through the night shadows. "By the time the paramedics got there, she'd lost consciousness. She never woke up after that, and she died twenty minutes later. Best I can tell, that promise was the last thing she ever heard."

Tears shot to Teagan's eyes, and even though she fought

them with every tool in the shed, she knew it was a losing battle.

Adrian drew a rough inhale, but continued, as if the story had been shaken up and uncorked and needed a place to go. "After that, I threw myself into work. The kitchen was where I belonged, and I'd sworn to my *nonna* that I'd be there a hundred percent, with no regrets. Carly and I had been close in culinary school, and she got a gig as a sous-chef at this place in the city. The owner brought me on as a line cook, mostly for grunt work, but I didn't care. I just wanted to be around the food. I wanted to be where I belonged."

"But something happened." Teagan's reply was a statement, and Adrian confirmed the words with a tight nod.

"Working in a professional kitchen, especially one in a cutthroat city like New York, doesn't bring a whole lot of sanity. The work's exhausting, the schedule's worse, and days off are about as foreign as little green men. Carly was married to her first husband by then, and it had only been a few months since my *nonna* had passed. I was cool being in the kitchen, but in the odd hours I wasn't . . ."

"You were lonely," Teagan finished, knowing all too well how those odd hours felt. How many nights had she curled up after finishing a tour at the station or a shift at the Double Shot, pretending the ache in her chest was heartburn and not heartache?

"Yeah." Adrian shifted, his chair scraping against the hardwood floor. "I started seeing another line cook, and for a while, everything was great. Carly got promoted and made me her sous-chef, and even though I fell for Becca pretty fast, I thought I'd found someone who really got me outside of the kitchen. It was impulsive, but I loved her. For that little scrap of time, I thought everything was great."

"You thought," Teagan repeated, her heart starting to patter with foreboding.

"Becca was married."

Teagan jerked back in shock, her shoulders clapping against the wooden backrest of her chair. "Married?"

"To a cop," Adrian added, tugging a hand through his hair. "She told me they were separated and getting divorced, but she conveniently forgot to tell *him* that. He found out we'd been having an affair, and they had a huge argument."

Teagan could barely eke out a nod over the surprise thrumming through her, but he continued to pour the story out.

"Becca came to the restaurant, shaken and crying. She said her husband had hit her, and I just snapped. I tore out of the restaurant in the middle of a shift without thinking, and I didn't stop until I'd found the guy and beaten the hell out of him."

"It sounds like he deserved it," Teagan managed, but Adrian cut the sentiment short.

"He might've, if he'd actually laid a finger on her."

Anger bloomed, fresh and hot in Teagan's veins. "She *lied* to you?"

"Of course, I didn't find out until after I'd already been peeled off her husband by three very pissed-off cops, one of whom just happened to be all buddy-buddy with the guy and all of whom decided my shoulder would look nicer outside the socket than in."

"Oh God, your scar tissue." She'd assumed his previous injury had been accidental. But now the whole thing made perfect sense.

Perfect, heartbreaking, horrible sense.

Adrian nodded. "Becca changed her story to save face with her husband, tried to make it look like I was unhinged and just attacked the guy, and with the other cops' statements, the DA bought it without a second thought. Becca and her husband reconciled, and they both testified that I'd assaulted him without provocation."

Teagan's mind spun on its axis, and her knowledge of the system caught up with Adrian's story in a gut-sinking rush. "Assaulting a police officer is a B felony." God, no wonder he'd done time on a first offense.

"All it took was one good, impulsive shove out of line, and I lost everything. Becca's husband's attorney threw the book at me, and the judge let it stick. The only thing that saved me from doing more time was Carly's testimony, both at my trial and when I made parole."

"She sounds like a good friend. One who believes in you," Teagan said.

"That's just the point," he shot back. "The minute I got sprung from Rikers, I swore I'd live up to what she'd said, that I'd do right by her word and what my *nonna* wanted for me. I swore I'd never lose everything on a crazy, impulsive risk again, not for anything."

Adrian broke off, his voice turning to gravel and his stare to pure steel. "All I've wanted for the last five years was to keep my head down and live my life in the kitchen where I belong. But then I wrecked my bike, and I spent all this time with you, and I didn't mean to, but . . . *damn it, I just . . . I can't . . .*"

Teagan's heart slammed behind her breastbone. "You can't stay."

"No. Don't you get it? I can't *not* stay." The words burst from Adrian's mouth, knocking the breath straight out of her lungs. "As insane as it sounds with everything tumbling down around me right now, being with you is the only thing that makes me feel like I'm really living with no regrets.

The risk, the food, none of it matters. There's only you. You're the only thing that makes sense."

"But . . . you just said—"

He halted her words with a slash of his hand. "I know what I said, but I also know what I feel. It would be bullshit for me to tell you that I have all the answers. Hell, I don't have the first clue how to handle the mountain of risks outside that door. But it would be even bigger bullshit for me to tell you I want to do anything other than stay."

Adrian stood, laying waste to the space between them in a single, breath-stopping rush. His big, capable hand reached up to cup her face, a gentle brush of skin on skin, and his touch vibrated all the way through her.

"Please, Red. I want you with no regrets. Let me stay."

Chapter Twenty-One

Teagan arced up toward his body without hesitation, and Christ above, Adrian wanted nothing more than to drown in the absolute heat of her red, ripe mouth. Everything about her—from her sassy, *dare me* attitude to the quiet, understanding nature that had made her listen as he'd aired out every stitch of his dirty laundry—it was all so gorgeous and stubborn and just so fucking perfect, Adrian didn't care what he was up against.

The only risk that mattered was the risk of not being with this woman.

"This is insane," Teagan murmured, clutching the sleeves of his T-shirt with hot, needy fists, and he wrapped his unhurt arm around her back to lock them together from shoulder to hip.

"I don't care." Adrian parted her lips with his own in one fluid stroke, stealing the deep-seated sigh coming up from her chest before breaking off to kiss the soft skin of her neck. "I meant everything I said. I want you. Just you."

"Oh God, I want you, too." Teagan pulled back, her cheeks flushed with desire, and her liquid copper stare hit him right in the sternum.

"I want you to stay."

Her mouth found his in a flawless combination of eager and sweet, and he dove in without thought. Tracing the extravagant curve of her lower lip with his tongue, Adrian tasted and teased, and although the dark impulse shooting through his blood screamed at him to rip Teagan's clothes off without lingering pleasantries, the certainty filling his mind kept him steady.

The more he kissed her, the more he wanted, to the point that his only option was to take Teagan so hot and slow, there'd be nothing left of him when they were done.

"Adrian, please." Her husky, sex-soaked whisper bordered on begging, and the sound shot straight to his cock. "Take me to bed."

"No." He cupped the hollow where her neck dipped into her shoulder blades, breathing in the combination of rosemary and total want pouring off her skin. She froze in his grasp, but before she could put the nonverbal protest to words, he slanted his mouth over her ear.

"I belong in the kitchen, remember?"

Teagan's sharp inhale acquiesced as Adrian slid his tongue from her ear to her collarbone, feathering his lips over the delicate yet pounding pulse point at the base of her throat. Lowering his hand to the back of her rib cage, he swung her from the café table to the narrow pantry door, giving in to the hurry-up urge just once as he pressed her up against the wooden surface with an agonizing thrust of his hips.

Teagan's stare glittered with need, pinning him into place while she slid her hand up the length of his thigh, and the suggestive move deleted *once* from his vocabulary.

"God, you are so hot right now." Adrian rocked against the tight cradle of her hips, his knees nearly giving out at the delicious friction of rough denim under her soft fingers.

"You didn't think I'd let you have all the fun, did you?"

She made another up and down pass over his button fly, but his hand shot out to snap up her wrist and pin it directly over her head.

"Yes."

With one deft scoop of his free fingers, Adrian hooked the hem of Teagan's T-shirt and yanked it upward, exposing creamy skin bound by white lace. The blush that still covered her face trailed over the swell of her breasts, shading the tight buds of her nipples a dark, sexy-as-sin pink beneath the thin layer of material barely covering them.

He wanted to taste her until she screamed.

Angling himself against her for better access, Adrian lowered his face to the deep V between Teagan's breasts, edging the lacy border of her bra with a sweep of his tongue. He nudged the fabric aside, tasting every inch of the smooth curve of her breast before closing his lips over her bare nipple with a groan.

"Don't stop."

Teagan's voice broke from her throat on a tremble, her unencumbered hand knotting in his hair with just enough pressure to sting sweetly as she strained against his mouth. Powerless to do anything but oblige, Adrian dropped the hand over her head, removing both her T-shirt and the lacy fabric under it with brisk motions. He returned his attention to her now completely bare breasts, slipping his arm around Teagan's back to splay his palm and fingers over the center line of her rib cage, guiding her right back to his hungry mouth. So slowly he thought it might kill him outright, Adrian drew her back to his greedy lips, swirling, sucking and tasting until he'd coaxed her into everything from a whisper to a scream.

"Oh God," Teagan said, the oath breaking over a cresting moan. "Don't you dare . . . *stop*."

"That's it," he breathed, sending a heavy exhale over the

damp peak of her nipple. "Let me take care of you. Come for me, Red."

He lowered his mouth back to her body, anchoring her to the door with his frame as he laved her harder and faster with his tongue. On a final, keening sigh, Teagan's spine went bowstring taut, arching beneath his mouth as she shuddered out his name. Adrian scaled back his touch in slow sweeps, pressing soft kisses to the curve of her shoulder and dropping his arm around her waist to hold her close.

"You are so beautiful. Christ, I can't take my eyes off you."

But in an instant, she'd curled her fingertips over his biceps, gaining just enough momentum to switch their positions by swinging him against the pantry door.

"Good. Then you can watch while I return the favor."

In the space of time it took Adrian to relearn how to breathe, Teagan had dropped to her knees, springing the top two buttons on his jeans with nimble fingers. A few flame-colored strands fell loose from her ponytail, framing her wicked smile as she peered up to meet his stare. Without breaking eye contact, she skimmed both hands up his legs, working the rest of the buttons on his jeans to free him from the constraints of the denim.

"Wait," Adrian warned, but his traitorous cock jerked at the enticing stroke of Teagan's hands diving beneath the waistband of his boxer briefs, and oh, hell, he was going to die from raw, hard want, right here in her kitchen.

"Not this time." Teagan lowered the black cotton and denim just enough to expose him from his hips to the tops of his thighs, and Adrian ground out one last-ditch effort at control.

"You can't . . . ah, God."

Every last one of his thoughts short-circuited and spun

out as the movement of her hands was replaced by the mind-altering glide of her mouth.

Caught in an erotic trance at the sight of Teagan kneeling between his thighs, Adrian sucked in a lungful of air that got exactly nowhere. With one hand pressed against his hip for leverage and the other wrapped firmly around his rock-hard erection, she turned the tables on him with one long slide of her tongue. The pure, wet heat of her mouth followed over and over again, and the flawless sensation coupled with the pressure from her hand had him fighting for control. Her fingers uncurled against the bare skin on his hip, guiding him into a rhythmic tilt against her mouth. On a groan, Adrian's hand fluttered to the silky crown of her head, and the touch had her lifting her gaze to lock eyes with him without slowing her movements.

She had to stop. Right. Now.

Dropping to hook his arms beneath hers, Adrian pulled Teagan to her feet, righting his clothes with a well-placed yank before drawing her close.

"You make me lose my mind," he said, slanting his mouth over hers in a punishing kiss she returned with matching need.

"Do you trust me?" Teagan murmured, trailing a line of barely there kisses over his jaw.

"Yes." His answer flew from his mouth on a breath of surprise, but it was the truth. "I trust you."

"Then go ahead and lose your mind. I promise I'll take care of you."

She threaded her fingers through his to lead the way down the darkened stretch of hallway on the opposite side of the kitchen from the foyer, not stopping until they'd crossed the shadow-lined threshold of her bedroom. Just enough moonlight spilled past the curtains to reveal the curve of Teagan's form as she pressed a kiss to his mouth.

Adrian's T-shirt rasped over her naked shoulders, and even though his need to feel her skin to skin bordered on desperate, he didn't rush. Instead, he ran his fingers over Teagan's body in slow strokes, tracing the length of her neck, memorizing the slope of her belly, drinking in the flare of her hips.

If he had a million years to discover her, he'd want a million and one.

Wordlessly, Teagan slipped out of the rest of her clothes before liberating him from the rest of his. The combination of silvery light from the windows and the adjustment of his eyes to the dark let him watch as she moved toward her bed, propping herself on her knees in the bedsheets. He stepped in to kiss her, and God, how could anyone be so soft and yet so strong and firm at the same time?

The kiss went from slow and sexy to right fucking now in the span of a breath, and Adrian deepened his motions to meet every one of Teagan's soft little moans. Dividing the cradle of her hips with his own, he pressed against her body until she'd reclined over the mattress, her knees listing open in hot invitation. Adrian shifted to his side to ease the weight of his frame off his injured arm, smiling into the fold of Teagan's shoulder as the lean muscles in her inner thigh tightened under his touch. He dragged his fingertips slowly forward, lingering in the crease between her leg and her hip before sliding over her core.

Impulse sizzled through Adrian's veins as he thrust into the slick heat between her legs, burying his thumb in the soft knot above his fingers. Teagan's answering cry of approval only pushed him harder, and he strained to keep his balance on his impaired arm as he worked her closer and closer to the edge.

"Do you know how badly I want to be inside of you?" he whispered, but the words had barely finished passing his lips before Adrian found himself flat on his back, covered by nothing more than the warm, wanting woman and his insane need to have her.

"Yes," she whispered back, swinging from the bed only long enough to grab a condom from his discarded jeans. Even the gentle motions of fitting it into place made Adrian's cock ache in demand, and he gripped Teagan's hips as she replaced her body over his. She fastened him with her gaze, her eyes glinting with desire and emotion, and even though the scant light of her room shadowed the connection, Adrian still felt the full force of it in his chest.

"Let me in, Adrian. Let me take care of you."

Teagan sank down, the space between their bodies becoming nothing in one breath-stealing thrust, and going slow never stood a chance. Adrian canted his hips, tilting her closer until he could reach around to palm the gorgeous swell of her ass to control every movement, pushing deeper into her with each unforgiving thrust. Rather than shy away or try to slow down, Teagan rocked right back against him, giving and taking and giving again until her warm, wet body went rigid around him.

"Oh God." The oath left her lips as more reverence than curse, and Adrian locked her relentlessly into place as he arched off the bed to fill her. With need that bordered on despair, he levered himself up from the mattress, seating Teagan to the hilt in his lap and holding her there as she unraveled in his arms.

Only, instead of going boneless in her release, she knotted her long, strong legs around the small of his back to adjust to her new position. She rolled her hips over his in a torturously sinful glide, squeezing just as tight and hard as Adrian had only moments ago, until a dark, familiar tingle broke free at the base of his spine. He struggled for the last thread of control in his grasp, but then Teagan looked down at him, her cinnamon-gold stare penetrating him like a palpable touch.

"Your turn. Come for me, Adrian. *Please*."

His release rushed up from every direction, shuddering through him in a heated wave of pleasure-pain, but Adrian didn't fight it. His mouth parted over the sleek column of her neck, and he surrendered to every last impulse as he came with a groan. Teagan held him fast in her arms as the intensity subsided, the earthy, sweet scent of rosemary filling him up as her hair tumbled down over both of their shoulders. Her chest rose and fell against his, her heartbeat sending a pattern over his skin that grew calmer with each breath.

They sat, locked together in silence and bedsheets, and for the first time in his thirty-two years, Adrian felt like he belonged somewhere other than the kitchen.

Teagan's eyes fluttered open just as the last strains of purple predawn light gave way to smudges of orange and pink through her bedroom window. The thick smattering of oak trees and tall pines around her cottage sent a kaleidoscope of shadows through the sheer white curtains, and she watched the patterns shift over the carpet at her bedside with a swirl of at-odds emotions uncurling in her chest.

She wanted to be wary, to throw on the prickly suit of armor that had served her so well for her entire adult life so she could push her vulnerability away with a nice, mean shove and go back to self-preservation mode. The only problem was, when Adrian had looked all the way into her last night and said he wanted her no matter what, Teagan had trusted him to stay.

And that trust hadn't budged or faded all night long.

Teagan shifted under the covers, slowly turning to her

side. The strong angle of Adrian's jaw was lax in sleep, the heavy fringe of his eyelashes sending shadows over his cheeks. Her dark green comforter draped over his imposing frame at the waist, and the corded muscles of his bare chest rose and fell in steady rhythm. Moving one scant inch at a time, Teagan propped herself up on an elbow, leaning over Adrian's body to examine the scrolled letters inked heavily into his right forearm.

Vivere senza rimpianti. He wanted her with no regrets.

But sometimes, regrets didn't happen in the moment. Sometimes, they happened only after everything was lost.

"It's a little early for good morning, don't you think?"

The rumble of Adrian's voice caught Teagan completely unaware, and she jumped about a mile off the bed at the same time his arms shot out to hold her close.

"Gah! I didn't know you were awake!" Her heart slapped around in her rib cage, and she squinted through the gray shadows of her bedroom to take him in with a critical eye. Nothing about him had changed, from his position flat on his back to his closed eyes and relaxed breathing, but his heartbeat kicked a faster rhythm beneath her palm.

"You're awake," he pointed out, shifting her against his side so her body fit under his uninjured arm. He trailed lazy circles over her back, sliding his fingertips from shoulder blade to spine and back again.

"Yeah." Teagan's pulse wound down at the steady, warm pressure of Adrian's arms around her, holding her tight, and she wordlessly relaxed into his touch. "Guess I just popped up for a second."

"It's early as hell, and I know you're tired. Go back to sleep." Adrian leaned down, filling her drowsier-by-the-second senses with his cinnamon-spicy scent before pressing a kiss to the top of her head.

"I should get up. I can't go back to sleep," she mumbled,

making a feeble attempt to resist the yawn welling up from her throat. But Adrian's body framed hers, all hard lines and strong angles, and damn it, everything about him felt perfect on her skin.

"You can. I told you, I've got you, Red. I won't let you go."

As Teagan's eyes drifted shut and she gave in to the exhaustion in her body and the pure, bright trust in her heart, she knew that Adrian was telling the truth.

And she was falling in love with him.

Chapter Twenty-Two

Adrian shifted his weight against the passenger seat of Teagan's Corolla, inhaling the woodsy-sweet scent of rosemary as her ponytail rode the early June breeze coming in through the open windows. Neither one of them had said much as they'd finally woken up and gotten ready to go to work, but that was fine with him. He'd spilled enough marbles last night to last him another decade.

And even when he'd told Teagan the darkest part of his past, the part that should've scared her the most, she hadn't run. She hadn't shut him out or shoved him away.

She'd let him stay.

Teagan cleared her throat, the soft sound pulling him back to the tight confines of the car. "You're awfully quiet over there."

"Sorry. I must have been zoning out." Okay, so it was a lame response, but he was pretty sure *sorry, I was just sitting here thinking that despite the fact that it's going to get my heart crushed like an overripe tomato and my ass thrown back in jail, I might be falling in love with you* would make him sound like an absolute wing nut.

Jesus. Nothing about this could end well.

"Oh. Okay." For a minute, nothing but silence filled the

space between them, until Teagan broke it with a curse. "Sorry, no. It's not okay. Look, I'm not any good at subtlety, so I'm just going to say this. I know things got a little crazy last night, and we both said some emotional stuff. But if you're, you know, having second thoughts—"

Adrian's head snapped up. "Having what?"

"Second thoughts about staying," Teagan repeated, pressing her lips into a thin, strawberry-red line. "Why else would you be sitting there looking all freaked out and not saying anything?"

Oh hell. "I'm not freaked out because I'm having second thoughts."

"You're not?"

Adrian closed his eyes for just a second before turning against the front seat to face her as completely as he could.

"No, Red. I'm freaked out because I'm *not* having second thoughts."

"Oh. *Oh,*" she said, the second word wrapped tight in re- alization, and she pulled into the Double Shot's parking lot and put the car in *park*. "Really?"

"Really. I know the odds are stacked mile-high against us, but I don't care. I need to live my life with no regrets, and that means helping you all the way through this street fair, no matter what the risk." Unable to help it, Adrian kicked one corner of his mouth into a half smile. "Did you honestly think I'd changed my mind?"

"No." Teagan dropped her hands to her lap. "I don't know. I trust you. I guess I'm just . . . scared."

Adrian leaned across the cramped space of the front seat, cradling her cheek in his palm. Sunlight streamed in through the car window behind her, illuminating her hair to a fiery red gold and showing him every inch of the honesty on her face, and suddenly, there was no *might be* about it.

He was a total fucking goner for this woman. Even if being with her was dangerous as hell.

"Not gonna lie, Red. We've got a lot in our path, and Lonnie's obviously been doing his homework." Adrian pressed a kiss over her mouth, quick and reverent. "But we're going to get through this together. I'm not taking off on you. Not now."

This time, Teagan eked out a tiny smile. "Okay." Her eyes flicked to the restaurant over his shoulder, growing serious again as she returned her gaze to his. "But if you're going to stay, we need a game plan. The bar is a risky place for you to be, now more than ever. Your parole officer is out for blood, and if he finds out—"

"Oh, I'll deal with Big Ed," Adrian said, his heart pounding a fresh load of adrenaline through his veins. The guy had gone too far, bullying him and threatening Carly. Felony record or not, that shit was going to stop, today.

"I agree that you need to talk to him, Adrian, but you also need to *think,*" Teagan shot back, her tougher side making a not-so-surprised appearance. "You said yourself he's just salivating for the chance to drag you back to jail. If you go at him full throttle, you might as well be gift-wrapping yourself for express delivery."

Shit. As badly as Adrian wanted to let loose on Big Ed once and for all, Teagan had a point. Still . . . "He went too far this time. I'm sick and tired of these bullshit power plays."

"So end them," Teagan said, the words so direct and matter-of-fact that he had no choice but to listen. But he'd been sucking up Big Ed's veiled threats for the last three years because he'd had no other choice. How the hell was he going to make them disappear now, when he needed them gone the most?

Unless . . .

"Okay. Big Ed's threats work for the same reason Lonnie's do, right?"

"Leverage," Teagan agreed, and oh holy hell, this just might work.

"But if he doesn't have any, he'll have no choice but to back off." Adrian pushed a hand through his hair, hope percolating in his chest. "I wonder what my attorney would think of him putting the screws to a high-profile character witness like Carly."

Teagan's eyes flashed with coppery surprise. "You're going to call your lawyer?"

"I'm going to meet leverage with leverage," Adrian corrected, the idea snapping into place. "Big Ed crossed the line, and he needs to back off. I'm just going to motivate him to do it. I don't want to call my lawyer unless I have to, but it's past time for some pushing back."

"Threatening him is a little risky," Teagan said, her face unreadable. "Do you think he'll bite?"

"I think it's worth a shot. Look, I've put up with Big Ed's bullying for three years because a part of me believed I deserved it for screwing up so badly. But he's messing with more than just me now. I need to do *something*. If it works, he'll let up on Carly and we can focus on getting Lonnie paid back."

Yup. And that just might be the biggest Hail Mary in the history of the two letters *I* and *f*.

But Adrian stuffed down the thought. "We've got two weeks to make this street fair work, and like you said last night, it's gonna happen. I'll deal with Big Ed. We'll make this work."

"And what about Carly?"

The question slapped him with a twin pang of surprise and don't-go-there. "What about her?"

Rather than get huffy or defensive, Teagan's voice went straight for matter-of-fact. "If you're going to deal with this, you need to deal with *all* of it. Carly's your boss, not to mention your best friend, and whether you like it or not, she's caught up in this, too."

"She kicked me out of the kitchen," Adrian argued, but Teagan countered his defensive pull backward with a single brush of her hand.

"Temporarily, yes. But Carly's had your back for the last five years. Do you really think she'd put you on leave without a good reason? Or that it didn't hurt her like it hurt you?"

"What?" Considering the utter shock reverberating through his chest, it was the best Adrian could muster. He'd been so caught up in the pain of being tossed from the one place he'd thought he needed, he hadn't ever considered that Carly's reasons for doing it might actually be sound. Or that putting him on a leave of absence would certainly have been hard for her, even if she thought it was right.

But Carly *had* been right. He really hadn't been living without regrets, in the kitchen or out. Only he'd been too torqued up trying to muscle through each waking moment to see what had been right in front of him the whole time.

Oh fuck. He was such an *idiot*.

"You're not an idiot," Teagan said, and Adrian realized he must've uttered the curse out loud. She leaned in, the end of her ponytail brushing softly over his chest as she kissed his cheek. "You're just kind of prickly, that's all. And maybe a little thickheaded. I'm sure Carly knows."

Adrian swallowed back a healthy dose of dread. As tempting as it was to tamp down his emotions with a fresh layer of tough-edged denial, closing himself off was what had gotten him into this mess to begin with.

Plus, as much as it scared the hell out of him, he trusted Teagan.

Enough to let her in.

"The stuff with Big Ed, I can fix. But I don't know how

to make this right," Adrian admitted, reaching across the center console for Teagan's hand, and damn. How did the simple feel of his fingers laced between hers make it so much easier to breathe?

"You want to live with no regrets, don't you?"

He nodded, and she lifted their entwined hands, pressing his palm over his breastbone with her own.

"Then stop being afraid of what's in here and just tell Carly how you feel."

"You think she'll listen?" Christ, Adrian wouldn't be surprised if she punched his one-way ticket to voice mail purgatory.

Teagan said, "If she cares about you like I think she does? Yeah, I do."

She pulled back, the corners of her mouth tugging into the sassy smile Adrian knew by heart.

"But for the record, Superman? It probably wouldn't hurt to lead with a giant apology. Now go make some phone calls. It's about time we had a little good news around here."

Adrian hit the *end call* icon on his cell phone and sank back against the couch in the Double Shot's office, trying like hell to get the bitter taste of talking to Big Ed out of his mouth. As curdled as the conversation had been, Adrian's not-so-subtle promise to include his lawyer on their exchanges if Big Ed didn't leave Carly alone had hit its mark, and the surly old crank had agreed—albeit grudgingly—to back off. He hadn't backpedaled a bit on letting Adrian know he still had both eyes on the situation and one hand on the door. If Adrian fucked up, Big Ed *would* still drag him upstate.

And that had been the easier of his two personal calls.

Although he'd tried her both at home and on her cell phone, the best Adrian had been able to do was leave Carly two messages saying he needed to talk.

Now he just had to hope she'd call him back.

Finding his feet, Adrian slid his phone to the back pocket of his jeans and aimed his heavy-soled boots toward the stairs. They had a hell of a workload in front of them today, and knowing Teagan, she'd already jumped in with both feet first with a yippee-ki-yay on her lips.

Despite the bone-wearying planning sessions they'd all been grinding out during the Double Shot's off-hours, Adrian and Jesse had been cutting it millimeter-close with the final menu for the street fair. Everything else had fallen into place over the course of the last week, from the setup to the entertainment to the contract with the brewery. But if they wanted to make enough money to turn Lonnie into nothing more than a bad memory, the food had to go above and beyond and above again, and Adrian was going to do everything within his power to make that a reality.

This street fair had to work. He couldn't leave Teagan in danger.

"Hey, slick. How's the coleslaw coming?" Adrian moved through the Double Shot's kitchen, claiming his spot next to Jesse at the prep station beside the grill.

"Good, I think." Jesse reached past the scattering of ingredients on his cutting board, snapping up a tasting fork from the plastic container at his station. Scooping up a healthy bite of the dish in question, he handed over the fork with the same quiet efficiency he gave to all his kitchen tasks, and no way could Adrian deny that the guy had come a long way from washing dishes in the last three weeks.

Especially after he tasted the coleslaw.

"Damn, Jesse. That's a whole lot better than good." Adrian savored the creamy tang of the just-right flavors before heading over to the warmer. With careful motions, he plated two pulled pork slider sandwiches in the paper-lined red plastic basket in front of him, adding a ramekin of the freshly made coleslaw and a decent handful of seasoned fries before looking up at Jesse with a now-or-never exhale.

"You think she's going to like it?" Jesse asked, his eyes flicking to the counter with an even measure of uncertainty and hope, and Adrian slid the basket from the prep station as he set his sights on the swinging door.

"Only one way to find out."

He edged into the dining room with Jesse following hot on his heels, and suddenly, his pulse kicked a brand-new batch of get-up-and-go through his veins.

"You two look like you're up to no good." Teagan pushed back from her go-to spot at the end of the Double Shot's bar, late-morning sunlight scattering patterns across the hardwood floor behind her. She brushed a wayward strand of hair behind her ear, splitting a suspicious glance between him and Jesse. Her eyes crinkled at the weight of the smile on her lips, though, and damn. Adrian felt that smile from his baseball hat to his boots.

"That sounds about right," he said, depositing the basket on the polished bar top at her side.

Both amber brows rose. "What's this?"

"Lunch."

Teagan's laugh popped out, and man, he thought he'd felt her *smile* everywhere. "Adrian, it's ten forty-five in the morning. I know I usually skip lunch, but this is a hell of a preemptive strike, don't you think?"

"Humor me."

Anticipation swirled in Adrian's gut as she lifted one of the slider sandwiches from the basket and took a big inhale. Her eyes sent an appreciative flick over the buttery-gold roll and the honey-brown pulled pork spilling out from the edges, but the small taste she took was merely polite.

Until about two chews in.

Teagan's lashes arced upward, framing the surprise in her eyes with a coppery fringe. Her spine went ruler-straight against the back of her bar stool, and she took another bite, then a third in rapid succession to polish off the tiny sandwich completely.

"I swear on my eyes, this has got to be the main course in heaven every single night."

"You like it?" Jesse asked, his voice tinged with hope and a healthy dash of pride.

Teagan leaned over the bar to grab a utensil roll from the caddy at the drink station, plucking the fork from within to dig into the coleslaw. "Like it?" she mumbled, scooping up another bite before continuing. "It's going to take all my restraint not to lick the liner in the basket. And, oh my God, this coleslaw is insane."

At that, Adrian chuffed out a laugh. "Take that as a *yes, slick.*"

"Hell, yes, it's a yes!" she crowed. "If we serve this at the street fair, everyone will come back for seconds—no, thirds. Please, please, for the love of all things sacred and holy, tell me you two can make this happen next Saturday within budget."

"Oh, I don't know," Adrian said, trying on his best this-is-iffy expression. "It might be kind of tough. What do you think, Jesse? Can we make this happen at cost for the street fair?"

"Nope." Jesse slid a hand over his close-cropped high and tight, but his goofy grin put him in the same basket as Adrian in the truth-telling department.

"You guys," Teagan said, but the warning faded in her

throat as Adrian planted his palms over the gleaming stretch of mahogany directly across from her.

"Jesse knows a guy who knows a guy who agreed to rent us the smokers dirt cheap, and I cashed in a couple favors with one of the distributors at the resort." He leaned in to peg her with a smile that came up right from his bones.

"Which puts us in just *under* cost. So yes, Red. We're a go for the street fair. The menu's set and all orders have been placed and confirmed."

"You finalized the entire menu? Without asking me?"

For a second that felt like the rough equivalent of ten, Teagan said nothing, and oh shit, maybe he'd pissed her off. They'd talked about keeping the menu streamlined to stay within budget, and doing one main dish extremely well seemed better than offering three or four half-assed choices. Especially since they could use the smokers for both pork and chicken, and provide a variety of sides. It had been a no-brainer when Adrian had finalized the orders right before calling Big Ed. He'd wanted to surprise Teagan to ease her mind.

But right in this moment, he just hoped she didn't want to surprise him with her right hook.

"I can't believe you did that," she said, her hands coming up to cover her mouth. Crap. *Crap!* He needed damage control, fast.

"I'm sorry we didn't tell you, but we were running out of time, and Jesse and I put the recipes together kind of fast over the last day or so. I thought it would make things easier on you if I just took care of it, and—"

Teagan cut off his words by grabbing the shoulders of his T-shirt and hauling him in for a long, hot kiss. "I love it. I love everything about it."

Adrian's shock met his relief in a head-on collision. "You do?"

"Except for the messing with me part, yeah," she said wryly, not unwinding her fists from the gray cotton stretching over his shoulders. "This whole thing is totally coming together. You two are seriously incredible."

He brushed his mouth over hers, unable to hold back. "Incredible, huh?"

"O-kay," Jesse said, clearing his throat twice over a relieved laugh. "I'm going to go be incredible somewhere else. Like waaaaay in the back of the kitchen. I'm glad you like the menu, boss. I'll see you guys, uh, later."

The soft thunk-*thunk* of the swinging door finding its way closed prompted a chuckle from Adrian's throat, and Teagan pulled back to slide him a glance loaded with thought.

"You've really taken Jesse under your wing. Brennan, too."

"Broken as it is," Adrian flipped back, lifting his cast as he leaned against the service counter behind the bar. "Anyway, they're both working their asses off. It's way more them than me making this place go right now."

"Bullshit," Teagan countered, although with more smile than sass. He should've figured she wouldn't cage her thoughts. After all, being coy definitely wasn't her bag. "We're *all* making this place go right now. You included."

Adrian shrugged, but he couldn't deny how good it felt not only to hear the words, but to know deep down that they were true. "I promised you I'd help."

She slid off her bar stool, turning the corner to walk behind the bar without taking her eyes from his. "I like your brand of help."

"Mmm. I like that you like it." He folded her against his body, and the way she fit, snug and warm in all the right places, did nothing to keep his impulses in check. "You know, we're ahead of schedule this morning, and Brennan's going to be here any minute." Adrian skimmed his tongue over the soft skin of her collarbone, smiling darkly at the goose bumps appearing in the wake of the movement. "We could take an early lunch."

Teagan's laughter vibrated against his chest. "You are extremely bad."

"You like me that way," he said, repeating the slow string of kisses in reverse.

"I do," she sighed, barely a whisper. "I lo—"

The heavy squeak of the front door moving on its hinges had Adrian pulling her in a protective jerk from the entryway, but he had zero armor against the soft gasp that accompanied the sound of the door.

Because it belonged to Carly.

Chapter Twenty-Three

"Oh God, I'm so sorry." Carly's voice, familiar and yet rusty in Adrian's mind, struck a direct bull's-eye into the center of his chest. "I bumped into the bar manager in the parking lot, and he let me in. I got your message, but I shouldn't have . . . I can just—"

"Wait." Teagan slipped around him, her eyes moving over Carly from her trademark dark French braid to the tiny yet definite swell of her belly that hadn't been there even three weeks ago. "You must be Carly. Come in."

Surprise dominated Adrian's chest as Teagan offered Carly the welcome that lay lodged beneath his sternum. He stood, completely frozen to the rubber mats behind the bar, with his pulse moving in a thousand directions, watching Teagan walk toward the spot where Carly appeared equally frozen by the door.

"Teagan O'Malley. My dad owns the place." She extended a hand, inviting Carly in with a nod of her head.

"Carly di Matisse. Carter," she added, her face flushing. "Sorry to, um, interrupt."

"Not at all. It's nice to meet you," Teagan said, swinging her gaze to Adrian. "I'm going to go help Jesse with prep so you two can catch up."

She threaded a quick glance between him and Carly, giving a tiny nod before slipping past the swinging door. The muffled *clink* of pots and pans being put to use filtered past the heavy silence in the dining room, and the sounds of the kitchen, coupled with the reassuring look in Teagan's eyes as she left him to it, made him kick his feet into gear.

Adrian might not know the right words to express his feelings, but he sure as hell needed to try.

"I'm glad you came." He rounded the bar, hooking his fingers beneath the back of one of the stools to flip it upright and turn it toward Carly. "You want to sit down?"

"Sure." She crossed the hardwood to settle herself at the bar, taking a quick visual inventory of the dining room before sending a longer gaze back in his direction. "You look really good."

"Thanks. But to be fair, the last time you saw me, I'd just gone ass over teakettle on Rural Route Four," he reminded her, moving back behind the mahogany to pop the lid on the cooler beneath the bar. Grabbing a carton of orange juice, he poured her a glassful, the simple motions knocking his unease down yet another notch.

Carly bit her lip. "No, I mean . . ." She fumbled to a stop, reeling back whatever she'd meant to say. "Look, you and I have never beat around the bush with things, so I'm just going to come out with it. I know you're really mad at me for telling you to take time off, and maybe I shouldn't have made assumptions about what you need. I didn't mean to shut you out. But—"

"I'm not mad at you." The words shot from Adrian's mouth, hitting his ears before they'd even registered in his brain, and Carly pulled back against her bar stool.

"You're not mad." The words betrayed her disbelief, and okay, it was time to start manning up with the truth.

"Well, I *was* mad. But I was also an idiot, because you were right."

"I'm sorry." A shot of surprise streaked over her expression. "What did you say?"

Adrian met her wide-eyed stare across the bar. "You were right. I needed some time off to figure out what was really important. I wasn't living with no regrets. In fact, I wasn't really living at all."

He might have hated every ounce of Carly's six-weeks-no-exceptions mandate at the time, but the truth was, if she hadn't put him on leave from La Dolce Vita, he wouldn't have ended up here at the Double Shot, helping Teagan.

And wasn't hindsight just a bitch and a half?

"I was worried," she said, fiddling with the end of her braid over one shoulder. "And mad at you, too." That got a tiny smile out of her. "But mostly just scared you'd lost track of who you are."

"You've always had my back, *gnochella*. You're a better friend than I deserve." Adrian straightened, stabbing his boots into the floorboards with purpose. "And I talked to Big Ed this morning. You don't have to worry about him harassing you anymore."

Carly scoffed, but Adrian caught the relief beneath the gesture. "Yeah, he's a peach. Can't say I'll miss him when your parole is up next month."

"You took a huge risk telling him you'd seen me and that I was fine."

"I know. Jackson already read me the riot act. But I'll tell you the same thing I told him. I didn't lie to your parole officer, Adrian. I told him you were fine, and you are." She paused, taking in the quiet hush of the Double Shot's dining room. "But I should've known you wouldn't stay out of the kitchen."

Carly's smile was too bittersweet to hold any of the

zing she'd likely wanted to pin to the gesture, and Adrian jumped to reassure her.

"I know you meant for me to take time off to heal, but Teagan's a paramedic, and I stuck to the doc's orders. I'm not cooking. Well, not really. I'm still stuck with this thing." He held up the arm trapped in its fiberglass stockade. "But the physical therapist says my shoulder is healing even better than she expected, so once the cast comes off in a couple of weeks, I should be good to go back and start cooking again."

Her dark brow popped. "You want to come back to La Dolce Vita?"

For a brief flash of a second, both *yes* and *I don't know* fought a turf war for Adrian's response, and really? Was he losing his mind?

"Of course I want to come back. I belong in the kitchen."

"Not to put too fine a point on it, but you're in the kitchen now," Carly said, and oh shit. He'd never considered that she'd think he didn't want to come back to work.

"I am. But me working here is temporary. Teagan needs the boost, and I'm on board with helping her. But she knows that once I'm clear, I'm not staying. Well, not in her kitchen, anyway."

"But you're staying with her otherwise?" Rampant curiosity covered Carly's face, and Adrian's gut knotted in an all-too-familiar trip toward lockdown status.

"Yeah." He stretched the word all the way out before letting it go. "It's kind of a long story."

"Oh. Okay." Carly nodded, taking a sip of her juice. She'd always sensed and respected his need for a wide berth with personal stuff, and his born-in survival instinct had always kept him from doing anything other than take it, carte blanche. When his *nonna* died. When he fell in love with Becca. When he lost control of everything around him and got arrested.

But for the first time, Adrian didn't want to stuff his feelings aside or pretend they weren't real.

He was tired of guarding who he was for fear of being rejected.

"Move over," he said, taking the handful of steps needed to eliminate the bar between them, and Carly sat up so fast, a healthy splash of orange juice sloshed over the rim of her pint glass and onto the napkin beneath.

"Why?" she asked, but Adrian didn't budge. Instead, he pulled down the bar stool next to hers, angling himself against the black leather cushion with a grin he hadn't felt in far too long.

"Because I want to get comfortable, that's why. This is gonna take a while."

Teagan slung a blue and white kitchen towel over one shoulder, breathing in the spicy punch of chili powder and smoked paprika so deeply, she could feel the pop of flavors on her tongue.

"Gotta hand it to you, Superman. I never thought of adding chili to the menu in the beginning of the summer, but this smells too good to pass up."

Adrian stepped in behind her, and the insinuation of his nearness alone sent Teagan's pulse into a lather. "Throw a couple of seasonal vegetables into a dish, and you'd be shocked what you can get away with. Plus, it stays cool here in the mountains until at least June, so this should go over well on the trial menu."

"Along with everything else," she said over a laugh. "I swear I think each idea you've come up with over the last four days has tasted better than the last."

"Oh no, you don't." He pushed her ponytail over one shoulder of her dark red T-shirt, leaning in to watch her movements from where he stood. "You're the one who cooked those dishes. All I did was advise."

Teagan gave a less than ladylike snort, melting into the hard, sturdy plane of Adrian's chest with a smile and sigh combination that felt so freaking good, it should really be illegal. "The best you're going to get out of me is that we're even on this little endeavor. Take it or leave it."

"You drive a hard bargain, Red." His mouth brushed over the sensitive skin of her neck, his dark and sexy smile threaded all the way through his words. "But I'll take it."

With a week and a half to go until the street fair and all the planning locked in place, she and Adrian had been able to take a look at some of the downward trends the Double Shot had spiraled through lately. Adrian's suggestions for some subtle yet definite changes to the menu by testing new dishes as daily specials had generated several great ideas over the last few days—not to mention a lot of rave reviews from Brennan, Jesse, and the waitstaff as they taste-tested the recipes. With Adrian spearheading the concepts and Teagan channeling her energy into executing them just right, they'd come up with plenty of options to give business a boost. If the plan worked, they'd pull off a much-needed brightening to both the menu and the restaurant's income while still keeping the Double Shot's tried-and-true classics.

Teagan trailed a wooden spoon through the stockpot in front of her, admiring the bright yellow burst of corn kernels peppered throughout the burnished brown chili. "It was really nice of Carly to sit down and talk with me about how she's using the produce grown on-site at the resort to boost La Dolce Vita's menu. I had no idea it could work so seamlessly."

"It takes a lot of hard work to set it up. Carly's a true testament to that. But yeah," Adrian agreed, kissing her neck one last time before stepping back to grab a battle-tested pot holder from the shelf above the oven. "The results are worth the effort. Being able to use fresh produce grown on-site is a huge win."

She nodded, mentally pouting at the loss of his body so close to hers but willing her mind to stick to the topic at hand. "Obviously, we don't have the space or funds for that kind of project here. But Brooks Farm is right in Beale-town, and to be honest, I'd kind of forgotten how much produce they grow."

"Plenty of restaurants work out deals with local farms. We could take a look at the ordering overall, see where you might be able to scale back on some of the prepackaged stuff to replace it with fresh ingredients. A lot of the time, the commercial items are more expensive anyway. Then if you want, I can go with you to talk to whoever runs the farm."

Adrian bent down low to slide a nine-by-thirteen pan of perfect, golden corn bread from the belly of the oven next to the spot where Teagan stood at the burner. She was tempted to tell him to take it easy using both hands in the kitchen, but damn, her mouth was too busy watering.

And then she caught sight of Adrian's gaze on her, intense and hungry and oh so hot, and all rational thought flew out of her brain. God, she wanted to let go, to give in to the delicious need swirling deep in her chest and fall to-tally, irrevocably, insanely in love with him.

But her tried and true survival instinct made her bite back the feeling, the same way she'd tamped down the words she'd very nearly uttered when Carly had walked into the bar the other day.

You might be in love with him, but what if he leaves anyway?

"Okay, sure," Teagan said, shaking off the thought. Adrian had made no bones about his intention to stay with her, even after he went back to work at La Dolce Vita and she returned to the station in a couple of weeks. Though her father's health wasn't a hundred percent, he'd finally taken a turn for the better and was steadily improving. Once she found a full-time cook to replace Lou and help her dad manage the bar, plus implement these new changes to the menu, things would look up even further.

Maybe then she could finally lose the ominous pang beneath her breastbone.

Teagan planted her boots into the kitchen tile, her resolve bracketed down nice and tight. "I'd love help getting all the options together for how to boost business and lower cost. I'm going to need all the details I can get before I talk to my father about the menu anyway."

"You think he won't go for the changes?" Adrian asked, turning the corn bread out onto the cutting board of the adjacent workstation and slicing it with methodical care.

At that, she had to crack a smile. "I think he's a little stubborn, especially when it comes to change. But business has been flagging for a reason, and it's possible the place just needs a few small changes. We've come up with some great ideas, so I'm hoping the old man cuts me a break in the listening department."

"Ah," came a familiar voice from the alcove by the side door, and Teagan's heart made a hard leap against her rib cage. "I knew my ears were burnin' for a reason, pretty girl. But whatever you're cookin' up in here smells good enough for me ta consider givin' ya the benefit of the doubt."

"God, Da!" Teagan splayed one hand over her chest and the other across the back of Adrian's shoulder in an effort to stay his lightning-fast defensive stance in front of her. "You can't sneak up on me like that." She slipped around Adrian, whose expression morphed to recognition as he took in the exchange, and she served her father with a stern frown even as she moved to pull him in for a hug.

"Looks as if I'm not the sneakier of us," he tossed back as they parted, sliding a pointed glance at her cooking partner, and ohhhhhkay. This wasn't going to be awkward at all.

Just as long as the kitchen floor crashed open to devour her in one giant gulp.

"Right!" Her cheeks went thermonuclear, and she hauled in a breath that barely made the trip past her windpipe. "You remember I told you I had someone, um, helping me out in the kitchen? Well, this is Adrian. He's a chef at the restaurant at the resort. Adrian, this is my father, Patrick O'Malley."

"It's nice to meet you," Adrian said, his voice laced with quiet caution, and her father stepped in to squarely meet his handshake even though Adrian's palm eclipsed his two to one.

"Likewise." Her father flashed her with a look that read *well, that explains a lot*. Ugh, great. She was as transparent as she felt. Her father's red-gray brows slid upward as he took Adrian in from his scuffed black motorcycle boots to the finger-combed tousle of his hard-edged platinum hair, and Teagan braced for impact.

"Teagan mentioned you've been runnin' the kitchen together the last few weeks," he said, settling his gaze back on Adrian's. "It looks as if I owe you a debt of gratitude."

Adrian's head snapped up, as if it was the last thing on earth he'd expected her father to say, and holy crap, that made two of them. "Oh, ah, it's not a problem. I had some time off from the resort." He skimmed his free hand absently over his cast before locking both arms down at his sides. "I'm just happy to help."

True to his ingrained charm, her father tipped his head with a boyish grin that defied most of his years. "Well, I'm grateful for it. Without you, I suspect this one would've worked herself into an early grave. As it stands, I'm shocked to my shoes ta see her in the kitchen without any fuss."

Oh no. Not a chance. She didn't care how relieved she was that her father seemed okay with Adrian in the kitchen.

If they ganged up on her, even playfully, she was toast.

"Excuse me, I don't fuss," Teagan said, pinning the words with a hearty dose of *we're so not talking about this*. She stepped back toward the stove to give the pot a stir, surprised to find the motion soothing. "And if I work too hard, it's because I learned from the best."

"Ah, see how she turns it into a compliment so I can't complain? Tricky girl."

"Mmm. A wise old man once told me you catch more flies with honey than vinegar. I'm just taking his lead."

Her father placed a hand over the center of his plaid flannel shirt, feigning injury despite the glimmer of a smile. "Old man! How you wound me."

"Oh, come on. I said you were wise," Teagan pointed out, although her own smile escaped without permission. She tapped the edge of the wooden spoon on the lip of the stockpot, balancing the utensil over a spoon rest on the counter before she turned to give her father an appraising look. "So how come you're out here today? You're supposed to be taking it easy before your appointment with Dr. Riley this afternoon."

"Bah, taking it easy is boring. Anyway, I was hungry. Thought I'd see what ya had brewin' down here. Looks like my intuition served me well, and not just with the food."

Her father eyeballed both her and the stockpot on the

burner with obvious interest, and her gut knotted. There was no point in delaying the inevitable now that her father had clearly overheard her conversation with Adrian, and truly, the Double Shot's books were running on fumes. Sure, the street fair would take care of the immediate cash flow crisis, but in the long run, they needed more than a quick fix for a slow problem.

"Okay, Da. You're right. But obviously, things around here need to change a little when you come back. Maybe it's time we took a look at how to make those changes work for the better." Teagan swallowed past the knot tightening in her throat. "I don't want you to get healthy only to come back and burn out again. I want the restaurant to be really successful, like you've always dreamed."

Before her father could answer or she could scoop in a shaky breath to continue, Adrian's gravelly voice filtered through the quiet of the kitchen.

"I'm going to let you two talk." He turned to move down the line toward the swinging door to the dining room, and Teagan's protest flew from her mouth before she could even register forming the word.

"No."

But it was twined around an identical objection, and both she and Adrian halted midstep to stare at her father.

"No. These ideas for changin' things, they've come from both of ya, haven't they?" he asked, but Teagan shook her head. Adrian might've come up with the specifics, but she'd been the one to push for something different in the first place. If her father was going to take exception, it should be with her.

"No, Da. This was all my—"

"Yes."

For the barest sliver of a moment, Adrian's eyes flashed green gray with apology, but then he planted himself at

Teagan's side with resolve rolling off his huge frame in waves.

"I don't mean any disrespect, Mr. O'Malley. The Double Shot is your restaurant. But yes. The suggestions for changes came from me, and I stand by them. Just like I stand by your daughter."

Deafening silence battled with the slam of her heartbeat in her ears as Teagan stood perfectly still between the two men, unable to do anything but breathe. Finally, the corners of her father's mouth twitched upward, displaying the charismatic smile she knew by heart.

"I told ya when I got here, I'll give ya the benefit of the doubt. I'm not makin' any promises, but I'm not fool enough to let pride get in the way of savin' my bar. Now do an old man a favor and fix up a bowl of that chili, would ya? Looks like the three of us have got a lot ta talk about."

Chapter Twenty-Four

Teagan balanced one filled-to-the-brim grocery bag on each hip while gripping the handle of a smaller one in the opposite palm from her keys, wishing like hell she'd figured out how to knock on Adrian's door *before* she'd arrived on his threshold. Still, she wasn't about to let a little bit of wood and steel keep her from hitting the kitchen. Adrian would probably commandeer the steaks she'd grabbed at Joe's as soon as she got past the doorframe, but that would free her up to mess with the potatoes and maybe even sneak in a glass of wine before they ate. With less than a full week to go now until the street fair, they'd likely be working around the clock getting the last-minute details hammered into place. While she'd originally balked at taking her usual Monday night off, deep down Teagan knew she needed to recharge in order to make it through the grueling work marathon of the upcoming week.

The thought snapped her to attention in front of Adrian's doorframe. When the hell had food and wine and leisurely dinners snuck into her go-'til-you-drop repertoire? This week would surely be gone in the time it took her to blink, and instinct screamed that she had no business doing anything other than prep, prep, and more prep.

Except everyone at the Double Shot had *been* prepping for the last two weeks straight. Even Carly and her staff at La Dolce Vita had pitched in to lend a hand, and with Carly's friend Sloane offering to take up the social media charge, getting the word out past Bealetown and Riverside had suddenly been a snap.

Plus, letting Adrian take care of her, just a little, felt more than deliciously good. It felt right. And Teagan trusted it.

She trusted *him*.

"You gonna just stand there looking pretty, or do you want to come in?" Adrian's rough-around-the-edges voice yanked Teagan on a direct flight back to reality, and she jumped at his sudden appearance in the doorway.

"Oh! You startled me," she squeaked, and sweet Lord in heaven, would she ever get used to the way that dark, sexy smile slid right beneath her skin?

"Sorry," he said, pausing to brush a kiss over her mouth as he leaned in to take one of the bags. "I saw you pull up a minute ago and figured you might need a hand."

"You were waiting for me?" Teagan asked, her belly going warm and tight, and Adrian kissed her again, his smile parting over her surprised sigh.

"What can I say? I missed you."

"I bet you say that to all the girls who show up on your threshold," she joked, but Adrian snapped the sass right from her lips.

"Nope. Just you, Red. I only want you."

"Mmm." Her mouth parted to return his kiss, and for one long, provocative second, Teagan considered skipping the meal and having Adrian for dinner instead. "Dinner first. You must be hungry."

With one last nip at her bottom lip, he conceded, turning to toss a smirk over the thick muscles of his shoulder. "Stickler."

"I prefer to think of it as being disciplined," she flipped back, cradling the remaining larger bag in the crook of her elbow as she followed Adrian into the now-familiar comfort of his apartment. "Plus, there are steaks in that bag and I'm starving."

"Jeez, woman. Why didn't you say so?" He moved over the scuffed linoleum in the tiny kitchen, unloading the contents of the bag she'd handed over. "So how did your father's test results look?"

"Pretty good, actually." Teagan slid the remaining bags to the counter, focusing on the larger one first. "Dr. Riley said there's already been some noticeable difference in his blood sugar levels and his cholesterol has come down significantly. The tests from a couple of days ago are the best ones yet. Just as long as he gets enough rest and keeps eating well, he should be good to try working part-time in a couple of weeks."

"But you're still worried." Adrian's words were a statement, and of course, they were spot-on.

"I can't help it. I don't know if he'll ever be able to handle a full-time workload along with managing the bar, and so much is riding on this street fair." Her voice broke, unexpected emotion welling up from deep in her chest. Damn it! She needed to stay strong if she was going to take care of this.

But then Adrian abandoned his spot by the refrigerator to gather her close, and denying how good his arms felt around her would've been like saying air was a perfectly optional luxury.

"Hey." He dropped his ever-stubbled chin to put his gaze level with hers, and God, how could he look right into her with one dark stare? "I know we've got a lot on the line here. But the street fair is going to work. We'll come up with the money to pay Lonnie off, and then you can work on finding a new cook."

Teagan nodded, dropping her forehead to the warm, wide plane of his chest as the swirling fear she'd been pushing back all week long took shape on her tongue. "I want to believe that. I really do. But there's so much at stake now. My father could lose the bar. You could go to jail. Lonnie could hurt us all. I just—"

"Teagan, stop."

The sound of his voice on her name stunned her to silence, and he slid his palm upward to brush her cheek. "You trust me, right?"

Her knees threatened to give out in rapid-fire succession, but the only word she could say was, "Yes."

"We have a good, solid plan. I swear to you I'm going to do everything I can to make sure it works. Whatever happens on Saturday, we're going to get through it together, okay?"

It sounded great in theory. But . . . "What if Lonnie calls Big Ed, or worse? Just because he's been quiet lately doesn't mean Lonnie's not a huge threat, especially to you, Adrian. What if . . ." She broke off, traitorous tears burning hot beneath her eyelids. "What if I lose you? Then what?"

Adrian stiffened, his eyes flickering with dark gray intensity that shot through every part of her. "You're not going to lose me."

"How can you be sure?"

"Because I love you."

Teagan's breath rushed out in a hard gasp. "You . . . what?"

But Adrian didn't flinch. "I know it's crazy, but I couldn't care less. All this time, I thought I belonged in the kitchen, and yeah, in a way, part of me does. But none of it matters as much as being with you."

He pressed against her, so close that his heart pounded a wild, steady rhythm against her chest, and still, he didn't falter. "So whatever it takes to make Lonnie disappear and keep you safe is what I'm going to do. I love you, Red. I belong with you, and I promise you I'll never leave."

He captured her mouth in a kiss that matched the words, both proprietary and needful, and Teagan gave in to it without thinking twice. She arched up, meeting him stroke for stroke as the kiss became deeper, and all at once, she knew beyond measure that Adrian meant what he'd said.

No matter what happened, he was hers and he'd never leave.

Breaking from his lips to pull him in tighter, Teagan knotted her fingers in Adrian's hair, notching her body against his to whisper in his ear.

"Oh God, I love you, too. I don't ever want to be without you."

His mouth was back on hers in less than a breath, taking, giving, and taking again until she felt almost drunk with want. Teagan pushed up on the balls of her feet, muscles squeezed tight as she desperately gripped Adrian's shoulders, angling for more. As if she'd broadcast the thought out loud, his hands shot low over the back of her hips, digging into the denim there as he yanked her up onto the counter at her back.

"Oh . . ." Teagan slipped from her haze just long enough to realize that other than to put away the perishables, dinner had become a dim afterthought. "We should . . . aren't you . . ."

"No." The fingers on Adrian's free hand slid up to skate over her lips, a hard tingle building beneath his touch. "The food can wait. I only want you. Let me take care of you."

The kiss that came next was so insistent, so punishing and pure that Teagan gave in. Every stroke brought her closer to the next, every slide of their lips, tongues and teeth making her boldly want the one that came after, until she was certain she would shatter from the need building under her skin.

Where Adrian usually took his time, he was now urgent, cupping her neck with hot fingers to keep her locked in close to his body. Teagan met the move with equal want, knotting her legs around his waist to bring them level, face-to-face and body to body. Her hands found the hard stretch of his shoulders, the column of his neck, the soft yet stinging brush of stubble on his jaw, and oh God, she would never have enough.

"You are so fucking beautiful," he grated, lacing his fingers through her hair to expose her from ear to collarbone. Heating her skin with a line of openmouthed kisses, Adrian lowered himself to the hollow of her shoulder, grazing the edge of his teeth over the wildly sensitive skin there, and Teagan lost her breath on a moan.

"Now. Please, now," she rasped, unable to throw her thoughts into anything more cohesive. But the demand between her thighs refused to loosen, every touch threatening to drive her crazier than the one before it.

To her absolute surprise, Adrian complied, lowering her from the counter in one swift pull. She was conscious of her legs beneath her, movement down the hallway, the early-evening shadows starting to color his bedroom through the blinds, but her mind could only focus on one true thing.

Adrian's eyes glinted, green gray and full of desire, as he stared right into her, and Teagan wanted nothing more than to let him have her, to let him care for her and really love her.

She knew he would never leave.

Wordlessly, Teagan covered the small space between

them, stopping only when she was less than an arm's length away. Adrian reached for her, but she pressed a palm to his chest, her hair tumbling freely over her shoulders as she shook her head. Her heart pounded against her breastbone, but it didn't stay her movements. Teagan reached across her hips, grasping the thin hem of her T-shirt to lift the cotton over her head and toss it to the floor. Her boots and jeans followed, and she didn't linger for even a second as she removed the swath of white lace from her breasts or her panties from her hips.

"I'm yours, Adrian. Don't make me wait."

He stepped in toward her, guiding her back toward the bed until her legs hit the soft fall of sheets still in disarray from the night before. Teagan lay back, pulling Adrian with her, and the friction of his clothes on her bare, aching skin shot a spear of heat right to her core. He braced his frame over hers just long enough to kiss her once before descending the plumb line of her body, parting her knees with the width of his shoulders as he pulled her flush with the edge of the bed and knelt down on the floor. Hooking his fingers beneath her hips, Adrian held her against the mattress, sliding his tongue along the length of her inner thigh before hitting home.

"Oh *God*." The words erupted from Teagan's throat on a ragged cry, and she grabbed at the loose skein of bedsheets at her side. But Adrian didn't hold back, exploring her center with bold, sure strokes. His pleasured exhale sent a bolt of warmth over her core as he guided the cradle of her hips into a slow and steady tilt that quickly had her on the brink of release.

Without breaking the rhythm of his movements, Adrian shifted just slightly to let his thumb glide over her folds and linger, and the combination of his mouth and hands—both working where she so desperately needed them—pushed her right over the edge. Teagan's orgasm crashed all the way over her, and Adrian worked her through every breathless wave. Finally, he slowed his contact with her oversensitive skin, just enough to let her come back to her body before shucking his clothes with decisive intent.

Teagan moved back over the bed, surrounding herself in the heady cinnamon scent of Adrian's skin on the dark blue sheets. Her breath hitched and pulled at her lungs, going even tighter in her chest as Adrian angled himself against her. Nudging her thighs apart again, he divided the midline of her body, pausing for the briefest of moments to roll on a condom before covering her chest with his. The muscles in Adrian's shoulders went taut as he bent to gather her bottom lip between his own, brushing her mouth with the wicked tip of his tongue before pulling back to look at her.

"I'm yours right back, Red. I want you so much."

Teagan's lips curled into a smile, and nothing in her life had ever felt so vital or so flawless.

"Then take me," she said.

He thrust forward at the same time Teagan lowered her hand to the spot where they were so nearly joined, circling her fingers around the full length of his cock to coax him closer still. Her hand rose and fell in a sinful rhythm as she slanted her hips under his, the lust-blown ache Adrian had just eased already rebuilding between her legs. But he wasted no time answering it, thrusting hard against her palm before sinking into her heat with a groan.

"Ah, God. So hot." The waning sunlight filtering through the room outlined the sheer intensity on Adrian's face as he buried himself deep in her body. Teagan's knees listed even wider apart, wordlessly begging him to fill her again and again. Pressing forward to clasp them together from shoulder to thighs, Adrian quickened the rhythm of his hips, pinning her to the mattress with each powerful thrust.

"Yes. *Yes*." Teagan slid both palms to the tight space between her own hips and the bed, pushing herself upward to meet Adrian's unrelenting movements. The added contact turned her ripples of pleasure into a shock wave, and oh God, how had she ever thought she'd be able to hold anything back from him?

"Adrian, please. I—"

All other thought scattered apart as she climaxed, hard enough to force the breath from her lungs in a keening cry. Adrian's muscles tensed and flexed against her skin and inside her body, and she squeezed her legs around his thick waist, tipping up to eliminate any space between them even as he continued to thrust. Sound left his throat on a pleasure-soaked groan, and with one last near-punishing push, the tension in his body unraveled as he came with a shout.

Adrian's weight pressed against her, heated skin on skin, until both of their breathing steadied. He shifted to the center of the bed, but only enough to reclaim his own weight and tuck her back in at his side. The shadows slanting through the blinds stretched farther over the carpet, marking the minutes as they fell from the clock, and even though time was clearly passing, Teagan didn't move.

She wanted this moment, with Adrian's body all warm and strong and *hers,* to last forever.

Finally, when they couldn't deny that the rest of the planet was indeed still spinning away outside Adrian's bedroom door, Teagan slipped from the bed to gather her clothes. She felt Adrian's eyes on her from the bed, watchful and reverent, and she pulled her T-shirt over her head before giving in to his gaze.

"Are you hungry?" she asked with a grin, padding over to the bed on bare feet, and Adrian lifted a brow over a high-octane, sexy-as-sin smile.

"Never thought you'd be happy to get into the kitchen,"

he said, levering up to kiss her before snagging his own discarded clothing from the carpet, and oh no. She might be all boneless and borderline goofy from the pair of religious-experience orgasms he'd just given her—not to mention the *I love you*s behind them—but no way was Teagan going to acquiesce.

"And I never thought you'd be happy to stay *out* of the kitchen."

She dodged the pillow Adrian winged in her direction just before impact, letting out a peal of laughter before scooping it up to throw it right back. The pillow glanced off his shoulder before falling to the bedsheets with a *whump*, and Adrian's expression lit into *oh really?* territory.

"You want to eat, right?" His arms threaded into a thick knot over his freshly replaced T-shirt. Menacing as he was, Teagan matched the gesture, although the ear-to-ear smile pulling at her lips probably canceled out the serious factor.

"Sure do, Superman."

His rough-hewn laugh was tipped in mischief. "Then you'd better hightail it to the kitchen, before I decide not to let you."

Teagan weighed the odds for exactly point-four seconds before heading down the hallway, her shoulders feeling as light as they had . . . well, as far back as she could remember. Humming under her breath, she popped the refrigerator door with a soft *whoosh*, collecting the steaks before nudging it closed with one hip. She went through the motions of getting things prepped, and everything from washing her hands to seasoning the meat sent even more relaxation through her body and her mind.

"So what's this?" Adrian asked, jerking his chin at the sole grocery bag still on the counter as he moved into the kitchen to stand next to her.

Even more warm and fuzzy bubbled up in Teagan's chest, and God, she had it so bad. "Oh, I almost forgot! I got you a present."

"You did?" He stilled at the counter, his surprise evident.

But Teagan reached into the bag with a smooth—albeit careful—sweep of her hand. "Yup. Your place is kind of bare, so I thought you might like it. Plus, it made me think of you."

For a distortedly long minute, Adrian simply stared at the item cradled between her palms, finally lifting his gaze to hers.

"You got me a cactus?"

She blinked. "Well, yeah. You know, tough and prickly. Plus, you're not a throw pillow kind of guy, remember?"

Teagan took a step backward on the cool linoleum. She'd meant it as an endearment, but maybe the cactus had been a bad idea. Clearly, Adrian liked his rootless environment, with his few sparse belongings all in order and ready to go. She'd seen the little potted cactus at Joe's Grocery and thought of him instantly, so she'd just bought it, but maybe . . .

"You're right, I'm not."

Adrian was on her then, taking the brown ceramic dish from her hands. But rather than balk or clam up his emotions, he wrapped his arms around her to pull her close.

"I'm the kind of guy who's in love with you. And nothing's going to stand in the way of that. Ever."

Chapter Twenty-Five

Adrian sat back in the extra chair in La Dolce Vita's small but tidy office, his chest full of *yes, yes, and more yes* but his gut brimming with dread. He'd gone over the impending street fair no less than a trillion times in his head, and while the plan itself was damn near flawless, there was one giant roadblock Adrian simply couldn't avoid.

Their success hinged on Lonnie keeping his word, and there was a zero percent chance the sleaze basket was anything other than violently untrustworthy.

"Hey, sorry to keep you waiting. I got caught up planning specials with Bellamy. I swear that woman is a culinary tour de force," Carly said, handing over a plate full of biscotti and a steaming mug of coffee. She plopped down into the chair behind the desk, running the flat of her palm over her belly before gesturing to the cookies in a *gimme*like wave.

"No sweat," Adrian returned, sliding the dish to the no-man's-land on the desk between them. "She's come a long way in a couple of years, huh?" When he'd first laid eyes on Bellamy, she'd had damn little practice to go with her promise. But hell, if she was responsible for the perfectly golden, chocolate-studded biscotti at his elbow, she'd come even further than he'd thought.

"I know, right? Even I have no clue how she gets her pie crust so frickin' flawless." Carly crunched into a cookie, making a blissed-out face before brushing the crumbs from the corners of her mouth. "So is everything okay? You sounded kind of serious on the phone."

"That's because I am." Shit. There was no way to slice this other than right down the middle, and Carly probably didn't expect any less from him, anyway. "There's more than just a little fund-raising going on behind this street fair at the Double Shot."

"There is." Carly's words held no hint of a question, and Adrian scraped in a deep breath. Fuck, this was going to be difficult, and more than a little dangerous. But the bottom line was that he trusted Carly, and no matter what, he had to protect Teagan if things went south.

Even if he didn't have a clue how to do that.

"Yeah." Without pause, Adrian dove into the story, giving Carly enough details to fill her in but not so many as to scare the hell out of her entirely. But from her wide-eyed, holy-shit expression as he finished twenty minutes later, he'd been only partially successful in not freaking her out.

"Jesus, Ade," she breathed, the words shaky. "Do you have any clue how totally dangerous this is?"

"I wouldn't be sitting here if I didn't. It's possible, maybe even probable, that once Lonnie gets his money, he'll do like he promised and become a ghost." After all, the best way to run a successful business—even a nefarious one—was to take your profits where you got 'em. "But I trust the guy about as far as I can throw a baby grand. I know the street fair will do its job, but . . ."

"You don't think Lonnie will do his," Carly finished,

and Adrian gave a shrug so tight, his shoulders might as well have been vacuum-packed.

"I think he's a bully. But he's a well-armed, cagey-as-all-get-out bully, and unfortunately, he's also not stupid. A bar like the Double Shot could launder his dirty cash from here to kingdom come. The easier he makes this, the more I'm not sure it makes sense that he'd let an opportunity like the Double Shot slip away with a simple payback."

Carly's dark brows jacked downward, outlining her confusion. "I don't get it. If Teagan's father *does* pay him back, what does Lonnie have as leverage?"

The needling disquiet that had built in his belly every time Adrian thought of Lonnie's radio silence made a comeback tour, and he swallowed hard to keep it in check. "Not what," Adrian said, the words grim as they stuck in his throat. "Who."

"You think he'd threaten Teagan to get her father to launder his gun money?" Carly gasped, her back going stick-straight and rigid against the cushions of her desk chair.

"I don't know," Adrian admitted, hating the words. "Like I said, he might just take the money and go back under the filthy rock he slunk out from. But something about how hands off he's been lately doesn't pass the smell test, and I can't sit back and take the risk." His gut doubled down, the adrenaline perking in his veins just begging for an outlet. "Not with Teagan."

"You're in love with her," Carly said, her tone as unreadable as her expression. Adrian had always gone big-brother-bulldog with regard to Carly's love life, and she returned the favor in spades. Hell, after the Becca disaster, Adrian's current fast track to the head-over-heels routine probably had her protective hackles up.

Nope. All the best-friend doubt on the planet wouldn't

keep him from defending the way he felt. "I know things between me and Teagan happened fast, but she's not like Becca. She's . . ." *Gorgeous. Everything. Mine.* "Different. And I can't let anything happen to her."

"I know."

Whoa. "You do?"

But Carly just shook her head and gave a knowing smile. "Please. We've had each other's backs for a decade, *gnoccone*. It's all over your face that you're in love with her. And it's all over hers that she's nothing like Becca. Plus, I hate to break it to you, but I actually know a thing or two about being in love. I can call it when I see it."

Relief spun through Adrian's gut, but it was short-lived. "So you know where I'm coming from, here." He'd sworn to Teagan he'd do whatever it took to keep her safe.

Trouble was, he had no plan for how to make that an unequivocal reality, and with the street fair happening in just five days, time was running out.

"I do. And I agree that you need some kind of assurance if you want to keep this jackass from coming back for seconds," Carly said. "But I have to be honest. You don't have a lot of options, especially if you want to keep this on the down-low to avoid attracting attention from Big Ed."

Though the guy had backed off of Carly as promised, he'd made no bones at all about the fact that he'd still haul Adrian back upstate at the slightest whiff of impropriety.

And damn it, Lonnie reeked like a landfill on the hottest day of July.

"There has to be something," Adrian grated, lowering his empty coffee mug to the desk with a hard *thunk*. "This dirtbag is running guns and exploiting people when they're vulnerable, right here in Pine Mountain. He needs to go down."

Carly sat bolt upright, opening her mouth to speak but then clamping her lower lip between her teeth at the very last minute.

Too late. Damage done. "What?" he asked, leaning in to search her expression for any bread crumb, however small. "Carly, if you have any ideas, I need to know. *Please*."

"Well . . ." She paused, but then muttered a curse in Italian. "Screw it, you're not going to let up until I tell you anyway. There might be a way you can get the insurance you need to keep Teagan safe. But . . ." This time, her pause was accompanied by tears gathering in her dark eyes. "It's iffy, and you'd be risking everything in order to do it. And I do mean *everything*, Adrian."

But his answer had started springboarding from his mouth before Carly even finished her last sentence.

"Done. Now tell me what you're thinking."

Teagan didn't even bother to trap her idiot grin between her lips as she double-, then triple-checked the pantry inventory on the computer in the Double Shot's office. For the last four days, everything had been all systems go with street fair preparations, right down to the commercial-grade smokers Jesse had gone to pick up from his buddy in Riverside just this morning. With the food delivery Teagan had supervised and signed off on a few hours ago, nothing was holding them back from launching into the final countdown for the street fair, with the key to breaking Lonnie's smarmy stranglehold so close, she could practically smell sweet freedom.

Things couldn't be coming together more perfectly if Teagan had scripted them line by happy-ending line.

"Hey, boss." Brennan stuck his head in the office doorway, shifting his weight to lean against the wooden frame.

The poor guy had bent over backward for the last few weeks, running the front of the Double Shot while coordinating all the volunteers and safety specs for the street fair. No wonder he looked like he could take a load off.

"Give me good news and I'll give you some back," Teagan said, her idiot grin going for maximum wattage as she waved him past the threshold.

Brennan sank into the chair across from her, nearly black brows raised in a who-are-you-and-what-have-you-done-with-my-coworker expression. "I just got off the phone with Hunter Cortland, down at the Cold Creek Brewery. Everything he finalized with us in this morning's meeting is a definite go, and we're all set for that early A.M. drop-off. I take it you were able to sweet-talk the rental guy into giving us the tents early?"

"Yup." Teagan snapped up the dog-eared master copy of the schematic and unfolded it with a flourish. "Carly's restaurant manager, Gavin, and Shane were nice enough to run out to Bealetown to pick them up in Shane's truck, and they're on their way back now. We should have plenty of time to get the tents set up in the parking lot before it gets too dark, which will put us ahead of schedule. Then we can double-check the food prep for the morning, get the smokers set and ready to go, and everyone can get a little shut-eye."

In order to keep everything on a manageable timetable for setup, Teagan had made the executive decision to close the Double Shot for tonight's dinner shift. While it might pinch a little to lose the income from a Friday night, the four of them needed to be game-on for this street fair, from right this moment until the last sandwich was served tomorrow.

"Okay. Sounds good," Brennan said, but his expression made him a liar.

"What?" Teagan asked, her pulse flaring. "Is something wrong with the setup?"

"No." Brennan brushed a palm over the back of his neck before exhaling a heavy breath. "Nothing's wrong with the setup. In fact, nothing's wrong at all. Everything's perfect. And that's kind of the problem."

"I don't understand," Teagan said, unable to rein in a chirp of relieved laughter. "How is smooth sailing a problem?"

"Because it's *too* smooth. Look, don't get me wrong, I want nothing more than for this street fair to work so your father can get the bar back to rights. But Lonnie's given your old man an awfully wide berth for someone who owes him that much cabbage, especially now that time is running out. Doesn't this feel a little bit off to you?"

Frustration welled in Teagan's throat, but she tamped it down. The last thing she needed was to get gruff-and-tumble with someone who was on her side.

"No," she said, absolutely firm. "Look, I'm not going to lie and say we didn't get a little lucky that Lonnie kept his word about leaving us alone until the month was up, but that doesn't mean anything's wrong. Lonnie hasn't made any other threats, and the only leverage he has over this place is what my father owes. He's greedy, and he wants to get paid. Adrian feels sure that Lonnie will disappear once we pay him off, and I trust that."

"I know you do, but . . ." Brennan paused, as if he was choosing his words with the same care he'd use to handle a highly combustible substance. "When was the last time you really talked to him about it?"

"Last week, I guess," Teagan said, surprised to realize that she'd had so little time alone with Adrian lately that she couldn't pinpoint the answer to Brennan's question. "Why?"

"Do you remember two days ago, when Adrian said he had a PT session?"

What the hell did that have to do with anything? "Yeah. He's getting his cast off in about a week, so the therapist wanted to take a look at his mobility."

Brennan's voice went soft and deadly serious. "No, she didn't, Teagan. He wasn't there."

"E-excuse me?"

"He wasn't there," Brennan repeated. "And he's been acting kind of weird ever since then. I can't put my finger on it, but he just seems . . . I don't know. Almost detached. Are you sure you can trust him?"

"Of course I can trust him," Teagan said, finally finding her voice even though it was two octaves too high. "Jesus, Brennan! You went all the way to Riverside to check up on Adrian's physical therapy just because you think he's acting weird? We're all supposed to be in this together."

"No, I . . ." Brennan winced, redirecting his words. "Look, I know you two are tight. I get it. But I'm your friend, and this place is my livelihood, too. I hope to hell I'm wrong, but my gut is telling me I'm not. Something's not right here."

"Of course something's not right," she countered, her determination barging in and taking charge. "We're all exhausted from trying to save the bar from Lonnie. But the solution to the problem is right in front of us, and we've planned it to the damned letter. The street fair is going to work, just as long as we all back each other up."

For a fraction of a second, Teagan's rib cage tightened with the urge to protect what lay beneath it, her old, sewn-in defenses welling up like blood from a nasty scrape. Okay, so now that she had time to think about it, Adrian *had* been kind of off-kilter this week, but truly, with his parole officer still one foot out the door and the threat of paying off Lonnie literally days away, the stress was enough to rattle even the toughest person. Plus, planning and prep had taken up literally all of their waking hours for the last week straight. All four of them were harried as hell. So Adrian had clammed up a little and skipped a PT session. Big deal.

He'd told her—no, he'd *sworn* to her—that they were in this together and that the street fair would take care of everything.

And Teagan believed him. She had to.

"Look." She blew out the breath that had been plastered to her lungs, her chair squeaking roughly as she turned to face Brennan head-on. "We're all spread pretty thin from the last few weeks, and Lonnie's threats have everyone on edge. I know you're worried, but we can't afford to fall apart now. Not when we're so close."

Brennan studied her for a minute that lasted a month, but finally, he said, "I'm sorry. You're right. I'm sure the Adrian thing is just a mix-up. I guess Lonnie's got my imagination on overdrive."

"It's okay," Teagan said, relief spinning through her chest hard enough to make her a little dizzy. "Lonnie's had us all pretty torqued up over the last couple of weeks."

She planted her boots into the threadbare carpet beneath the desk, unfolding her spine as straight as it would go before adding, "But in two days, we won't have to worry about him ever again."

Chapter Twenty-Six

Adrian scrubbed the already-damp shoulder of his T-shirt over his brow in a half swipe, half shrug, losing the battle with the heat in the Double Shot's kitchen. His movements felt slow, awkward, and clunky like a pair of steel-toed boots being run through a dryer, and he stopped to reset himself for the fortieth time this hour. The food was right in front of him, washed and prepped and ready to rumble. He should be able to make this happen from a coma, for Chrissake.

He needed to get his shit together, like yesterday.

"Hey," Teagan said, appearing in the tile-rimmed alcove leading into the kitchen from the side door. "How's it going in here? Your arm's not hurting, is it?"

All it took were those few sparse words as she moved to stand next to him at his workstation, and okay, yeah, now he could breathe deeply enough to make an impact. Because he only had a week left to go with the fiberglass nightmare on his arm, Teagan had reluctantly given in and agreed to let him cook for the street fair as much as the cast and his pain threshold would allow. While finding a groove was admittedly a little rough, Adrian couldn't deny that he'd missed the electric high of having his hands on the food. Although he was limited in some aspects, for the most part he'd held his own. Except for the last hour or so, anyway.

"Nope. Everything feels fine," Adrian said, giving the double batch of coleslaw a showy one-handed flip in its stainless steel bowl to grand-slam the sentiment home. "How's setup going outside?"

Teagan brightened, even though her eyes showed the toll of the grueling workday. "The tents are almost all set up, which puts us ahead of schedule. Of course, it doesn't hurt that Shane and Gavin stayed to help, although I did promise to feed them dinner for their trouble. Jesse and Brennan are working on putting together the smokers right now." The corners of her mouth perked into a demi-smile. "Of course, I promised to feed them, too."

"Of course." Damn, this woman was a natural in the kitchen. How had she fought it all this time? "There are some burgers left in the lowboy from last night's service, and we can dish up some fries and a bit of this coleslaw to go with them. Should be plenty to go around."

"Great, thanks." She moved to the hand-washing sink by the pass-through, tucking her chin over her shoulder to angle a shuttered glance at him as she cranked the faucet. For a second, Teagan said nothing, as if she was simply taking him in on the sly, but then her brow dipped down low over her troubled eyes, and man, Adrian couldn't wait to erase the worry from her face forever.

"You skipped lunch again, didn't you?" he asked, teasing just enough to loosen the obvious triple knot in her shoulders.

Bingo. A smile softened her strawberry-red mouth. "I might've. But Brennan and my father and I were swamped getting everything finalized with the brewery guys." She paused, her hands going still beneath the stream of water rushing over them. "So you were here by yourself all morning, huh?"

Adrian sent his mixing spoon through the jewel-toned coleslaw mixture in purposely even strokes, spinning the bowl over the countertop with surgical precision. "You guys were off-site, and Jesse was gone for a few hours picking up the smokers in Riverside," he agreed, choosing his words with extreme care. Her expression didn't sway.

"I just haven't had a chance to really talk to you lately, other than for work. I'm worried about you. I'm worried about all of this."

Adrian pulled up a tasting fork's worth of coleslaw to plug it into his pie hole. But neither the bowl in his grasp nor the creamy-sharp perfection of what was in it could smooth out the sudden tilt in his gut.

"We're ahead of schedule, and we have a solid plan." He dropped his hand to his hip, skimming it over the cell phone in his pocket before cutting a direct path to the sink. "Everything's going to be fine." Adrian stepped in to press a kiss to the back of her neck, and damn. Her shoulders were right back to Defcon Triple Knot.

"I know," she said, jacking her hands back into motion all at once. "I'll just be happy on Sunday, when this is all over."

"Sunday?" he asked, his instinct snarling to life like a junkyard dog waking up from too short a nap.

"Yeah. Apparently Lonnie likes his money fresh." Teagan's eye-roll outlined what little disdain her frown left open to interpretation. "He called my father about twenty minutes ago. They set up a meeting at the pool hall where Lonnie hangs out in Bealetown. Real classy establishment over on Hanover Street. Anyway, we're supposed to meet him there on Sunday with the payoff."

"Hold on." Fear and adrenaline skidded through Adrian in a big, fat cocktail of *oh hell no*. "You're not going to meet Lonnie."

Teagan whipped around, tiny droplets of water arcing off her hands. "I just had this argument with my father, and I'll tell you exactly what I told him. I'm standing by him no matter what. He's not going to hand over that money alone."

Adrian grappled for a deep breath, doing his level best to keep his voice steady. "And I'll second what I'm sure your father told you right back. Going with him to the exchange, especially on Lonnie's turf, is a bad idea. Not to mention dangerous as hell."

Of course, Teagan didn't even flinch. She turned to nail him with an amber glare. "The two of you can gang up on me if you want, but my going with him is the *only* possibility. Look, I don't like making this payoff in unfamiliar territory either, but Lonnie wouldn't budge. This is my father, Adrian. I'm not leaving him."

Shit. *Shit*. He couldn't let this happen. He needed an alternative, and he needed it right fucking now. "Let me go instead. I'll make sure he's safe."

"No." Teagan stepped in, bringing their bodies close enough to touch, and yet he felt the space between them hurtling outward like a giant chasm. "I know you'd keep him safe, I do. But you've only got a few weeks left on your parole. Waltzing in to a gun-running loan shark's place of business to knowingly make an illegal transaction could land you back in jail faster than any of us can blink, and . . ." Now, her voice did hitch. "Just like I'm not going to lose my father, I'm not going to lose you, either."

Adrian hated himself. He really, really did. "You're not

going to lose me. Please." The emotion behind the word grated and stung upon delivery, but he knew asking her like this was his last hope. "Just tell me when you're meeting Lonnie on Sunday so I can go instead."

Teagan's eyes were shot through with glittery tears, but the stalwart determination behind them punched holes in Adrian's chest.

"I'm sorry. But I can't."

And she turned to walk out of the kitchen.

Teagan sat with her back to the bricks on the Double Shot's exterior, forearms draped over the propped-up knees of her jeans as she watched the morning dew illuminate the soft stretch of grass by the side of the building. Although it was still crack-of-dawn early, the mug of coffee at her side had long since gone cold, which was fitting, really, since Teagan felt the exact same way.

She'd tighten her hoodie around her shoulders, maybe even zip the thing up to her chin, if she didn't know beyond a doubt that a hundred hoodies wouldn't do a damn bit of good.

Teagan's chill came from beneath her own skin.

The hinges on the side door squalled briefly as they creaked into action, and a familiar footfall echoed in her ears.

"Lost in thought there, pretty girl?" Teagan's father asked, extending a fresh mug of steaming coffee in her direction.

"A little, yeah." She got to her feet, brushing her hands over her denim-encased hips before wrapping her fingers around the mug. "Is everything okay in the kitchen?"

But her father waved off her concern. "Right as rain. Jesse and Adrian started that first round of pulled pork in the smokers last night, and they're finishing it up in the indoor ovens right now. The next round is already in the smokers, lookin' as good as it smells. The food is all set, love."

Teagan nodded, letting her eyes roam down the side lot toward the canopy tent strung over three stainless steel drums, all chugging out lazy streams of white smoke and perfuming the air with the woodsy scent of summertime barbecue. The other tents had been set up throughout the parking lot in methodical rows, streamlined to direct the flow of traffic yet guide everyone to the various concessions in a way that made each of them naturally accessible. With the food going to serving stations in several different tents, plus the two beer-tasting areas, the healthy handful of smaller refreshment stands, and the stage Carly's husband, Jackson, had been able to build with a few guys from his contracting company for the live music, this street fair was a right-now reality that had the end of their problems well within sight.

Now, if Teagan could only get the anvil off her chest, everything would be stellar. While her father had made it clear that he was less than thrilled with her decision to accompany him tomorrow no matter what, at least he was still speaking to her.

Adrian? Not so much. Though he hadn't gone the complete cold-shoulder route, things had been way more business than usual ever since she'd told him about tomorrow's payoff.

But even though his pulling away stung, she wasn't about to budge.

"Okay." Teagan shook herself back to the present, taking a long draw from her mug and letting the bold, warm brew ride all the way to her belly. "I'll go ahead and check in with Brennan to make sure Hunter's on his way with those kegs."

"I take it back, ya know."

Her father's words stopped her short on the pavement, and Teagan turned to serve him with a quizzical stare.

"You take what back?"

"You don't always catch more flies with honey than vinegar. It was your hard work and grit that got us here." He paused, nodding his auburn-gray head toward the avenues of crisp canopies and food stands. "I don't know how ta thank you."

"Don't be ridiculous," Teagan said, too shocked to do anything other than stare. "You're my father. Of course I'm going to stand by you no matter what."

Her father chuffed out a soft laugh, scattering the steam rising up from his coffee cup. "You are true ta form, I'll give you that. Just like your mother that way."

"I'm nothing like Mom." The challenge was out before she could curb the words, and damn it, this really wasn't how she wanted to start the day.

But her father simply smiled. "Ah, but ya are. And I'm grateful. You get all your fire from her. It's what I loved the most."

Was he kidding? "She left us when we needed her, Da. Aren't you angry?"

"Of course I'm angry, love." His eyes flashed, brief and hard. "Your mother was no saint for what she did. But I loved her, and I can't overlook the gift she gave me in you. You can think you're nothing like her, and that's all well and good. But whether ya like it or not, she shaped who ya are. I'll always be grateful ta her for that."

Teagan opened her mouth, the argument hot on her tongue, but it stopped just short of delivery. Her father had made so many sacrifices, working as best he could to raise her on his own, and she'd always love him.

But no matter how badly she burned to renounce anything

that even whispered of Colette O'Malley, Teagan knew in that instant her father was right.

In her own way, her mother had forged the bond between Teagan and her father. And though her leaving had hurt Teagan so much for so long, there really was no denying that it had strengthened that bond into the devotion the two of them shared. Teagan would've loved him no matter what. But part of *why* she cherished what they had so much was because of the way they had it—just Teagan and her father.

Her mother really *had* shaped who she was. And it was time for Teagan to stop being afraid of that.

"I love you, Da." Teagan slid her arms around her father to rest her cheek on the soft flannel covering his shoulder, and the embrace chipped away at the cold that had wrapped so tightly around her just moments ago.

"I love you too, pretty girl," her father returned, his voice rough with emotion. "Tough as ya are."

Teagan pulled back, a tentative smile rising up from her chest, warming her heart on its way to her lips.

"Let's go put all that toughness to work, huh? We've got a street fair to open."

Chapter Twenty-Seven

"Hey, boss! We need another warming tray of chicken over at the tent by the stage, we're already down a keg of summer ale at the big tasting station, and Annabelle said the line at the main entrance is starting to get pretty long. What're you thinking?"

Teagan's brain prioritized the information on autopilot as she dished up a pulled pork sandwich and a heaping scoop of coleslaw for the eagerly waiting teenager in front of her. "Here you go, Lucas. When you're done with that, come back for seconds, you hear?" She plucked the next ticket from the queue, turning toward Brennan without even breaking stride. "There are backup trays of food in the kitchen, but check with Adrian or Jesse before you dig into them. If we get low on kegs, Hunter said he'd bring more over—he's at the brewery today until five. And let's get another two volunteers at the door, one to take money and another with water and lemonade to keep everyone cool if there's a wait. Good?"

"I've gotta hand it to you," Brennan said, after passing the directives on through one of the walkie-talkies they'd borrowed for the fair. "You're an event-planning force of nature. We're barely four hours in, and this thing is already going full throttle."

"Tell me about it." Teagan laughed, grabbing a red and white cardboard food tray and filling it with crisp-golden fries and a hot dog from the portable grill before passing it to the young teenaged girl making doe eyes at Lucas. "I haven't taken a breath since we opened the gates at noon."

"Yeah, well, you might want to gear up. It looks like the local radio station in Riverside is playing the band's new single and telling everyone they're here today." Brennan gestured to the stage across the parking lot, where a handful of guys in jeans and backward baseball hats were putting the finishing touches on a sound check.

"That and the Twitter blast that Sloane just did should hook us a nice second wave of people for the evening," Teagan said, filling another ticket. She turned on her heel to keep her momentum going, but was met by a thick chest and a stoic frown.

"You needed this?" Adrian asked, dropping his eyes to the stainless steel warming tray in his grasp. Her heartbeat worked fast in her chest, radiating a solid ache outward from her breastbone at Adrian's closed-off expression.

"Oh yeah, thanks. Down at the tent by the stage. Looks like we're about to get a lot of people incoming. The radio station apparently just gave us a shout-out, so . . ." Teagan paused on purpose, nurturing a tiny glimmer of hope that maybe he'd at least give her a smile.

Negative on the smile, or on emotion of any kind. "Roger that. Jesse and I will turn over another batch of chicken and pork."

And then he was gone.

"Great." Gripping her spatula with tight fingers, Teagan reached for the next ticket in the queue, but Brennan's words stopped her cold.

"Gigantor's got his eye on the prize today, huh?" His voice was soft, but the last thing she was in the mood for was yet another man she knew telling her what an epically bad idea it was for her to go with her father tomorrow.

Teagan caged her thoughts, opting for a simple nod. "I guess." Desperate for something to keep her hands occupied, she reached around him, but her too-hard yank tore the slip of paper curling out from the printer right down the middle. "Crap," she muttered, fumbling for both halves.

"Okay." Brennan rounded the corner of the makeshift workstation, turning his palm up to wave his fingers at the shredded ticket and her spatula in a *hand it over* motion. "Even forces of nature need to take a break, and we're about to get weeded. So go. I've got you covered for a few."

"Come on, Brennan. I don't need a break," she protested, but damn, he was quick on the draw. How had he moved into her spot so fast? And now he had her spatula, too?

He arched a dark brow in her direction, and wow. Who knew he had such a serious and-I-mean-it face? "I don't care what you do, as long as you don't do it here. I'll even go after you if it makes you feel better. But you need a break."

"Fine." Teagan's grumbling gave way to the sigh collapsing from her chest. She could stand to go check on the kitchen anyway, and truthfully, it was past time for her and Adrian to air out this distance between them. "I'll be back in fifteen."

As Teagan moved through the crowd, she had to admit that despite her unease over Adrian, the rest of the day was a raging success. From the looks of the people spilling down the walkways, eating and laughing and eating some more, that success was only going to grow as the day turned into evening.

Brennan was right, she thought as her chest lightened

with a shard of happiness. They *had* planned a hell of an event.

But every last scrap of percolating bliss screeched to a halt as Teagan caught sight of Adrian standing by the roped-off side entrance to the Double Shot. His body language was dialed up to its highest don't-fuck-with-me setting, fists jammed over his jeans-clad hips as if he were ready to use them for more than just posturing. The two guys in front of him looked equally joyless, one roughly the size of a lumberjack, the other half as big but twice as pissed as he pulled his broad shoulders down and back to answer Adrian's defensive stance gesture for gesture. Teagan narrowed her eyes as she peeled off from the crowd and got closer, sweeping the scene in a fast, critical assessment.

Oh God. Was that a gun holstered beneath the big guy's open jacket?

"Sorry to interrupt, gentlemen. I came to check on my kitchen," Teagan said, not caring one bit that she'd ripped their conversation to a thudding halt from ten paces away. All three men jerked toward her, the two she didn't recognize taking a wary step back at the same time Adrian surged forward, and Teagan's gut twisted with a hard yank.

Both guys were wearing gun holsters, and neither of the freaking things was just for show.

"Kitchen's fine. Everything's right on schedule," Adrian said, his voice matching his expression in the perfectly unreadable department. But then he backed it up with nothing but dead air, and *oh hell no*. Something was very wrong.

The smaller of the two men shifted toward her, a polite smile suddenly taking shape on his classically handsome face. "I'm Detective Shawn Winston, Bealetown PD. This is my partner, Detective Brett Allen." He flipped his badge from the back pocket of his jeans while Teagan's pulse went ballistic in her veins, and it took every molecule of calm she could muster to offer up a pair of steady handshakes.

"Teagan O'Malley. My father owns the bar, and I'm in charge of the street fair. Anything I can do for you?"

"Actually, yes, ma'am, there is. I'd like to ask you a few questions, if you've got a minute." The detective gestured to the door leading to the Double Shot's kitchen, but Teagan had watched enough cop shows to know the divide-and-conquer routine when she saw it. Until she could figure out what these guys knew and what they were after, she wasn't letting Adrian out of her sight.

Even if he was still impersonating a poker-faced statue.

"Sure thing, Detective," Teagan said, matching the man's businesslike smile without budging from the pavement. "What do you need to know?"

He hesitated, but thankfully didn't push the issue of going inside. "Detective Allen and I are following up on a phone call we received from the New York Department of Corrections a couple of days ago. From an Officer Ed Piazi?"

Adrian flinched from his post by the side door, so slightly that if she hadn't been standing right next to him, Teagan likely would've missed it.

"Ed Piazi?" she repeated, her brows snapping together for a brief second until her brain slammed to a stop in both recognition and understanding.

Big Ed was calling in the cavalry.

Teagan swallowed past the sandstorm in her throat, zeroing her gaze specifically on the two detectives, because damn it, if she looked at Adrian now, her composure would topple. "I've never met anyone by that name."

"Mr. Piazi is Mr. Holt's parole officer," Detective Winston replied, his bluer-than-blue eyes sharpening over her as he took a step closer. "You are aware that Mr. Holt is on parole in the state of New York."

Teagan's spine snapped to attention at the same time she felt Adrian coil tightly next to her, but she refused to step back in response to the detective's advance. Cop or not, no way was she going to let this walking, talking male-model knockoff intimidate her. Even if he did have a Glock strapped to his rib cage.

Her tone came out nice and fluid, although she deserved an Academy Award for the performance. "I'd imagine there are thousands of people in that situation, Detective."

"Is that a yes, Ms. O'Malley?"

"Yes," Teagan agreed after a pause. "I know he's on parole." As much as she wasn't going to be strong-armed by the guy, going evasive would only rouse suspicion.

Detective Winston nodded at his partner, retracing his steps to give both Teagan and Adrian some space to breathe. "We're checking in with Mr. Holt here as a courtesy to Mr. Piazi. Just to make sure everything's been going as . . . expected since Mr. Holt's injury. He's been working for you in an advisory capacity, is that correct?"

"No."

"No?" The detective's magazine-cover mouth parted in surprise, and Teagan took full advantage of the chance to scrape together her equilibrium. If Adrian's parole officer was sniffing around for violations, he was going to have to go somewhere else.

"No. Adrian and I are involved on a personal level. He's been giving me advice while I take care of the restaurant on a temporary basis for my father, but I'm not paying him." She capped off her words with a deep breath and a look dead-center into the detective's eyes. "Adrian doesn't work for me or my father, and he never has. So if Mr. Piazi is questioning the integrity of his work release status, I can assure you, those concerns are baseless. Anyone on my staff will tell you the same thing."

An interminable minute dragged itself from the clock, then another before Detective Winston finally took a step back. "I see. Well, it looks as if you were right, Mr. Holt. This does change things."

"I told you." Adrian's voice sounded rusty from lack of use, but the words panged through Teagan all the same.

"We'll adjust things on our end," Detective Winston continued over a clipped nod, his cross-trainers scuffing the sun-bleached asphalt as he turned toward his partner. "Just do us a favor, and don't do anything stupid. Thanks for your time, Ms. O'Malley. You two have a nice afternoon."

Teagan watched the detectives retreat into the street fair crowd, not daring to move an inch until they were both entirely out of sight.

"Adrian," she breathed, her knees threatening to go on strike as she turned toward the spot where he stood in the doorframe, but he shut her down with one tight shake of his head.

"I need to get back to the kitchen," he said, the words perfectly modulated and devoid of emotion, but she grabbed his arm to halt him. She'd watched him grow more and more distant over the last handful of days. No way was she letting him cram something like this down. Not when he'd promised they'd get through this together.

"Screw the kitchen. Talk to me." Teagan stepped into Adrian's path, her palms making a soft landing on the hard plane of his chest. "Look, I know you're still mad at me about tomorrow, but don't keep shutting me out. I—"

Adrian's eyes snapped over hers, and the steel-gray intensity of his stare knocked the breath from her lungs. "You can't go with your father tomorrow, Red."

"We've been over this. I'm not letting him go do this payoff alone."

"We *have* been over this," he ground out, his heart kicking a faster rhythm against her hand from beneath his T-shirt. "Let me go instead so we can end this whole thing once and for all."

Shock burst out of her mouth in a hard chirp. "Are you kidding me? Adrian, your parole officer sent local detectives to find you, *out here,* to poke around for dirt on your work release. They're begging for a reason to drag you in, and they're clearly watching. I'm not serving you up on a silver platter. I told you . . ." God damn the traitorous waver in her voice. "I won't lose you. I can't."

For just a breath, Adrian's expression went utterly soft, the hard lines that had bracketed his eyes for the last week straight disappearing as he looked all the way into her.

But then he took a step back, letting Teagan's hands slip from his chest. "Then I guess we have nothing to talk about."

And as she watched him retreat to the kitchen, the truth hit her like a ten-ton wrecking ball.

Sometimes you could lose someone even when they were standing right in front of you.

Chapter Twenty-Eight

Every muscle in Teagan's body throbbed with the burn of complete overuse, but even as she slumped over the end of the bar from her favorite perch, she had to let out a bittersweet smile.

They'd done it.

The street fair had gone well past dark, with the over-twenty-one crowd enjoying the beer and the band until the last song played at around ten P.M. Their crew of staff and volunteers had managed to break down the outdoor food service areas with efficiency while the party flowed on. Brennan and Jackson and Shane had taken care of the crowd, while Jesse and Adrian handled the kitchen so she could do the books with her father.

Sixteen thousand, one hundred and forty-seven dollars later, Teagan had finally let out the first honest to God breath of relief she'd felt in over a month. With the cash bundled nice and tight in the office safe and the meeting with Lonnie set, the only thing Teagan could do now was wait out the rest of the night.

And hope that Adrian would start speaking to her again when everything was over.

"Hey." Jesse's quiet greeting startled her from her reverie, and she shot upright over her bar stool.

"Hey. Is everything okay in the kitchen?"

"Yeah, of course." Jesse skimmed a hand over his barely there military skull trim, shaking his head as he moved behind the bar. "You ever going to stop trying to take care of all of us?"

"Probably not," Teagan admitted, her smile as worn thin as she felt.

Jesse fished two bottles of beer from the cooler, liberating the caps with a fast snick of his wrist. "Thank you."

Huh? "For what?"

"For taking care of all of us. I know everybody gives you a hard time about it. But it . . . means a lot to me. So thanks."

"Oh." It was the only word she could manage past the sudden burst of surprise taking over her brain. "I, uh. You're welcome."

Jesse nodded once, passing one beer over the bar while lifting the other in her direction. "Guess we've earned this, huh? Brennan hit the kitchen a little while ago and told us we'd made enough to pay Lonnie off."

"Yeah. My father refused to go home and rest until we were sure, but Bellamy was nice enough to stick around and give him a ride." The sheer exhaustion on her father's face had been plain, in spite of his obvious happiness and relief. He'd agreed to start looking for someone to work full-time in the kitchen in order to lighten his workload, and within a week or two, she'd be back at the station, jawing with her partner, Evan, and driving the ambulance like she'd never been away.

"Well," Jesse said with a smile. "Here's to good plans in bad situations."

But before Teagan could get her beer halfway to her

lips, Brennan appeared in the doorway from the kitchen, looking as serious as a five-alarm fire.

"You put the money upstairs, right? All of it?"

"Of course," Teagan said, her palms going cold and slick over the bottle in her grasp. "My father and I put it in the safe about an hour ago, just before he left. Why?"

Brennan's eyes went pitch-black. "Because it's gone."

"What?" She and Jesse let loose with the startled word at the same time. "That's impossible," Teagan continued. "I locked the safe myself. Anyway, the side door's bolted and Adrian's in the kitchen. No one could've gotten past him."

"Adrian's not in the kitchen." Jesse's words burned a path all the way through Teagan's gut as he swung his gaze between her and Brennan. "He took off about twenty minutes ago, as soon as we were done with breakdown. Said he was beat and wanted to go home. He didn't tell you?"

"No." Teagan's brain pitched hard as she grabbed for rational thought, for any explanation at all that would make sense.

Let me go instead so we can end this whole thing once and for all . . .

Oh. My. God.

Teagan flew out of her chair, making it halfway across the floor before even registering her legs beneath her body.

"Jesse, I need you to stay here and finish closing everything down. Shane's still outside, so ask him if he'll stay with you. Brennan, I need you to make sure my father's safe at home. Don't argue!" she snapped as he opened his mouth. "Just do it. And call me the second you get there, do you hear me?"

"What're you going to do?" Brennan asked, but Teagan had already swiped her keys from behind the bar.

"I'm going to Adrian's apartment. He's got a lot of fucking explaining to do."

* * *

Adrian pulled his cell phone from his back pocket, hitting *ignore* to kill the vibration even though the move took a serious potshot at his gut. Replacing the thing in the pocket of his jeans, he shifted the nylon strap of his gym bag over one leather-bound shoulder, doing his best to hide his cast and calm his nerves. The pool hall was exactly as seedy as his gut had told him it would be, and Adrian soaked in a good visual of the building from the neon-lit parking lot, memorizing every exit and each dark corner. No matter how well prepared he was, there were still a hundred ways this could go south—a cold, hard fact he'd known the instant he'd lifted Lonnie's phone number from Patrick O'Malley's cell phone at five thirty this morning. Even throwaway cell phones popped up in a person's call history, and as much as Adrian hated not just his actions but what they would get him for his trouble, he stood by what he'd done.

Teagan couldn't be here. Even if she'd never forgive him for this.

Well . . . if he lived through the night, anyway.

Bulldozing past the thought, Adrian kicked his boots into gear, the steady cadence of his footfall keeping time with his racing pulse. He paused for just a second on the crumbling threshold, closing his eyes and sending up his first prayer in almost a decade.

I get it now, Nonna. *I love her with no regrets.*

A wall of stale smoke and bad intentions hit Adrian in the face as he stepped into the ugly, narrow box of the main room, the muted *click* of the pool balls and the conversations hovering around the tables both halting at his presence. The hitch lasted less than five seconds, but there was no doubt in his mind that every eye in the place was on him, and on him hard. Luckily for Adrian, at two o'clock in the morning, even disreputable pool halls weren't that heavily populated.

"Can I help you?" The bartender crossed his arms over his dingy muscle shirt, his hard-edged expression suggesting that nothing on the planet could help Adrian now that he'd had the balls to walk into this place, but Adrian served up a look just as mean, along with a haphazard shrug.

"I'm looking for Lonnie Armstrong," he said, angling both his hurt arm and the gym bag against the bar and out of sight.

The bartender's laugh was as oily as it was humorless. "This business?"

"No. I'm here because I like his winning personality." Adrian pressed forward to cancel out the guy's menacing frown. "Tell him Adrian's here, and I've got what he's looking for."

At the implication of either money or merchandise, the bartender's eyes narrowed to slits. He picked up a cell phone, swiping at the screen before putting it to his ear. After a minute's worth of muttering back and forth, the guy hung up and jerked his chin toward a narrow hallway lined with cheap, fake, wood paneling.

"Second door on the left. Knock unless you want to get shot."

Fucking great.

Arian adjusted his leather jacket for maximum coverage before placing his fist dead center in the heavy steel door, and what do you know? It felt pretty good to give the thing a decent whack. He scanned the rest of the hallway, taking in the other two doors marked as restrooms, as well as the crooked exit sign at the very end of the corridor.

After the longest minute of Adrian's life, Lonnie's brother, Trigger, cranked the steel door inward on its hinges. Holy shit, Trigger was still built like every inch of a double-wide trailer, and he stared down at Adrian with a big, fat nobody's-home in his eyes. But it was too late to fall back now, so Adrian jerked his chin to the open real estate over Trigger's massive shoulder and worked up some bark to go with his bite.

"I'm assuming you girls don't want to do this in the hallway."

A sound that started as laughter but ended in something more like a smoker's hack echoed from behind The Great Wall of Trigger, who stepped back to reveal Lonnie in all his crooked, gun-running glory.

"Well, well. You are just a bad penny, aren't you, Mr. Holt?" Lonnie's hand dropped to the small of his back, just briefly enough to indicate the weapon surely concealed there. "Gotta say I was surprised to get your phone call a little while ago, what with already havin' set up a meetin' with Mr. O'Malley tomorrow."

He pushed off from the flimsy particle board desk in the back of the office space, motioning Adrian inside as Trigger pulled the door shut with a heavy *bang*. The room barely exceeded storage closet status, topping out at maybe nine feet square and not a window or another exit in sight. Adrian stepped toward the desk, shifting so his back was to the wall rather than the door as he pegged Lonnie with a stare.

"That's me. Full of surprises," he said, and Lonnie's smile became all teeth.

"I hate goddamn surprises. You're lucky yours involves money."

Lonnie moved close enough for Adrian to smell the greasy stink of his skin, bringing them face-to-face in front of the desk, and Adrian fought the deep-down urge to lay him out clean. Instead, he loosened the bag from his shoulder and handed it over.

"It's all there. The whole fifteen large O'Malley owes you."

"You won't mind if I don't trust you," Lonnie said, pulling back to swing the bag to the desk. He jerked his chin at Trigger, who unzipped the bag and went to work with a cash counter as if it was just another day at the office. Adrian waited out the screamingly silent handful of minutes until the magic number flashed on the digital readout.

But Lonnie never moved his predatory stare from Adrian's face, not even when Trigger gave him the nod, and shit. This was the only time in his life Adrian had hated being right.

"Looks as if we've got a problem, Mr. Holt."

"You got your money," Adrian challenged, battening down the this-is-bad flying through his gut.

"Yes. But see, my meeting—my business—was with Mr. O'Malley. And he's not here."

Trigger's cell phone sounded off in a loud buzz, and Adrian forced himself to stillness as he calculated his next step. "O'Malley's not coming, Lonnie. I told you on the phone—you want the money tonight, you get to deal with me."

Lonnie's face bent into a frown, but whatever answer he was going to pop off was cut short by the low murmur Trigger put in his ear.

"Well! Turns out you ain't the only one full of surprises, Mr. Holt." He gestured toward the door, and when a no-nonsense knock echoed through the room, all the air vanished from Adrian's lungs.

"Looks like your girlfriend came to represent the old man." Lonnie's expression went from dark to deadly in less than a breath. "And if I can't have him, believe me, son, I *will* take her instead."

Any hopes that Teagan had held on to for a simple cash exchange were demolished as soon as the flinty-eyed bartender pushed her through the door to Lonnie's office. The bare-bones space couldn't have seen a good cleaning in years, the grime coating the walls like a promissory note of what would happen if you stuck around the place long enough. But she was here to end this, once and for all, tonight.

Relief-tinged anger churned in her belly as Teagan caught sight of Adrian on the right side of her peripheral vision, although she forced her stare forward to the spot where Lonnie stood. Giving Adrian a full look would either blow what little composure she had or tempt her to murder him on the spot, and she couldn't afford either right now. As soon as Brennan had called her to say her father was safe at home and had no clue where Adrian was, she'd slapped the facts together fast enough. But she wasn't going to let Adrian throw his freedom on the line by making this payoff alone.

No matter what it would cost her.

"Aw, look! It's my favorite cherry!" Lonnie stood front and center at a desk by the back wall, wearing a jeans and T-shirt combo that had seen better days and a scummy I-own-you smile that made her want to knock him into next week. "Come on in and have a seat, sugar. You're just in time."

Teagan took as few steps inside the office as possible, turning her back toward the wall even though it angled her face-to-face with Adrian. "I'll stand, thanks. Since this won't take long." She gestured toward the stacks of money just behind Lonnie's position in front of the desk. "I see you got the money my father owes you. So we should be square."

Lonnie's laugh slunk through her bones. "Oh, honey, as I was just explainin' to Mr. Holt here, we're far from square. See, this fifteen grand is what your daddy *borrowed* from me. But it ain't what he owes. The way I do business, there's interest on cash borrowed."

Teagan's gut sank like a stone, but she didn't stand down. "You're a gun-running loan shark, Lonnie. The way you do business is illegal."

Lonnie's stare went from predatory to murderous, and he sharpened his gaze over her like a double row of razor wire. "Watch your mouth, cherry, or I'll watch it for you."

Adrian shifted forward at the threat, only a half step ahead of Trigger, but Lonnie was faster on the draw than either of them. The square-nosed black handgun he whipped from the small of his back sent fear careening through Teagan's chest, sucking all the oxygen from the room as everyone froze.

"Your boyfriend here is a bit uppity," Lonnie said, one hand on the gun and his gaze split between her and Adrian, but oh God, she couldn't rip her eyes from the weapon in his grip.

"Don't," Teagan whispered, the word a plea rather than a demand, and Adrian let out a barely audible breath in response.

Do not look. Do not show Lonnie how much Adrian matters.

Do not give away that he's everything.

Lonnie relaxed by a hair, lowering the gun to his side but still keeping a tight hold on the thing as he clucked his tongue at Teagan. "I always knew this guy was gonna be a problem. So here's how it is. Your old man owes me more than this, and I want it now."

"We came up with the fifteen thousand," Adrian ground out, and oh God, the sound of his voice was heaven and terror at the same time. "What more do you want?"

"Five grand interest, or I'm in the books at the Double Shot tomorrow."

"*What?*" Teagan barked, realization settling in like a dread-soaked delayed reaction. "You were never going to let my father go with a payoff, were you?"

"You got me, Mizz O'Malley." Lonnie held up his hands in mock surrender, his cowboy boots clacking hard against the floorboards as he stepped behind the desk. "But at the end of the day, I'm a businessman just like your daddy. Opportunities like the one at the Double Shot don't grow like apples. I let y'all be for a few weeks so you'd come up with some cash for me—although I gotta say, I never had you pegged for all of it. The fifteen grand is nice, but now I want my real due, and I'm gonna take it."

Icy cold tendrils of panic speared through Teagan's veins. "You can't use the Double Shot to launder your gun money."

Lonnie nodded toward Trigger, who started shoving the piles of cash back in the bag lying open on the desk. "Oh, but I can. The problem with gun money is that it doesn't clean itself, and this pool hall is startin' to raise suspicion. I knew the minute I laid eyes on you that I could play you and your daddy off each other to get what I really wanted. The devotion's just touchin'."

He placed his free hand over his T-shirt, flashing a condescending smile before his expression morphed back to dark and deadly. "But it is gonna be your downfall. Now you, Mr. Holt, are my problem. You're a wild card. Truth be told, I didn't think you'd stick around after I sent my associate to the bar. I'm not quite sure what to do with you now."

Sweat bloomed over Teagan's forehead, even as her hands balled into fists. She opened her mouth to tell Lonnie to leave him alone, to let Adrian walk and she'd find a way to get the five thousand—to get *anything*—but Adrian's voice stopped her dead.

"Why don't you hire me?"

Lonnie's stringy head snapped back in shock, and even Trigger's normally blank eyes went wide from his post beside his brother as the uncut shock of Adrian's words reverberated in Teagan's skull.

"No!" she shouted, finally setting her eyes fully on him, and Adrian's gray-green stare pierced right through her with finality and remorse.

"Even trade, Lonnie. You leave the O'Malleys alone, and in exchange, I'll come work for you. Nine months in Rikers gets a man a very unique set of skills, not to mention contacts. You want in on some big-time New York gunrunning? I can get you there. But you need to walk away from the Double Shot. Now."

Tears stabbed at Teagan's eyelids, born of both sadness and pure anger. Adrian's strange behavior, his pulling back to become more detached, his insistence that he make the exchange in her place made sudden, flawless sense.

He'd planned to trade his freedom for hers all along, only she'd been too blind to see it.

Lonnie shook his head, slinging the bag over his shoulder without loosening his grip on the gun. "Damn, son! You *are* full of surprises after all. But here's the thing. As tempting as your offer is, I don't trust you."

He tossed a look from Trigger to the spot where she stood, pointing the weapon at Adrian at the same time Trigger closed in on her to lock his arms around her body.

"*Wait*." The word fired from Adrian's mouth just as

Lonnie hit the Glock's safety with a *click*, and Teagan fought twin urges to fight and vomit.

"You don't want to shoot me, Lonnie. And you don't want to hurt her." Adrian lifted his hands, his voice oddly loud and slow as he stepped all the way back toward the wall. "You're a businessman, remember? The Double Shot is nothing compared to what I can get you in the city. Why don't you put that gun down, tell your brother to let the girl go, and we'll talk about it?"

The silence wreaked havoc on Teagan's eardrums, a strange thud making its way into her consciousness past the terror in her throat. But then Lonnie nodded at Trigger, who loosened his anaconda hold on her shoulders and shoved her toward the door.

"Go before I don't let you," Lonnie hissed, putting his gun on the desk. Teagan scrabbled for purchase on the grime-slicked floor, turning to protest as Trigger yanked the door open to push her into the hallway, but a jumble of testosterone-fueled shouts and the slam of heavy footsteps cut her off.

"Bealetown PD!" came the bellow from the main room, and Lonnie swung with a savage glare.

"You fucking set me *up?*" he spat, face contorting as he turned toward Teagan.

But before Lonnie could face her fully, Adrian snarled from across the room, "No, asshole, *I* set you up. You fucked with my woman, and now you're going to pay the price."

At the same moment Detective Winston burst through the open door, Lonnie snatched his gun from the desktop and shot Adrian in the chest.

Chapter Twenty-Nine

The ear-shredding blast of the gunshot shock-waved through Teagan all the way to her marrow, and she screamed as Detective Winston followed it with three remorseless rapid-fire taps of his .45. Lonnie jerked back, each of the bullets slamming into his chest in a perfect cluster, but the only thing Teagan saw with clarity was Adrian's huge form lying lifeless on the floor.

"*No!*"

Gut-scrambling terror clawed at the back of her throat as she rocketed forward to hit her knees, yanking Adrian's coat from his chest. Oh God, oh *God,* the bullet hole in his T-shirt was center mass, and Teagan let loose an unholy scream.

"Adrian! Don't you dare leave me! I need you here, you big, giant pain in the ass. You can't *leave!*"

Voices flew over her head, snippets of movement and sound filtering past the sharp-edged ringing in her ears, but nothing registered. A set of hands fell gently on her shoulders, but Teagan reared back in blind rage.

"I'm a paramedic, and if you touch me while I treat this man, I will *end* you."

The grasp disappeared, and her hands flew over the

expanse of Adrian's chest, desperate to assess his injuries. The skin beneath her fingers was utterly rigid, and damn it, she needed to see what she was dealing with. With a swift yank, Teagan laid waste to Adrian's T-shirt, blinking in absolute confusion at what lay in front of her.

Bealetown Police Department.

What. The. *Hell?*

"Kevlar?" she breathed, shock and relief and pure pissed-off anger crashing together in her veins. "You're wearing fucking *Kevlar?*"

Her fingers skimmed the reinforced center plate directly over Adrian's heart, the sharp-edged fragments of the spent bullet biting her fingers from its craterlike resting place. She cut a direct path to Adrian's carotid, which thumped a fast yet strong rhythm against her fingertips. When she dropped her cheek to his face, his breath fanned out over her cheek.

He was perfectly, wonderfully, stunningly alive.

"Adrian? Can you hear me? It's Teagan." Not wanting to aggravate any injuries he might've sustained from the impact, she opted to run a hand down his face rather than go for the standard firm shake to rouse him. Her training kicked her body into motion, and she cradled Adrian's head between her palms to stabilize him in case he'd hit it on the way down.

"We've got a rig incoming in three," said a voice from her side. "This one's DOA, and the scene is secure. Is he stable?"

Stunned, she jerked back to look at Detective Winston, who was standing over Lonnie's lifeless body as his partner and two other detectives led a zip-tied Trigger out the door.

"Yes. You planned this all along?" Teagan breathed, the pieces coming together through her thick fog of emotions.

He nodded. "We set it up last week. My vice unit has

been tracking this asshole for months, but we needed an informant, someone who would turn on Lonnie. You made it a little tough on us by not budging on the drop-off, although Adrian told us you wouldn't," the detective said, holstering his gun to step in and kneel next to her. "But he'll be okay. A nine to the chest plate hurts like a bitch. Good news is, he'll come around in a minute."

As if on cue, Adrian groaned, blinking his eyes open as he fought to get up. "Red?"

All of Teagan's moxie self-destructed at the sound of his voice. "Hey, hey. Take it easy," Teagan said, not letting go of her clasp on his head even though tears rolled down her face. "I'm right here. Everything's fine, but you've got to be still, okay?"

"Lonnie?" he wheezed, his gaze widening in concern.

"It's done, and you're going to be fine. Even though you scared the hell out of me."

"I'm . . . sorry. For being an ass this week. I couldn't . . . tell you." Adrian winced, but Teagan brushed her fingers over his lips.

"Paramedics are going to be here in a minute. Just sit tight."

Adrian looked up at her, grabbing her fingers with a dark smile, and Teagan had never seen anything so beautiful or perfect in her life.

"Did you . . . just shush me?" he asked.

"Only because I love you." She dipped her lips to his forehead as two paramedics appeared in the doorway, closing in fast. "But do me a favor, would you?"

Adrian's eyes locked onto hers, bright green and wide open. "Anything, Red."

"Let's make this our last trip to the hospital, yeah? I'd like to keep you around for a while."

* * *

Adrian pushed up the sleeves of his chef's jacket, running a hand over the rows of buttons with a smile that tasted as bitter as it did sweet. Gripping the handle on the skillet in front of him, he coaxed the contents over the low flame. It had been two weeks since he'd taken Carly's advice and set up the meeting with Jackson's friend at the Bealetown PD. Detective Winston, along with everyone else on Bealetown's vice squad, had jumped at the chance to let Adrian wear a wire and work his way into the pay-off in order to nail Lonnie for the laundry list of crimes he'd committed. Shutting Teagan out and going cloak-and-dagger in order to make the informant meetings and get a plan together had been a tall freaking order, but Adrian had known she'd never have gone along with the plan if he'd told her about it. The whole thing had nearly been blown to bits when Teagan had caught him talking to Detectives Allen and Winston on the day of the street fair. Thankfully, Winston had been quick with the cover story about checking on Adrian's parole. God, he'd hated every second of lying to her, but he would do it again in a second if it meant keeping her safe.

Even if she *had* let him have it once he'd recovered from his bruised sternum.

Adrian moved the skillet off the burner in front of him with his now cast-free left hand, his heart kicking up a notch at the sound of the door opening over his shoulder.

"What are you doing here?"

Adrian took a minute to drink in Teagan's surprise, and damn, even in her careworn navy blue paramedic uniform, she was totally exquisite. A few wisps of red hair fanned down from her ponytail, and she looked exactly the same as the day they'd met.

"I'm making scrambled eggs. Even money says you skipped lunch at the station, and you need to eat before tonight's shift."

"But you're not supposed to be here. It's your first night back at La Dolce Vita," she said, but he cut her off with a shake of his head.

"It's my first night back at work," he corrected, moving to plate the eggs with a smile that felt tailor-made for his face. "And as of this morning, there's been a change to my work release status."

Teagan's bag hit the floor at her side with a heavy thump, her eyes going perfectly round. "I'm sorry?"

"Well, it's kind of a funny story. See, when Detective Winston's boss called Big Ed and let him in on how I'd helped them catch the nastiest criminal in the Blue Ridge, they worked out a deal. Detective Winston is overseeing the rest of my parole. The paperwork came through today."

Although Big Ed had fought it at first, once he'd discovered the truth of what had gone down with Lonnie, he'd had no choice but to go with Lieutenant Miller's suggestion-slash-order to back off for the remainder of Adrian's parole. And since the lieutenant had a few good friends at the NYPD, he assured Big Ed there would be plenty of people keeping an eye on how he treated his parolees in the future as well.

Adrian had received a formal apology along with the paperwork.

"I don't understand," Teagan said, bringing Adrian back to the kitchen with a shake of her head. "I mean, I'm glad about the deal, but what about La Dolce Vita?"

"I resigned last week. Bellamy's going to take over as Carly's sous-chef."

It had rattled his chest harder than Lonnie's nine millimeter to offer Carly his resignation, especially since both she and Bellamy had cried as he'd handed it over. But Adrian would never be far from his family at La Dolce Vita, and it was time for him to face his life with no regrets.

Teagan reclaimed her voice after a moment of clear surprise. "So you're going to work here?"

"Your father puts on a tough interview. But when I proposed handling the kitchen here with Brennan as my bar manager and Jesse as my sous-chef so he could focus on being the GM as his health allowed, he was pretty interested. Of course, he did say all final hires have to go through his second-in-command."

She laughed, and no doubt about it, he was home. "But you're a chef. Don't you belong in a fancy kitchen?"

Adrian took a step toward her, then another until he was close enough to breathe in the sweet rosemary scent he loved more than anything. "Don't you get it? I don't belong in a place. Not even a kitchen." He moved his hand to the slim space between them, the center of his palm spreading over her heart. "I belong here, with you. I love you, Teagan. I want you without regrets, forever."

"Oh." Her eyes filled with tears, but her sassy smile refused to let them fall. "Well, I suppose you must be serious if you're actually using my name."

Adrian laughed, cupping her face. "How about we make it even and you use mine back?"

"You want me to marry you?" she gasped, and yeah. Now the tears fell.

But Adrian caught each one. "Yes, Red. I want you to marry me."

"Okay," Teagan said, her mouth perfect on his as she pressed up to kiss him. "But let's eat first. If you want me forever, you're gonna need all the strength you can get."

Recipes

Adrian's Pulled Pork Sliders

This recipe will have people coming back for seconds . . . and thirds! The rub can also be used on chicken breasts. The result is just as tasty.

<u>Ingredients</u>:

  3 Tablespoons dark brown sugar
  1½ teaspoons smoked paprika
  2 teaspoons chili powder
  1 teaspoon ground cumin
  1 teaspoon salt (kosher preferred)
  ½ teaspoon ground ginger
  One 3-pound pork shoulder
  Barbecue sauce of choice
  8–10 sandwich rolls (split and toasted)

<u>Directions</u>:

Combine all dry ingredients in a bowl. Mix well. Cover pork shoulder generously with mixture and cook in a slow cooker on low, 8–10 hours, until extremely tender. Shred with two forks and place is a serving bowl. Add sauce to taste, and enjoy!

Jesse's Not-Your-Average Coleslaw

Putting a personal spin on recipes is a Pine Mountain staple. This slaw is mayo-free, but it makes up for the flavor with a tangy kick from honey mustard.

Ingredients:

¾ cup prepared honey mustard dressing
2 Tablespoons red wine vinegar
⅓ to ½ cup olive oil
1 teaspoon each kosher salt and freshly ground black pepper
One (16-ounce) bag of coleslaw mix

Directions:

Place honey mustard in a medium bowl. Mix in red wine vinegar until combined. Slowly whisk (don't stir! You're making an emulsion—doesn't it feel fancy?) olive oil into the mixture in a steady stream. Don't be afraid to take your time. Season with salt and pepper. Add slaw mix to cover completely. For great results, serve immediately. For even better results, serve over pulled pork sliders!

Gnocchi for Two

Adrian makes his gnocchi by hand, and he makes it look easy as well as sexy. Since pasta by hand is a tricky business unless you're a big, burly chef, I'm substituting packaged gnocchi for this dish. It goes from pot to plate in five minutes. My kids always ask for more!

Ingredients:

> 1 package potato gnocchi
> 1¼ sticks of butter (10 Tablespoons)
> ½ cup granulated sugar
> 1–2 Tablespoons cinnamon (to taste, if you're feeding
>   your kiddos in particular)

Directions:

Cook gnocchi according to package directions, drain well and set aside in a serving bowl. Melt butter in a saucepan over low-medium heat, stirring occasionally. Stir in sugar and cinnamon, mixing well and warming through (about 2–3 minutes). Pour sauce over cooked gnocchi to combine. Serves 3–4, and is deceptively filling!

Make a Christmas visit to Pine Mountain

this October with Nick Brennan's story,

ALL WRAPPED UP!

Nick Brennan's boots sounded off against the neat stretch of pavement in front of his apartment, and he inhaled a deep breath full of frozen air and screaming back pain. He'd learned to cope with an extended and somewhat brutal version of winter upon moving to Pine Mountain two years ago.

The pain was a little more difficult to swallow, but then again, the snap, crackle, and pop running the length of his spine was more rule than exception. After two and a half years, Brennan had learned to suck it up and lock it away.

After all, there were worse things than blowing out a couple of vertebrae. Not to mention worse ways to deal with the pain.

Brennan stuffed back the thought, popping the locks on his Chevy Trailblazer and sliding into the well-worn driver's seat. The Double Shot's staff schedules weren't going to write themselves, no matter how much his back creaked like a hundred-year-old staircase, and he needed to get to work, stat. Brennan might've closed the bar last night, and yeah, the four before it too, but his friends Adrian and Teagan needed all the help they could get.

With business booming under the new management of

the burly head chef and the owner's daughter, busy shifts were a foregone conclusion, especially around the holidays. Not that Brennan minded. All that work kept him moving forward, and that was a good thing. Because going back?

Not an option.

The handful of country miles between his apartment complex and the small-town bar and grill started flashing by in a late-morning slideshow of snowy pine trees and mountain backdrops, and Brennan cracked his window to take another deep breath despite the December chill in the air. Dwelling on the past and the physical pain that went with it only spelled trouble, and he forced the muscles in his shoulders and back to unwind as he slid more air into his lungs.

Wait . . . was that smoke?

Brennan's pulse catapulted into go-mode, his heart triple-timing it against his sternum even though he refused to let his movements follow suit. With his senses at Defcon One, he methodically scanned the narrow road in front of him from shoulder to shoulder, scooping in another lungful of air as he lasered his focus through the bare trees to the sky overhead.

Fuck. Definitely smoke. Enough to mean very bad things.

And it was getting stronger by the second.

Brennan swung the Trailblazer around a familiar bend in the road, whipping gracelessly into the parking lot of Joe's Grocery. His palms went slick over the steering wheel as the building came into view past the tree line on either side of Rural Route Four. Black smoke funneled from the far end of the clapboard building near the roofline, billowing with enough density to kick his oh-shit meter up another notch. Fueled by nothing more than pure instinct and hard-edged adrenaline, Brennan threw his SUV into *park* and laid waste to the distance between his sloppy parking job and the front entrance.

"Joe!" Relief uncurled in his chest at the sight of the store's owner standing outside the front door, despite the obvious panic on the older man's face. "What happened? Are you hurt?"

"No." Joe shook his head, eyes glassy and breath puffing around his face from the cold. "Caleb and I were stocking produce when all of a sudden the fire alarms started going berserk. I did a quick look for people in the aisles, but by the time we got Michelle from the register at the front and told everyone to get out, smoke was all over the place."

Jesus. Something must be burning back there, and *fast*.

"Okay. If everyone's out, we need to move away from the building and call nine-one-one." Brennan turned toward the opposite side of the parking lot, where the two college-aged kids on Joe's staff stood alongside a smattering of shoppers, thankfully all far enough from the building to be out of harm's way.

For now, at least. Fires could turn on a dime and leave nine and a half cents change, and the smoke now steadily pushing at the expanse of windows on Joe's storefront was thick enough to make Brennan twitchy.

Right. Time to go. "Come on." He turned to lead Joe across the parking lot, ready as hell to let the Pine Mountain FD have at the building so he could get out of here and slide back into the shadows, when an ungodly scream stopped him cold.

"Matthew? *Matthew!*" The woman belonging to the noise came hurtling around the corner of the building from the back, her head whipping from side to side in a panicked search.

"Whoa!" Brennan looped an arm around her waist to

stop her midstride as she angled herself toward the front door. "You can't go in there."

"My little boy!" She struggled against his grip, turning to fix him with a wild-eyed stare. "He was in the bathroom, but I can't find him. I think he's still inside. Please, you have to let me go!"

Realization punched Brennan's gut full of holes. "Ma'am, it's not safe inside. You need to wait for the fire department."

"No." She shook her head, vehement. "No, I don't see him anywhere. He's not out here. I'm going back inside!"

For a split second, the entire scene froze into place. Black smoke, foreboding and malicious, pushed from any exit it could find. The heat pouring off the building, demolishing the chill of winter from twenty feet away, was a clear-cut sign of a large, active fire within. Brennan's brain screeched at him to restrain the woman and fall back, to let the fire department get here and secure the scene, to *not* act impulsively in a way that could cost him everything. Again.

But then he caught sight of the propane tanks Joe sold in the summer, lined up in a chain-link storage locker against the side of the clapboard building, and he was done thinking.

"Joe, get my cell phone out of my truck and call nine-one-one. Tell them you have an active fire with reported entrapment. Round up everyone on the outside and stay as far away from the building as you can until they get here. Go now." Brennan flipped his keys to the older man, scanning the grocery store for the best strategic point of entry. Dammit, despite all the possibles, this still had *spectacularly bad plan* written all over it.

He turned toward the woman, purposely slowing his words and movements so he didn't spook her further. "The last place you saw Matthew was the bathroom in the back of the store?"

"Y-yes," she sputtered. "When the alarm went off, I looked all over, but I couldn't find him. I thought . . . maybe he got out another way, but . . . oh God. He's only seven. You have to help him. *Please*."

Serrated echoes of a different voice yanked at his chest from the depths of two and a half years ago, stealing the breath from his lungs and cementing his body to the asphalt.

You don't have time for this. Your only job is to get this kid. This. Kid. Right fucking now.

Before Brennan could register the movement, the past was gone and his boots were crunching over the frost-encrusted gravel strip leading to the side of the building. The bathrooms were in the back of the store, and he needed to start there and work forward. Just because Matthew's mom hadn't seen him there didn't mean he *wasn't* there, and it was the last place the kid had been for sure. With the fire alarm going full bore and the building full of smoke, they could've missed each other, and at seven, Matthew had to be terrified.

Probably enough to hide.

Jacking the neck of his long-sleeved thermal shirt up to cover his nose and mouth before zipping his black canvas jacket tight, Brennan clattered to a stop by the side door marked EMPLOYEES ONLY. Although it was ajar, he laid a quick hand on it to assess the temperature, relief splashing through him at the relatively cool feel of the steel panel. This had to be where Matthew's mom had exited the building. Calculating his surroundings with every move, Brennan swung the door open and stepped inside the space, squinting hard against the thick curtain of smoke issuing up from the floor.

Christ. Until it had a place to go, this smoke was

going to be a major roadblock. He needed to find Matthew. Yesterday.

"Matthew!" The acrid air scraped a path into Brennan's lungs, but that didn't stop him from crouching down low and drawing in another ration of breath. "Call out, buddy! I'm here to help."

But the bathrooms and the small office beside them turned up empty, and Brennan banged both doors closed behind him in an effort to isolate his search field and contain some of the heavy smoke. The heat had gone from zero to unbearable in about three seconds flat, and between the sweat stinging his eyes and the smoke clogging his path, visibility was pretty much nil.

Nope. No way was he leaving without this kid.

"Matthew!" Swiping an arm over his brow, Brennan tried again, the bellow burning in his chest as he called out over the clanging smoke alarm. "I'm here to get you out!"

The only answer was the incessant bell and the soft, underlying *whoosh* of unseen flames that told Brennan he needed to haul ass unless he wanted to die trying.

Pushing forward, he bent even further for breathable oxygen as he quickly checked the employee break room and made his way toward the main section of the store. Despite the high overhead ceiling, the normally wide-open space was cloaked in hot, soot-filled air and thin stretches of orange flames, and Brennan coughed hard against the sucker punch rattling through his lungs. Fully on his hands and knees now despite the bite of the linoleum through his jeans and the screaming tightness in his back, he forced Matthew's name past the charred taste of smoke in his mouth.

Process of elimination told him the boy had to be somewhere in this room, so Brennan shuffle-crawled toward the wall to start a strategic search. Yes, he needed to move as fast as possible, but speed wouldn't matter for shit if he missed the kid altogether. Starting in aisle one, Brennan clambered down the smoke-obscured rows, instinct thrumming through him as he shoved past metal shelves and cardboard displays. The first four aisles turned up empty, each one hotter and more smoke-laden than the one before it, and damn it, where was this kid?

Brennan sucked in a raw breath to call out again when a deep chill of fear plucked down his spine.

What if Matthew *had* gotten out safely? What if the boy was outside, right now, wrapped up in his mother's arms, while Brennan was trapped inside?

What if history was cruel enough to repeat itself?

The barely there sound of a cough sank hooks into every inch of his attention, and he whipped toward it without pause. "Matthew?" The word flung past cracked lips, and Brennan crawled forward as fast as he could, searching wildly. "Call out, Matthew! I want to help you."

"I'm here."

The wavering reply sent a shock wave of relief through Brennan's chest. A set of saucer-wide eyes blinked out from an oversized shelving unit half-full of cases of water, and holy hell. Brennan never would've seen the boy hiding there if he hadn't hitched.

"Hey, bud. I'm going to get you out of here, but we've got to hurry." He didn't want to frighten Matthew any further, but they'd been running out of time since the minute Brennan had crossed the threshold.

"I want my mom," the boy said, coughing over the words, and Brennan instinctively pulled the collar of Matthew's shirt over his nose and mouth to match his own.

"I want to get you to her." Brennan calculated the distance between their location and the front door in his mind, weighing it against the return trip to the back of the store. The front door was the fastest route out, for sure.

Just as long as it wasn't blocked.

"Come on." Brennan stomped on the thought and reached for Matthew, who thankfully slipped from his hiding spot to crawl next to Brennan on the floor. Other than looking tearstained and terrified, he didn't appear to be hurt, which was a huge mark in the win column. With one economical move, Brennan swung the boy to his back, and even though his muscles seized in pain from the added pressure, he aimed himself full-on at the exit.

"Hold on as tight as you can, okay?" He stabbed his boots into the linoleum in a wide stance, balancing Matthew's weight with the need to stay as low as possible. Between the smoke and the tall shelving on either side of them, visibility was limited to only a few feet forward, but Brennan still covered the space with confidence. He'd memorized all the exits by his third trip to Joe's, and by the sixth time, he could find the front door with his eyes closed.

Some instincts were sewn in forever.

Brennan rounded the corner at the end of the aisle, sweeping his gaze in a lightning-quick one-eighty before tipping it upward. Flames sparked like bright orange pinpricks through the haze of black smoke, covering a huge section of the far wall, and what little breath he had left shot from Brennan's lungs, making him dizzy. *Shit*, this fire had moved fast, changing the game with each passing second. Which meant he was only getting one chance at the door.

And dizzy or not, he needed to take it *now*.